P9-EMH-616

Her face brightened. "You can get me invited as your mistress!"

Gavin stared at her. Few people could astonish him; the impetuous Lady Haversham had done so twice. This was the most novel invitation he'd ever received. And oddly enough, the most intriguing.

He trailed his gaze down her body, lingering over her ample bosom and the black fabric that hid what he'd discovered was a trim waist and nicely plump arse. When she blushed, he nearly laughed aloud. The woman screamed innocence, so why the devil was she offering to be his paramour?

"I'm sure I could play the fawning female well enough," she said. "How hard could it be to act the role?"

His smile vanished. "You're suggesting that you pretend to be my mistress?"

She blinked. "Of course. What else?"

"If you're willing to risk scandal by pretending to be my mistress, you might as well be my real one."

She looked alarmed by the very idea. "Why would I want to do that?"

"The obvious reasons," he said. "Entertainment, companionship . . . ," he bent close, " . . . pleasure."

One Night with a Prince is also available as an eBook

Acclaim for Sabrina Jeffries!

"Sabrina Jeffries' wit, passion, and ardent characters will enthrall you."

—Christina Dodd

"Anyone who loves romance must read Sabrina Jeffries!"

—Lisa Kleypas

And praise for her previous works of romantic fiction

The Royal Brotherhood Series

IN THE PRINCE'S BED

"A traditional Regency told with sparkle and energy . . . the chemistry among all the characters—not just the hero and heroine—ensures that there's never a dull moment in this merry romp. . . . The attraction between the protagonists is electric, and it's consistently entertaining to watch them juggle their various secrets. Fans of historical romances will find the simple pleasures of this novel irresistible."

—*Publishers Weekly*

"Delightful, sensual, and poignant, Jeffries' latest brings humor and pathos to a richly peopled tale. This is a delightful start to a new series featuring a trio of heroes to die for."

—*Romantic Times*

MARRIED TO THE VISCOUNT

"Jeffries' enticing tale will have readers rooting for the outgoing and upbeat Abby while she tames her dreadful viscount. It's an enjoyable and lusty read."

—*The Oakland Press*

DANCE OF SEDUCTION

"The biting, humorous repartee and slowly building sexual tension, along with a cast of utterly delightful characters, will have you captivated from the first page to the chilling climax. This delightful and passionate romance is guaranteed to win your heart and earn a space on your keeper shelf."

—*Romantic Times*

"One will be wonderfully light of heart at its end, and pleasantly sated by Ms. Jeffries' wickedly nimble prose."

—*Heartstrings*

AFTER THE ABDUCTION

"Ms. Jeffries has created a delightful, light-hearted tale with winning characters and sparkling romance."

—*Romantic Times*

"I would recommend *After the Abduction* to anyone, but those who love Regency type historicals definitely won't want to pass this one by."

—*The Word on Romance*

Also by Sabrina Jeffries

Sabrina Jeffries

One Night with a Prince

POCKET **STAR** BOOKS

New York   London   Toronto   Sydney

An *Original* Publication of POCKET BOOKS

 A Pocket Star Book published by
POCKET BOOKS, a division of Simon & Schuster, Inc.
1230 Avenue of the Americas, New York, NY 10020

ISBN-13: 978-0-7434-7772-7
ISBN-10:   0-7434-7772-3

First Pocket Books printing July 2005

10   9   8   7   6   5   4   3

POCKET STAR BOOKS and colophon are registered trademarks of Simon & Schuster, Inc.

Cover design and stepback art by Alan Ayers
Handlettering by David Gatti

For information regarding special discounts for bulk purchases, please contact Simon & Schuster Special Sales at 1-800-456-6798 or business@simonandschuster.com

Manufactured in the United States of America

To Rexanne Becnel, the best critique partner ever—what would I do without you?

One Night
with a
Prince

Chapter One
London
Autumn 1815

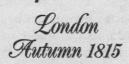

*When choosing a lover, I made sure we
both agreed to the terms of the liaison, so
there would be no recriminations later.*
—Anonymous, *Memoirs of a Mistress*

Sometimes having half brothers was a bloody nuisance.

Gavin Byrne scowled at them both. The youngest—
Alexander Black, the Earl of Iversley—was the only one of
them whose mother had waited until he was full-grown to
tell him that his real father was the Prince of Wales. Next
came Marcus North, the Viscount Draker, whose massive
build and scandalous past still had society calling him the
Dragon Viscount. Draker had known their father most of
his life and did not consider that a *good* thing.

It was Draker's study that they stood in now. And it
was Draker who was behind this insanity.

"You want me to do *what*?" Gavin bit out.

Draker exchanged a glance with Iversley. "Perhaps our
older brother is losing his hearing."

Iversley chuckled. "Perhaps so, now that he's in his
dotage."

Gavin rolled his eyes. "I could whip you pups with one
hand tied behind my back. And if you think wounding my

vanity will provoke me into doing this, you've obviously forgotten whom you're dealing with. I was manipulating men before you grew hair on your ballocks." Though he should have suspected something when Draker asked him to arrive early for dinner. Gavin selected a prime cigar from the oak box on his brother's desk. "Why in hell would I do a favor for Prinny anyway?"

"For the reward, of course," Draker said. "Prinny is offering you a barony."

Ignoring the instant leap in his pulse, Gavin lit his cigar. A title wouldn't make up for spending the first twenty years of his life being called Byblow Byrne to his face, and the last fifteen being called it behind his back. It couldn't erase the stigma of being Prinny's unclaimed bastard.

Besides, he already possessed everything he required. His gentlemen's club had made him wealthy beyond his wildest expectations, he never lacked for a woman in his bed, and his friends were all viscounts, earls, and dukes.

All right, so perhaps those friends weren't the enduring sort, more interested in his wit than his welfare. And perhaps he was sometimes painfully aware of that invisible line of illegitimacy that separated him from them, despite his royal blood. But that was nothing to him. "Why should I care about a barony?"

"If you don't care for your own sake," Iversley said, "consider your future children. Your first legitimate son would inherit the title."

Gavin snorted. "That's no incentive. I don't plan to marry or sire a 'legitimate son.' With luck, I won't sire any children at all."

"Then consider this." Draker eyed him closely. "Titles are bestowed in Parliament by the Regent himself. It's the closest you'll ever get to having Prinny acknowledge that you're his son."

Now *that* gave him pause. The idea of Prinny being forced publicly to give a title to the bastard he'd denied for years was enormously tempting. Even if it was only a fraction of what he wanted from the man. "He agreed to that?"

"He did," Draker said.

Gavin chomped down on his cigar. "That doesn't mean he can't renege."

"He won't," Iversley insisted.

"He has before." His brothers knew what Prinny had done to Gavin's mother.

"I'll make sure he keeps his word," Draker said.

"Ah, yes," Gavin said dryly. "Now that you and our sire are such fast friends, you think you have some influence over him."

Draker snorted. "We'll never be fast friends, but to his credit, he's begun to regret his past actions. So yes, I have some influence over him."

Gavin shook his head. "I swear, you and Iversley have gone soft. Ever since you settled down with your pretty wives, you see the world through a haze of sentimental nonsense."

Hearing envy creep into his voice, Gavin ruthlessly squelched it. He didn't envy his brothers their contented marriages. He *liked* his life—liked being his own man, liked his easy, nonthreatening liaisons with the married women who turned to him for a few hours of wickedness here and there.

He liked being essentially alone and rootless.

A scowl knit his brow. "So what must I do to gain this dubious reward?"

Iversley relaxed. "It's nothing, really. Convince Lord Stokely to invite a certain widow to the annual house party he throws for his gambling friends."

"How do you know about that?" Gavin asked.

"Prinny has his spies," Draker put in.

Gavin knocked some ash from his cigar into the tin bowl Draker kept for that purpose. "I take it that the woman is one of them? Or one of his mistresses?"

Iversley shook his head. "She's definitely *not* Prinny's mistress. And I would guess, having met her, that she's not a spy either."

"Stokely is very particular about his guests. They have to be adept at whist and comfortable with wickedness, not to mention discreet. Is she?"

Draker looked blank. "I'm sure she can be discreet, under the circumstances. I suppose she could pretend to be comfortable with wickedness, but I have no clue if Lady Haversham is any good at—"

"Wait a minute—the Marchioness of Haversham? *She's* the one you want Stokely to invite? Are you insane?"

That seemed to catch Draker off guard. "She's not your average marchioness," he said defensively. "She's General Lyon's daughter."

"That's probably why the bloody chit nearly blew my head off a year ago," Gavin said.

Draker blinked. "You've met her?"

"If you could call it that." An image rose instantly in Gavin's mind, of a small, raven-haired lass with a very large gun. "I rode out to speak to her husband at his estate about his mounting debt at the Blue Swan, and she put a hole in my cabriolet—not to mention my hat."

Iversley smothered a laugh. "You mean, she didn't take a liking to you at once, like the other ladies in society?"

Gavin arched one eyebrow. "Apparently the good Lady Haversham didn't approve of her husband's gambling. She was reloading her repeating rifle when Haversham himself came out and coaxed her inside. Otherwise, I'd probably be missing a crucial piece of my anatomy."

He shook his head. "That termagant could never blend in at Stokely's, even if the man would invite her. She's clearly opposed to gambling, and probably wickedness, too." Gavin scowled. "I take it she didn't tell you of our disastrous first meeting?"

"No," Draker admitted. "And if it was so disastrous, why did she choose your name from among the list of guests Prinny procured?"

"She probably wants to get close enough not to miss this time," Gavin said. "With Haversham dead, she's settling old scores. How did he die, anyway? Did she shoot at him, too?"

"Nothing like that."

"Well, *I* didn't kill the man, if that's what this is about. He paid me in full right before he died, so I had no reason to wish him dead."

"She knows that. Besides, he died in a fall from a horse." Draker poured himself some brandy. "And how he died has nothing to do with it."

"But you don't know what does," Gavin remarked.

"Prinny wouldn't say, so you'll have to ask her yourself." With a sly glance, he added, "Unless you're too afraid of the woman to talk to her."

Gavin snorted. Yet another attempt to coerce him by pricking his pride. Hadn't Draker learned by now that he could see through such ploys? "I'll let the woman speak her piece. But she'd better be unarmed for the meeting."

Iversley shot Draker a smile. "What do you say, Draker? Shall you search Lady Haversham now or shall I?"

"She's *here*?" Gavin growled. "Have you lost your mind? You let her in your house, around your wife and son? Did you lock up your firearms first?"

Draker scowled. "We had to arrange a meeting between you and her that no one would find suspicious, so you're both here for dinner. But she can't be as bad as you say. The woman seems perfectly amiable, if a little . . . well—"

"Mad?"

"Forthright."

"If that's what you call it," Gavin muttered. "Fine, go fetch the wench. After I hear why she wants to drag me into this, I'll consider your proposal."

Draker nodded and left the room with Iversley. Only a minute passed before Lady Haversham herself marched in. Up close, she was prettier than he remembered, despite her awful widow's weeds and lopsided coiffure. She also looked quite fierce for a woman who came up only to his chin—a little spitfire with snapping green eyes and an impudent nose.

He stubbed out his cigar, though he wasn't sure why he bothered. Despite her title, Lady Haversham was no lady. She was a soldier in skirts.

"Good evening, Mr. Byrne." She thrust out her black-gloved hand as boldly as any man.

Gavin took it in a firm grip, then in one quick motion, jerked her around so he could clamp an arm about her waist and hold her still from behind while he smoothed his other hand down her starched wool gown.

She began to struggle. "What the devil—"

"Be still," he growled. "I'm making sure you didn't pack a pistol in some pocket."

"Oh, for pity's sake," she muttered, but stopped fighting him. After a moment of enduring the indignity of having his hands on her, she snapped, "My pistol is in my reticule, which is sitting in Lord Draker's drawing room. All right?"

The woman was a walking arsenal. "All right." He released her, not because of what she'd said, but because running his hands over her petite but surprisingly womanly figure had perversely aroused him. He didn't want her to know it, however—the female was liable to shoot off his cock for its impertinence.

She faced him, crossing her arms over her chest. "Well? Will you help me?"

Nothing like going to the heart of the matter. "Why me?" he countered. "The last time we met, you weren't exactly impressed with my credentials."

A small smile touched her lips. "You mean I nearly put a hole in your credentials. I suppose I should apologize for that."

"That would be a good start."

She lifted her chin. "I was only trying to save Philip from certain ruin."

"Ruin! Your husband paid off his debt easily enough."

A weary sadness passed over her face. "Yes, he did. He gained the money by selling to Lord Stokely something belonging to my family."

Suddenly, things began to make more sense. "That's why you want an invitation to Stokely's. To retrieve your property. Or more accurately, to steal it."

"If I could *buy* it back, I would. But Lord Stokely won't sell."

"You asked him?"

"His Highness asked him." When Gavin's eyes narrowed, she added hastily, "On behalf of my family, of course."

Not bloody likely. Prinny didn't have a philanthropic bone in his body. Whatever her property was, Prinny clearly had a vested interest in it. Otherwise, he would never offer Gavin a barony to help recover it.

"How can you be sure it's at Stokely's estate? He has a town house. He might even possess a special vault at a bank."

"He would never let it that far out of his sight. Besides, his town house has only a couple of servants in residence; it would be too easy to break into. He wouldn't take that chance."

"Yet you think he'd take the chance of inviting you to attend his party, knowing that he has something you want that he won't sell to you."

"He doesn't know that I know he has it."

"I beg your pardon?"

"My husband told Lord Stokely that he'd received it from Papa, when in reality, Papa had given it to *me,* and Philip had stolen it without my knowledge. I didn't even realize it was gone until Lord Stokely wrote to His Highness about it and the prince summoned me to London."

"Why in God's name would Stokely write His Highness?"

She blinked, as if realizing she'd said too much. "I-I have no idea."

Liar. For the moment he let it pass. "And how does this tangled web concern me?"

She arched one eloquent eyebrow.

"Ah, you've decided I should help you steal your property back because your husband sold it to pay *me.*"

"If he hadn't gambled with you—"

"—he would have gambled with someone else. Your

late husband's weakness for cards isn't my problem, Lady Haversham."

"I should have known a man like you would have no conscience."

"Yes, you should have." When she glared at him, he added, "It's all moot, anyway. There's only a slim chance I could help you even if I wanted to."

"What do you mean?"

He laughed mercilessly. "Stokely only invites a certain type of person to his house party, and you're not it."

"Because I'm not a gambler."

"Because you're not a certain *sort* of gambler." Gavin lit a new cigar and took a long puff. "However, I might consider retrieving your property for you—"

"No," she said tersely. "I have to retrieve it myself."

What the bloody hell could this mysterious property of hers be? "At least tell me what you wish to steal and why."

She stiffened. "I can't do that. And if you insist upon it, I shall have to ask someone else to help me."

"Fine. If I can't get you into that party, though, no one else can."

An expression of sheer incredulity spread over her pretty features. "Didn't they tell you that you'll gain a barony out of it?"

"I've succeeded very well until now without one, so that's not much of an inducement."

"What if I said that helping me would be a service to your country?"

He laughed. "That's even less of an inducement. What has my country ever done for me that I should put myself out for it?"

She looked exasperated. "It's not as if it would be much trouble for you. You merely need to convince Lord Stokely to invite me to his house party. Just tell him I'm your whist partner or something."

"Do you play whist with any competence?"

She stuck out her chin. "I can manage well enough."

The chit was lying again. Badly. "Stokely is always my partner." Gavin dragged hard on his cigar. "Besides, his house party includes a very scandalous set—his friends would shock you."

"I'm not that easy to shock. Remember, I spent many years abroad. I've seen more than the average English-woman."

He'd wager she'd never seen anything like Stokely's party. "All the same, it can't be done. Stokely only invites longtime gamblers whose playing he knows."

She frowned. "Other people on the guest list don't fit that description—like Captain Jones."

"True, but his mistress, Lady Hungate, does. That's also why Lord Hungate and *his* mistress will be there. You only get an invitation to Stokely's by being a serious gambler or a serious gambler's lover, spouse, or mistress."

Her face brightened. "Why didn't you say so? You can get me invited as your mistress!"

He stared at her. Few people could astonish him; the hot-headed Lady Haversham had done so twice. This was the most novel invitation he'd ever received.

And oddly enough, the most intriguing.

He trailed his gaze down her body, lingering over her ample bosom and the black fabric that hid what he'd discovered was a trim waist and nicely plump arse.

When she blushed, he nearly laughed aloud. The woman screamed innocence, so why the devil was she offering him this?

Dropping her gaze from his blatant one, she said,

"You're not taking a mistress to the affair already, are you? I know that you and Lady Jenner—"

"Not anymore." He stubbed out his cigar. "I'm between mistresses at present. But you can't be serious about this."

"Why not? I realize I'm not the sort of female you generally prefer—"

"You mean, the sort who don't shoot at me?"

She scowled. "I mean, the statuesque, blond, shameless sort rumored to hang on your arm at every social event."

"You seem to know a great deal more about me than I know about you."

"Your preference for a certain type of female is legendary. I can't alter my height and my coloring—or the fact that I get what I want using my brain, not my bosom—but I believe that with some tutoring, I could make a convincing enough mistress."

"You'd require more than tutoring." Taking her by surprise, he snatched out the demure black fichu tucked into the bodice of her gown. "You'd have to shed these abysmal widow's weeds, for one thing. No one would ever believe I'd go about with a woman dressed like a crow."

Her gaze locked with his, fiercely defiant. "And I suppose you'll expect me to cut off my unfashionably long hair and torture it into silly curls—"

"No, nothing so drastic." He liked long hair and he couldn't wait to take hers down. "But you could use the services of a lady's maid to dress it better."

She stiffened. "I *have* a lady's maid. She's just not that good with hair."

"A lady's maid who doesn't dress hair. Of course." He ran one finger along the too-high line of her bodice. Her nicely filled bodice. "And I assume she's also responsible for your prim gowns."

She thrust his hand aside. "I can acquire more fashionable gowns if necessary."

A smug smile touched his lips. "Ah, but can you learn to tolerate my lascivious touch?"

"I'm sure I could play the fawning female well enough. How hard could it be to act the role?"

His smile vanished. "You're suggesting that you *pretend* to be my mistress?"

She blinked. "Of course. What else?"

His disappointment surprised him. "If you're willing to risk scandal by pretending to be my mistress, you might as well be my real one."

She looked alarmed by the very idea. "Why would I want to do that?"

"The obvious reasons—entertainment, companionship . . . pleasure. It's not as if you have to protect your virtue. Widows can do as they wish." Just how far would she go to gain her "property"?

He bent close and caught a whiff of her scent—exotic, unfamiliar, and more spicy than sweet. Amazing. He would have expected the chit to bathe in lye. That glimpse of the real woman further intrigued him.

"Having you as my mistress is the one thing that might induce me to help you," he said in his best seductive whisper.

To his surprise, she burst into laughter. "You don't even *like* me."

"Not when you're shooting at me." He skimmed his finger along her jaw, exulting when her breath quickened. "But if you were to focus all that fierce energy on pleasing a man in bed—"

"As if I know anything about that." She pushed his hand away with another laugh, but this one was strained. "I'm a respectable woman, for pity's sake."

"My mistresses generally are. That doesn't mean they can't enjoy themselves in the bedchamber."

Her amusement vanished. "May I be frank, Mr. Byrne?"

He bit back a smile. "When have you ever not been?"

"I would prefer to be your pretend mistress. If you don't mind."

"Ah, but I don't need a pretend mistress. I can have a real one whenever I wish."

Her eyes narrowed. "Are you saying you won't help me unless I become your mistress in truth?"

"That's exactly what I'm saying." It was less a bluff than he'd like. The idea of making Lady Haversham his mistress had begun to hold a certain appeal.

Take care, man, he cautioned himself. It was fine to desire the woman, but her usefulness lay in the property that Prinny seemed so eager to have her regain. Gavin meant to get more than a barony out of this. He would settle for nothing less than Prinny's public confession of how he'd wronged Gavin's mother.

Never mind that it might cause a scandal that Prinny could ill afford these days. Gavin wanted the record set straight. But he needed leverage for that, which Lady Haversham might provide—*if* he didn't let his lust for the woman run away with him.

A long sigh escaped her. "Oh, all right. I suppose I can endure having you lie atop me and do your business if I must."

That brought him up short. "Lie atop you and—"

"I endured it well enough with my husband, so a few encounters of the sort with you won't hurt me."

Her heavy sigh alerted him. She was calling his bluff, but doing it in a way designed to put him off, the clever chit.

"Ah, but if you shared *my* bed, it would be—"

"Yes, yes, it would be sheer bliss with you. Of course."

Her sarcasm didn't fool him, either. "Then we're agreed."

She stiffened. "I don't think it's quite fair for you to ask an additional payment for your services when His Highness has already offered you a barony." When his eyes narrowed, she added hastily, "But I'll meet your price if I must."

Now she was trying to reduce his seduction to a mercenary act. But her shaking hands gave her away—this was all bluster. Damn, but this must be important to her—and to Prinny.

He ought to keep pressing her to see how far she'd go, but the truth was, he liked his women willing. What pleasure would there be in taking a woman to bed who didn't want to be there? If he agreed to her scheme, though, he'd have plenty of time to bring her round. And that would make the pleasure even sweeter in the end.

When he said nothing, she added, "Shall we seal the deal now? You gentlemen are usually quick with your swiving, so I could throw up my skirts, and you could take care of matters before anyone guesses—"

"Enough, madam, you've made your point." Not the point she thought she'd made, but an effective one nonetheless. "Where did you learn a word like *swiving*, anyway?"

She eyed him coolly. "I've spent most of my life in the company of soldiers. My father is a general, remember?"

"Right." Which was why, when pressed to the wall, she had tried to outmaneuver him. Little did she know that it would take an army of general's daughters to outmaneuver *him*.

"Very well," he said smoothly. "I agree to keep this a masquerade only." The relief in her eyes at not having to share his bed pricked his pride. "For the moment."

"Are you sure?" she snapped. "Because I could still—"

"Watch it, my sweet," he said in that soft, deadly tone that men knew to beware. "Best to stop while you're holding the winning hand." He dropped his gaze to her trembling mouth. "You won't get another."

He walked to the door and opened it. "Now run along like a good little girl and let the men talk. My agreement with you is conditional upon whether His Highness will agree to certain terms of mine. And they don't concern you."

Though she bristled at his insulting dismissal, she nodded and headed toward the open door. "Thank you for your help, Mr. Byrne."

"No need to be formal. If we're pretending to be lovers, call me Byrne as everyone else does." He arched one eyebrow. "Or feel free to call me 'darling.'"

An inelegant snort escaped her. "Feel free to call me Christabel."

"For God's sake, how did a general's daughter get such a fanciful name?"

"I had a mother, too, you know." With that she stalked out, her lovely hips swinging.

As heat rose in the wrong places, he marveled at the perverse intensity of his attraction to her. She had a mother, did she? Then it must be some Amazon or fairy queen or succubus from hell. No mere Englishwoman could possibly have spawned that whirling dervish of a female.

A whirling dervish who thought to put him off by implying that his lovemaking would be a chore, or worse yet, a business transaction. But that wouldn't last long. He would have the Widow Haversham begging for him to take her if it was the last thing he did.

He'd built a fortune on his ability to mix business with pleasure, so he would play her game for now, but in the end he'd have it all—her mysterious property, his revenge upon Prinny, and a willing Christabel in his bed.

"Well?"

Iversley's voice snapped him out of his reverie. He looked up to find his brothers approaching. After they entered the room, he shut the door. "I'll do it."

"Excellent," Draker said.

"But I have an additional condition. I want a private audience with Prinny when it's done."

"Why?" Draker asked.

"I have my reasons."

Draker eyed him intently, then sighed. "I'll see if he'll agree to that."

"He'd better if he wants me to help Christabel."

"Christabel?" Iversley said.

Might as well tell them the plan. They'd hear of it soon enough. "Stokely will only invite the good widow if she's my mistress. So she will be."

Draker drew himself up. "I hope you did not coerce that poor woman—"

"Did I mention that she'll be my *pretend* mistress? We're perpetrating a deception like the one you and Regina perpetrated with your pretend courtship."

"It may have started out as a pretend courtship," Draker retorted, "but it didn't stay one for long."

A smile curved Gavin's lips. "Exactly."

"I thought you didn't like Lady Haversham," Draker snapped.

Gavin thought of Christabel's soft, curvy body pressed to his, of the quickening of her breath when he'd touched her—of the stubborn will that he would greatly enjoy bending to his own. "She grows on a man."

The overly moral Draker frowned, but Iversley burst into laughter.

"What's so funny?" Gavin asked.

"Draker's pretense with Regina eventually led to marriage," Iversley said slyly. "Or had you forgotten?"

When Draker began to chuckle, too, Gavin retorted, "Don't worry. I have no interest in marriage." Only once had he even considered it, as a green lad of twenty-two. But Anna Bingham had cured him of that nonsense.

"Women have a way of changing a man's mind," Iversley said.

"Not bloody likely." His idiot brothers' sly winks and knowing glances annoyed him. "Besides, Lady Haversham appears quite happy with her current situation."

Draker lifted one eyebrow. "That could change, too."

"For God's sake, you're as bad as your wife, with her talk of connubial bliss and falling in love. Contrary to what Regina seems to think, some bachelors actually have no interest in love."

The disaster with Anna had taught him that there were lines even "love" didn't cross, that his preference for sophisticated women could only be assuaged in illicit physical liaisons. No respectable woman would marry him unless she was after his money, and he had no desire to endure such a hypocrisy of a marriage.

Besides, the more adulterous affairs he engaged in, the more cynical he became about marriage, his brothers' happy unions notwithstanding. Any woman worth her salt married for financial or social advantage. Would Katherine or Regina have married his brothers if they hadn't had titles?

He didn't explore that question further, for it made him uncomfortably aware of the main difference between him and his half brothers. Their mothers' husbands had claimed each of them as legitimate sons. Gavin's mother hadn't had that choice, which was why he would be Byblow Byrne until he died.

Unless he became the Baron Byrne. He certainly liked *that* idea. Especially if forcing Prinny to set matters straight and acquiring the intriguing Christabel as his real mistress were part of the bargain.

"So it's settled," he said, ready to change the subject. "I'll get Christabel onto Stokely's guest list, and our sire will hand me a barony."

"Yes, it's settled," Draker said.

"We're glad you agreed to this," Iversley added. "It's time you got something more from our alliance than entertainment."

"Don't worry. When this is done, I intend to get a great deal more than entertainment from it." When Iversley looked speculative, Gavin added quickly, "This calls for a toast." He poured brandy all round, then lifted his glass. "To the Royal Brotherhood of Bastards."

They all echoed the usual toast, then drank. When he went to refill Draker's glass for the second toast, his half brother shook his head. Gavin glanced to Iversley, who was clearly toying with his glass to avoid having it refilled.

"You two really have gone soft," Gavin muttered, then refilled his own glass and raised it defiantly. "To our noble sire," he said loudly. "May he rot in hell."

Chapter Two

What an insane bargain! As Christabel gazed round Lord Draker's dinner table, she wondered if she'd made an enormous mistake. Play Mr. Byrne's mistress? At a house party with sophisticated sorts like these ladies and gentlemen? She must have been mad to suggest it.

Though truly, she'd been fortunate Mr. Byrne hadn't called her bluff and demanded that she be his real mistress. What would she have done?

She choked back a hysterical laugh. As if she could please a man of his scandalous tastes. If she were capable of *that*, her beloved Philip would never have taken a mistress.

The usual low ache began in the pit of her belly, and she stifled an oath. It didn't matter now, did it? Compared to Philip's other betrayal, it was nothing. So why couldn't she stop thinking about it?

Because of that Mr. Byrne with his flirtations. He'd stirred up all sorts of . . . naughty feelings that should have stayed buried with her husband.

And Mr. Byrne probably didn't even *mean* his flirting! It was merely his nature, which meant he must have some other motive for agreeing to her plan. He was just that sort of devious scoundrel. Nothing she'd seen this evening had changed her initial opinion of him one whit. He was the Prince of Darkness himself—polished, more handsome than she remembered, and possessed of an Irishman's glib tongue. She didn't trust him. She didn't approve of him.

She found him utterly fascinating.

Of course. She always found the wrong sort of men fascinating. That's why she'd ended up here in the first place.

"Do try some of the galantine, Lady Haversham," Lady Draker said from her post at the end of the dinner table. "Our cook is famous for it."

Christabel blinked at the fair-haired viscountess. Which of the dishes before her was a galantine? That's why she hated coming into society. She always floundered in the morass of rules and French words. Not to mention the expectation that she—a mere general's daughter— knew how to behave as a proper marchioness.

"If I may," Mr. Byrne said, and offered her a dish.

Oh, the aspic-covered thing. "It does look delicious," she lied as she took some. She ventured a bite, relieved to find it edible. She only prayed that Lord Stokely didn't have a French cook, or she'd never make it through his meals.

Perhaps Mr. Byrne could help with that, too. For a notorious owner of a gaming club, he seemed perfectly adept at navigating the treacherous social waters, perfectly at ease in this august company.

Then again, Mr. Byrne was rumored to be the prince's natural son, like Lord Draker, which would make them

half brothers. That might explain it. It might also explain
His Highness's willingness to ask the two men to help her.

His Highness—oh dear. He would *not* be happy when
he heard the outcome of the meeting. He'd wanted Mr.
Byrne to act as a go-between only—not dangerously involved in the entire scheme.

But what else could she do? Lord Stokely was threatening to have her family's letters published if the prince
didn't meet his outrageous demands. And the prince had
made it painfully clear what could happen to Papa if she
didn't get them back.

"Would you like some of these, Lady Haversham?" Mr.
Byrne asked from beside her, startling her.

Forcing her attention to the heavy platter he balanced
easily in one hand, she sighed with relief when she recognized it. "Oh, yes, I *love* oysters."

The sudden gleam in Mr. Byrne's eye gave her pause.
"Do you?" He scooped three out of their shells and onto
her plate with the silver serving spoon. "Do I dare hope
you're also inordinately fond of pomegranate and Spanish fly?"

"What's Spanish fly?" she asked when the two ladies
turned beet red, and their husbands scowled.

"Stop teasing the poor woman, Byrne," Lord Draker
said sternly. "Can't you see she has no idea what you're
talking about?"

Christabel bristled. Perhaps she didn't understand exactly what had brought that sensual huskiness into Mr.
Byrne's voice, but she wasn't a complete fool. "I know it's
probably wicked." She shot Mr. Byrne a side glance. "He
seems to think women find wickedness attractive in a man."

Mr. Byrne grinned. "Some women do."

"Only the shameless females *you* consort with." Hearing a choked sound from across the table, she glanced at their hostess, and hastily added, "Present company excepted, of course."

"Oh, don't worry," Lady Iversley said with a laugh, "we're entirely in agreement with you about Byrne's shameless females."

"You see, Draker?" Mr. Byrne said. "You needn't try to protect Lady Haversham from me. The woman can hold her own very well."

"So we heard," Lady Draker put in. "Pulled a rifle on you, did she?"

Christabel wanted to sink under the table in mortification. Papa and his fellow soldiers might find the tale of her encounter with Mr. Byrne amusing, but this company would surely be shocked.

Oddly enough, however, the only one showing disapproval was Mr. Byrne, who glowered at Lord Draker. "You *told* Regina?"

With a smug expression, their host served himself the last of the roast pheasant. "How could I resist? It's not every day that you get shot at by a woman."

"And you no doubt deserved it," his wife added with a small smile.

Christabel tipped up her chin. "He did indeed."

"Yes," Mr. Byrne snapped. "Like a fool, I tried to collect my due after your husband ordered his banker not to honor his note. What was I thinking?"

His sarcasm—and his lies—infuriated her. "Philip said you allowed him credit, then reneged."

"Haversham lied."

"He would never have done something so dishonorable," she said stoutly.

"Oh? Have you forgotten why you're here?" *Because your husband stole your property to gain money to pay his gambling debts?*

He was right, of course. Everything she'd thought about Philip had been turned on its ear since his death. "I should have shot you when I had the chance," she mumbled.

"So you really did fire at Byrne?" Lady Iversley's eyes sparkled with curiosity.

"She put one hole in my cabriolet and one in my hat," Mr. Byrne said.

"For all the good it did. He kept riding toward the house, cool as you please. You'd think people shot at him every day."

"They do," he said. When she glanced at him, startled, he had the audacity to wink at her. "You'd be surprised how many dishonorable gentlemen roam London. But that's never stopped me from getting what I want."

His gaze dropped to her mouth, and a delicious shiver swept down her spine. Blast him. How could she be attracted to this unrepentant devil?

She sighed. How could she not? Women leaped into his bed for good reason. Look at him—he was built for the bedroom, with his tousled hair and night blue eyes and that cocky smile promising paradise in his arms.

She jerked her gaze from his. Paradise, hah! Men didn't give women paradise. Not a lasting paradise, anyway.

But as the dessert course replaced the dishes of sautéed this and fricasseed that, she couldn't take her mind from Mr. Byrne.

Her mission would be so much easier if she understood him. But he differed markedly from the bluff foot soldiers, courteous officers, and practical field physicians she'd grown up with. Even on Philip's estate,

Rosevine, the men had been easy to read, their roles simple to define.

Everything about Mr. Byrne unsettled her. She'd always been a good woman. Unsophisticated, unfashionably forthright, but good.

He made her want to be bad.

She stiffened her spine. Surely she wasn't fool enough to fall prey to a charming scoundrel *again*.

Lady Draker daintily dabbed custard from her lips, then cleared her throat. "Have you been in town long, Lady Haversham?"

Christabel stabbed a stewed plum. "Just a few days." Long enough to answer His Highness's summons and discuss what to do about the politically sensitive letters Lord Stokely had bought from Philip. The ones that would destroy her family if she didn't get them back.

"Then Katherine and I can show you the latest amusements." Lady Draker flashed her a cheery smile. "When were you last in town?"

"It's been years." When that seemed to startle her hostess, she added, "My mother died when I was young, so I grew up traveling with Papa and the army. That's where I met my husband."

"The marquess?" Lady Iversley said, sounding surprised.

"He was just a second son then, with a lieutenant's commission. He inherited the title and estate after his elder brother died unexpectedly in our sixth year of marriage. That's when we returned to England."

"How long ago was that?" Lady Draker asked.

"Four years."

"Go on with you!" Lord Draker exclaimed. "Ten years married? You couldn't be a day over twenty-five."

She laughed, flattered in spite of herself. "I married young, but not *that* young. I'm nearly thirty."

"A very youthful thirty," Mr. Byrne put in, the faintest hint of a soft Irish burr humming along her senses. "Yet you never came with the marquess to kick up your heels in town."

"There was so much to do at Rosevine that I spent all my time there." Let them think what they would. Her life with Philip—which, in their final years, was mostly spent without Philip—was private. "Of course, now that Philip's cousin has inherited the estate and the title, I'm no longer mistress there. Fortunately, the new Lord Haversham allowed me to remain until he took up residence recently. Even then, he was generous enough to let me use the town house for my stay in London."

She was grateful to the young man for that—otherwise, she would have had to lease a town house she could ill afford on the tiny settlement Philip had left her.

Mr. Byrne cast her a searching glance. "But the man's generosity is temporary, no doubt. Once the season begins, the new marquess will be looking for a wife to go along with his title. He won't want his sister-in-law and her staff hanging round."

His perception startled her. "True. I suppose I'll lease a cottage somewhere until Papa returns from France."

"Ah, yes, General Lyon," he remarked. "Still hunting the stray supporters of Napoleon, I suppose."

She nodded, a lump filling her throat. She wasn't really sure *where* Papa was at the moment. That was the trouble. The army was cleaning up after the war, and Papa was difficult to reach. "But as soon as he returns, I'm sure he'll retire to the country somewhere, and I'll go with him."

"You prefer country to town?" Lady Draker asked.

She preferred not playing a marchioness, and no one would let her dispense with that in town. "I'm more comfortable in the country, yes," she hedged.

Lady Iversley smiled. "I certainly understand that. If not for our friends here, my husband and I would probably never leave Edenmore."

My husband and I. As pain sliced through Christabel, she forced a smile. She and Philip had once been of a single mind, too. But he'd changed after leaving the army. He'd started inventing reasons for racing off to town. She'd been too relieved at not having to go with him to realize he was going off to gamble and drink. And apparently visit a mistress.

She'd thought he was happy with her. How could she have been so naïve?

"If you haven't been to town in a while, you probably haven't seen Week's Mechanical Museum," Lady Draker put in. "Marcus and I are leaving town for a few days later in the week, but we could take you there tomorrow—"

"Out of the question," Mr. Byrne interrupted. "Lady Haversham and I are going for a drive tomorrow, aren't we, lass?" When she blinked at him, he added, "And you said you'd be ordering new gowns in the morning, too."

Yes, fashionable gowns. The sort his mistress might wear. "Of course." She pasted a smile on her face for Lady Draker. "I'll be busy tomorrow. I'm so sorry."

Lady Draker glanced from Christabel to Mr. Byrne, her eyes narrowing. "No need to apologize. But if you change your mind—"

"She won't," Mr. Byrne put in.

The steel in his tone made Lady Draker stiffen. She glanced pointedly at the clock, then cast Mr. Byrne a smooth smile. "I believe it's time for the gentlemen to have their port and cigars." She rose with a polished grace that Christabel envied. "Come, ladies, let's retire to the drawing room and leave the men to their fun."

When Christabel hesitated, unsure how she'd fit in with these two ladies she barely knew, Mr. Byrne leaned over to whisper, "Don't worry—you'll be fine. Didn't you say your pistol is in the drawing room?"

Casting him a glare, she left with the other ladies. But as she followed them up the stairs, her stomach began to roil. How would she ever complete her mission successfully when the mere idea of making polite conversation with the elegant Lady Draker and the well-spoken Lady Iversley made her sick with apprehension?

It would be far worse at Lord Stokely's estate. She could easily guess the sort of female who would be there: sophisticated ladies of rank who could effortlessly entertain twenty people at dinner, then dress themselves in the height of fashion to meet their lovers in the boudoir the next morning.

Christabel didn't even *have* a boudoir, unless you could count her modest dressing room littered with her failed attempts at needlework and souvenirs from her travels. And although she could load a rifle as well as any guardsman, fashion a field dressing out of an old petticoat and some twine, and tell a naughty joke about a harem in Turkey, she knew nothing about entertaining guests of the lofty sort.

Then again, perhaps that wasn't so important for a mistress. And the naughty joke might even be acceptable. She sighed. The trouble was, she didn't know *what* was acceptable.

As they entered the refined drawing room that well suited the fashionable Lady Draker and Lady Iversley,

Christabel searched for something appropriately refined to say.

She didn't get the chance. As soon as they sat down, Lady Draker turned to her, eyes alight. "Lady Haversham, you simply must tell us what's going on. My husband is being surprisingly close-mouthed."

"So is mine," Lady Iversley put in. "What in the dickens were you and Byrne discussing so privately earlier this evening?"

"I can't tell you," Christabel said bluntly, taken off guard by the sudden feminine assault. "It's a matter of strictest secrecy."

"Involving you and Byrne," Lady Draker prodded.

"Yes." She smoothed her features, straightened her spine, and folded her hands in her lap as she'd seen haughty ladies do. "That's all I have to say."

"He's helping you with an estate matter?" Lady Iversley probed. "Or is this about the debt your husband owed to him?"

Dear Lord, they weren't the least put off by her attempt at a marchioness's manner. And they seemed very inquisitive ladies. Perhaps if she told them *something*, they'd let her be. "My husband paid his debt to Mr. Byrne before he died. All I can tell you is that Mr. Byrne and I are engaged in a rather delicate . . . business transaction. But I really can't say one word more about it."

"Business transaction?" Lady Draker looked skeptical. "When he's undressing you with his eyes, taking you for drives, and discussing aphrodisiacs?"

"Aphrodisiacs?"

"Foods to increase one's appetite for lovemaking," Lady Iversley explained.

"Oh," Christabel muttered, hot color suffusing her cheeks.

"All of which is rather more intimate than one usually gets with business associates," Lady Draker continued.

Christabel scowled. "I still can't discuss my connection with Mr. Byrne."

Lady Iversley leaned over to take her hand. "I'm sorry, I know we must seem rather . . . er . . ."

"Nosy?" As soon as the tactless word left her mouth, she groaned.

Lady Iversley merely laughed. "Yes, nosy. But we're only concerned. Don't misunderstand us—Byrne is a dear friend to both our families, and we adore him for that, but he isn't the marrying sort."

Lady Draker nodded. "Believe me, we've tried and tried to marry him off."

"He pokes fun at the very idea of marriage," Lady Iversley said with a sigh. "Though that doesn't stop women from falling in love with him, even when he states outright that he has no interest in a respectable connection."

Christabel withdrew her hand from Lady Iversley's. "Thank you for your concern, but I assure you I'm no more interested in marriage than Mr. Byrne. And I'm perfectly capable of handling myself around him. Unlike some women, I'm not the least bit impressed by rumors that he has a royal connection—"

"Impressed?" Lady Iversley shook her head. "Trust me, he succeeds with women despite, not because of, his 'royal connection.' His Highness's public refusal to acknowledge Byrne as his son and those nasty rumors he spread about Byrne's poor mother practically ensured that the man would never gain any advantage from *that*."

"Now, Katherine—" Lady Draker began.

"It's true, Regina, and you know it," Lady Iversley said. "The prince may be a friend of your family's, but he treated Byrne and his mother very wrongly. No boy should be forced into the streets to help support himself at the age of eight."

"At eight!" Christabel said, horrified at the very idea. If His Highness had treated him so ill, why was he willing to help her? She had to know more. "What sort of job could he have found at eight?"

"Running errands for the blacklegs. That's how he got his start in gambling. He was ten when he started helping with the E-O tables at the races."

Christabel knew about blacklegs and Even-Odd tables from Philip. The blacklegs were swindlers in the gaming world. As for E-O, authorities had been trying to stamp out the low form of roulette for years, but it persisted at the races, where E-O table runners descended to offer gambling to anyone who would play. The game was foolish at best and shady at worst, run by scoundrels who often got into fights with customers suspecting them of crookedness.

"Dear Lord, that's young to be working an E-O table." Christabel's heart ached at the thought of any ten-year-old boy forced into such an environment. "Did he run his own?"

A voice came from the open doorway. "Not until I was twelve." Mr. Byrne strolled into the room, casting Lady Iversley and Lady Draker a dark glance. "But that was after the fire."

Christabel sucked in a breath. She'd heard that his mother died in a fire, but hadn't realized he'd been only a boy when it happened.

"Eavesdropping, Byrne?" Lady Draker asked.

A hint of defiance touched his brow. "Always. Actually, I've come to tell you I must dash off. An emergency has arisen at the Blue Swan." Lady Draker began to rise, but he shook his head. "No need to get up. I can show myself out." He turned to Christabel. "I'll come for you tomorrow at 2:00 P.M."

"So late?"

"I run a gaming club, remember? Two o'clock is first thing in the morning for me." He bent to clasp her bare hand, then pressed a lingering kiss to it that made her skin feel all shivery. Eyes gleaming, he murmured, "Until tomorrow, my sweet Christabel."

Blast him. She'd been feeling sorry for him until he'd exposed her lie about their being involved only in a business transaction. Mindful of her companions, she forced a cordial smile. "I shall see you then, Mr. Byrne."

Though he lifted an eyebrow at her formality, he released her hand to stroll toward the door. But he paused on the threshold to flash the other two ladies an arch glance. "Try not to elaborate on my wicked exploits for Lady Haversham. I hate repairing holes in my cabriolet." With a wink at Christabel, he left.

As soon as they heard his footsteps descending the stairs, Lady Draker muttered an unladylike oath. "That man is up to no good. We wouldn't blame you if you shot at him again," she told Christabel.

"I can't," Christabel said woefully as she held up her reticule. "I forgot the balls for my pistol at home."

Lady Draker stared at her blankly. "You brought a pistol with you?"

"Of course. London is by no means safe."

Lady Draker burst into laughter. "Oh, heavens, you're perfect for him."

"Perfect," Lady Iversley agreed. "Blunt, practical, and as suspicious as he."

"He doesn't stand a chance," Lady Draker told her friend. "She'll never let him get away with a thing."

"Never." Lady Iversley leaned toward Lady Draker confidentially. "I've always said he needs someone who would keep him in line."

"Exactly. Someone with intelligence, who can match him step for step."

"He chooses frivolous women on purpose, you know," Lady Iversley pointed out. "It makes it easier for him to discard them—"

"For pity's sake," Christabel cut in, "what on earth are you talking about?" Both ladies blinked at her as if the writing table had just up and spoken to them. "My association with Mr. Byrne isn't what you seem to think—"

"Oh, please," Lady Iversley broke in, "we're not fools. Perhaps *you* believe your association is about business, but it's perfectly clear that Byrne intends to—"

"Yes," Lady Draker broke in, with a warning glance at her friend. "What Katherine is trying to say is that you should have a care for your reputation. If you are seen going for a drive tête-à-tête with Byrne, society may assume . . . well . . . how to put this delicately . . ."

"That I'm his mistress?"

Her candor seemed to shock them, but there was no point in continuing her claims about a business association. Neither of them would believe it now. Besides, they'd hear the gossip soon enough.

"And what if society does think I'm his mistress?" Christabel said, trying for a nonchalant tone. "I don't care."

Lady Draker's eyes narrowed. "We merely want to make sure that you know what you're about."

Lady Iversley added, "You don't seem the type to . . ."

"Take a lover?" If she couldn't convince these ladies, how would she ever convince Lord Stokely? "I suppose you think I'm too short and plain for a man like Mr. Byrne."

"Not at all," Lady Iversley said. "You're too innocent."

"And respectable," Lady Draker added.

"You'd never even heard of an aphrodisiac," Lady Iversley pointed out.

"I didn't know the word," Christabel admitted. "But I'm aware of the idea, having spent my life around soldiers. And as a widow, I have no attachments."

She'd thought that would end the discussion. She was wrong.

"An interesting point," Lady Iversley told Lady Draker. "Byrne has never shown interest in a widow before. He only likes women he can hand back to their husbands when he's done."

"So you think his interest might be more serious?" Lady Draker asked. "He *is* taking her for a drive tomorrow, and that's unusual—"

"Excuse me," Christabel said, rising abruptly. Mention of the drive reminded her that she was supposed to order new gowns. But she had no clue where to go for inexpensive attire Mr. Byrne might find suitably fashionable for his mistress.

She must catch him before he left. Already she could hear him requesting his carriage, and these two ladies clearly didn't need *her* here to continue this outrageous discussion. "I forgot to ask Mr. Byrne something. I'll be back in a moment." She hurried from the room. From the top of the stairs, she spotted him about to go out the door. "Wait, Mr. Byrne!" she called as she hurried down.

He halted in the doorway. As she approached, he said dryly, "I thought you were going to call me Byrne."

"If you mean to be informal, why not have me call you by your Christian name?"

A smile touched his lips. "Because only my mother ever called me Gavin."

His poor, dead mother. The thought of anyone, even the wicked Mr. Byrne, being all alone in the world saddened her.

"Did you have something you wanted to ask?" he said.

"Oh, yes, I forgot. What dressmaker should I use for my new gowns? I have no idea who might specialize in the sort of gowns you ... well—"

"Want my mistresses to wear?" His eyes twinkled. "Don't worry, I'll bring a dressmaker tomorrow to consult with you before our drive."

"No one too expensive, mind you," she said.

He cast her a speculative glance. "I think you'll be pleased with my choice." He lifted his hand to finger the high collar of her gown. "And one more thing, Christabel. Don't wear black tomorrow."

Chapter Three

*A mistress must gain as much as she can
from any liaison, for who knows how long
her charms will last?*
—Anonymous, *Memoirs of a Mistress*

Don't wear black tomorrow.

Right. Christabel surveyed the contents of her armoire with a sigh. Black muslin with lace trim, black dimity with braid trim, black fustian with pearl buttons. Even her riding habits were black. A truly dismal selection.

"I told you, milady," said Rosa, her Gibraltan lady's maid, "we dyed *all* your gowns black. Every one. You ordered it so."

"And you *listened* to me?" Christabel slumped onto the bed. "What were you thinking?"

Rosa had been with Christabel from the beginning of her marriage, first as a maid-of-all-work, then as a lady's maid. Since they were nearly the same age, Christabel regarded her less as a servant than a sister. A very opinionated, often annoying, sister.

"I always listen to you," Rosa retorted with a toss of her lush black curls. "Especially when you are—how do you say in English—pigheaded. You said you would mourn his lordship forever."

Christabel winced. That was when she was still in the throes of grief, before she'd learned what Philip had been doing behind her back. Now another of her rash and impulsive acts had returned to haunt her.

"Go on, say it." Christabel lay back to stare at the ceiling. "I was a fool. You disapprove of my not keeping at least one gown undyed."

"It is not my place to approve or disapprove," Rosa said primly.

Christabel snorted. "And when did this sudden subservience make itself known? Shall I call in a doctor?"

"Very well, if you must know my opinion, life is too short to spend it mourning a man. Any man."

Christabel sat up to hug her knees. "But especially Philip, right?"

Rosa's manner softened. "Oh, my lady, he wasn't worthy of you. You deserve a better husband. Perhaps this Mr. Byrne—"

Christabel began to laugh hysterically. "No, indeed. He's not remotely the marrying sort."

Rosa frowned. "But good enough to share your bed?"

Christabel stopped laughing. She hadn't dared reveal the real reason for her sudden connection to Byrne—even loyal servants like Rosa gossiped, and this must be a masquerade in the truest sense. So she'd told her servant that she'd found a protector.

But that wasn't the source of Rosa's frown; oh no. Rosa believed that a woman should engage in scandalous liaisons whenever possible. It was part of the "life is too short" philosophy she'd embraced after her cheating soldier husband had got himself shot in a French brothel. Rosa was also practical enough to realize that a woman had to do what she must to survive sometimes.

So something else must be bothering her. "I thought you approved of my taking a lover?"

"It is not for me to—"

"Stubble it, Rosa. What's annoying you now?"

"I only want to make sure he's a good man. And men who aren't ever interested in marriage with anyone are generally . . ."

"Scoundrels. I know." She managed a smile. "Does it help that he's a charming scoundrel?"

Rosa eyed her askance.

"I don't intend to remarry anyway, so it hardly matters."

After this scheme with Byrne, no one of her rank would probably have her. Which was fine. Truly. She would return to traveling with Papa and spending her time with soldiers. What did she want with a lordly husband? She'd be better off with some sergeant who might appreciate her talents with firearms.

And who would never presume to court a widowed marchioness.

She swallowed the lump in her throat. She might consider remarrying if it meant she could have children. But she was clearly barren—ten years of marriage with no babes amply demonstrated that. Tears stung her eyes. No man with rank or property or any hopes for the future wanted a woman who couldn't give him heirs.

So what difference did it make *what* she wore for an outing with that devil Byrne? She thrust out her chin. None whatsoever. And if it annoyed him, so be it.

Brushing away her tears, she left the bed. "All right, let's get this done. Which of the awful things should I wear?"

"It matters not. They are all ugly in black." Rosa shot her a sly glance. "Thank heaven your new lover is purchasing you gowns."

"He's not purchasing me gowns. He's merely helping me choose them." She only prayed she didn't go too deeply into debt while buying them.

"What?" With another frown, Rosa took down the dimity gown and helped Christabel into it. "Will he expect you to pay for everything? You cannot afford—"

"We haven't worked out the financial arrangements yet." She eyed Rosa askance. "And what happened to 'it is not my place to approve or disapprove'?"

Rosa ignored her, refusing to hand Christabel the fichu she generally wore with the gown. "You should at least show your bosoms. He is a man, after all."

Christabel sighed. There was no question about Byrne's manhood. And showing some bosom might allay his annoyance at her. "Very well." She sat down at the dressing table. "But can you do something more sophisticated with my hair?"

"I shall try. But you should cut it off and curl it like the other ladies."

Christabel bit back her retort. That was easy for Rosa to say—*she* had natural curls, not Christabel's straight hair. Christabel wasn't about to let the feckless Rosa anywhere near curling irons. Or scissors, for that matter.

By the time Byrne and the dressmaker were announced, Rosa had piled Christabel's thick, unruly hair rather presentably atop her head. Leaving the room, they headed off down the hall. But when Rosa spotted the man from the top of the stairs, she pulled Christabel aside. "Isn't that the gambler you shot at last year?"

Would nobody ever forget that? "I'm afraid so."

"*Madre de Dios,* he is *forcing* you to be his mistress, isn't he, because of the shooting? I knew it! You would never take a lover by choice—you are too much the strict

Englishwoman for that. But to be forced . . . no, I will not let him do this. I will march right down and tell that scoundrel—"

"You will do nothing of the sort." Christabel grabbed her maid by the arm. "I'm not being forced. Have you ever known me to be forced into anything?"

When Rosa raised her eyebrows, Christabel added, "All right, so I did let Philip get around me occasionally, but he was my husband. This isn't the same." She lowered her voice to a whisper. "I find Mr. Byrne . . . interesting, that's all. And you *have* been saying that my life needs a change, that it's too dreary."

"*Si*, but you should not make the change with a gambler!"

"He's a man of property, not a gambler. He owns the Blue Swan."

That gave Rosa pause. "Ah, I have heard of it. A very lofty gentlemen's club. He must be quite rich." Rosa peered over the edge of the landing, her black eyes assessing Byrne with renewed interest. "I remember now—he's the one they call Bonny Byrne. Well . . . he *is* rather handsome. A fine dresser, too." The maid frowned. "You really should have kept one of your pretty gowns undyed."

"They weren't all that pretty anyway." It was hard to have pretty gowns when your husband spent all his money at the tables. "Now come on, let's go down."

"Perhaps the muslin gown would have worked when it was still pink," Rosa went on as they descended. "But no, a man like him expects something more."

Truer words were never spoken. Did he *have* to look so . . . so bonny? His auburn hair was wind-tossed from his drive, but the rest of him . . . Lord help her.

The perfectly cut riding coat of dun kerseymere showed

his chest and broad shoulders to fine advantage, especially since he eschewed the high, pointed collars and elaborate cravats most fine gentlemen seemed to wear. Instead of his chin being lost in a froth of linen, his modest collar and simply knotted cravat accentuated the masculine lines of his square jaw.

Even from here, she could see the dressmaker, a portly woman twice his age, casting him flirtatious smiles. Who wouldn't? The man's doeskin breeches could have been painted on him. Christabel had seen cavalrymen with less muscular calves and thighs—clearly Byrne did more with his days than sit at gaming tables.

The one thing she could find no trace of in his lean form was His Highness, his supposed father. Then Byrne shifted his gaze to them, and she saw the resemblance. It was in his eyes, the same unearthly blue as the prince's.

Eyes that narrowed with disapproval when they spotted her gown. He waited until they'd approached and he'd introduced the dressmaker before saying, "I see you're still intent on your widow's weeds."

"They suit me," she lied.

"No, they don't." He added in a huskier tone, "You were made for satins and silks, Christabel."

"Satins and silks are expensive, sir," Rosa cut in.

As the dressmaker scowled at Rosa's impertinence, Christabel said through gritted teeth, "Forgive my maid, but she's foreign and has decided opinions."

Byrne's lips twitched as he turned his unsettling blue gaze on Rosa. "And where do you hail from, miss?"

"Gibraltar." She presented it like a badge of honor.

He said something in a foreign tongue, and Rosa blinked. It was the first time Christabel had ever seen her maid startled.

"You speak Spanish, sir?" Rosa asked.

"A bit." His ingratiating smile took in both of them. "In my business, it pays to know a smattering of other languages."

Rosa nodded, though she still looked wary. But when he rattled off more Spanish, she cast him a cautious smile. Her short response, however, must have been saucy, for he burst into laughter. After a second she even joined him.

Then he said in English, "Rosa, why don't you show Mrs. Watts where we'll be doing the fittings for your mistress's gowns? Her footmen are waiting to bring in bolts of fabric."

Before Christabel could stop her, Rosa took the dressmaker off.

Christabel turned to Byrne with a frown. "I thought this was a consultation."

"It's also a fitting. I want Mrs. Watts to get started on your gowns right away. She's making it her first priority."

"I can't afford that!"

"Ah, but I can. And the quickest way for people to learn that you're my mistress is if they hear I bought you expensive gowns."

She considered that a moment, torn between pride and practicality, as footmen marched through the vestibule to the parlor, carrying bolts of muslin and sarcenet. "I suppose you do this all the time," she grumbled.

He took that for the acquiescence it was. "Occasionally. Although fortunately, my mistress's husbands generally pay for their gowns."

She stuck out her chin. "Then I'll pay you for mine later."

"I'm getting a barony out of this—that's payment enough." He slanted her a glance. "Besides, if I let *you* pay for them, you'll probably buy the coarsest linsey and plenty of dimity and fustian."

Because that was all she could afford. "That's practical for the country. And we are going to be in the country, aren't we?"

"Trust me, no one at this affair will be dressed in fustian. I mean to see you in gauze and silk and sheer muslin." He bent close to murmur, "*Very* sheer muslin."

Ignoring the sudden racing of her pulse, she said, "Is that what you said to Rosa in Spanish?"

"I told her I could afford satins and silks. And I told her I would treat you well." His eyes gleamed with humor. "She said that if I didn't, she'd feed me my privates for breakfast." At Christabel's groan, he chuckled. "Do you find your servants on the battlefield, for God's sake? Do you test them on marksmanship and swordplay before you hire them?"

"Very funny. Rosa is a soldier's widow. That taught her to be fierce."

"Much like her mistress." He drew her aside to avoid a footman carrying a particularly large bolt of rose satin. "God help the poor fellow who waylays you two in some dark alley. He's liable to have his head shot off."

She sniffed. "Sometimes a woman has to defend herself."

"And sometimes, my sweet, she should allow a man to defend her."

"As long as that man isn't the same one she needs defense from."

He shot her a seductive smile. "In which case, there are more effective ways of bringing him to his knees than shooting at him."

She fought to ignore the sensual pull of his dark flirta-tions. "As if you would know—have you *ever* let a woman bring you to your knees?"

"I do it in bed all the time." He scoured her with a wicked gaze, then lowered his voice to a whisper. "I can't wait to be on my knees with you."

A vivid image of him kneeling between her parted thighs rose in her mind, shocking her. "You'll be waiting an eternity for that," she shot back, as much to convince herself as him.

He merely laughed. The audacity of the man! Did he have *no* intention of holding to their bargain? Or could he simply not help trying to seduce any woman within reach?

Well, it wouldn't work with her. She refused to let his flirtations make her imagine what he'd be like in bed. Or wonder if he would be gentle or rough. If he would leave her feeling vaguely dissatisfied afterward the way Philip always had—

Oh, Lord, how could she even think about such things with her husband freshly in the grave?

Byrne drew her into the nearby dining room out of the way of the trooping footmen. Glancing around, he caught sight of a portrait over the mantel that she'd brought with her from Rosevine. His eyes narrowed. "Your father?"

"How did you know?"

"The uniform." He smiled. "And the resemblance. You have his fierce green eyes and stubborn chin."

"Thank you," she said, pleased. Most people said she looked nothing like Papa, because he was tall and gaunt, with gray-streaked chestnut curls utterly unlike her long, dark locks.

"Does he know about your scheme?"

She eyed him warily. "How could he? He's fighting the French right now."

"But you didn't write him."

"I thought it best not to bother him."

"And Prinny?" Byrne lifted one eyebrow. "When he learned that your 'property' had been sold, why didn't *he* approach your father?"

Because there was no time. In one month, Lord Stokely would make good his threats unless she stopped him. It would take a month at least just to reach her father and bring him back to England.

But if she told Byrne that, it would raise more questions in his too-inquisitive mind. So she shrugged. "I suppose His Highness thought it best to deal with me, since it was *my* husband who sold my family's property."

Byrne flicked her a glance. "If your father did know of your scheme, what would he think of it?"

Trying to ignore Papa's stern eyes staring down at her, she clasped her clammy hands together, and lied. "I have no idea."

"I doubt he'd approve of your sacrificing your reputation for 'family property.'"

"With luck, he won't hear of it." But of course he would. And no, he wouldn't approve. She was his "little soldier," his "Bel-bel"—he would want no man sullying her good name.

But what use was her good name when his was about to be destroyed? She refused to watch "Roaring Randall" be vilified in the papers as the man responsible for the greatest scandal in royal history.

Worse, as the prince had pointed out, if the letters weren't retrieved, Papa might very well hang for treason. How could she take that chance?

Papa should never have kept those letters after he'd been ordered to destroy them. But like any military strategist, he'd thought to protect himself—and his family—in case the drastic actions he'd taken on the prince's behalf ever came back to haunt him.

Which was precisely what they'd done. Because of her husband, the man whom her father had cautioned her against. She only wished Papa had barred her from seeing Philip. Then she wouldn't be in this position now.

She sighed. No, she would have found a way to elope. At the time, she'd chafed at Papa's many restrictions. Never mind that they'd been designed to protect her. She'd wanted light, air, freedom.

She'd found it in Philip, a gentleman officer too charming and solicitous for a woman of her limited experience to resist. What a naïve fool she'd been.

"Mr. Byrne? My lady?" came a voice from the vestibule. Grateful to be dragged from her thoughts, she walked out of the dining room with Byrne to find Mrs. Watts standing there. "We are ready for your ladyship's fitting now."

Once they were in the small parlor, the dressmaker banished Rosa with the excuse that there was no space for the maid. But after the maid stalked out, Mrs. Watts explained in a confidential tone, "I find that ladies' maids only get in the way. Best to leave matters of dress to the experts, don't you think?"

"Certainly," Christabel replied, flummoxed by the dressmaker's lofty pretensions. But as the dressmaker brought out a book of fashion plates for them to examine, it became apparent that the expert she referred to was Byrne.

While Mrs. Watts took notes, he flipped through the book, barking orders faster than the dressmaker could write them down. "She'll need at least five chemises, seven evening gowns, three riding habits, eleven walking dresses with matching pelisses or spencers—"

"That's too many," Christabel protested.

"We'll be in the country a week." Skimming his hand down to rest just above her hips, he added, "And I intend to have you in and out of your gowns frequently."

As the dressmaker discreetly dropped her gaze, Christabel glared at him. He was enjoying his role of lover far too much.

Leaving his hand on her waist, he went on. "She'll need new petticoats—silk, preferably—a few nightgowns of very fine linen, and dressing gowns."

"And shawls," Christabel added.

"No shawls." Byrne dropped his gaze to her bosom. "A woman should flaunt her . . . assets."

Heat rose in her cheeks despite her efforts to contain it. "Then perhaps I should do without gowns entirely," she said sweetly.

His eyes gleamed. "An excellent idea. We'll stay in my room the whole time."

Blast him. She tipped up her chin, determined to have the last word. "I need my shawls. I get cold."

"I'll keep you warm enough, don't worry."

"Byrne—" she began in sheer exasperation.

"Oh, all right." He turned to Mrs. Watts. "And a shawl."

"Three shawls," Christabel said.

"*One* shawl," he countered. "In silk." When she frowned, he added, "If you want more, you'll have to pay for them yourself."

He knew perfectly well she couldn't afford such things. "Then I'll just use my old ones."

"Of wool, no doubt."

"As a matter of fact, yes."

He groaned. "Fine. Three silk shawls." Her triumphant glance made him add, "But don't think I'll let you wrap yourself up like a mummy after I've gone to the trouble of buying gowns that display your charms." He lowered his voice to a confidential murmur. "Either play the part or don't. Stokely will be suspicious enough as it is."

Her face fell. He was right. "Very well, one shawl will do, I suppose."

The next hour was taken up in sorting through a dizzying array of fabrics, styles, and colors.

The fabrics were the most exquisite she'd ever seen or touched. She'd never cared much about clothes, but then she'd never had gowns made of fabrics like these—silks that flowed over one's hand like water, muslins so soft and delicate she feared tearing them with a single touch. As a lieutenant, Philip hadn't been able to afford such. Then, along with his estate he'd inherited a mountain of debt, which he'd built higher every year.

But Byrne could clearly afford them. Either that or he was mad.

Madness *would* explain his outrageously bold color choices—brilliant reds, vibrant blues, and dramatic greens. Didn't he realize she wasn't one of his stunning society ladies, who could easily wear clothes that drew attention to themselves?

When she protested, he told her, "Trust me, they'll suit you perfectly."

"But I thought pink and cream were the fashion." That's what Philip had always preferred her to wear.

"For schoolgirls coming out, not for a grown woman. And certainly not for you."

When Mrs. Watts held particular fabrics up to her face for him to choose, Christabel saw in the mirror what he meant. Even she could see that the rose satin made her cheeks glow a healthy color, and the holly green crepe made her eyes sparkle. She'd always looked rather sallow in her pink gowns.

The fact that he'd been right perversely annoyed her. "You seem to know a great deal about women's clothes."

His slow smile sparked something hot low in her belly. "I know what I like." His gaze dropped to her mouth. "And what makes a man desire a woman."

A delicious shiver coursed through her. Curse the randy devil, he also knew what made a woman desire a man. Him and his smiles and extravagant gifts and commanding voice—all designed to send a female's pulse into a frenzied gallop and melt her resistance into a puddle.

Well, he wouldn't do that to her. No, indeed. She'd already allowed one man's flatteries and flirtations to tempt her into an unwise marriage; she wasn't about to let it tempt her into an illicit liaison with a devil who put his own gain above his conscience. If he even possessed a conscience.

Once they'd settled on the gowns, Mrs. Watts drew out her measuring tape. "If you will come this way, my lady . . ." Mrs. Watts led her to a corner of the room where a little dais had been built to accommodate a previous resident's passion for exhibiting. "Stand up here, please. And forgive me, but you must remove your gown so I can measure you in your corset."

"Of course." As she mounted the little steps, she glanced expectantly at Byrne, who responded by taking a seat in her favorite armchair. "Byrne! You can't watch this."

"Why not?" The sneaky devil had the audacity to smile. "It's nothing I haven't seen before."

He was taking this role too far, and he knew it. "Which is why you don't need to see it now," she persisted.

"Ah, but I have to make sure everything is done to my specifications." He glanced at the dressmaker. "Don't mind me."

Mrs. Watts's plump cheeks turned a rosy sheen, but she gave him a cursory nod. That's what Byrne's extravagance bought him—compliance from dressmakers and servants.

Fine, she would let him watch her be measured. She couldn't very well quarrel with him in front of the dressmaker. Besides, he *was* paying for the gowns. She supposed he had a right to have a say in it.

But his extravagance would not buy *her*. He'd find that out soon enough.

Pretending she didn't care in the least if he saw her half-dressed, she stared him down as the dressmaker helped her remove her gown. Watching him proved a mistake, however, for once she stood atop the dais in her corset and chemise, her pride forced her to keep looking as his gaze roamed wherever it pleased.

It took all her strength to fight a blush. No man had ever gazed upon her like that before. Even Philip had never really taken the time to look at her. A lusty soldier, he'd been quick to join her in bed, and just as quick to retire to his own when he was done.

Somehow she suspected that "quick" wouldn't apply to Mr. Byrne. While Mrs. Watts took her measurements and scribbled them in her notebook, he did some measuring of his own. His eyes lingered on her bosom with disquieting interest, then examined her cinched-in waist and too-ample hips. When he was done with his thorough assessment, his heated gaze made a leisurely trip back up her body to fix on her face.

And in his eyes, she saw the truth that he wasn't even bothering to hide. He would stop at nothing to have her in his bed, bargain or no.

She cursed as a wayward thrill coursed down her spine. The impudence of the man! Well, she would just show *him*. She turned to the dressmaker with a smooth smile. "I do hope my friend hasn't embarrassed you too much with his antics. Sometimes he can be most outrageous. I wouldn't be surprised if after he chose all these gowns, he changed his mind about them and refused to pay."

Mrs. Watts didn't so much as frown.

Worse yet, Byrne merely chuckled. "Mrs. Watts has dealt with me often enough, my sweet, to know that I pay my bills with admirable regularity."

Christabel glared at him. So much for trying to shame the man into behaving.

Ignoring her frowns, he turned his attention to the dressmaker. "And speaking of payment, I'm willing to pay more to have these gowns finished in three days."

Mrs. Watts eyed him with a wily gleam. "It will be a great deal more."

"Whatever it costs."

The woman smiled broadly. "Very good, sir." Then she untied Christabel's chemise and pulled it down to form a line across the very top of her breasts. "Now, milady, for your evening gowns, is this an acceptable neckline?"

"No," Byrne said, before Christabel could even answer.

Mrs. Watts pivoted to him like a dog following the bounce of a ball. She pulled the chemise down a little more. "Here, then?"

"Lower," he said.

As Christabel seethed, Mrs. Watts went down another half inch. "Here?"

"Lower."

"Perhaps I should simply pop out my breasts and serve them on a platter," Christabel grumbled.

As the dressmaker coughed to hide her laugh, Byrne raised one eyebrow. "While that sounds intriguing, my sweet, when we're in public you'd best keep them in a gown."

"*In* being the important word," she retorted.

Mrs. Watts continued to hold the chemise in its present position, her gaze fixed on him. "Sir? Is this all right or not?"

He glanced from the dressmaker to a glowering Christabel, then back to the dressmaker. "That'll do for now, I suppose. We'll see how the gowns look once they're done."

With a nod, Mrs. Watts finished her measurements. "Will that be all, sir?"

"No. She needs something to wear for the next few days, so if you could alter one of her old gowns, something she wore before she went into mourning—"

"She can't," Christabel broke in. "We dyed all my old gowns black."

"*All* of them?"

She stuck out her chin. "Yes."

"Bloody hell. At least that explains why you persist in wearing them." He turned to the dressmaker. "Could you make her mourning gowns a bit less . . . severe? And have one of them ready in the morning?"

"Certainly, sir."

He rose and strode to the door. "I'll call her maid to fetch them."

As he opened the door, Rosa practically fell into the room. Christabel rolled her eyes. Rosa would never go meekly off when there was gossip to hear.

"Forgive me, sir," Rosa babbled, "I was merely coming to tell my lady—"

"It's all right, Rosa," he broke in. "Just go bring us the prettiest of your mistress's mourning gowns, will you?"

"But they are all ugly, senor."

"What a surprise," he said dryly. "Very well, then take Mrs. Watts with you. She can assess which ones are best for alteration."

Rosa and Mrs. Watts went off, and Byrne closed the door. Only then did she realize they were alone. And she was dressed most scandalously.

He seemed to realize the same thing, for his gaze took outrageous liberties as he surveyed her scantily clad form.

To her chagrin, her pulse leaped in response. "For pity's sake, go see to your horses or something. We can finish this without you. Go on, go away and leave us in peace."

"And let you dress yourself like a nun? I think not."

His nonchalant assumption that this masquerade gave him the right to tell her what to wear frustrated her. "I should warn you, just because I let you get away with these outrageous flirtations in public doesn't mean I'll allow them in private. Furthermore," she lied, "I shall elaborate on your abominable treatment of me in my written report to His Highness. And when your father hears—"

"What did you say?" He'd gone abruptly still, his eyes turning gray as a sudden tempest.

Too late, she remembered that he had good reason to dislike his father. "I-I said I will make a report to—"

"No, you called His Highness my 'father.'" He advanced up the dais's steps swiftly, trapping her atop it. "If you're to play my mistress, Lady Haversham, there are some things you should know about me. For one, His Highness is not my father."

She blinked. "But I thought—"

"He did sire me, yes, no matter what the bloody arse claimed to the world. But there's a vast difference between producing seed and being a father. Only one person raised me, and she's the only one who counts. That fool at Carlton House had nothing to do with it, so I don't give a bloody damn what you tell him."

Backing her against the wall, he scowled down at her. "And one more thing—I don't take kindly to threats. I respond by doing exactly what I've been warned not to do. And if you think my flirtations were outrageous before—"

Taking her off guard, he caught her chin in a firm grip and brought his mouth down on hers.

The kiss was hard. Commanding. And very, very thorough. With provoking insolence, he sealed his mouth to hers as if he had every right to do so. But when he tried making the kiss more intimate, she wrenched her mouth from his.

"What do you think you're doing?" she demanded, fighting to ignore the silly pounding of her heart and the deplorable quiver in the pit of her belly.

His smoldering gaze seared her wherever it settled. "I'm kissing my pretend mistress."

"Stop it." She cast a furtive glance to the door. "The servants might see us."

"Good. Servants are notorious gossips, so let's put on a good show for them." Then he kissed her again.

Except that this time he succeeded in invading her mouth with his tongue, erotically, possessively. And she didn't stop him, blast it.

Worse yet, she liked it. She tried not to compare his

slow, drugging kisses to Philip's sloppy, eager ones, but it was hard to ignore the difference. Her husband's kisses had always been a brief prelude to a quick tumble. Byrne's kiss was an end in itself, hot, heady, and intoxicating. He fed on her mouth as if he'd been waiting half his life to taste it. The sensation made her dizzy.

His hand skimmed down her throat, and she waited, on the edge of disappointment, for him to grab her breast and squeeze it roughly the way Philip always had.

Instead, Byrne curved his hand around the side of her neck, caressing her throat with his thumb, up and down, back and forth, to mimic the heated plunges of his tongue between her lips.

Oh, heavenly day. He drove the very air from her lungs, which might explain why her knees were going weak and her head growing faint. With leisurely care, he thrust, probed, caressed . . . made love to her mouth.

But only her mouth. How very intriguing.

Though he'd settled his other hand on her waist, he merely stroked her ribs with it. He didn't paw her breasts or cup her between the legs or squeeze her bottom, all of which Philip would have done within seconds after starting to kiss her.

And Byrne's peculiar restraint was having the oddest effect on her. She felt restless and unsatisfied. She found herself *wanting* his hand on her breast. Lord help her— what kind of a wanton was she?

She tore her lips from his, seeking breath and . . . respite? Relief from the liquid heat he fed with each newer, bolder thrust into her mouth? "That's enough," she somehow managed to whisper. "You've made your point."

His breath warmed her cheek. "My point?"

He turned to nibbling her ear, and oh, what that did to

her. She thought she would come out of her skin. She could barely think, much less answer. "That if I threaten you, you'll feel free to . . . take . . . certain liberties."

"Ah. *That* point." He tugged on her earlobe with his teeth, then pressed an openmouthed kiss to her neck.

"So you can . . . stop now. I got your point."

"And I got yours—that you don't mind my taking certain liberties."

The truth of it didn't make it any less insulting. She jerked back. "I didn't say that."

"You didn't have to." His smugly masculine smile roused her ire, especially when he followed it with a sweeping, proprietary caress of his hand from her ribs to her hip. "I dare say if I took you to bed right now, you wouldn't protest."

His arrogant assumption drove her over the edge. Reaching down, she grabbed his privates and squeezed, just enough to warn him. "I don't take kindly to threats either, you randy Irishman. We made a bargain. You agreed to the terms, which didn't include kissing or anything else. So if you try that again—"

"You'll what? Maim me?" His voice held nothing but sarcasm.

She blinked. Most men retreated when faced with serious bodily harm.

But of course Byrne wasn't most men, as evidenced by his erection, growing harder and thicker and heavier in her hand by the moment. Nor did his angular features show even an ounce of concern for his precarious position.

He actually leaned closer, shoving his . . . *thing* into her hand. "Go ahead. I dare you." His eyes were steely bright as he lowered his voice to a menacing whisper. "See how far you get."

Her mouth went dry. Dear Lord, what now?

She was saved by the door opening, and the dress-maker saying cheerfully, "I think we've found two gowns that will—Oh, dear. I-I'm sorry, I'll come back."

"No, stay," Christabel called out, grateful that Byrne's back was to the door. Releasing his privates, she started to withdraw her hand, but he gripped it before she could.

When her gaze flew to his, he hissed, "Next time you touch my cock, it had better be under much more enjoyable circumstances. Understood?" Only then did he let go.

As he turned to face the dressmaker and Rosa, cool as you please, it was all Christabel could do not to throw something at him. He was in for a surprise if he thought that she'd ever touch his cock in *that* way. He'd just reminded her of the dangerous devil who lay beneath the smooth, charming façade, and there was no way she was ever sharing a bed with *that* man.

Chapter Four

*I learned early on to guard my secrets. A
man will keep them faithfully as long as
he's sharing your bed, but once he discards
you, all his loyalty is lost.*
—Anonymous, *Memoirs of a Mistress*

The warmongering female had actually threatened to
unman him! Shaking his head, Gavin settled back in a
chair to watch as Mrs. Watts marked one of Christabel's
black monstrosities for alteration.

Christabel pretended to ignore him. The bloody chit
was a real piece of work. One minute she responded to
his kiss with all the fervor of a dockside tart, and the next
she loosed that fiery temper of hers.

He'd infuriated many a mistress, but none had ever
dared to grab him by the ballocks and vow to maim him.
Even the boldest ones knew better than to tempt fate
with him.

But not Colonel Christabel, oh, no. She made a habit
of tempting fate. And every time she did, it only stoked
his desire higher. If she continued it, he'd soon be walking around with a bloody Maypole in his trousers.

*Careful, Gavin. You've got bigger matters at stake than
some female, no matter how pretty.*

"Tighten the bodice, too, would you, Mrs. Watts?" he called out, venting his annoyance at himself by annoying Christabel. "Make it nice and snug."

"I'll try, sir, but it will take time. The trim makes it impossible to simply double the fabric. It would make the seams too thick."

"Like Mr. Byrne's skull," Christabel grumbled.

Gavin waited until she looked at him for his response, then said, "It's not my skull that's thick right now, lass."

With her cheeks flaming, she jerked her gaze from his. Good. Let *her* be uncomfortable for a change.

This arousal was bloody inconvenient. He ought to be trying to unearth her secrets, instead of dwelling on the sheer pleasure of kissing her.

But the woman had quite a talent for kissing, whether she knew it or not. There'd been none of those coy female tricks he was used to from his mistresses—no false air of innocence or fake shyness or pretense of propriety, all meant to stimulate his jaded palate, though they usually served only to irritate him. Even if people weren't honest anywhere else, they should at least be honest in bed.

Like Christabel's kisses. In their honesty, they'd been more erotic than those of any sophisticated courtesan. Her mouth had tasted of currants and cinnamon, like a Christmas pudding, sweet and warm and generous. It was nothing like the perfumed mouths of the practiced society women, who only gave enough to get what they wanted—a pleasant romp with a man who wouldn't interfere in their marriages or expect anything of them other than enjoyment.

Christabel didn't want a pleasant romp from him. Nor was she willing to buy what she wanted with kisses. And the fact that she'd still responded to his kiss with such generosity of feeling intoxicated him. Made him want more. A great deal more. And soon.

He couldn't wait to take down her "unfashionable" hair, wrap it about his hand, and feel it tumbling over his chest, his belly, his cock.

"Mr. Byrne!" said a sharp voice.

He snapped to attention. Damn, there he went again. He looked up to find that Mrs. Watts had started unbuttoning the marked-up gown to remove it.

And Christabel was glowering at him. "If you don't mind—"

"I don't." There was no way he'd let the chit throw him out now. The more unsettled he kept her, the more likely she was to let something important slip. "I've already seen you in your corset, my sweet."

She stayed Mrs. Watts's hand. "But I still prefer to have privacy."

"And I still prefer to watch." He motioned to Mrs. Watts to continue, then added, "Besides, your chemise and that long corset are so prim and proper, you might as well be wearing armor."

She looked skeptical, as well she should. Armor it might be, but it highlighted her figure so temptingly that Gavin's blood pounded in his temples as Mrs. Watts slipped the gown off her.

It still astonished him to find such a lush form hidden under the voluminous fabric of her widow's weeds. He liked women with some flesh to them, and she was built as if made for him, with plump breasts, full hips, and a rounded belly reminiscent of that painting of Venus rising from the sea. Christabel might be short, but she wasn't short on curves. He itched to touch them, to taste every inch of that sweetly abundant flesh.

A pity she had to don her damned ugly gown again. She seemed to think so, too, for after she was dressed, and he was speaking to Mrs. Watts about a few final matters, he noticed the widow running her hand slowly over the rose satin that was to be made into an evening gown for her.

He bent close to Mrs. Watts and lowered his voice. "The rose gown—what would it cost to have it finished in time for her to wear tomorrow evening?"

The dressmaker followed his gaze, then named some exorbitant sum.

"Done." This had nothing to do with any sudden urge to please Christabel, he told himself. It was merely another tactic for keeping her off guard.

"And your lady will need the matching pelisse and—"

"The whole ensemble. Whatever it takes."

Beaming her approval, Mrs. Watts hurried off to gather up her wares.

While she bustled about, Gavin strolled up to Christabel. "Mrs. Watts works with a milliner and a cobbler who will make sure you have bonnets, caps, slippers, and any other matching fripperies. As for reticules—"

"My present reticules will be sufficient. I don't need all that." With a sigh, she turned from the satin as a pilgrim turns from temptation.

It reminded him of his boyhood, when he'd watched futilely as his mother tore her gaze from the rich gowns in shop windows that she couldn't afford, thanks to Prinny. And that he couldn't afford to get for her. "Yes, but you want 'all that,' don't you?"

She lifted her clear-eyed gaze to him. "It doesn't matter what I want. You've already spent too much as it is."

"Let me be the judge of that."

Her features hardened. "You'll expect something in return."

"Yes, I'll expect you to wear the gowns," he snapped.

"You know what I mean. And gowns weren't part of our bargain."

He frowned. The idea of her feeling obligated to accept his advances because he'd bought some clothes didn't sit well. It smacked too much of a whore's transaction with her customer. And Christabel, like his mother, was no whore. "Think of it as my way of atoning for my part in your current situation."

"Is that what it is?"

"No. But if that makes you feel better—"

"I would feel better if you wouldn't spend so much money on me that I can't repay without ... without ..."

"Sharing my bed?"

She stuck out her chin. "Yes."

"One thing has nothing to do with the other. If I'm to convince Stokely to invite you to his party, you have to dress well. My reward has already been established; this is simply part of earning my barony."

She eyed him skeptically.

His exasperation grew. "Consider it this way—if I didn't spend money on clothes for you, I'd spend it on loose women, wine, and song. By taking the gowns, you're saving me from other wicked pursuits." He bit back a smile. "And I know how keen respectable women are on saving men from wickedness."

"Not *this* respectable woman." A sad little frown marred her smooth brow. "The last time I tried saving a man, I failed spectacularly. I don't plan to try again."

Haversham, no doubt. And why did her cynicism annoy him? He was just as cynical, if not more so.

She picked up a monstrous reticule and a shawl she'd draped over a nearby chair. "Are we going for a drive or not?"

He eyed her reticule suspiciously. "It depends." Before she could stop him, he snatched it from her and peered inside. Lifting one eyebrow, he dug out her pistol. "I'm not going anywhere with you carting a loaded pistol."

"It's not loaded," she protested.

"Then it's no use to you at present anyway." He shoved it into his coat pocket, then offered her his arm. "Shall we go?"

"Now see here, that belongs to me!"

"And you'll get it back upon our return."

She sniffed. "So we actually *are* going for a drive then? I thought you might have said that last night just to disguise what we were really doing today."

"That was part of it. Iversley and Draker know the true situation between us, but I cautioned them not to tell their wives. So the ladies would naturally assume the worst if they heard about my buying you gowns. You seemed to be enjoying yourself at dinner, and I didn't want to make things awkward for you."

Taking his arm, she let him lead her into the hall, where the servants handed her a horrid black bonnet. "Then you shouldn't have kissed my hand and called me 'my sweet' when you took your leave."

She had a point. But hearing them tell her about his sordid childhood in the streets had provoked him. He had spent his life amassing a substantial fortune, yet no one could forget where he'd begun.

That was Prinny's fault, and Gavin meant to make the man atone for it, one way or the other.

"Well, as you say, it hardly matters." He led her outside and down the steps to his cabriolet. "They don't move in

Stokely's circle, so you'll have little occasion to see them."
He cast her a side glance. "Unless you plan to take society
by storm after this is over."

"Hardly. I'll have enough trouble with *this* scheme.
Once I have my property back, I'll retreat to the country
and never show myself in London again."

He helped her up onto the perch, then climbed up beside her. "Do you hate town that much?"

"Actually, I like town. It's society that terrifies me."

"Yet you'll throw yourself upon its mercy for the sake
of family property."

"I have no choice."

He set the horses off at a smart pace. "Speaking of your
property, do you know where Stokely might keep it? His
estate is rather large." And her answer might give him an
idea of what the bloody thing was.

"I have no idea," she said coolly.

"Where did your father keep it?"

"In a strongbox."

So the object was small. Jewelry perhaps? But how
would that affect Prinny? "How do you know Stokely isn't
keeping it in a strongbox or even a safe?"

"I don't. If he is, I'll have to find a way into it. Or take
the entire thing with me. Surely he won't have more than
one." She paused. "Do *you* know how to break into such
things?"

"I can get into any safe, I promise you." Though she
would undoubtedly disapprove of his methods. "And if
your property was in a strongbox in the first place, how
did your husband get his hands on it? Or even know
about it?"

At her long silence, he glanced over to see her face suf-
fused with shame. "I told him." She caught him staring

and cast him a defiant glance. "Before Papa left for France last time, he gave me the strongbox. He explained what I was to do with the contents if something happened to him. When I brought the box home and wouldn't tell Philip what was in it, his curiosity was roused. He badgered me about it, asking why I didn't trust him. It already galled him that Papa didn't."

A defeated sigh left her lips. "I couldn't stand to see him so hurt. Philip had been distant toward me, and I thought if I could show him how much faith I had in him—" She shook her head. "It probably sounds silly to you."

"Not at all." Haversham had been exactly the sort to play on his wife's affections to get what he wanted.

"Well, it sounds silly to me, especially now that I know that while he was begging me to tell him the family secrets he was also trotting off to London to—"

When she stopped there, he prodded, "To do what?"

Color filled her pretty cheeks. "Gamble. And . . . and other things."

Other things. Gavin wracked his mind, but could think of no other vice he'd heard of Haversham engaging in. Strong drink? As he recalled, Haversham had swilled his share of Gavin's brandy when he was at the club. Still, if she'd grown up around soldiers, she had to be used to that. A mistress? Not that he'd ever heard.

Whatever it was, her closed expression made it clear that she didn't wish to discuss it. Very well, he'd get it out of her later. Besides, that wasn't the important thing right now. "So you gave him the key to the strongbox, did you?"

"No, indeed, I'm not that much a fool." She scowled. "But his steward knew how to break into such things—he was that sort of person."

Gavin bit back a smile. "Like me, you mean."

When she tossed her head back, the wind nearly carried off her large-brimmed bonnet. "It does take a certain sort of scoundrel to break into things."

"It does indeed." And another sort to betray his wife for a gambling debt. No wonder she distrusted gamblers. Gavin began to wish he'd exacted a different sort of payment from Lord Haversham. "So he never confessed what he'd done?"

As their speed increased down a long stretch of road, she grabbed for her bonnet ribbons. "I never even guessed they were missing until it was too late. After the prince summoned me, and we spoke, I immediately went to check the contents of the strongbox, only to find that they were gone."

He pounced on her slip. "'They'?"

"It," she said hastily. "The contents."

"You said 'they.'"

The panic in her eyes was unmistakable. "You misheard me."

"Ah." *Misheard you, my arse.* She'd said it twice. So there was more than one piece of property. A whole set of jewels? Documents? Documents made more sense, in light of Prinny's interest in the things. But what sort of documents?

"So where are we going?" she asked brightly.

He smothered a chuckle. He'd never heard a more blatant change of subject. Despite her testy demeanor and aggressive stance, she was at heart an honest person. Keeping this secret was probably killing her.

Which is why he'd have to make it easy for her to unburden herself when the time came. Surely if that idiot Haversham could get it out of her, Gavin could do so.

He'd simply get her into his bed, where she belonged. No woman could keep silent for long when cocooned in the intimacy of the bedchamber.

"Byrne?" the fetching female prodded. "Where are we going?"

To bed, I hope. "Rotten Row, of course." He flicked the ends of the reins at her. "Why? Do you want to drive?"

Her face lit up. "Oh, could I?"

He'd been joking, but how could he resist when she looked as if he'd just offered her the keys to the city? "Do you know how to drive a cabriolet?"

"I've driven a phaeton. It can't be any harder than that."

"A phaeton? And you didn't turn it over?"

"No, indeed!" She looked insulted. "I'll have you know I've never turned a vehicle over in my life."

Suppressing a grin, he handed her the reins. "Then try not to turn this one over, will you?"

Her eyes went wide, then she broke into a smile of such delight, he didn't even mind risking his cattle. "I won't, I swear," she said in a rush.

She took control of the cabriolet as if born to it, expertly controlling his team of matched grays, settling them at once when they showed some rebellion.

"You enjoy driving, do you?" he asked.

"The only thing I love better than driving a rig like this is riding my gelding. In the country, I either ride or drive myself everywhere I can."

"That explains why you do it so well. I've never seen a woman—and few men, for that matter—handle a rig so competently."

Eyes twinkling, she glanced over at him. "Some of us women *do* have abilities beyond the bedchamber, you know."

He chuckled. "Then I shall have to hire you as my coachman. It would certainly liven my jaunts about town."

She threw her head back and laughed. None of that ladylike tittering for Colonel Christabel, oh no. Hers was a hearty, deep-throated laugh that resonated deep inside him. And when her bonnet flew off to go tumbling down the road, she only laughed harder, her pretty cheeks flushing with the sheer joy of being in perfect control of her fate on such a pleasant day.

When was the last time he'd gained joy from that simple a thing? Not since he was a very young boy, almost certainly. Before his mother had exhausted all attempts to get Prinny to continue her annuity. Before they'd moved from lodging house to lodging house, each one meaner than the last.

Before the fire that had tossed him into the cold world at twelve to fend for himself.

Shaking off the dark memory, he laid his arm behind her back. "I noticed that your butler wears an eye patch. Why?"

"He went blind in one eye when a stray bullet shattered his cheekbone."

"Not one of your bullets, I hope."

"No, indeed! He was in the war. But after he was wounded he could no longer serve in the army, so we hired him."

"You and Haversham? Or just you?"

She shrugged. "He was in my husband's regiment. I couldn't very well let the man starve, could I?"

"Some people would."

Her lips tightened into a fierce little line. "Then they don't properly appreciate the sacrifices our soldiers make to keep them safe."

He eyed her consideringly. "So you really *do* find your servants on the battlefield."

"A few. Five, I think. No, six. I always forget about Cook, since he was a chef long before he served in the navy."

"Quite the military household you have there. I suppose I should be happy you were the *only* one to shoot at me that day."

A smile played over her lips. "I shall have to issue pistols to my staff."

"That sounds exactly like something you'd do." And oddly enough, it didn't dampen his desire for her one whit. Christabel was a bracing tonic after all his coolly sophisticated mistresses.

He frowned. That might prove a problem for their scheme. Would his friends believe he'd changed his preference in mistresses on a whim? Or would they—and possibly Stokely—suspect a deeper reason for the change?

Perhaps he should test the waters before they went any further. What day was it? Tuesday. Perfect. What he had in mind would have the added advantage of showing Christabel exactly what she was getting herself into.

"Change of plan," he told her. "Give me the reins."

She did as he said, though her face showed her disappointment. "Why? Where are we going?"

He took the next turn, heading them off toward Cheapside. "Somewhere you can learn firsthand how to be a proper mistress."

"Now see here, we agreed—"

"Not like that. Believe me, when I get ready to seduce you, you'll know it. Right now we're going to a card party."

She looked perplexed. "How will that teach me to be a proper mistress?"

"You'll see."

Chapter Five

❦

*As mistress to an earl, I witnessed many a
scandalous event, but none so outrageous
as the secret card parties.*
—Anonymous, *Memoirs of a Mistress*

Christabel was ready to throttle Byrne. He refused to say
a word about where they were going, no matter how
much she plagued him.

And that comment of his—*when I get ready to seduce
you.* Hah! Did he think she'd fall into his bed the minute
he decided he was "ready"? Bonny Byrne indeed. He was
more like a Prince of Sin, trying to corrupt anything in
skirts.

Look at how he tooled the vehicle to ensure that she
touched him as often as possible. At first she'd thought
him merely a bad driver, but it soon became apparent
from the way his spirited horses followed his every com-
mand that his motions were intentional. If she slid away
on the seat, he took a corner fast to throw her back
against him. And every time he did it, she marveled at the
taut muscles in the thighs plastered to hers, the fine control of his whipcord of an arm.

By the time they drew up in an alley behind a nonde-
script town house in Cheapside, Christabel's blood was

thundering in her veins. Despite her determination to ignore him, he made touching him an addictive enjoyment.

Which was, of course, what he intended. To make her want him, crave him . . . desire him. It wasn't going to work, no matter how much he tried. It *wasn't*.

As he helped her down, she glanced uneasily around the alley. This looked less a place for a card party than a place for secret assignations. A little iron-barred door led into a high-walled garden amazingly lush for the middle of town.

When he produced a key to unlock the door, her suspicion that the place might belong to him deepened. Until he brought her up the path of the garden and in the back way to a kitchen, where his appearance threw the servants into a tizzy.

"Monsieur Byrne! What a delightful surprise!" exclaimed a tall, spindly fellow sporting a chef's hat and a thick French accent. "If I had known you were coming, I would have sent to ze butcher for a leg of lamb."

Byrne laughed. "We won't be here for dinner, Ramel. And I doubt your mistress would approve."

With a snort, the chef lowered his voice. "*La canaille* upstairs with Lady Jenner do not appreciate fine lamb— for them, I only make *le boeuf*." He said it as if beef were beneath his abilities. "But for you, it should be lamb with *petits oignons*—"

"Monsieur Ramel!" a female voice barked from beyond the kitchen doorway. "Where's the tea we called for over ten minutes ago?"

When the woman entered to find Byrne and Christabel standing there, she halted abruptly. "What the devil are *you* doing here?"

"My lady," the chef said hastily, "Monsieur Byrne came in the back way—"

"Good afternoon, Eleanor," Byrne told the woman.

Even Christabel had heard of Byrne's torrid affair with the Countess of Jenner. So *this* was the famous whist-player, who won and lost thousands of pounds at the tables without blinking. Did she always wear such outrageously low-cut gowns? And hadn't the chef mentioned guests?

Tossing back the blond locks that flowed shockingly unbound over her shoulders, Lady Jenner frowned at Byrne. "You can't come up. I'm unwell."

"Relax, I know all about your Tuesday afternoon card games."

Lady Jenner's eyes narrowed. "Who told you?"

He arched one eyebrow.

The buxom female groaned. "I swear, I don't know how you unearth everyone's secrets. But we don't allow strangers, so if you've come to play, you'll have to get rid of your friend."

"We've come to watch." Byrne settled his hand in the small of Christabel's back. "And my friend isn't a stranger. She's Haversham's widow."

Lady Jenner cast Christabel a withering glance. "*You're* the Marchioness of Haversham? The woman who wouldn't accompany her husband to town because, as he put it, 'she's too afraid of society'?"

Christabel bristled. "What? I've never been afraid of anything in my—"

"Yes," Byrne said, giving Christabel's waist a warning squeeze. "This is the same woman. As you can see, Haversham's description wasn't entirely apt."

"Still, we can't be sure she won't gossip."

"I'll vouch for her discretion." Byrne lazily surveyed the kitchen. "But if you don't want us to stay, I could always mention to your husband the purpose to which you're putting the town house you inherited from your family."

"Damn you, Byrne." She pouted in that fetching manner only certain women could pull off. "Very well, I suppose if you only wish to watch . . ."

"That's all. I want Lady Haversham to see truly excellent whist-playing, and I thought at once of you and your friends."

That seemed to soften the woman's temper. "We *are* the best."

"That's why we're here." A devilish gleam appeared in his eyes. "To assess the competition for Stokely's party."

"You and Stokely won't win the pot this year, I promise you. We'll lead you a merry dance." She shifted her gaze to Christabel, running it down her awful black gown with an impudence bordering on insult. "If you're planning to play at Stokely's, Lady Haversham, I do hope you're better at it than your husband was."

Christabel's curiosity got the better of her. "You played cards with Philip?"

The woman's laugh grated on her nerves. "Of course. We played him when we needed to plump our pockets after a loss. Dreadful player, your husband."

With another grating laugh, she turned and gestured to them to follow, leaving Christabel to shake with impotent rage. All right, so Philip had been awful at cards, but it was still a cruel thing to taunt a man's widow with.

Suddenly, she felt Byrne's hand soothingly stroke her waist. "Pay Eleanor no mind." Byrne led her after their hostess. "The only thing she excels at besides playing cards is being a hellcat."

Christabel stifled a gasp at his bluntness.

"Is that why you became my lover, Byrne dear?" Lady Jenner remarked from ahead of them in silky-sweet tones. She began to climb a rather narrow staircase. "Because you enjoyed bedding a hellcat?"

"That's why I became your *ex*-lover," he shot back. "I have better things to do than serve as your scratching post."

Lady Jenner had reached the top of the stairs, where she now stood waiting for them. Catching sight of Christabel's shocked look, the countess apparently misunderstood the source of it, for she said with a sly smile, "I take it that Byrne didn't say you'd be meeting one of his mistresses here."

Christabel managed to smooth her features. "*Former* mistresses, you mean."

The woman shrugged. "We come and go. He has so many." A gloating smile touched her lips. "As a matter of fact, there are two more here this afternoon."

Christabel forced a smile of her own. "Good. Then I'll have the chance to determine for myself if they're as tiresome and stupid as he claims."

That wiped the smile right off Lady Jenner's face. Turning abruptly, she headed down a dimly lit hall.

As they followed, Byrne murmured, "I believe Eleanor has met her match."

She cast Byrne a wary glance. "Is that why we're here? To see if I can hold my own around your former mistresses?"

"Among other things. Think of this as a rather extreme example of what you might encounter at Stokely's party. If you can stomach this, you can stomach anything. We'll watch them play at whist and scandal." He skimmed his hand up her spine. "And we'll give the cardplayers the chance to watch *us*."

"Watch us do what?"

He kissed her cheek, then whispered, "Pretend to be man and mistress, of course. So if I were you, I'd hold that quick tongue of yours. Watch, learn, and listen. And try not to look shocked. Your reactions are entirely too transparent."

That was her only warning before they entered a most licentious scene.

Three players were ranged around a card table as Lady Jenner took her seat on a settee drawn up to it, making the fourth. There were four other guests in the moderately sized drawing room, and most of the eight were behaving indecently.

A blowsy brunette in a low-cut day gown was curled up on a chaise longue beside a pointy-nosed fellow with thinning hair, her hand rubbing his thigh as he examined his cards. An exceedingly handsome young gentleman in his shirtsleeves shared Lady Jenner's settee, draping his right arm across the back so he could tangle his fingers in her unpinned hair. Then there was the gray-haired matron who divided her concentration between her cards and the fierce-looking fellow in an unbuttoned uniform jacket, who leaned over her shoulder to nibble her ear.

But most wicked of all was the slender, reddish blond female who actually sat upon a portly man's lap, giggling as he sipped from a glass of brandy.

"Byrne!" exclaimed the portly man as he caught sight of them. "Fancy seeing you here." He leered at Christabel. "And who is *this* fair creature?"

As Christabel stiffened instinctively, Byrne squeezed her waist in warning. "This is Lady Haversham. A very good friend of mine."

Apparently, that was code for "mistress," because the women exchanged knowing glances, and the men joined the portly man in leering at her. Though bile rose in her throat, Christabel forced a smile for their benefit.

Then Byrne performed the introductions. Names flew at her so quickly she couldn't take them in: Talbot, Markham, Bradley, Hungate, Talbot again . . .

Two Talbots? She must have misunderstood.

"There's only one chair left," the countess said matter-of-factly, gesturing to a heavy walnut *bergère* a short distance from the card table. "You can share it."

"All right." Byrne shoved the chair closer to the table. Then before Christabel could react, he took a seat and hauled her onto his lap.

She froze. She'd never sat across a man's lap in her life, not even Philip's. It was the most intimate thing she could imagine—save activities reserved for the bedchamber. In shock, she swung her gaze to Byrne, only to find him watching her with an impudent smile.

Deliberately, he stretched his arm out on the chair behind her rigid back and settled his other arm across her waist, his taunting gaze daring her to protest.

"I can call for one of the servants to carry a chair for you up from the dining room if you're uncomfortable, Lady Haversham," their hostess said slyly.

Christabel forced herself to relax, to lean back against his arm. "No need to go to that trouble," she managed. "I'm fine here."

"Fine, indeed," Byrne murmured, giving a whole new meaning to the word.

He splayed his fingers over her belly, sparking her temper. His head was close enough that the bracing scent of his shaving oil filled her nostrils, and his breath practically scorched her cheek. How dared he take advantage of the situation to hold her so scandalously?

She glanced around the company, only to find that no one regarded her presence on Byrne's lap as the least bit strange or alarming. Except perhaps Lady Jenner, who shot her a malevolent look. Or did she? Seconds later the countess was regarding her cards in apparent deep concentration.

None of the other women even showed a hint of jealousy. And two of them had been his mistresses! But which ones? The red-haired woman? The brunette in the appallingly naughty gown?

She didn't want to know. That would mean she cared, and she didn't. Not one whit. All she cared about was her mission, and if she must play a scandalous lady to gain the letters, she'd do it.

But that didn't mean she had to like it.

"Do you play, Lady Haversham?" asked Mr. Talbot, the pointy-nosed gentleman.

"She's going to be my partner at Stokely's," Byrne answered for her.

Christabel shot him a questioning glance he ignored. Yesterday, he'd refused to let her partner him at the house party. What had changed his mind?

Lady Jenner looked just as surprised by the admission. "You're not partnering our host as usual?"

"Not this year, no."

The countess regarded Christabel with new antagonism. "For your sake, madam, I hope you're better at whist than your late husband. Byrne detests losing."

Mr. Talbot threw a card on the table. "Stokely has to invite her first anyway. And you know how he feels about bringing new people into our cozy group."

"I don't go unless she goes," Byrne drawled. "And since she'll be with *me,* he should know he can trust her."

Mr. Talbot shrugged. "If you're not partnering him, why should he bother?"

"Because Stokely can't resist a challenge. He'll invite her out of sheer curiosity to see who I threw him over for."

Christabel began to sweat. Dear Lord, she should never have lied to him about her whist-playing.

"In any case," Mr. Talbot said, "the man never invites anyone after he's sent out his invitations, and ours arrived last week, didn't they, my dear?"

The flame-haired female answered, not the woman with her hand on Mr. Talbot's thigh. "Yes. We were in town when they came."

We?

From her seat on the portly gentleman's lap, the flame-haired woman batted her long lashes at Byrne. "But I'm sure he'll make an exception for you. Stokely's party wouldn't be the same if you weren't there."

"Don't waste your flirtations on Byrne," Lady Jenner said snidely. "Can't you see he's presently occupied? The man may be incapable of faithfulness to a woman, but at least when he's with her, he gives her his full attention." Lady Jenner shot Mr. Talbot a cold glance. "Unlike your husband there."

Christabel's mouth fell open.

"Yes, they're married," Byrne hissed in her ear. "And yes, they're both here with other lovers. Wipe that shock from your face."

Unable even to comprehend such blatant debauchery, she swung her gaze to him. But that proved a mistake, for when Byrne saw her outrage, he took immediate measures to hide it.

He kissed her. Before the entire roomful of people, he kissed her, slowly, leisurely, as if it were his right. His mouth was hard and thorough, commanding her response, leaving her no choice but to play the part, though her every feeling revolted at the idea of behaving so intimately in front of other people.

She forced her eyes closed and her lips apart to admit the heated thrusts of his tongue. And as if it weren't bad enough that she had to put on this shameless display, she could feel his arousal grow hard and insistent beneath her bottom—

"For God's sake, Byrne," Lady Jenner said peevishly. "Did you come here to watch us play or to make love to your mistress?"

Christabel tore her mouth from his, grateful for the reprieve. Byrne's warning glance kept her mute as his broad hand shamelessly stroked her belly. "Both." He shifted his gaze to Lady Jenner. "We're not the only ones enjoying ourselves. Unless I miss my guess, that's Lieutenant Markham's hand rubbing your thigh under the table. At least, I hope it's your thigh."

Christabel had to bite her tongue to keep from gasping.

The lieutenant started to yank his hand out, but Lady Jenner caught it and held it still. "Don't pretend you care what Markham and I do, Byrne. We both know you don't waste time on jealousy after you're done with a woman."

"Ah, but you're wrong," Byrne said in a lazy drawl. "I don't waste time on jealousy even *before* I'm done with a woman."

As Lady Jenner scowled and the men laughed, Christabel forced a smile. How she wished she could leap from Byrne's lap and stalk off. But she dared not. So she sat there, chafing at the harsh reminder of his true character.

And how could anyone be so very wicked? Oh, he might kiss well, but he had no tender feelings, for her or anyone else. If she ever succumbed to his advances, she'd end up being the same to him as one of these women—a discarded plaything to trade public insults with and nothing more.

Perhaps he'd had a conscience once, before he'd been forced to work in the streets as a boy, but sadly that had ruined him forever. Because the Byrne before her now clearly had no morals, no scruples. Otherwise, he couldn't be so comfortable here.

Lord, she'd never even imagined that such nonchalance about infidelity existed among the nobility. When Byrne said they were a fast set, she'd imagined ladies who wore too much rouge and gentlemen who made the occasional bawdy comment. No wonder he'd tried to warn her.

But if she wanted her father's letters back, she had to play her part and be convincing, no matter how disgusting she found it.

Pasting a look of lazy contentment on her face, she relaxed against Byrne's chest. His quickly drawn breath gave her a measure of satisfaction. He thought she couldn't handle this, but she would prove him wrong.

She met the portly gentleman's leer with a sultry smile. When she realized Mr. Talbot was watching her, she deliberately covered Byrne's hand on her waist with her own, then rubbed it as she'd seen Mrs. Talbot rub her lover's chest.

She could feel Byrne's heated gaze on her, feel his arousal harden again beneath her bottom. The Prince of Sin, no doubt about it.

Then she felt his mouth against her ear. "Very good, lass. Keep that up, and even *I* might believe you a wanton." He slid his hand along the underside of her breasts. "Now it's time for you to pay attention to the players, if you're to partner me in whist. Watch Talbot, the best of the lot. And Eleanor's partner, Lady Hungate. She's good, too."

From then on, Byrne was all business, explaining the intricacies of their plays in heated whispers. Christabel forced herself to attend, even though his arousal didn't abate, and her shocking surroundings grew no less shocking.

Before long, she realized that his arousal came as much from the game as from her. She and whist were both challenges to be mastered. Well, he might have mastered whist, but he would never master her. No, indeed.

"Your whispering over there grows tiresome," Lady Jenner said just as Byrne explained a particularly perplexing move that Lady Hungate, the gray-haired lady, had made. "Can't you stop your flirting for even one moment, Byrne?"

"We're discussing strategy. Strategy is the key to winning at whist."

"I thought good cards were the key to winning at whist," the countess retorted. "But let's see who's right. We're almost finished with this rubber—why don't you and your new 'friend' play the winners? It'll give *us* a chance to assess your playing the way you've been assessing ours."

Panic rose in Christabel's chest. Oh no, not now, not here. She hadn't even played a practice game in two years!

But before she could think of an excuse, Byrne tightened his grip on her waist as if in warning, and said, "Why not?"

Lord help her. She was in deep, deep trouble.

Chapter Six

Beware those women who regard all other
women as rivals, for they delight in
spreading misery wherever they go.
—Anonymous, *Memoirs of a Mistress*

Much as Gavin hated having Christabel leave his lap, it was time to test her abilities. He suspected the wench had lied to him about her facility for whist. He'd done his best to refresh her on the rules with his explanations about strategy, but if she were truly inexperienced, she could botch it anyway.

That would either hurt their cause . . . or help it. Although Stokely would be angry that he'd lost his longtime partner to a poor replacement, it might be like spilling blood in the water to draw the shark. Stokely might invite Christabel if only to show Gavin what a mistake he'd made in choosing her.

It was a calculated risk, but one Gavin was prepared to take. Because he now realized that she had to be his partner as well as his mistress for his plan to work. Once she was at Stokely's, Gavin needed her in plain sight at all times. Otherwise, during one of his heated games with the others, she might retrieve her "property" and be off before Gavin could get his hands on it.

But first he had to make sure Stokely invited her. And that meant she must keep her wits about her and stay in her role as wild-living marchioness. It would be hard enough to tempt Stokely into inviting a stranger—if he caught even a whiff of Christabel's lofty morals, they were done for. So Christabel had to convince the man's friends that she could be as debauched as they were.

At least playing cards would take her mind off the wickedness around her. And after tonight, he wouldn't bring her around Stokely's set again until he'd thoroughly prepared her to look them in the face without blinking.

"Well, Byrne?" Eleanor asked. "Are you going to play or not?"

He stared down at his cards and heartily wished he'd started out with better luck. All his trumps were low, and he held only one court-card. Christabel would have to carry the hand. If she could.

To his surprise, she acquitted herself very well even though her cards were nearly as bad as his. They lost the hand, but it was a respectable performance.

He smiled encouragingly at her as he took up the deck to deal. "Let's hope for better cards this time, my sweet, to show off your competent playing."

When she beamed at him, he realized he'd never had a mistress whose smile was genuinely warm. Calculated, yes. Flirtatious, certainly. But when Christabel smiled, really smiled, her whole heart showed in her face. It had the perverse effect of dampening his ardor. If he used her family's property for his own purposes, he'd almost certainly demolish her joy, and that thought was oddly lowering.

He took up his cards with a frown. He was being ridiculous. This situation was no different than any other. He was going after what he wanted as he always had, heedless of the effect upon other people. So no mere smile would deter him.

He forced his attention back to the game. His cards were just as bad that hand. If he hadn't dealt them himself, he might have guessed foul play was involved. But he'd played enough through the years to know that luck came in streaks. A clever man could win despite luck's vagaries.

"Some brandy, Byrne?" Markham poured himself a glass.

"Not at the moment," Gavin retorted. And never when he was at the tables.

Christabel made a bad play, and Talbot snorted. The man stood behind her, drinking a glass of wine as he stared down at her cards. His mistress, bored by a game in which her lover wasn't involved, wandered over to the window to look out at night falling over the city.

But Talbot paid his mistress no attention. He was too absorbed in trying to look down the front of Christabel's gown. "It's too bad we're not playing Whist for the Wicked. We'd have Lady Haversham in her chemise in no time."

Stiffening, Gavin frowned at his former mistress. "I should have known you could never keep silent about that."

Eleanor shrugged. "I had to tell Talbot—I knew he would find it perfectly delicious, the way you and I divested that little cheating couple of their attire. They thought they were so clever, so sure to fleece us, even after we proposed such outrageous stakes. But I don't imagine they complained too much about losing the clothes on their backs after a night in our respective beds."

Gavin shot Christabel a warning glance, but there was no need. She kept her face carefully blank, though he fancied he could see revulsion in her tightened lips.

"What is Whist for the Wicked?" Markham asked.

Talbot chuckled. "A game Eleanor and Byrne invented."

"A *private* game we invented," Gavin said tersely.

"Since when do you keep anything private, Byrne?" Eleanor said. "Or has the good Widow Haversham reformed you?"

To his surprise, Christabel said, "Why would I do that? Then he wouldn't be any fun anymore."

Gavin bit back a smile. Perhaps the woman could manage this after all.

"Pray continue, Mr. Talbot," his wily pretend mistress went on. "Explain the rules for your wicked whist game."

"Gladly, madam." Talbot's eyes gleamed as he gazed down Christabel's bodice. "The stakes are any item of clothing or adornment on one's person—coat, gown, jewelry, watches, etc. A man's purse and a woman's reticule are excluded, as are other nonattire items, such as weapons. For every point the opposing team gains, the members of the losing team each have to give over an article of attire."

"That's ridiculous," Lady Hungate put in. "The stakes are deplorably uneven. A watch can hardly equal a stocking."

"That isn't the point," Talbot retorted irritably. "The point is to strip both members of one team down to nothing. The game ends when one side is naked."

Though Christabel swallowed convulsively, she kept her gaze fixed on her cards. "And do you and your friends play this game . . . often?"

Eleanor laughed. "Not as often as Talbot would like."

"Don't listen to them, Lady Haversham," Lady Hungate said as she rearranged the cards in her hand. "This is the first I've even heard of it. Appalling idea—taking off one's clothes before a group of cardplayers. Mr. Talbot and Lady Jenner are only trying to shock you. It's their favorite pastime."

"Then they're in good company with Byrne," Christabel remarked.

"Oh, Byrne isn't as shocking as he sometimes seems." Lady Hungate cast him an arch look. "Boys will be boys."

Gavin stifled a chuckle. Lady Hungate was the only former mistress whom he counted as a friend, even if she was the biggest hypocrite in London. They'd made abysmal lovers—she'd had tastes too bizarre even for him. But he still enjoyed talking to her; her gossip sources exceeded his own by a mile.

"Speaking of boys," Eleanor said, "a few weeks ago I ran into that young card cheat Byrne and I played in wicked whist. The fellow said little Lydia had left him to work in some dress shop the day after our game. It seems his mistress didn't approve of his manner of making a living, and adamantly refused to help him cheat people anymore. You wouldn't know anything about that, would you, Byrne?"

Gavin concentrated on his cards, though he could feel Christabel's gaze boring into him. "Why should I?"

"You seemed rather taken with the pretty young Lydia, as I recall."

Hard to be "taken with" a girl little more than eighteen. Especially when she stared up at you with haunted eyes, utterly bewildered to have ended up naked in a stranger's bedchamber instead of her card cheat lover's arms. What was he supposed to do with a chit like that? Not bed her, that's for sure.

"Don't be absurd, Eleanor. The girl was nothing more than a night's entertainment. I haven't given a thought to her since." He played his only decent card, trumping her king. "And you would be better served paying attention to your game than annoying me with stupid questions."

"Indeed, she would," Lady Hungate said tersely, as they finished the round with a surprising win for Gavin and Christabel. "Stokely is going to eat us for breakfast if you don't attend better than this, Eleanor."

To his and Christabel's misfortune, Eleanor began to pay better attention at once. They'd had some luck with that last hand, but neither his skill nor their luck could continue the wins. Christabel's playing simply wasn't sophisticated enough to beat the likes of Eleanor and Lady Hungate. Nor did the other distractions in the room help—Talbot's leering down her bodice, Markham's lewd jokes, and Talbot's wife kissing her lover with her husband right there in the room.

It was a scene straight out of some obscene novel, and clearly Christabel couldn't blot it out. More than once, she played out of suit, forcing him to ask if she didn't have a card in suit after all. And her strategy for trumps was deplorable.

Unfortunately, the more she lost, the worse she played. Unsurprisingly, the good widow Haversham was a sore loser, and in keeping with her tempestuous nature, she allowed her emotions to affect her playing.

They lost the second game, and Eleanor sat back with a gloating grin. "Well, Byrne, I do hope Lady Haversham's prowess in bed exceeds her prowess at whist. You'll need her to console you after you lose every single rubber at Stokely's house party. *If* he even invites the two of you, that is."

Christabel bristled, but before she could say anything, Lady Hungate responded. "Don't be an idiot, Eleanor," the matron said coolly. "The woman is clearly only trying to lull you into letting down your guard at Stokely's. You should know Byrne well enough to realize he'd never let his lust overtake his judgment. If he says the woman can play cards expertly, then she probably can."

As Eleanor's face fell, Gavin stifled a laugh. Leave it to Lady Hungate to punch holes in Eleanor's armor. He couldn't have done it better himself.

"They've found you out, Christabel," he said smoothly. "Next time we play, you'll have to show them your true mettle."

After a second's surprise, she fell right in with Lady Hungate's lie. "I *was* showing them my true mettle," she said with a secretive little smile sure to give Eleanor pause. "I can't imagine why Lady Hungate would think otherwise."

"Let's play again then," Eleanor snapped, taking up the deck of cards. "I'd like to see this 'true mettle' of yours."

"Certainly," Christabel said mutinously.

Gavin wasn't about to let her pride destroy the illusion Lady Hungate had so conveniently created. Taking out his watch, he made a show of examining it. "Sorry, Eleanor, but we're done for tonight. I have to be at the club in a couple of hours, and before that I'd like to . . . escort Lady Haversham home."

Eleanor scowled at him, but she knew his habits well enough to accept his reasons. Gavin's favorite time for lovemaking had always been right before he left for the club. He'd often "escorted" Eleanor home . . . and right up to her bed, whenever her husband was dining with his own mistress.

"Very well," Eleanor said, pouting. "Perhaps we'll see you next Tuesday."

"Perhaps," he said noncommittally. He stood and rounded the table toward Christabel. "Shall we go, my sweet?"

She had the good sense not to gainsay him. "Of course." She rose and took his arm. "Thank you, Lady Jenner, for a most enlightening afternoon."

They'd already started for the door when Eleanor said, "And thank you, Lady Haversham, for clearing up a little question I had about your late husband."

Bloody hell. He'd almost extricated them from this situation without incident. He tried to keep Christabel moving, but she halted, turning to face her adversary with a look of sheer belligerence. "Oh? What question is that?"

Alarm bells rang in his head, especially when Eleanor skimmed her gaze down Christabel's black-gowned form with clear contempt.

"Why he was always leaving his wife at home to run to town. I see now that he was only searching for more—" Eleanor paused to fluff her long blond hair with one hand "—stimulating company."

Damn the bitch for her petty vindictiveness. Lady Hungate might have succeeded in covering up Christabel's incompetence at cards, but in the process, she'd made Eleanor regard the widow as an enemy.

Gavin attempted to steer Christabel toward the door, but she wrenched free to stride right up to where Eleanor sat gloating.

"If your company is so wonderfully stimulating," Christabel said, planting her hands on her hips, "then why did Byrne leave you for *me*?"

Eleanor's glee abruptly vanished. "Don't be absurd, he did not—" She glanced to Gavin. "You couldn't possibly have been dallying with this . . . this mouse when we were still . . ."

Gavin arched an eyebrow. "You're the one who said I'm incapable of faithfulness." Not waiting to endure more of her temper, he turned to Christabel. "Come, lass, I find myself direly in need of stimulation."

They left Eleanor sputtering behind them.

But as soon as they were in the narrow hall, Christabel marched off toward the stairs like an officer hastening into battle.

He caught up to her at the top of the stairs. "Christabel—"

"Teach me to be an expert at whist," she hissed.

He started to remind her that supposedly she already was, then thought better of it, considering her present mood. "All right."

Lifting her skirts, she scurried down the stairs. "Teach me how to eviscerate that . . . that witch. I want her to lose so spectacularly that she can never hold her head up among you and your abominable friends again." Tears welled in her eyes, tears she brushed away with furious swipes of her hand. "I want to humiliate her! I want . . . I want . . ."

"I'll teach you whatever you wish." He laid his hand in the small of her back to guide her toward the kitchen. "As soon as we're away from here."

That seemed to remind her that this was neither the time nor the place for such a discussion. She remained mute as he led them past the kitchen staff, and held her tongue while his tiger brought round his cabriolet.

But once he took up the reins, and they headed out into the night, she slumped in her seat and said, "I hate

her! That . . . that horrible, wicked woman practically admitted that she'd been Philip's mistress!"

"I seriously doubt that Eleanor ever spent one second
in your husband's bed," he said smoothly. "She was
merely trying to provoke you."

"Do you think so? Really?" The hope in her voice set
his teeth on edge. Faithful to her or not, Haversham
didn't deserve her concern.

Not that Gavin cared how she felt about her late husband. He didn't. Not in the least. "Come now, can you
imagine Eleanor *ever* sharing the bed of a bad whist-
player? And we both know Haversham couldn't play whist
to save his life."

"But that Lieutenant Markham—"

"—plays almost as well as I do. When he isn't seducing
Eleanor."

Shifting her gaze to the road ahead, Christabel chewed
on her lower lip for a moment. Then she uttered a heartfelt sigh. "If it wasn't Lady Jenner my husband took up
with, then who was it?"

Ah, so that *was* the "other thing" she thought Haversham had come to London for. "Are you sure he took up
with anybody?"

"Don't pretend you didn't know."

"If Haversham had a mistress, I never met her."

"He must have been discreet."

"Then how do *you* know about it? It isn't the sort of
thing a man tells his wife."

"I heard about it from . . . someone else."

"Who?"

"It doesn't matter. The point is, I know that he had one."

"Did you learn about it before Haversham died?"

She shook her head. "After."

"Then you don't know if it's true. You can't even ask him, and you only have that other person's word for it."

"What possible reason could the . . . person have for lying?"

"You'd be surprised by the reasons people have for lying."

She sighed. "After tonight, I don't think anything would surprise me."

She was such an innocent, despite her marriage, despite her travels abroad, and despite her recent disillusionment about Haversham. She had no clue how dark a place the world could be.

She'd never seen a man gutted for not paying the blacklegs, or women whose love of gin so consumed them that they allowed their children to starve, or—

Bloody hell, what had brought all that to mind? He'd put those days well behind him. "I did warn you what to expect of Stokely's friends."

"I know." She stared over at the newly rising half-moon. "And that's more than I did for you."

He made the turn onto her street. "What do you mean?"

"I should have warned *you* that I can't . . . that I'm not . . ." She clasped her hands tightly in her lap. "I lied to you about being good at whist."

"Did you?" he said dryly. "I hadn't guessed."

He heard her snort even over the horses' hooves beating the cobblestones. "I couldn't have played worse if I'd tried."

"Ah, but you did try. Didn't you hear Lady Hungate?"

A reluctant smile touched her lips. "I can't believe she thought I was doing it on purpose. Your friends have very devious minds, all of them."

"Yes, they do." He didn't bother to enlighten her about Lady Hungate's true motives, especially since he wasn't quite sure what they were.

A long silence fell. Finally, she said in a low voice, "The thing is . . . I'll need money to gamble with, and as you probably know—"

"Haversham left you with little."

"Exactly. He paid you with what he got from Lord Stokely, but he had so many other debts . . ." She trailed off with a sigh.

He clenched his jaw. The fact that she'd been left struggling because of her heedless husband's gambling gnawed at him. "It was my idea to have you go as my partner, so I'll take care of your part of the stakes."

He could feel her eyes riveted on him. "What if I lose too much?" she asked. "I'm not the player that you are. Perhaps you shouldn't partner me in whist after all. I could just pretend to be your mistress—"

"That might not ensure that Stokely invites you to his party. But if you're my partner, he'll almost certainly do so. So it's best to hedge our bets and have you be both." Drawing the cabriolet up in front of her town house, he brought it to a halt, then leaped down. "Besides, I thought you wanted to eviscerate Eleanor."

A fierce light sparked in her eyes as he helped her down. "I do."

"Then I'll simply have to teach you to be an expert at whist." He offered her his arm. "Beginning tonight."

Her gaze shot to his. "But . . . but I thought you had to go to your club."

"Not for a couple of hours. That's plenty of time for a lesson."

"Here?" she said uncertainly.

"Not on the street," he quipped, "but your parlor would be suitable. Of course, it has been a long day for you, so if you don't have the energy to play well into the night like Eleanor and the others—"

"No, no, I can do it." The door at the top of the entrance stairs opened, and she let him lead her inside, where the footman took her pelisse and her bonnet. "Just let me get the cards from Philip's old study."

"Certainly," he said, handing his overcoat and hat to the footman.

Trying not to grin, he headed for the parlor. So Eleanor and her silly taunts about Haversham had touched a sore spot, had they? He would make good use of the widow's competitive streak.

Because one way or another, he meant to have Christabel. And every single one of her secrets.

Chapter Seven

*Something as innocent as whist can be a
prelude to seduction.*
—Anonymous, *Memoirs of a Mistress*

Christabel fetched the cards and headed back to the parlor, then froze just outside the door. Dear Lord, perhaps letting Byrne into her home so late at night was a mistake. He'd clearly been aroused by her sitting on his lap earlier. What if he tried to act on it?

She mustn't let him stay. She would tell him she'd changed her mind.

But when she entered the parlor to find that he'd already pulled the card table out from the wall and set chairs before it, she faltered. He did have a point about hedging their bets. She did need to learn how to play better if she was to partner him. And they didn't have much time before the house party . . .

"You found the cards?" He seemed oblivious to the intimacy of the small room where earlier he'd seen her half-dressed.

Surely if he were bent on seduction, he wouldn't be sitting down at her card table. And it wasn't as if he could stay the night—he had his club to hurry off to.

"Yes." She set the deck on the table. Still nervous, she stood there uncertainly. "Would you like some refreshment? Wine? Brandy?"

"No. And none for you either."

She blinked. "Why not?"

He shuffled the cards, then pushed them toward her for her to cut. "I'll let you in on a secret. Half of winning at cards consists of staying sober when no one else is. It gained me many a trick when my cards were against me. I learned that from General Scott. He won two hundred thousand pounds at whist primarily by abstaining from drink at the tables at White's."

"Oh." She sat down. If Byrne were so bent on winning that he would eschew strong drink, then he clearly wasn't thinking about seduction. She cut the cards, then handed them back to him, intrigued when he began to deal two piles. "How can we do this when we don't have four people?"

"We'll play two-handed whist. The strategy is different, but it will teach you how to use your trumps more effectively. That was your weak area tonight."

"I see." She squelched a niggling disappointment at his focus on the cards. She didn't *want* him to try seducing her, for pity's sake. Not at all.

"For the first few hands we won't keep score, and after each trick, I'll tell you how you might have improved your play. Once you've grasped the rules, we'll play a real game with real stakes."

She nodded. He finished dealing them each thirteen cards, then set the other half of the deck aside and turned up the top card.

"Now, the thing about two-handed whist is . . ."

For the next hour, Byrne's entire attention was on the

cards. And on beating her. She caught on to the rules fairly quickly, but couldn't figure out how to beat him. Every time she thought she had him, he tossed onto the table a card she'd forgotten to account for. Nor did it help that he could predict, almost to a card, which cards *she* held. It was uncanny.

It was infuriating. Losing to Lady Jenner had been bad enough; losing to him was maddening. And she couldn't even claim that her surroundings distracted her. Byrne allowed no jokes, no pointed questions, nothing but his matter-of-fact explanations of where she'd gone wrong in her play.

After losing four rounds to him, she was eager to wipe that calm expression off his face. Well into the fifth round, she examined her cards, then played the ace of spades with a flourish.

"I told you never to lead with the ace," he said.

She tipped up her chin. "Unless I had the king, too."

"Are you strong in trumps?"

Blast, she'd forgotten about that rule. "No."

He trumped her ace with a two and took the trick. "How you handle your trumps is everything in whist, Christabel. Tell me how many trumps you think I have left in my hand."

"Two," she snapped, without stopping to think.

He raised that maddening eyebrow of his. "You're angry."

"Of course I'm angry. I'm losing. Again."

"You can't let losing make you angry."

"Why not?" she said belligerently.

"Because anger impairs judgment, and impaired judgment makes one play badly. Whether ten pounds or ten thousand ride on your hand, you must leave emotion out of it. Take no greater risks if you're losing than if you're winning. Play to the cards you have. Always. The only thing that matters is the cards."

How could he be so blasted sensible about all this? It was unnerving. "You should write a book," she complained. "*Rules of Card Play According to Mr. Byrne.* No drinking, no emotion . . . no fun."

"I didn't get where I am by playing for fun." He rearranged his cards. "Nor did any of Stokely's set. They're very serious about their whist. So you must be serious, too, especially if you mean to take on Lady Jenner."

Suitably chastened, she mumbled, "All right."

"I find that taking deep breaths helps to calm violent emotions. Try it."

Feeling rather silly, she took one breath, then another and another, surprised to find that it did banish any lingering vestiges of bad temper.

"Good," he said. "Now concentrate. Think about the cards that have been played and the ones you saw me take from the pile."

"Very well." She forced herself to work back through the hand.

"How many trumps do I have left?"

She hesitated, then said, "Five?"

"Six. But that's good." He held up his eight remaining cards, then took one and threw it on the table. It wasn't a trump. "I gained three from the stock in the first half, one of which I played earlier, which leaves two that you know about—"

"Enough." She reexamined her cards in light of his comments and the card he'd played. "How in blazes do you remember every card?"

"One must if one is to win at whist."

"No doubt you also excelled at mathematics in school," she muttered.

He kept his gaze fixed on his cards. "I've never been to school."

The edge of bitterness in his tone tugged at her heart. "Never? Not even before your mother—"

"Lost the annuity Prinny gave her? Not even then."

"What annuity?"

He stiffened. "I thought Regina and Katherine had told—" He broke off. "Clearly not. Never mind."

"Tell me. I want to know. I thought your mother was just the prince's—"

"Whore?" he snapped.

"No, of course not." He wasn't so calm now, was he? "But . . . well . . . from the gossip I heard, they had a brief affair, and that's all. She wasn't even really his mistress."

"That's what *he* says. It makes it easier for him to justify his treatment of her. She's just a whoring actress, right? A little tart he can take at his leisure, then discard without a thought. At least I don't leave my mistresses destitute."

She played a card. "Because you only choose married women as mistresses," she said dryly.

"Exactly. Their husbands will support them and claim any children I inadvertently sire. But I'm not leaving some bastard of mine to struggle and starve and—" Breaking off with a curse, he tossed a card down. "Play."

She didn't. "Tell me about the annuity, Byrne."

"Fine." He lifted his glittering gaze to her. "You want to know the truth about your friend, the prince? Prinny promised my mother an annuity if she would publicly declare that I wasn't his son. She agreed, poor naïve fool, thinking that the money would do me more good than any claim to royalty."

He laughed bitterly. "The money didn't last, of course. Once Prinny decided to 'marry' Mrs. Fitzherbert illegally, she demanded he put his mistresses aside."

"You can't blame her," Christabel said stoutly. She'd met Mrs. Fitzherbert only once as a child, but that meeting remained branded in her memory. The woman was the noblest she'd ever known.

"I don't blame her—I blame *him*. Putting his mistresses aside did not mean he had to leave them destitute. Yet he conveniently waited until Mother's claim that I wasn't his had spread, then cut off her annuity."

A muscle worked in his jaw. "After that, it was just a matter of a word here and a nasty statement there, until he had everyone believing I was some product of my mother's many supposed customers. She lost her job as an actress, and he didn't even care. Bastard."

She said nothing, her heart in her throat. No wonder he'd had to run with the blacklegs at eight.

Was that why the prince had suggested that she turn to Byrne, of all people, for help? Did His Highness now feel guilty for what he'd done? Perhaps he'd thought to make amends by offering Byrne an easy chance at a barony.

But that was also why the prince had made it clear that Byrne should only be asked to get her the invitation, nothing more. Because involving him further in her mission was dangerous. *He* was dangerous.

Panic gripped her. She'd brought him into the thick of it by suggesting she pretend to be his mistress and even his partner! Yes, she'd had no choice, but still . . . Oh Lord, what had she done? If Byrne found out what was in the letters, he wouldn't hesitate to use them against His Highness. Never mind that he would cost the prince his throne in the process. And destroy her and her family.

Well then, she must never let him know what was in them. Never.

"So that's why I never went to school," he went on. "We couldn't afford it. I'm what is popularly termed *self-taught*. Although Mother taught me to read, I learned the rest on my own." He flashed her a ghost of a smile. "And luckily I inherited my actress mother's gift for mimicry. It has served me well."

Of course. That's why he used such overly precise and formal language. He'd had to work at it, had to learn proper speech and manners and behavior by watching his betters, so he was more conscious of it than those born to it.

Hiding the pity that she knew he'd loathe, she said lightly, "Consider yourself fortunate to miss school. I hated it, particularly mathematics."

"I'm surprised you were even taught it." He eyed her over his hand. "Isn't that unusual for a woman?"

She shrugged. "Papa wanted a son. Mama died before he could have one, so he pinned his hopes on me. He taught me how to shoot and ride and hunt . . . and solve equations. That's why I'm completely inept in the feminine arts."

"Not completely inept," he said with a faint smile. "You kiss very well."

Absurdly, that pleased her. "Do I?"

He chuckled. "Play, damn you, play."

She sloughed off a low card in another suit to save her trumps, knowing it would lose her the trick but hoping it might win her the next few.

"You should have trumped while you had the opportunity," he murmured, then proceeded to lead her out of her trumps, thus winning the rest of the tricks.

As he gathered up the cards, she fidgeted in her chair. "Give me another chance. I'll try harder this time."

"Bloody right you will." He shuffled the cards. "This time we're playing a real game. With real stakes. You're never going to make an effort unless you have something tangible to lose."

She scowled. "Like what? You know I have little money."

"I'm not talking about money."

When her gaze shot to him, he wore that hooded look that would turn any woman's heart to mush. Even hers. Her pulse began to race. "Then what are you talking about?"

He rose and went to the door, which he closed and locked, sending a frisson of alarm down her spine. "Risking the clothes on your back." Coming up behind her, he bent to set the deck on the table before her. Then he pressed his mouth to her ear, and added in a heated whisper, "I'm talking about Whist for the Wicked." Her heart thundered madly when he sat down, his eyes gleaming. "I can't think of a better way to motivate you to improve your playing."

"I am not going to— I would never—"

"Why? Afraid you'll lose?"

"Absolutely! You're a seasoned gambler, and I've only begun to learn. Of course I'll lose."

Reaching across the table, he took the deck and shuffled the cards, slowly, methodically. "There's no 'of course' about it. If you concentrate on remembering the cards, you'll have a fighting chance. And I suspect you'll be far more likely to concentrate if the consequence of not doing so is that I see you naked."

Naked. The word perversely sent wanton thrills along her every nerve. This afternoon with the dressmaker had been bad enough, when his thorough examination of her half-clothed form had made her blush like a silly schoolgirl. But if she were forced to bare her breasts and her belly and . . . and . . .

"No," she said firmly. "You're trying to seduce me."

A rakish smile touched his lips. "That would be a fitting end to the evening, but you've already said that sharing my bed doesn't interest you. So I hardly see how one of us being naked will change that."

She eyed him askance. "Really, Byrne, I'm not a fool."

"No, but you claim to find me unappealing. Are you saying you've changed your mind? That you consider one of us being naked too great a temptation for your virtue?"

"Don't be ridiculous." But the idea of Byrne sitting naked in her parlor lodged in her brain. If she happened to win—which was unlikely—she would get her revenge upon him for his high-handed behavior earlier, when he'd made her strip down to her corset and chemise in front of him.

"You already have the advantage," he said. "You females wear more clothes than we males. And if you lose, you need only sneak upstairs. While I'll have to drive home in my open cabriolet, wearing nothing but my overcoat and hat."

The ludicrous image swayed her further. "That does sound appealing."

"I'll make it even easier for you." His continued card shuffling sounded as loud as carriage wheels on cobblestone. "I'll give you four items of clothing before we start. You'll begin the game with a substantial lead. You'll have all my clothes in no time. *If* you play well enough."

"You'll cheat," she persisted.

"I don't cheat." He lifted one maddening brow. "I wouldn't have to cheat to win anyway, not when you're playing without a care for strategy."

Blast him. He knew it stuck in her craw that she couldn't best him. But could she really do any better if she concentrated? "What if I refuse your stakes?"

"That's your choice, of course." He leaned forward to set the shuffled deck before her. "But consider this—the more clothes you take off, the more distracted I'll become. You might actually win." His smooth smile taunted her. "And you know you want to win."

She weighed her options. She didn't want to stop the lessons until she'd proved she wasn't a complete ninny at whist. But to encourage his wicked games was sheer madness. Look how disastrous Philip's gambling with Byrne's fast set had proved to be.

Still, wouldn't that make besting him even more satisfying? To march out of the parlor with his clothes in her hand? To watch him drive home through the streets of London wearing only his overcoat and hat? What a delicious thought.

"Cut the cards, Christabel," he said in a low murmur.

He thought he would win. Ha! She would show him.

She cut the cards and handed them back. "You said you'd give me four items of clothing to start. So take them off."

"Certainly." He stood and rounded the table. Reaching inside his coat, he withdrew her pistol. "I believe this is yours, madam."

She seized on it eagerly. "Now I have something else to remove if I lose."

"No weapons, remember?"

"Oh, right." She set the pistol on a nearby chair.

Removing his watch, he handed it to her, followed by his coat and waistcoat. She draped the items over her pistol. But when he unbuttoned his shirt, alarm swelled in her chest. "Aren't you going to take off your cravat first?"

"I can remove my clothes in any order I please. Those are the rules."

"Oh." She hadn't thought about what effect *his* nakedness might have on *her*. She tried not to stare as he worked the collar of his shirt out from beneath his tight cravat. "Are there other . . . rules to this ridiculous game that I should know about before we start?"

"Any item of clothing or adornment counts—my watch, for example, or your earbobs." He smiled. "If you were wearing any."

Blast it all. Next time she was with him, she would definitely wear jewelry.

He unfastened his cuffs. "We'll score the thirteen tricks that count by using regular whist rules—whoever wins the hand gains one point for each trick won beyond six." Dragging his shirt free of his trousers, he raked her with a devilish gaze. "And for every point, the winner gets a piece of the loser's attire."

Abruptly, he pulled his shirt off over his head. She tried not to gape, but that was impossible. Even with his cravat covering part of him, she could still see ample proof of his sculpted chest and finely hewn arms. The silky dusting of reddish brown hair surrounding his flat nipples appeared also around his navel, then trailed down in a thin line to disappear beneath his trousers.

His markedly bulging trousers.

Blushing, she jerked her gaze back to his face, only to find him grinning. "If you want to see more, all you have to do is win my trousers and drawers."

"I-I . . . was not—" she stammered. "I-I did not mean—"

"Of course not," he said smugly, dropping his shirt into her lap. "There's your fourth item. Good luck gaining the rest."

Snatching up his shirt in a fit of temper, she started to toss it over with the other items. Then she caught a whiff of his scent—a tonic mingled with sweet oil and pure male musk. How long had it been since she'd smelled the distinctive scent of a man? It seemed like forever.

A groan escaped her lips. It was all she could do not to lift the linen to her nose and inhale. And wouldn't he delight in that, the arrogant wretch? Setting the shirt firmly aside, she snapped, "Deal the cards, sir."

To her satisfaction, she won the first hand, though only by one point. He didn't seem perturbed, but merely removed his ruby cravat pin and laid it on the table between them as she gathered up the cards.

Uneasily, she placed the pin with the other items. "Can you afford to lose this? It looks rather costly." She shuffled the cards, then pushed them over to him.

With a chuckle, he cut them and passed them back. "Don't worry—I never risk more than I can afford to lose."

"Another of your gambling rules?" She dealt the next hand.

"Absolutely. Only a fool goes into debt playing cards."

Then thank God they were only playing for clothing, because she lost the next hand. Badly. So badly that he took every trick save one. Blast it all.

His eyes gleamed at her across the table as he gathered up the cards. "Six points. That means six items of—"

"I know what it means." But which items would be least mortifying to remove?

Inspiration struck. Hiding her smile, she removed a hairpin and laid it on the table.

As she reached for another, he jerked upright in his chair to growl, "You can't count those, for God's sake."

"I most certainly can. You said 'items of clothing or adornment.' You got to take out your cravat pin—how is this is any different?"

Glowering at her, he shuffled the cards with jerky snaps of his wrists. "You must have twenty of those at least."

"At least," she echoed smugly as she removed another.

Unfortunately, she needed every single one to hold up her heavy hair. After the fourth pin, she felt her coiffure droop. After the fifth, it fell entirely, sending a few pins pinging upon the floor. Frantically, she grabbed for the mass to make sure the other pins didn't fall.

As he regarded her half-fallen hair, his gaze began to smolder. "You can't play cards while holding your hair, Christabel."

She released it gingerly, wincing when two more pins hit the floor. "We'll count one of them against this hand and the rest toward my future losses."

His voice was low, husky. "Oh no, lass, those don't count. They're no longer items of adornment once they leap from your body of their own accord. Otherwise, you could claim every speck of dirt that fell off your boots."

"But—"

"That's only logical, Christabel," he said firmly.

Curse him for being right. "Blasted logic," she muttered as she plucked out one of the few remaining pins and plopped it on the table.

That's when the battle began in earnest. She forced herself to play as he'd trained her, to contain her anger, to concentrate on every card he laid down. And her efforts paid off—as they headed into the last trick of that hand, she was winning by two points.

"Hah!" She played her last card with a flourish, beating him by three points. "Take that, you wily rascal!" She tossed her head back, which cost her the rest of her hairpins, but she didn't care. She didn't need those pins anyway. She could beat him without them.

Yet her success didn't seem to annoy him at all. Removing each of his boots, he came around the table in his stocking feet to hand them to her. With a gloating smile, she placed them on the pile of clothes, then turned back to find him unbuttoning his trousers. Right in front of her.

Her mouth went dry as he slipped them off to reveal the short stockinette drawers beneath, stretched taut over his full arousal. Lord help her.

Because she couldn't seem to look away. He was so very . . . large. The stockinette enfolded his erection with such loving attention to detail that she could even make out the heavy weight of his ballocks.

"Do you want to keep playing, lass?" he asked in a husky murmur. "Or shall we turn to more enjoyable entertainment?"

Swallowing hard, she forced herself to meet his gaze. Sheer hunger shone in his face, so raw and palpable it made her breath quicken.

Dear Lord, she must be mad to be playing this game. Or perhaps she was mad not simply to give in to his seductions. Here was her chance to discover if it could be as heavenly as some women claimed, as all of *his* women must think, anyway, judging from how eager they were to share his bed.

But seizing that chance was far too dangerous. Lovemaking with Philip had fallen far short of heavenly, yet it had been enough to turn her into a weak-spined ninny, willing to let him wrangle out of her the family's most volatile secret. Only imagine what she might do if Byrne pleased her in bed. She'd probably give him the keys to the blasted kingdom.

She'd already had her heart broken by one man's betrayal; she didn't want to try for twice. "Let's keep playing."

His eyes flared hot, but he merely nodded. "Whatever my lady wishes."

But as he dropped his trousers in her lap and strolled back to his chair, her gaze trailed inexorably down his very fine buttocks, then to his surprisingly muscular thighs, then to—

She blinked. "You've got a knife strapped to your calf." His boot normally hid it from view.

"Yes." He took his seat. "It's easier and safer than carrying a pistol." Flicking his hand toward the cards, he added, "It's your deal."

She gathered up the cards and shuffled, then handed the deck over for his cut. "But why—"

"I go to and from my club at all hours, sometimes with large sums of money. I didn't get where I am by handing my earnings over to cutthroats." He cut the cards and handed them back to her. "A better question might be why do *you* carry a pistol to a dinner party?"

She dealt the cards. "As you just admitted, London is dangerous."

"So is carrying a loaded pistol."

"Not if you need one."

He shot her a searching glance, ignoring his cards. "When did you need a pistol? Few women carry them. Come to think of it, few women know how to grab a man with intent to maim. What happened to you?"

She picked up her own cards, trying to appear nonchalant. "I was accosted in an alley in Gibraltar once."

"What were you doing alone in an alley?" His clipped words reflected the sudden tension in his posture.

"You'll think me a complete ninny if I tell you."

"Try me."

"I was seventeen, young enough to be foolish. Papa had always said that if I needed to go out, and he wasn't available, I should take a footman or send to the barracks for an officer. But I knew that either would report my movements to him—they always did." She fanned out the cards in her hand, but didn't see them. "I'd noticed this amazing sword for sale that I knew he'd like for his birthday, and I wanted to surprise him. So I thought that if I just popped round to the shop myself—it was only a few streets away—I could purchase it and be home without anyone the wiser. And . . . well . . ."

"Well what?" he prodded.

"There was a shortcut through an alley that would get me there in minutes." She frowned, remembering. "Except that just as I neared the street, three scruffy local men blocked the alley. And they sort of . . . took a fancy to me."

He let out a low curse.

"If they'd realized I was English, they might not have come near me for fear of reprisals, but my hair is dark, and the light in the alley wasn't the best. They assumed I was fair game, and since they were clearly scoundrels—"

He paled. "Did they—"

"No, they didn't get that far, thank heavens, though it was a near thing. One held my arms while the second covered my mouth and the third tried to lift my skirts. He probably would have succeeded if I hadn't managed to bite the hand of the man covering my mouth. As soon as he drew back his hand, I let out a scream fit to wake the dead." A faint smile touched her lips. "A British officer walking nearby heard me and came to my rescue. He routed them with his sword."

Byrne stared intently at her. "Haversham."

She nodded. "That's how we met." A sigh escaped her lips. "You should have seen him then, so gallant, so dashing in his red coat. When he brought me home, and they summoned my father, Papa couldn't stop praising his courage and quick thinking. It was only later that—" She broke off with a silent curse.

"Yes?"

"Nothing." She went on hastily. "Philip courted me for a year. Then we married. That's all."

He picked up his cards. "Is he the one who taught you how to grab a man by the ballocks?"

"No, Papa did that after the incident. Even though I had a suitor to protect me, he wasn't taking any chances."

"Your father taught you well," Byrne said wryly.

She snorted as she arranged her cards. "When I tried it on you this morning, I only managed to . . . well . . ."

"Arouse me? Ah, but that's because everything you do arouses me, lass," he said in that richly sensual voice that sent temptation coursing along her nerves.

Blast him. Just like that, he reminded her that he was sitting across from her, half-naked and erect. Desiring her.

"Play," she said tersely.

With a low, mocking laugh, he did.

They played a few minutes in silence. Then he said, "Did you ever use your maneuver on Haversham?"

"Why would I?" She played a card. "He was my husband."

"Not at first. A year is a long time to court. Didn't he ever try to put his hands where he shouldn't?"

She rolled her eyes. "This may come as a shock to you, but in many parts of society—obviously not the ones *you* frequent—such behavior from a gentleman to a lady is frowned upon. My husband happened to be a respectable man when I met him. He behaved respectably the entire year we courted."

He gazed at her over his cards, a sudden heat flaring in his face. "I wouldn't have lasted a year with you." His eyes drifted down to her mouth. "I would have been lucky to last a month."

Feeling color flood her cheeks, she jerked her gaze down to her cards, and realized she had no idea what had been played. "Stop that. You only flirt like that so you can distract me into playing badly."

"Is it working?"

She glared at him.

He laughed. "You credit me with more deviousness than I possess. Flirting comes naturally to me. Especially when I'm with a beautiful woman."

"Don't insult my intelligence. I've seen your mistresses in the flesh, and I don't begin to compare."

"You undervalue your attractions," he said tightly. "If I didn't find you appealing, I wouldn't be trying to beat you at whist merely for the chance to see you naked. I don't make such an effort with every woman."

"Just a large number of them."

He chuckled. "True."

The next few hands went badly, but though she blamed it on her poor cards, Byrne's lack of clothes was every bit as distracting as he'd claimed hers would be. It wasn't just what she could see either—like his muscles flexing when he played a card—but what she couldn't see. Beneath the table, was he still aroused? Did he intend to act on it? If he did, what would she do?

Worse yet, he didn't seem bothered by watching *her* remove her clothes. It only spurred him to better playing. He won hand after hand, gathering a point here, three points there. Her handkerchief, half boots, and garters went first, then her stockings and her petticoat.

How she wished she'd worn more than one petticoat. How she wished she'd ignored Rosa and worn her fichu. Anything—even a cheap iron ring—would be welcome.

She forced herself to ignore his half-dressed state, to concentrate on the cards, yet she lost to him by three points.

Gazing at her with satisfaction, he gathered up the cards. "It appears you're faced with a difficult choice. You can either remove your gown, corset, and chemise . . . or your gown, corset, and drawers. Personally, I think you should strip down to your drawers—"

"You *would,*" she said with a sniff. Rising from her seat, she reached up under her gown and deftly removed her drawers, then tossed them onto the table. "You've been trying to get a look at my bare bosom all day. I swear, you're the most infuriating man."

"You aren't the first woman to tell me so."

"I probably won't be the last either, judging from what I saw of your harem."

His mouth quirked upward at one corner. "You seem oddly interested in my 'harem' for a woman who doesn't wish to join it. Are you jealous, my sweet?"

"Of a man incapable of faithfulness to a woman? I'd have to be insane."

But the truth was, those women of his did indeed annoy her. She was starting to like him—though she couldn't imagine why—and it peeved her to think of being only one in a long string of women he had kissed and teased and—

"You're dawdling," Byrne said, jerking her back to the present. "The gown, remember? I've already seen you without it once today, so why be missish about removing it now?"

Because this was different. Because they were alone in a room of soft, lambent firelight, the heavy weight of night making her drowsy enough to loosen all her restraints.

Because if he looked at her tonight as he'd looked at her earlier, she might do something she regretted.

She shook off the thought. "You are such a beast." Planting her hands on her hips, she cast him a foul glance. "Well? Don't just sit there, for pity's sake. I can't take my gown and corset off by myself. Come help me."

Chapter Eight

❦

Men are cheats, both at cards and at love.
—Anonymous, *Memoirs of a Mistress*

Come help her? Did she have any clue what she was asking? He was liable to tear her gown off her. He'd never been this aroused in all his life, and his control was paper-thin.

He wasn't alone, either. Judging from her quick breaths and flushed cheeks, she was just as aroused. Unfortunately, she didn't *want* to be aroused. He wasn't sure why she persisted in resisting him. Had Haversham made her skittish of all men, or was it just him she feared? Either way, he meant to have her.

He rose and rounded the table, stifling a chuckle when her gaze swung right to his drawers. His cock grew impossibly hard, a state that only intensified as he began to undo her gown. He took his time, relishing the moment, drowning in her exotic scent. How had a woman who claimed to be "inept in the feminine arts" managed to acquire such an intoxicating perfume?

It made him wonder what other intoxicating surprises she hid beneath her practical exterior. A hennaed mons?

A jewel in her navel? Nothing she had or did would sur prise him. And he meant to uncover every secret.

He was halfway down her gown when someone tried the door to the parlor. His arousal came to a crashing halt, especially when the intruder knocked and asked in a concerned voice, "My lady? Are you there? It's very late, and I wanted to know if . . . will you be . . ." A low curse sounded in Spanish. "Should I retire?"

As Christabel stiffened, he gritted his teeth. Damn her meddling maid. Surely the chit knew they were in here to-gether. Why didn't she have the good sense to leave well enough alone?

Because the woman was protective of her mistress. And if he weren't careful, Christabel would seize this chance to escape.

When she moved toward the door, Gavin slipped his arm about her waist, and growled, "Oh, no, you don't, lass."

"What?" she said in feigned innocence.

"No need to let her in." Then Rosa might believe that her mistress wanted an excuse for ending the evening. "Tell her to go away."

"I will." She strained against him. "As soon as you let go of me, blast it."

"Get rid of her first," he commanded.

"Why should I?" Her uncertainty showed that she fought her own desires.

He made her choice easy. "Because the game isn't over, as you well know." The woman had an inherent sense of right, thank God. "You agreed to the game *and* the stakes. It would be dishonorable to renege simply because you're losing."

"What if I concede?"

"Then you'll have to take off your chemise and walk

out naked to meet Rosa. Are you ready to do that? When you can still win?"

She sighed. And he knew he had her.

"My lady?" Rosa demanded, shaking the doorknob until the door rattled.

"I'm fine, Rosa!" Christabel called out. "Mr. Byrne and I are playing cards. I don't know how late we'll be, so go on to bed, if you please."

"Very good, my lady," Rosa answered.

Gavin released a tense breath. For a moment there, he'd thought—

"Let go of me," Christabel demanded. "As you said, the game isn't over."

He released her at once. They had plenty of time yet. And he'd use every minute to beat down her defenses. "You still owe me a gown *and* a corset."

"Fine." She shucked off her gown, but was forced to let him untie her laces. He took his time, making sure she felt every brush of his fingers against her back.

After she shimmied out of the corset and turned to face him, he was pleased to find her blushing. "Here," she said with a gesture of defiance as she thrust the pile of fabric at him. "I wish you good use of it."

He stared down at her vile black gown, then made a quick decision. Walking over to the fireplace, he tossed her gown into it, where it promptly burst into a most satisfying blaze.

"Are you insane?" she protested.

She dashed across the room to rescue it, but he stayed her with one hand. "It's mine now, remember? And I pray never to have to see that ugly thing again. Come to think of it—" He tossed her corset into the fire, too.

"That was a perfectly good corset, I'll have you know!"

"Which you don't need tonight." He faced her, then froze.

The leaping fire, fueled by her clothing, illuminated her chemise so thoroughly that her nipples—her dusky, plump nipples—showed through the thin cotton. Not to mention that the fabric clung to her, tracing the shape of her heavy breasts, hinting at the slight fullness of her belly . . . barely veiling the triangle of raven hair between her thighs. "In fact, there's little that you do need, lass," he said in a guttural voice.

She followed his gaze, her eyes going round when she saw what he'd seen. With a muttered curse, she turned on her heel and hurried back to the table, giving him only a flash of the pale buttocks outlined by her chemise before she took her seat. But that flash was enough to spur him on. He walked back to the table as she tapped her fingers impatiently.

"Come on, Byrne." Grim determination now shadowed her features. "It's your deal. Prepare to be routed."

Routed? Not bloody likely. He wasn't leaving tonight without seeing her naked. Without having her.

By God, the woman was magnificent, especially with her dander up. Settling back into his chair, he shuffled the cards without taking his eyes off her. What a female! That flowing hair, those gem green eyes . . . the sweet flesh barely veiled by her thin chemise. It was all he could do not to attack her where she sat.

Steady, man, steady. You'll get your chance.

Bloody right he would. He handed the cards over for her to cut, and she did so with the fierce concentration of a player bent on winning. With a chuckle, he began to deal. Did she really think she could best him? He lacked only one point to have her where he wanted her.

But that one point eluded him. For the first time that evening, she focused her intelligence—which he'd already guessed was substantial—upon playing her cards to advantage. And luck was with her, too. By the end of that hand she'd gained four points, the most she'd gained all night.

Smug with her triumph, she settled back in her chair. "The garters and the stockings, Byrne. Hand them over. Or else give me your cravat and any combination of the rest."

"Or . . ." He stood and reached for the buttons of his drawers. "Perhaps I'd prefer to leave my stockings on." He lowered his voice to a teasing whisper, "So my feet don't get cold."

Her smile faltered. But then a sudden mutinous light glinted in her eyes. Leaning across the table, she growled, "Go ahead. I dare you."

Her deliberate echoing of his earlier words tempted him, but he suddenly had a better idea. "I'd rather have you take them off me yourself, once I win."

"If you win, then you won't have to—" It suddenly dawned on her what he meant. "Oh." She pursed her lips as she gathered up the cards. "I assure you, sir, that the only way you'll be naked tonight is if you lose. In which case, you alone will be removing your drawers."

"We'll see." Unable to suppress a smile, he removed his garters and stockings and tossed them across the table at her. "Your deal."

Her deal gave him abysmal cards. He eyed her speculatively. Could the chit have cheated? Surely no random deal could give him a hand so full of nothing.

But judging from her earnest concentration, her hand wasn't that grand either . . . which meant that all the good cards were in the stock. Damn.

The first thirteen tricks were a battle royal—both of them fighting to gain the best cards for their respective hands. She kept him on his toes, and he didn't know whether to be pleased at her improved playing—or annoyed that he'd actually have to work at winning.

And work, it was. He could steel himself to ignore her tousled hair, or the translucent fabric of her chemise that allowed him to see her nipples plain as day whenever she leaned forward to gain a card. What he couldn't blot out was the flare of excitement in her face when she gained a good card, or the satisfied purr she uttered every time she won a trick. Did she know how seductive that tiny little sound was? That he imagined her making it as he sucked those succulent breasts or thrust deeply into her—

"Stop dawdling, Byrne," she broke in.

He jerked his attention back to the table. "What?"

Her smile was self-satisfied. "The game. Don't be a sore loser. Play your last card, so I can claim my winnings."

Startled, he glanced at her tricks. Bloody hell. While he'd been salivating over having her in his bed, she'd managed to win most of the thirteen tricks. Even if he won this one, she'd win the hand by three points.

And only his cravat and his drawers were left. And the knife he kept strapped to his calf. Which didn't count.

He stared at her. She'd beaten him. The bloody chit had beaten him! He couldn't believe it. If it got out that Bonny Byrne had let a female distract him into playing badly, he'd never be able to hold his head up at his club again.

Damn her. That's what he got for giving her a lead at the beginning. If he hadn't, he'd have another chance at getting her chemise.

No, that's not what had sunk him. He'd broken one of his own rules—never start tasting the fruit of success before you've actually plucked it from the tree. And now he wouldn't get to taste it—or her—at all.

The hell he wouldn't.

He trumped her card and won the last trick, but that didn't dampen her enthusiasm. She sat back, triumph lending a fetching glow to her features that sent hot need thundering through his veins. "Take it off, Byrne." He reached for his cravat, and she said, "Wait! Not here."

He raised one eyebrow.

With a decided smirk, she pointed to the dais where she'd been measured earlier. "Over there. Stand up there to take your clothes off."

The way she'd done earlier today. He rose, smothering a laugh. She was so transparent. "Turnabout is fair play, is that it?"

Her gloating smile was her only answer.

He strolled to the dais, his mind racing. She thought to sit there safely distant while she watched him undress. That way she could dash from the room as soon as he was done, before he got any amorous ideas.

But he had an ace up his sleeve.

"Have you always had this flair for the dramatic?" He mounted the dais, then faced her. "Or do I just happen to bring it out in you?"

"My winnings, sir." She snapped her fingers. "I want them now."

Hiding his smile, he untied his cravat and held it out. "Come and get it."

"Leave it there," she said smoothly. "I'll gather it later."

"As you wish." He dropped it on the floor. Clever girl. She knew exactly what she was about. But so did he.

He bent to his knife, and she said, "What are you doing?"

"You won by three points. The cravat is one, the knife is another, and the sheath a third. I'm giving you your winnings."

Her smile vanished. "The knife doesn't count, as you well know. It's not an item of 'clothing or adornment.'"

"It is for me. I wear it every day."

"As a weapon! You *said* that weapons don't count."

"I've never had to use it as a weapon." He unfastened the sheath and removed the knife. *Come on, my sweet, let's see that famous temper of yours.*

"That doesn't matter! You're cheating, blast you!"

He said nothing, just laid the knife atop his cravat and unbuckled the sheath.

She shot to her feet. "You're not playing fair! I demand that you take off your drawers!"

Placing the sheath on the cravat, he straightened. "No."

Her mouth opened and closed like a fish's. "What? But you have to! Those are the rules!"

He shrugged. "I interpret them differently." He descended the dais, adding in a provokingly snide tone, "Now sit down and deal the cards like a good little girl."

She flushed. "I will not! I won, fair and square, and you know it. So take those drawers off this instant!"

He walked up to the table, waiting until he was in reach of her, before murmuring, "Make me."

Chapter Nine

*If you do not intend to share your lover's
bed on a particular visit, make your wishes
known immediately, even if you
must suffer his foul temper for the rest
of the evening.*
—Anonymous, *Memoirs of a Mistress*

How dared he! After he'd made her send Rosa away and
insisted that she play fair— "Take off your drawers,
Byrne," she demanded.

"Make me," he said again, cool as you please.

She saw red. Ooh, that was so like a man—to cheat,
then assume he'd get away with it!

With an oath, she strode up to him and seized the band
of his drawers. "I'll take them off of you myself, I will."

As she worked loose the top button, the fabric began to
bulge beneath her hands. That's when her good sense finally
kicked in. She jerked her hands back, but he caught one and
flattened it against his half-buttoned drawers . . . and the
erection beneath. His very solid, very dangerous erection.

"Go on," he said in a guttural voice. "You want your
winnings, don't you?"

Her gaze shot to his, but that proved a mistake. Because his expression of rampant need was the last thing
she saw before his mouth crushed hers.

Like a mare cornered by a stallion, she realized the

danger only when it was too late. Curse her unruly temper. And curse him for taking advantage of it, for thrusting his tongue so deliciously between her lips, for making her forget why . . . she . . . ought . . . to resist . . .

And now his hand was sliding hers inside his drawers to cup the heavy length of him, and her gut was knotting in a welter of fear and excitement actually to be touching it. Him. His flesh.

Dear Lord in heaven, she must be mad. Yet her hand moved of its own accord, stroking, caressing—

"Yes, lass," he whispered against her lips. "Yes, like that, yes . . ."

He returned to ravaging her mouth. But gone was the restraint he'd exhibited earlier in the day. He cupped her breast through the chemise, then slid her chemise off one shoulder so he could knead the naked flesh beneath with his warm, broad hand.

But when he squeezed her nipple, sending a shock of pleasure straight to her belly and below, she tore her mouth from his to murmur, "Byrne, please . . ."

She wasn't sure if she was begging for him to stop or to go on. Taking her by surprise, he lifted her onto the card table behind them, forcing her to release her grip on his . . . his thing.

The flimsy table wobbled under her weight, and she grabbed for his arms to steady her. "What in blazes do you think you're doing?"

His only answer was to tug her chemise down enough to expose one aching breast to his heavy-lidded gaze. "What does it look like I'm doing?" He bent his head to suck her nipple. Hard.

She nearly shot up off the table. "Oh, Lord," she moaned, even as she clutched his head close for more.

He happily obliged her, teasing her nipple with teeth and tongue, making her gasp and sigh and yearn. She'd never felt anything this intense with her husband, never. What sort of wanton was she, that she could only feel it with this blatantly immoral scoundrel?

"Blast you," she whispered. "You are such a . . . devious . . . devil . . ."

"I do try," he rasped, sliding his hand inside her chemise to find her other nipple and roll it between his thumb and forefinger in a motion clearly designed to drive her insane. "Do you like that, lass?"

"Yes . . . oh . . . yes . . ." When he removed his wicked hands so he could shove her chemise down to her waist, she caught his hands before he could touch her again. "Wait a minute—I'm not supposed to be naked. Only *you* are, you . . . you cheater," she accused him breathlessly.

His eyes glittered like the fiercest of foxes in some dark-forested night. "You won't be happy until I concede defeat, will you?" He shoved down his drawers and kicked them away. "There—you've got your winnings. I'm naked as the day I was born."

Her gaze shot inexorably to the flesh he'd bared, and her mouth went dry. Lord help her. She'd seen only one man naked in her entire life, and he'd been nothing like Byrne. Philip's member had been long, sleek, and slender. Easy to manage.

Byrne's didn't look easy to manage. It thrust boldly forward like the impudent scoundrel that it was—hard and huge and heavy. And unmanageable. Exactly like its owner.

Who was presently inching up her chemise—

"Stop that!" she protested, grabbing for his hands. "You mustn't—"

He cut her off with a long, needy kiss, the sort of soul-deep kiss she was rapidly growing addicted to. Philip hadn't been much for kissing . . . or for silken caresses, either. Love-making had been a basic need he satisfied as quickly as possible, often leaving her craving the inexplicable.

But even as Byrne's caresses built that same craving inside her, he began satisfying it. He fondled the breasts that craved his touch, fingered the nipples that yearned for his teasing, slid his hand up inside her thigh until his thumb found the pulsing center of all her cravings and . . .

"Byrne!" she cried as he rubbed her most impudently. She grabbed his hand. "I don't think you should—"

"Hush, my sweet, you think too much." He stroked her on that tender spot again, making her squirm on the table shamelessly.

Desperately, she fought to keep her sanity. "No doubt you've used . . . that line before."

"Hardly." He slid a finger inside her, and she gasped. "You met my mistresses—did they seem the type to need coaxing to misbehave?"

"No, but—"

"The trouble with you is that you have everything backwards."

Now he was thumbing her nipple with one hand and thrusting his finger inside her with the other. She couldn't catch her breath, couldn't halt the rush of sensations assaulting her.

He went on in a husky rasp. "When you *should* be using that clever brain of yours, playing whist, you let every emotion sway you. But let a man try to make love to you, and all you do is think."

He heated her cheeks and brow and temples with a series of kisses designed to do anything *but* make her think. She struggled against the fog stealing over her.

"There you go again," he murmured. "You're thinking. I can tell from your frown."

"If I don't ... keep my wits about me ... you'll destroy me."

He gave a low chuckle. "Such drama. Does this feel like destruction?"

He drove another finger deep inside her, making her rise up on the table with a cry of alarm ... of delight ... of pleasure. Blast him.

"You can think later," he added. "Right now, just feel and enjoy."

But if she gave herself to him in this, she would give herself in other ... more dangerous ... Oh, Lord, what was he doing to her?

She gripped his shoulders as he battered her defenses on every front, giving her another of his too-enticing kisses while he caressed her inside and out, her breast ... her nipple ... the soft, throbbing flesh between her legs. She'd felt a vaguely unsatisfying ache down there before, but Byrne's caresses sharpened it to a piercing need that grew and swelled and consumed her below, carrying her forward in a rush until she was arching into his hand and gripping his shoulders and reaching for something ...

She tore her mouth from his as the craving grew insatiable. "Oh, Byrne ... please ... oh yes ..."

"Is this what you want?" he whispered, his motions growing fiercer, his breath thick and heavy against her cheek. "Is it, lass?"

"I want ... I need ..." It hit her suddenly, a flood of exquisite sensations she'd never known. "Byrne, yes!" she cried out, as they swamped her senses. "Byrne ... oh, my word ... Byrne ..."

"I'm here." His hand slowed to a sensuous caress, gentling her, soothing her as she shook from the waves of pleasure rocking her body.

And when it was over, and the excitement faded to a sweet contentment, he nuzzled her cheek, and said again, "I'm here, my sweet."

For a moment, all Christabel could do was breathe and wonder and try to figure out how he—

"You're thinking again," he whispered, then laved her ear with his tongue.

"I'm not . . . I . . . what on earth was that? What happened?"

Moving his hand from between her legs, he drew back to stare at her. "You don't know?"

"Should I?"

His lips tightened into a thin line. "Haversham should have shown you, yes. But I'm not exactly surprised that he didn't."

His condemning tone stung. She leaped to defend her late husband. "You can't expect him to have been as wicked as you. He was a respectable man—"

"Who was too selfish to pleasure his wife." His eyes bored into her, unsettling her. "Unless you found what we just did unpleasant, don't excuse him for denying it to you."

She colored. "Perhaps he didn't . . . know how—"

"Then he should have learned." His hands caressed her thighs. "Trust me, that's the very least that a man . . . a lover . . . a *husband* should do for his wife. Though plenty of them don't."

"I see," she said inanely. And she did. So very much. *This* was why married women clamored to play the role of his mistress. They wanted this heady, addictive pleasure that their husbands wouldn't or couldn't give them.

He bent to kiss her cheek, then her jaw, then her throat. "Now I see why you balked at sharing my bed. Because you didn't know what you were missing."

"That wasn't why," she whispered without thinking.

"Then what was the reason?" He tongued the pulse in her neck that still beat so wildly.

Because if I share your bed, I'll lose myself.

She couldn't say that; it would give him an advantage.

Still kissing her neck and her hair, he moved in closer, the tip of his erect shaft brushing between her legs. Panic seized her. Oh, Lord, she'd already given him an advantage. He'd pleasured her, but he hadn't gained his own pleasure. And now he would expect to gain it in her bed. Unless—

Almost desperately, she reached between them to close her hand about his hot, rigid flesh.

He groaned. "Damn, that feels good."

Tentatively, she worked her hand up and down his shaft, rewarded by another heartfelt groan. She'd caught Philip doing this once, watched secretly as he stroked himself to release. If he could do it to himself, then surely she—

"That's enough," Byrne growled, catching her hand to stay it. "I want to come inside you."

"But I want to touch you as you touched me." Frantically, she searched for an argument that would convince him. "Philip never let me touch him like this," she whispered. Though it was true, it shamed her to reveal it. Still, if the choice was to let Byrne take her here, in her own parlor, like one of his wanton mistresses—

"Please," she continued, "let me touch you."

After a second, his hand fell away from hers. "If you want." He thrust into her hand. "We do have all night."

"I thought you had to be at the club."

"They'll send for me . . . if they need me," he choked out. "With luck, they won't."

Then he surprised her by lowering his mouth to suck her breast. It was like tossing kindling into smoldering embers—her blood raced hot again, and that insatiable flesh between her legs began to throb. Oh, no, no, she mustn't let him arouse . . . her . . . again. . . .

Praying she was doing it right, she increased the rhythm of her strokes. His response was heartening. With a choked gasp, he tore his mouth from her breast and began pumping his hips against her hand. She couldn't believe how fiercely firm he was, yet how silky soft his skin, like liquid velvet encasing steel.

"God . . . oh, God . . . yes, lass, yes . . ." he growled.

For the first time in her life, she understood what he must be feeling. And to think that *she* was the one giving this pleasure to him was intoxicating. Perhaps she wasn't entirely inept at pleasing a man.

She stroked him harder. "Is that what you want?" Drunk with her own exhilarating power, she consciously echoed his earlier words. "Is it, Byrne?"

With a heartfelt curse, he threw his head back, the muscles in his neck stretched taut. "You know . . . that it is . . . you bloody, teasing . . . minx." Reaching behind her, he snatched up the pair of drawers she'd tossed onto the table earlier and wrapped it about her hand and his aroused flesh.

"Damn . . . damn . . . damn!" he cried out seconds later as his seed, warm and thick like buttermilk, flooded her linen-bound hand.

As she witnessed the blood flush fill his face and heard his breath come raggedly from his throat, a strange awe stole over her. So even the fiercely controlled Byrne was human.

Perhaps he was not so very controlled after all. Perhaps he was even capable of real feeling—

No, how could she even think it? Yes, he enjoyed love-making fully—what else could she expect of a man like him? But he would never go beyond that, a fact that he'd made clear in every act, every word. He wasn't the sort of man to care for a woman beyond the bedchamber.

His head lowered, and his eyes slid open. "Well, well," he managed to gasp as his breathing slowed. "For a woman who never before experienced pleasure with a man, you are . . . quite talented at giving it."

Trying not to let the frank approval warm her, she dropped her gaze from his. "Am I?"

He wiped her hand clean on her drawers, then tossed them aside. "Oh, yes." Bending to press his lips to her cheek, he murmured, "Time to move to your bedchamber, my sweet, where we can be more comfortable."

A groan escaped her. He was not going to take this well, was he? "I . . . I would rather not," she evaded. "I'm tired, and you have to be at the club—"

"I don't, I told you." He nibbled her ear as he laid his hands on her waist. "And if you're tired, we'll sleep a while." A teasing note entered his voice. "Making love is even better in the morning."

"No, I can't." She drew back from him, her head lowered. She couldn't look at him. "I . . . I just can't."

His fingers curled into her waist. "You can't?" he said disbelievingly. "You mean, you won't."

She nodded.

Seizing her chin, he lifted her head until her gaze met his, now icy gray as a winter storm. "You never intended for us to share a bed tonight, did you? That's why you jerked my mutton."

"I . . . *What*?"

"You're a cock-chafer," he hissed. "You excite a man, then throw him out of your bed without giving him relief."

"That's not true!" she protested. "I *did* give you relief!"

A muscle jerked in his jaw. "Yes, I suppose you did. In a fashion. But it wasn't the kind of relief I wanted."

She sighed. "Byrne, you have to understand—"

"No, I don't. What are you so bloody afraid of, Christabel? That you might enjoy yourself? That you might discover you're secretly as wicked as the rest of us whom you hold in such contempt?"

She dared not tell him that she couldn't trust herself with him if she took him into her bed. But she could tell him some of the truth. If he could understand.

"I'm not like your other women, you know," she whispered. "I'm not willing to take a man in parts. I can't share your bed one day and blithely look the other way the next as you share another woman's bed. It isn't in my nature." Drawing her chemise up to cover her breasts, she slid her arms through the sleeves. "And it isn't in *your* nature to be faithful to a woman, is it?"

He was silent a moment, his eyes boring into hers. And even when he spoke, his answer wasn't an answer. "So you want marriage then." He spat the word as if it were loathsome.

She shook her head no. "I will never again place my future in the hands of some man who will end up—"

"Betraying you?"

She nodded.

A familiar calculating gleam entered his eyes. "Ah, but that's exactly why what I offer is better than any marriage." His hands rubbed her thighs, slowly, caressingly . . . temptingly. If Satan were a seducer, that was how he'd do it, too. "We can enjoy our pleasure without fearing that one of us will destroy the other—as spouses so often do. And when we tire of each other—"

"What if I don't tire of you before you tire of me? Two people needn't be married to destroy each other—just witness the havoc that Lady Caroline Lamb's behavior has wreaked upon her lover Byron and her own family."

He quirked up one eyebrow. "I somehow can't imagine you threatening me with a knife at a dinner party."

"Are you forgetting that I shot at you? If I came to care for you, and you treated me as you do your other women, I don't know what I might do. As I said, it's not in my nature to fall in and out of a man's bed without a thought."

His fingers dug into her thighs. "So you mean to remain celibate all your life? No marriage, no lover, no one but your aging father to keep you company?"

She swallowed. In typical Byrne fashion, he'd left out the most important thing—no children. Since she was probably barren, a new marriage would be difficult. Most men wanted women who could bear them sons.

With a sigh, she pushed his hands from her thighs and slid off the table. "I haven't thought that far."

"And no wonder." Refusing to move away, he planted his hands on the table on either side of her to keep her trapped there. He bent his head, his mouth brushing her ear as he lowered his voice to an achingly seductive whisper. "Until tonight, you didn't know what pleasure was. But now that you know—"

"I must be even more cautious." Drawing back, she managed a smile. "Besides, you don't want a jealous mistress who will demand to know where you've been, complain when you ignore her, and beg you to share only her bed. That's precisely the sort I'd be. I drove my own husband to gamble and drink and . . . who knows what." She couldn't keep the pain from her voice. "Only imagine what I'd drive a debaucher like you to do—commit murder, probably."

Anger flared in his face. "You didn't drive that fool Haversham into anything, damn it. From the moment I met him, I recognized him as one of those thoughtless arses whose thirst for the tables blots out any other consideration in his life. That isn't your fault."

His words were like a surgeon's knife probing flesh for a bullet. "Isn't it? If I had made him happy at home—"

"Did you ever refuse to let the selfish idiot bed you?"

"No, but—"

"Did you make sure he was well fed?"

"Of course."

"Did you plague *him* about where he'd been and what he was doing?"

"Not at first. To be honest, I was relieved not to have to play the marchioness in society when I didn't know the role."

"So he found you someone to instruct you, did he? Reassured you that you could learn those things? Did his best to help you feel comfortable accompanying him into society?"

His rather pompous dissertation began to annoy her. "Not exactly, but—"

"As I said, a selfish, thoughtless arse. Tell me, Christabel, when you first met him, was your husband a gambler?"

She stuck out her chin. "Moderately so."

"How do you know he was moderate? Did he ever

promise to be somewhere and then not appear, pleading headache or some other nonsense? Was he always the one to suggest cards as the evening's entertainment? Did his pay often mysteriously disappear—"

"Stop it!" She shoved his arm aside to escape his too-accurate description of a man whose proclivity for gambling even her father had questioned. Once she'd put some distance between them, she faced him. "You have the audacity to call him selfish and thoughtless when you daily show a complete lack of feeling for the women you bed—"

"The women I bed are as uninterested in my feelings as I am in theirs." Eyes glittering, he stalked up to her, apparently unconcerned that he was stark naked. "They want the same thing I want from them—pleasure and nothing more."

"Are you sure? Is that why Lady Jenner went out of her way to provoke me this evening? She was halfway to scratching my eyes out."

He went rigid. "Her pride was wounded, that's all."

"Perhaps. But even if you're right about her and the others, even if they did want only one thing from you, I can't be like them. So we're back to where we started. I simply can't be the sort of mistress you want. I know my own nature well enough for that."

A muttered oath escaped his lips. "Fine. Then perhaps we shouldn't play Whist for the Wicked anymore."

"And perhaps you should stop trying to seduce me."

He arched one eyebrow. "That, my sweet, is not in *my* nature."

Coloring, she bent to pick up his drawers where he'd left them on the floor. "Then perhaps you should go. Here, take these."

With a glance that would have frozen ice, he walked past her without taking them, headed for the door. "Keep them. You won them fairly."

"Byrne, please, at least let me call for your overcoat."

He stared at her with annoyance. "After tonight, your reputation will be severely tarnished anyway. Since that doesn't seem to bother you, why do you care if a few servants gossip about how I left your house naked?"

"I just . . . do."

His jaw went taut as he laid his hand on the doorknob. He hesitated, then cursed again and opened the door wide enough to call through it. "You there, footman! Bring me my coat."

There was a ruckus in the hall as someone hurried to do his bidding. Moments later, Byrne thrust his hand out and came back with his coat, then slammed the door.

"Your footman was limping. Another of your ex-soldiers?" he growled as he pulled on his coat and began to button it with jerky movements.

"Yes. He's missing a foot."

"Of course." He gave a harsh laugh. "Only you would hire a footless footman." He cast her a hooded glance. "You're the most maddening woman I've ever met, do you know that?" He laid his hand on the doorknob again. "I'll see you in the morning."

"What?" she asked, bewildered.

"Mrs. Watts is coming back, remember? After she leaves, we'll play cards again—*respectable* cards, mind you." He sneered the word *respectable*. "And tomorrow evening we'll go to the theater, so people will see us together socially. Unless you find that activity not respectable enough for a pretend mistress?"

"No, that's fine," she said, a little peevishly. After all,

she'd only told him the truth about what she felt. No need for him to be so childish about it. "I like the theater."

"Of course you do," he snapped. "Drama is your stock-in-trade."

But there was a bit of humor in his tone now, as if he, too, recognized that he was overreacting.

She let out a breath she hadn't even realized she was holding. "So we're . . . in agreement? About my not sharing your bed?"

"We will *never* be in agreement about that." He raked her with a long, heated glance that turned her knees wobbly. "But I'm not one to force a woman to my bed. I can wait until she goes there willingly." A devilish smile tipped up his lips. "Because that day *will* come. It always does."

And with that arrogant statement, he left.

Only then did she let out a breath. But even after she heard his cabriolet pulling away, she couldn't relax. She felt bereft, adrift. Restless. Roaming the room, she picked up a stocking here, a garter there, hardly distinguishing between his and hers as she piled them on a chair and prayed she could get them upstairs without the servants seeing.

She picked up his waistcoat, and his scent wafted to her again, a strangely male blend of sweet and musky. Holding the embroidered fabric to her cheek, she felt tears prick her eyes. How familiar this seemed—picking up a man's discarded clothes. Before Philip had ascended to the title and hired a fancy valet, she'd been the one to gather up his clothes after he returned from a long night out. But Philip's clothes had reeked of brandy; Byrne's reeked of *him*. And if she'd wanted—

No, she'd been right to refuse what he offered. Tempting as the man might be and much as she'd secretly love to experience the delights of sharing his bed, she would surely regret it in the end.

She sank into a chair with a sigh. Then why, oh why, did it feel as if she'd made an enormous mistake?

After a moment of driving in nothing but his overcoat, Gavin began to wish he'd accepted his drawers when Christabel had offered them. In early autumn, nights in London were plenty cool and damp. The fog seeped under his coat, chilling him to the bone. Damn Christabel for tossing him out when he could have been lying warm and cozy in her bed, making love to her with slow, easy thrusts—

"Bloody hell," he growled, as his cock stirred once more. The woman would be the death of him.

He reached for his watch, then realized she had it. But it couldn't be that late. He could always go to one of the better brothels to satisfy his lust. Though he rarely frequented whores, sometimes it was necessary.

Yet the idea was so unappealing at the moment that it silenced the clamoring of his wayward cock. Odd, that. The whole situation was odd. No woman who clearly wanted him—who aroused him, too—had ever refused him his satisfaction.

That must be the trouble—he hadn't *had* Christabel, so no other woman held any appeal. But that would end soon. He would have her, and when he did, it would be all the more worth it for the waiting. Unlike that idiot Haversham, he knew how to savor the anticipation of bedding a woman. He only hoped he didn't have to savor it too much longer.

At least one good thing had come of tonight. He now knew that his strategy would work. As she'd said, she wasn't like his other women. Which meant that once he seduced her—and he would, eventually—it would be easier to get everything he wanted from her, including the truth about her "property."

Of course, there were other risks involved. First, the obvious one—that he might get her with child. He'd always relied on the husbands of his mistresses to claim any child that might occur despite his preventive measures. Still, he'd been glad it had never happened. It would have unsettled him to know that some child of his was being raised as another man's.

But if he somehow got Christabel with child, there would be no husband to claim the babe. So he'd have to be extra cautious. They would both take measures to prevent it—there were sponges a woman could use. She couldn't possibly have any more desire to bear a bastard than he did to sire one.

So that left the second risk—that Christabel would become exactly the kind of mistress she claimed. That she'd turn into a jealous, unpredictable, possessive harpy. He chuckled as a sudden image leaped into his mind, of her dragging out her rifle to take shots at any other woman who demanded his attentions.

When he realized that the idea appealed to him, his humor faded abruptly. No self-respecting rakehell wanted a woman waiting impatiently for his arrival every night, hanging on his every word, gazing at him with a longing so profound that it—

He cursed under his breath. This was what came of dallying with respectable women. They put ideas in a man's head that he would never entertain otherwise.

He liked his life precisely as it was. He'd make her his mistress because he desired her, but he would teach her not to expect more of him than that. Surely even the indomitable Widow Haversham could be made to accept the way of the world eventually.

And if it meant that the light in her eyes and the passion in her heart were extinguished?

With an oath, he flicked the reins to speed the horses. That sort of thinking was what had led him to be a fool about Anna Bingham. Never again would he succumb to such dangerous sentimental nonsense. Never again.

Minutes later, he reached his town house in fashionable Mayfair. Before he even halted, a groom hurried out to meet him, and his youngish butler appeared in the window. Gavin paid well for such attention late at night—his hours were odd, and he didn't like to bother with rousing a servant. His entire household operated on the supposition that morning was night and night was morning.

In fact, this was early for him; his dire need for clothes had prevented him from going to the club straight from Christabel's. He halted his rig, handed the reins to his groom, and climbed down, cursing the lack of his boots when his feet hit gravel.

His butler came outside. "Sir, do you need assistance?"

"No, I can manage." Gavin gingerly took the few steps to the stone entrance staircase, then shook the stones from beneath his toes.

His butler said naught about Gavin's bootless, stockingless state; he knew better. But as Gavin climbed the steps, the servant hurried down to meet him instead of waiting at the top as usual. "I thought you'd want to know, sir—you've received a message from Bath. The messenger is waiting inside for your reply. I had just sent a footboy to the club for you when you drove up."

Bath. He tensed. "Thank you, Jenkins."

He took the remaining steps two at a time. A summons from Bath was never good. The messenger from Bath met him at the top and wordlessly handed him a sealed missive. Gavin groaned. Sealed missives were never good either.

He tore it open, then scanned the message swiftly. Though the tension left him, it didn't change what he must do. "Jenkins, as soon as that footboy returns, send him to the livery to have them ready my coach. I mean to leave in an hour. And bring me some paper and a pen. I have to write a note or two before I leave."

Jenkins nodded. "I'll take care of it at once, sir."

Gavin's jaunt to the theater with Christabel tomorrow night would have to wait. But he'd make it up to her. He'd find some bauble in Bath before he returned.

It shouldn't be too long. The message said the situation wasn't as dire as it could be. He'd go tonight, spend the day consulting with the doctor to make sure everything was indeed all right, stay there tomorrow night, and come back the day after next.

He'd only lose a day or two of preparing Christabel for Stokely's party. That shouldn't affect matters. It might even work to his advantage to have her stew a bit. She might be more eager to reveal the truth about her property if she thought he was losing interest in helping her.

His eyes narrowed. Come to think of it, Rosevine wasn't far off the road between London and Bath. Perhaps he should stop near there on the way back. A few guineas to the right gossipy villager might afford him a bit more information about her and her family. At the very least, he could learn something about the steward who'd broken into her strongbox. Plenty of lords kept on the previous title-holder's more experienced servants, so the steward might even still live at Rosevine.

It was time to start pursuing this from other angles, just to hedge his bets. Because whether Christabel knew it or not, he meant to discover the truth. One way or another.

Chapter Ten

*If you require faithfulness, buy a cocker
spaniel. No mistress ever gains it from
her lover.*
—Anonymous, *Memoirs of a Mistress*

*C*hristabel awakened alone after a tempestuous night of
erotic dreams. Byrne—curse his soul—figured promi-
nently in every one, him and his searing kisses and stealthy
caresses.

How would she make it through the next few weeks?
Or, for that matter, a week at Lord Stokely's, where everyone would expect them to behave as if they were intimate?
Byrne would certainly take advantage of *that* situation—
kissing and touching her at will, rousing her passions at
every opportunity.

Turning onto her side, she crumpled her pillow into a
ball that she cradled against her breasts . . . her too-sensi-
tive breasts that ached—

Lord help her! What was she doing? What secret po-
tion had the man given her to make her so aware of her
body? She never wanted to touch herself wickedly before,
yet last night she'd actually stuck her hand under the covers to stroke herself *down there*.

Worse yet, she'd liked it. Weren't respectable women

supposed to dislike such things? She'd always known she wasn't like other women, but she'd never guessed she was secretly a wanton. Not until Byrne came along.

With a sigh, she pressed her flaming cheek to the pillow. Perhaps she should simply let matters go where they would. The important thing was getting the letters, and wouldn't it be easier if she didn't have to fend him off constantly?

She groaned. Oh, Lord, it was already happening. She was already letting him persuade her into lowering her guard. Next she'd be confiding in him about Papa and His Highness and that fateful day twenty-two years ago . . .

A shudder wracked her. She mustn't let that Prince of Sin sway her with kisses and caresses, no matter how enticing. It was too dangerous. She would lay down some firm rules. No physical contact except when absolutely necessary. Their whist lessons would take place with the doors of the parlor open. He couldn't continue his seductions even if—

A tap at the door prefaced the arrival of Rosa with a breakfast tray. "Good morning!" the maid said cheerily as she set the tray down and went to open the curtains. "I do hope the extra sleep did you good."

Christabel shot up in bed. "Extra sleep—what time is it?"

"Nearly noon."

"Oh, blast," she muttered as she threw the covers aside. "He'll be here any minute, him and the dressmaker! I have to get ready."

She dared not let him guess what a restless night she'd spent. A rogue like him would know exactly why she'd overslept. And what—who—had consumed her dreams.

"If you are speaking of your Mr. Byrne," Rosa said, "a message came for you from him early this morning."

Christabel glanced at the tray, where a sealed note was indeed propped up between the coffee she couldn't live without and the plate containing the buttered scones that she ought to live without, but never did.

Why had he written a note? He'd be here himself in a few moments.

The note got right to the point:

> My dearest Christabel,
>
> I regret that I will be unable to accompany you to the theater tonight. Urgent business calls me to Bath. I am uncertain of how long I will be gone, but I will call on you directly upon my return. In the meantime, you may wish to read the books about whist that I am sending along. You may also wish to practice your Patience.
>
> Sincerely,
> Byrne

She gaped at the note, then balled it up in her fist. Of all the arrogant, presumptuous—They'd made a bargain, blast it, and now he'd trotted off to Bath without even considering her lessons!

Lessons. "Rosa? Were there books included with the note?"

"I believe so. The footman has them." Smiling to herself, Rosa gathered up the clothing Christabel had tossed onto a chair the night before. "So what does your Mr. Byrne have to say?"

"He's had to go to Bath on business." She tossed Byrne's note aside. "Lord only knows when he'll return."

"It will not be long, I wager, not when he left these behind." With a smirk, Rosa held up a pair of obviously male drawers. "Shall I have them cleaned and kept for his future visits?"

A blush rose in her cheeks. "You can burn them as far as I'm concerned." Leaping from the bed, Christabel paced the room. "I won them from him in a card game last night."

"You bested the gambler?"

"Yes, for all the good it did me."

Rosa started to smile.

"What are *you* smiling about?" Christabel said peevishly.

"Nothing." Rosa folded the waistcoat very carefully. "It is just . . . curious that you would win. Perhaps he was distracted?"

He'd been distracted, all right—with plotting how to get her out of her clothes and into his arms. And when that hadn't brought quite the success he'd expected, he'd rushed off to Bath without one whit of concern for the fact that Lord Stokely's party was less than two weeks away.

Had he done it because she'd refused to share his bed? Horrible thought. Could his passions be so powerful that one denial would send him off in a temper?

Somehow, that didn't sound like the controlled Byrne she knew.

"Do you wish to dress?" Rosa asked.

"Yes, of course." No matter what Byrne did, she still had to continue with their plan. And that meant meeting the dressmaker.

As Rosa helped her don another ugly mourning gown, Christabel's mind wandered back to Byrne's defection. What was in Bath that he might consider "business"? She'd never heard of his owning a club there. So if it didn't have to do with his gambling affairs—

She paled. What if it concerned a woman? He might very well have a mistress hidden away there, one who wouldn't hesitate to satisfy the urges Christabel had refused to satisfy exactly as he'd wished.

She waited impatiently as Rosa did up her buttons. So help her, if Byrne had a mistress in Bath—

And if he did? She had no hold on him. She'd never said he couldn't be with other women. He'd never protested Lady Jenner's claim that he was incapable of fidelity. So why should she assume that just because he'd kissed and caressed her, it meant anything?

Blast him! This was precisely why she hadn't wanted him to touch her. She'd known exactly how it would affect her foolish heart.

No, not her heart. Just her pride and sense of fairness. How dared he run off to Bath in the middle of their bargain? Practice her Patience indeed—when he returned, she would give him a piece of her mind, she would. The audacity of the man—to preach patience to her when he was ignoring their agreement!

A knock at the door jerked her from her thoughts. "My lady," said one of the lower maids, "the dressmaker is here."

"Tell her I'll be there shortly," Christabel called out.

Rosa forced her to a chair so she could put her hair into some semblance of respectability. As the brush flew through Christabel's tangles too swiftly for comfort, she tried to calm her irritation with Byrne. At least she could have a sensible discussion with the dressmaker today, without having to deal with the man's searing glances that said he wanted to fondle and kiss every inch—

She let out an oath as her knees went weak. Blast him for turning her into this silly female, capable of falling into a faint just because he smiled at her. Philip had never done that to her.

"There," Rosa said. "Good enough for the dressmaker, is it not?"

"Yes. And you should probably stay out of her way. She doesn't like having ladies' maids around." Before Rosa could protest, Christabel jumped up and hurried from the room.

Today Mrs. Watts had an assistant with her, a pretty young woman with riotous brown curls who dropped into a deep curtsy as Christabel entered the parlor. That was something Christabel would never get used to—the courtesies that came to her because of her now lofty station. She didn't really *feel* like a marchioness. She felt more like a general's daughter—his wayward daughter who had let him down. Certainly not deserving of any curtsies.

"My lady," the dressmaker said, "I've brought the gown Mr. Byrne wanted for tonight. Do you still need it now that he's had to rush from town on business?"

Did Mrs. Watts mean the altered mourning gown? But wasn't that supposed to be ready for *today*? Not that it mattered, with Byrne gone. "No, I don't suppose I need it for tonight."

"Because I can have it ready if you require it. After you try it on, we can make the necessary adjustments before we leave. Indeed, that's why I brought Lydia—she's quickest with a needle."

The name Lydia teased Christabel's memory. "It's fine, really. I don't intend to go out tonight."

"As you wish," Mrs. Watts said deferentially. "Then we shall just see how they fit. Move aside, Lydia, so her ladyship can see the evening gown."

Evening gown?

Lydia moved and Christabel spotted what was behind her, draped over the settee. It was the beautiful rose satin, done up in the most stunning gown imaginable.

"Dear Lord," Christabel whispered.

Mrs. Watts stiffened. "Does it not meet with my lady's approval?"

"No . . . I mean, yes . . . It's lovely. Just lovely."

The dressmaker relaxed. "Mr. Byrne will be pleased, then. He was most intent upon having it ready for tonight."

Their trip to the theater. He'd planned the gown for that.

Despite herself, she turned to mush. He'd probably paid an exorbitant amount to have it ready quickly, just because she'd admired it.

Tears filled her eyes. Just when she wanted to hate him, he went and did something like that.

"Do you wish to try it on?" Mrs. Watts asked.

"Yes, please," Christabel replied, not even bothering to hide her delight.

Once it was on and Mrs. Watts had turned her toward the mirror, her mouth dropped open. Who was that . . . that gorgeous creature staring back at her?

She'd never cared much about gowns, but then she'd never had a gown that made her look . . . pretty. The rose lent color to her cheeks, and the subtle cut of the skirt hid her rounded belly, drawing the eye instead to her nicely displayed breasts. And when she turned, the satin swirled around her hips, then clung lovingly to the curves.

A blush touched her cheeks. She felt naked and wicked, even though the gown showed no more than those of Lady

Draker and Lady Iversley two nights ago. But something in how it accentuated her "assets," as Byrne had put it—

"If the lack of embellishment disturbs my lady," Mrs. Watts said, apparently misinterpreting her long silence, "it will only take a day to add some satin roses around the hem."

"No, it's perfect," she whispered. "Absolutely perfect." And perfect for *her*. As Byrne somehow had known it would be.

"Once you add the matching reticule and the adorable little hat—" Mrs. Watts looked around. "Oh, dear, I must have forgotten them in the carriage." She frowned. "Unless I left them entirely—"

"Shall I fetch them, ma'am?" Lydia asked.

"No, no, I can't remember if I even brought them. I'll go myself, and if need be, I'll send one of the footmen back for them."

The dressmaker hurried out, leaving Christabel alone with young Lydia. The girl ventured near. "It looks lovely on you, my lady. Mr. Byrne will be entranced."

Entranced. An oddly sophisticated word for a mere seamstress's assistant. "Do you know him, then?"

The girl blushed. "Yes, my lady. He got me this position with Mrs. Watts."

Christabel blinked. Then it hit her all at once. *He said his little Lydia left him to work in some dress shop.* Lord help her, this was *that* Lydia, the fetching young thing Byrne had been "taken with."

"Of course he did," she said sarcastically. Strange that Lady Jenner hadn't roused jealousy, but this young woman did.

Her tone sent alarm flitting over the girl's features.

"Did he . . . that is . . . your ladyship knows how I met Mr. Byrne?"

"Playing whist, wasn't it?" she said dryly.

The girl looked positively panicked. "Oh, my lady, please don't have me turned out! I will do anything you wish, only don't tell Mrs. Watts about how Jim and I were card cheats. Please, I beg you, don't have me sent to the magistrate—"

"No, certainly not! Why would you think I'd do such a thing?"

The woman eyed her warily. "You're Mr. Byrne's mistress, aren't you?"

Christabel colored. "What has that got to do with it?"

"The mistress he had before—that Lady Jenner—she would have had me turned off for sheer spite."

"No doubt," Christabel muttered. "I, however, am not so beastly. But I admit to being confused. Doesn't Mrs. Watts know of your past already? I mean, since Byrne got you the position—"

"He told her I was the daughter of a tenant. From his estate in Bath."

She gaped at the woman. "Byrne has an estate?"

"Oh dear, oh dear, I wasn't supposed to tell, but I thought you would know, you being his mistress and all!" Tears filling her eyes, Lydia pleated and repleated her apron between her fingers. "He told me and Mrs. Watts not to tell anyone, and now I've gone and—"

"It's all right—I'll keep his secret safe," Christabel reassured the girl, but her mind was awhirl. Byrne really *had* gone to Bath on business. But who would have guessed that he possessed land, and outside of London, too? In all the gossip she'd heard about him, no one had ever mentioned it. "I've only recently become acquainted with Mr.

Byrne." And clearly the man shrouded whole portions of his life in secrecy. "I suppose you've visited his estate?"

"No, my lady. Why would I?"

"Because you . . . that is, you and he have . . ."

The girl's eyes went wide. "Oh no, we have never— I mean, not that I would mind, he's been so kind to me; but he never expected it, not even that night when Jim was so cruel as to leave me to him."

The blood pounded in Christabel's temples. "I thought you and your friend Jim played a rather wicked game of cards with Byrne and Lady Jenner."

The girl blushed. "Yes, we did. And when that awful woman—" She stopped herself. "Forgive me, I shouldn't speak of her like that."

"It's all right. She's a nasty sort, isn't she?"

"She enticed my Jim off to her bed," Lydia said hotly, "and left me to Mr. Byrne." Her tone softened. "But he was a gentleman, didn't lay a finger on me, even though I was . . . well . . . naked. He could tell at once that I—" She thrust out her chin. "I was raised for better, you see. My father was a gentleman farmer. Nearly broke his heart when I ran off with Jim. But I thought Jim meant to marry me, and once I was ruined, it just got worse and worse until . . ."

She trailed off with a heartbreaking sigh. "Anyway, Mr. Byrne said he could get me a respectable position if I wanted. That's how I came to work for Mrs. Watts."

"I see." Yes, she saw a great deal. Byrne talked like a scoundrel, but somewhere buried in his cynical soul was a kernel of good.

Mrs. Watts bustled back in with the other items, but as Christabel tried on the "adorable little hat," her mind was elsewhere.

What was she to make of the rascal? *The girl was just a night's entertainment.* She snorted. What a liar. He spoke as if he were the greatest debaucher in the world, yet he hadn't tried to force young Lydia—or Christabel—to his bed.

And he had an estate—an estate, for pity's sake! Next she'd be hearing that the man regularly attended church.

Careful, her conscience whispered. *This is how it begins—you soften toward a gentleman because he shows some merit, and next thing you know you're sunk. Byrne keeps secrets—that should be reason enough for caution. And he's helping you with this only so he can gain a barony. Don't forget that.*

She wouldn't. But neither would she assume that Byrne was entirely the devil that he seemed.

They were done, so she walked out with the dressmaker and Lydia as the woman babbled on happily about the gowns and when they'd be finished. Mrs. Watts climbed into the carriage, but as Christabel started back up the steps, Lydia excused herself to return to her side.

"Thank you, my lady, for keeping my secret," she whispered. "Mr. Byrne is lucky to have you for . . . a friend."

"I hope you're right." She waited until the girl entered the carriage, then strode back inside and found the nearest footman. "I understand that Mr. Byrne left some books for me."

"Yes, my lady, I have them right here."

As he handed them over, she said, "I'll also need a deck of cards. Do you know what happened to the ones I had last night?"

"They're in the study," the footman said. "I'll fetch them at once." When he limped back with them, he said, "Going to play a little Patience, are you?"

She gaped at him, then groaned. *Practice your Patience.* Of course. It wasn't whist, but at least it was cards. Byrne would consider that better than nothing.

Fine, she wouldn't disappoint him. Because when he returned, she meant to show him she could make him proud, even at Lord Stokely's.

Chapter Eleven

◇◇◇◇◇

> *I always hired servants of superior*
> *discretion and muscular build, because*
> *sometimes only a servant stands between*
> *you and a lover you wish to avoid.*
> —Anonymous, *Memoirs of a Mistress*

*B*y the evening of the second day without Byrne, Christabel was starting to fret. She'd read his books and practiced her Patience until she saw cards in her sleep. She was even wearing a new gown, rushed over to her by Mrs. Watts.

And still, no Byrne. What if he'd decided to spend a week in the country? What if he'd even begun to rethink their endeavor?

Such thoughts were plaguing her when an ornate card arrived for her. Certain that it was from Byrne, she eagerly opened it, astonished to find a gold-engraved invitation. To Lord Stokely's house party.

Her pulse began to race. Byrne had done it—she was invited. Astonishing!

She leaped to her feet. Unfortunately, only a week and a half remained, and she was little closer to being an expert whist player than before. Enough of this waiting around—she must locate Byrne. Or at least get a message to him at his estate about the invitation.

She called for her carriage but had no clue how to find

him. She didn't even know the address of his town house, much less his estate.

But Lord Draker would know. Wait, hadn't Lady Draker said they were going into the country around this time? And Lord only knew where the Iversleys lived. Besides, they might have gone into the country as well.

At least there was one place where enough people were well acquainted with Byrne to tell her what she needed. And fortunately, her coachman seemed to know the Blue Swan's precise location, for he went right to it.

As she climbed from the carriage, she hesitated. The brightly lit building on St. James's Street looked rather daunting. Sounds of distinctly male laughter filtered out into the night air, and the entrance door of solid English oak with its oddly austere brass knocker practically shouted, "No women allowed!"

She drew her new silk shawl more tightly about her, and her footman limped close. "Is there anyone you wish me to ask for, my lady?"

"No." She gathered her courage. "Wait here. I'll speak to the porter myself."

She didn't have to go far. The ancient servant, all starch and vinegar in his pristine blue livery, met her at the top of the stairs before she could knock. "Pardon me, madam, but this is a club for gentlemen only. If there is a particular gentleman to whom you wish to speak, I can give him your request that he meet you outside."

"I'm looking for the owner, Mr. Byrne." When the man's leathery features didn't change, she lied, "He and I had an engagement tonight, but he hasn't appeared or sent word. Perhaps you know where he is?"

The porter looked wary. "And whom shall I say is calling, madam?"

Byrne was *here*? How long had he been back in town? Her temper short, she nearly snapped, "Tell him his mistress is here," but no lady with any care for her reputation would say such a thing.

"I would prefer not to give my name," she said as imperiously as she could manage. "But I am a particular friend of his."

Her manner seemed to give the man pause. He scanned her new gown of green-spotted muslin with its matching hat and parasol, then glanced beyond her to Philip's smart town rig, which she'd inherited. Then his rigid features crumbled from proper to panicked. "Lady Haversham?" he whispered.

She blinked, then nodded.

"Forgive me, my lady . . . I must have mistook . . . Mr. Byrne is napping in his office. When he returned from Bath, he said to wake him by 7:00 P.M. so he could call on you. I must have got the time wrong. But he didn't say he was expected for an engagement, and I assumed—"

"It's all right," she said hastily, hiding her surprise.

"I am truly sorry, my lady, that my mistake caused you to have to come down here. I shall go wake him at once—"

"No, don't do that." She thought quickly. Now was her chance to see his famous club . . . and learn more about the enigmatic Byrne. "Let him sleep. If you will show me to his office, I'll just wait until he awakens." She arched one supercilious brow. "Unless that's not allowed."

The porter hesitated, but self-preservation must have won out over rules. "Mr. Byrne does occasionally have ladies in his office. I am certain he would not mind if you wait there." He lowered his voice. "And if your ladyship would be so kind as to tell him when he awakens that I did not mean for him to miss his engagement—"

"I'll simply say I came here early on a whim and begged you not to wake him." Which was the absolute truth. She cast the porter an indulgent smile. "He needn't know when I arrived, after all."

Relief flooded the elderly porter's face. "Thank you, my lady, thank you. Mr. Byrne has been very good to me, and I do not want to give him reason to question my ability to do him service."

The poor fellow's distress tugged at her heart, making her regret her little white lie. "I can't imagine why he'd do so—you seem perfectly competent to me."

"Thank you, my lady." He drew himself up proudly. "Some of the younger members complain that I am too old for the position. Fortunately, Mr. Byrne appreciates the advantages of having a man with experience."

She bit back a smile. "Of course he does. One always prefers experienced staff." And despite Byrne's teasing of her, clearly she wasn't the only employer with a soft spot for down-on-their-luck servants.

The porter frowned. "Oh, but look at me nattering on like an old fool while your ladyship is kept waiting." With a discreet nod, he indicated one corner of the building. "I am sure your ladyship would prefer to enter where you cannot be seen. Just have your coachman bring you round to the back. Knock on the green door, and I shall admit you myself."

"Thank you. Your help is much appreciated."

Back in the carriage, she dug a coin from the depths of one of her new matching reticules, all of which were too small to hold a pistol. No doubt she had Byrne to thank for that.

Once they'd driven round to the back, the porter let her in and accepted her coin with a nod and a murmured thanks. Before he led her down a private hall, she caught a glimpse of Grecian columns, surprisingly austere carpet, costly crystal chandeliers, and bronze busts displayed on pedestals. It seemed a very aristocratic club for a man who'd spent his boyhood with the blacklegs. He must have worked quite hard to make it so.

After ushering her into Byrne's office, the porter whispered, "Forgive me for saying so, my lady, but you seem too . . . er . . . good to be one of Mr. Byrne's 'particular friends.'"

"Do I? I wonder." She glanced over to where Byrne himself was sprawled along a couch in his shirtsleeves, with his waistcoat unbuttoned and his coat and cravat slung over the back. In repose, his features were oddly innocent. "I begin to think that no one is ever what they seem." On impulse, she clasped the porter's hand and gave it a quick squeeze. "Thank you again for your help."

Mumbling a response, the man blushed and left.

She wandered over to gaze at Byrne, whose exhaustion was plain in the drawn lines about his mouth and his grayish pallor. And she'd thought he hadn't cared about their preparations for Lord Stokely's party—he'd clearly driven himself hard to get to and from Bath in such a short time, while still taking care of whatever estate emergency had required his sudden attention. Poor man.

She reached out to stroke his whiskered cheek, then thought better of it. She didn't want to wake him until she'd had a chance to examine his office. Knowing Byrne's secretive nature, he would rush her off as soon as he awakened.

Strolling over to his desk, she noted the open account books. She knew a bit about accounting, having often overseen Philip's steward in his absence, so she thumbed through the pages, astonished by how carefully they were kept. The precise handwriting was Byrne's—she recognized it from his note. Despite never having attended school, he clearly grasped the concepts of accounting well enough to do it for his own business. Self-taught, he'd said. Amazing.

Next she turned to the neat arrangement of papers on his desk—the bills of lading, letters to licensing offices, crisply cut newspaper articles . . . and carefully marked gossip columns with names highlighted. She swallowed, remembering Lady Jenner's words about how he always seemed to know everything.

With a glance in his direction to determine that he still slept, she dropped into his chair and thumbed through the clippings. There were hundreds—from provincial papers, cheap London rags, shipping lists. Each had something marked—a line, a name, a date—and they were pinned together in groups. Some of them she understood—the ones about gaming laws were obvious. But the rest was so much Greek to her.

Then she spotted the satchel lying beside his chair, obviously thrown there in haste upon his arrival. With her blood pounding, she picked it up and opened it ever so carefully, casting surreptitious glances over to the couch the whole time.

Keeping it open on her lap, she examined the papers inside. Most of them had to do with his estate—she still could scarcely believe he had one—but there was one folded piece of foolscap stuffed down between two innocuous documents that drew her interest.

Stealthily she opened it. At first, she wasn't certain what it was—it looked like a hodgepodge of notes. Then she saw the word "Ilsley." Rosevine was two miles from Ilsley. And not far from the road to Bath either.

Fear crept up her spine. Quickly she scanned the paper, but most of it she couldn't decipher. Byrne apparently had some code for notes to himself. She did make out one notation that arrested her—the date she and Papa had left England for Gibraltar. In a panic, she examined the other notations, but couldn't tell if they mentioned anything important.

It didn't matter—Byrne's notation of the date meant he'd asked questions. And while he might not yet know what to make of the answers, he would surely figure it out eventually. Especially if he ever got his hands on Papa's letters.

Byrne's only possible reason for investigating her past was to discover what her property was, and that meant he hoped to use it for his own purposes. The scoundrel.

Not that it surprised her. But his active probing of her secrets made her task even more difficult. She needed him, and she dared not trust him. A potentially dangerous situation.

Some sound from the couch made her start. Hastily, she shoved the note into the satchel, which she set back where she'd found it. When she turned, it was to find Byrne staring at her through sleep-dazed eyes.

"Christabel?" he asked.

Her heart thundered in her ears. Had he seen her reading the note? What would he do if he had? She had a fox by the tail, and if she weren't careful, he would turn and bite off her hand.

"Hello, Byrne," she said, forcing a game smile to her lips.

He sat up to scrub his hands over his face. Then his gaze flicked from her to the satchel at her feet, but seeing that it was closed, he let out a long breath. "What are you doing here?"

"I came looking for you, of course."

A slow grin touched his lips. "Missed me, did you?"

She made a face. "Not a bit. You were supposed to be teaching me whist, and you ran off."

Leaning back against the couch, he looked her over. "At least you came dressed to give me a proper welcome. Stand up and let me see."

She rose, her hands suddenly clammy as she twirled slowly for his benefit. She wished she were elegant like Lady Hungate or even flagrantly sensual like Mrs. Talbot, instead of just a general's daughter in a lady's fancy gown.

And how silly of her to care what he thought, anyway. Although she knew he wasn't feigning his desire for her, he might be trying to seduce her in the hopes that he could find out her secrets. So she shouldn't let what he thought about her sway her.

Yet it did sway her. *He* swayed her. He'd made her desire him, curse his soul, and now she was rapidly sinking in over her head. It wouldn't be a problem if she were able to give and receive pleasure without a qualm, free to behave like some decadent descendant of the hedonistic Romans. But at her core she was a simple woman. She wanted something more from a man than pleasure, and Byrne would mock that as he mocked everything else— propriety, patriotism, loyalty, and honor.

Yet the heated glance he trailed down her form wasn't mocking, and the approval in his face seemed honest. "Come here," he said in a throaty murmur.

Despite all her caution, a thrill shot through her. "Absolutely not."

"Come here." Keeping his eyes riveted on her, he reached over to pat the suspiciously bulging pocket of his coat. "I have something to show you."

Curious, she edged closer to the couch. Without warning, he grabbed her and hauled her onto his lap, clamping his arm firmly about her waist.

"Byrne!" she protested as she tried to wriggle free. "You said you had something to show me!"

"I do. After you show me how much you missed me." He seized her mouth with his, and she melted. Even though she knew it was wrong and foolish and utterly dangerous, she melted. She *had* missed him. She'd missed this reckless way he made her feel, as if she were riding headlong into the dark night, where anything could happen and usually did.

For a moment, she let herself enjoy it. She tangled her tongue with his and reveled in the groan that erupted from his throat in response. She savored the slow, sensual caresses of his mouth and the deep thrusts that made her ache in every place he wasn't touching and caressing.

But then his hand slid inside her new gown to fondle her breast—her easily accessible breast—and his parted lips trailed down her throat, and the hunger began to gnaw at her— "No, Byrne." She pulled his hand out of her gown. "I didn't come here for that."

A growl sounded low in his throat, and for a second she feared he would ignore her protest. But then his hand went slack, his fingers curling around hers. He lifted his head to stare at her with that smoldering look that always heated her in the wrong places. "Didn't you?"

All right, perhaps deep inside she *had* come for this. But she couldn't allow herself to partake of it, not if she wanted to keep her wits about her. "No." She wriggled off his lap. She should tell him about the invitation, but first she wanted to glean what information she could about how he worked and what he was up to. "I came to see your club, of course."

With a sigh, he settled back against the couch. "And snoop through my desk no doubt. Find anything interesting?"

She trailed over to it, trying to act nonchalant. "Just a lot of clippings that make no sense." She picked up the top set. "Like these—you've marked the date of a ship's docking, then the price of nutmeg, then a society column's mention of a Miss Treacle's debut." She eyed him askance. "Are you choosing your mistresses from the paper now? Really, Byrne, isn't she a little young for you?"

He chuckled. "Miss Treacle is the daughter of Joseph Treacle, a merchant whose income was moderate until recently. The ship belongs to him, and its cargo was nutmeg, which is presently worth a great deal due to a shortage. We're nearing autumn, when nutmeg will be in demand, so his cargo will fetch a high price."

He rose and strolled to the desk. "His daughter came out four months ago, but gained no offers. Now he has the wealth to draw suitors, but no way to indicate that to the world without showing himself to be a vulgar cit, which would hurt her chances." He smiled. "So I invited him to join my club. He will accept, because my members are either eligible gentlemen, or friends and family to eligible gentlemen. Some of whom desperately need a wife with a substantial dowry."

Dear Lord, what deviousness. "So Mr. Treacle will join your club and gamble away that new fortune of his, much of which will land in *your* pocket."

He shrugged. "Only if he's a fool, in which case he deserves to lose it all. But if he's clever, he'll pay his membership fee, play a friendly game of hazard here from time to

time, eat my food, drink my liquor, and find a husband for
the sad Miss Treacle." His eyes gleamed. "It's to my advantage for him to be a fool, but it's really up to him, isn't it?"

She stared at him, torn between laughter and sheer exasperation. "You must be the most wicked man in creation."

Leaning against the desk, he crossed his arms over his
chest. "Unless a man is born to privilege, he has to be
wicked to succeed."

"But at what cost to his soul?"

He looked amused. "Haven't you heard, my sweet?
People not born to privilege don't have souls. They're
conscienceless and immoral, little better than animals. Or
so our good government would have us believe."

"You don't believe that, and neither do I. Everyone has
a soul."

His amusement faded. "If they do, they're headed for
disaster. Because a clever man dispenses with his soul as
early in life as he can possibly manage."

"And you're nothing if not clever." A weight of sadness
settled on her chest. Was that how he'd handled his
mother's death and his difficult situation? If so, no wonder he hated the prince. What man could live happily
without a soul?

Pushing away from the desk, he took the set of clippings from her and tossed it onto his pile. "Anything else
you want to know about my evil endeavors?"

"Actually, yes. Why didn't you tell me about the estate
you own in Bath?"

He grew instantly wary. "What makes you think I do?"

"Lydia told me."

Cursing, he left the desk to pace the room. "Never trust
a card cheat with a secret."

"Don't blame *her*—she thought I already knew. And

once she realized I didn't, she made me promise not to tell anyone else." Enjoying his discomfiture, she followed him. "But she did reveal a number of other interesting things. It appears from your treatment of her that occasionally you do indeed have a soul."

"Nonsense," he said gruffly, raking his fingers through his already disheveled hair. "I merely prefer to retire card cheats from their profession whenever possible. They make everything harder for those of us who profit from legitimate gambling."

"Yet you did nothing to help Lydia's friend Jim 'retire,' did you?"

"He was beyond help. Eventually some hotheaded gentleman will take care of him by putting a bullet through his idiot skull in a gaming hell."

"Probably," she agreed. "But this is getting off the subject. You still haven't answered my question—why didn't you tell me about your estate?"

"No need," he said with a shrug. "But it's not any great secret."

"Oh? Do the Drakers or the Iversleys know?"

He stiffened. "No."

"It's no great secret, yet your closest friends are unaware of it. Why is that?" Her eyes widened. "Oh no, you won it gambling, didn't you?"

"I did not—" He gritted his teeth. "I bought the bloody place fair and square. And if my friends learn of it, they'll be trotting out to see it and dropping in to visit. Here, I'm always at people's beck and call, so I like to have a place to go where I can gain some peace once in a while. All right, Lady Inquisitive?"

"All right." His explanation made sense, yet she sensed there was more to it.

"Now, are we done with all the questions? And if so, shall we adjourn to your house to practice more whist in case Stokely does invite you to his party?"

"Oh, I forgot! Lord Stokely's invitation arrived at my house this afternoon."

His eyes narrowed. "Already?"

"Yes." She retrieved it from her reticule, then handed it to him.

Frowning, he scanned the invitation. "Something's wrong."

"What do you mean?"

He tapped the card on his desk, his expression calculating. "This was too easy. Stokely hears about you playing whist at Eleanor's, and suddenly he's eager to invite you to his naughty card party? He knows something. He's probably guessed what you're up to."

Alarm coursed through her. "Then why did he invite me?"

Byrne's brow was furrowed. "Stokely likes to play games of all kinds, not just cards. He wants to toy with you, with us, dangling your property in front of you for his own amusement. Unless—"

"Unless what?"

"Have you ever met the man?"

"If I have, I don't remember. Why?"

"Because it would be just like him to invite you so he could seduce you."

She snorted. "You must be joking."

"Hardly." He used the invitation to trace a line along the exposed upper swells of her breasts. "You're a beautiful woman. Plenty of men would want you, especially dressed as you are now." He cast her a rueful smile. "My frequent attempts to bed you should be evidence of that."

It was time for frankness. Otherwise, he would keep trying to use seduction to find out her secrets. "You're only interested in bedding me because of my father's property, and you know it."

Surprise flickered in his eyes before he masked it. "You mean, because of the barony that helping you retrieve it can bring me."

With a sinking in the pit of her stomach, she noticed that he didn't deny the reason for his trying to bed her. "I mean, because of *everything* you assume it can bring you. Admit it: You're hoping that my property will contain something you can use for your own purposes. Otherwise, why go to Ilsley and ask questions?"

He frowned. "I see you went snooping in more than just my desk."

"You aren't the only one who can be devious."

"I wasn't being devious. I can't help you if I don't know what I'm looking for and why it's so important."

She glared at him. "Don't pretend that this is about your helping me, because we both know it's not."

She started to walk away, but he grabbed her arm, jerking her up close to him. "What's in the letters, Christabel?"

"L-Letters?" she stammered, her gaze swinging to his in a panic. "What do you mean, letters?"

"Your husband's old steward is an amazingly chatty fellow once he's had a few brandies in him. He was more than eager to boast of his great connection to the Marquesses of Haversham, especially the one who gave him a gold ring in exchange for help retrieving some letters from his wife's strongbox."

Her breath caught in her throat. Lord help her, how much did he know? Everything?

No, if he did, he wouldn't be asking her. "I can't tell you what's in the letters," she whispered.

"Because you don't trust me," he hissed.

"You're the man without a soul, remember? I'd be mad to trust you."

A grudging smile touched his lips. "True. But you still need me." He bent to press his mouth to her ear. "And there can be advantages to having a man without a soul on your side, my sweet. When it comes to deviousness, you don't begin to compare to me. If I knew what was in the letters, what Stokely means to do with them, and why you and Prinny want to prevent it, I could help you thwart him some other way than just by trying to steal them back."

She wrenched free of him. "I'm never going to tell you what's in them, so stop asking. You won't cajole or trick or seduce me into doing so, either. If you help me retrieve them, you will get your barony, but that's all."

When he merely stared at her with his typically smug expression, she bristled. "And if you persist in trying to bed me, then I'll find someone else to help me learn how to play whist well. I don't need the added distraction of having to fend off your advances whenever we're together."

"I'll try to keep my hands to myself," he said in a lazy drawl. "But you still need me to get you into Stokely's."

She tipped up her chin. "Not necessarily. I do have my own invitation."

His eyes gleamed at her. "I'd like to see you try attending Stokely's party without a protector. After a couple of days of dealing with *his* friends, you'll welcome the chance to fend off *my* advances. If he even lets you stay after I tell him what you're up to."

She gritted her teeth. He had her over a barrel, and he

knew it. "Fine. I'll play your mistress at Lord Stokely's. But I and I alone will look for those letters."

"Whatever you say."

Right. As if he would give up just like that. She'd have to keep her eye on Byrne. And make sure she got to the letters before he did.

Buttoning up his waistcoat, he walked over to the sofa. But when he picked up his coat, he paused. "I almost forgot. I brought you a gift." He pulled a long, slender box out of his coat pocket and turned to hold it out to her. "You see? I *did* have something to show you."

"Why would you give me a present?" she asked warily.

"To apologize for leaving you hanging while I 'ran off' to Bath." He waved it at her. "Go on, take it."

She did as he bade, her pulse doing a silly little dance. Philip had frequently given her gifts, yet she'd never felt like this when he did. Swallowing, she opened the box, then stared into it, perplexed. "You bought me a fan?"

"Not *just* a fan, lass." He took out the fan, both handles of which were intricately worked in a silver design. Instead of opening the fan, however, he pressed one of the little knobs in the design, and with a click a slender steel blade shot into place, protruding from one handle of the fan.

She gasped.

He moved the knob, presumably to lock the blade in position, then presented the fan/knife to her, handle first. "Now you won't have to carry a pistol."

Fascinated, she took the thing from him, examining the blade and the release mechanism. He showed her how to work it, and she practiced a few times. Then she opened the fan itself to see if it looked sufficiently fanlike. It did. "You found this in *Bath*?" she asked, captivated by the very ingenuity of it.

He chuckled. "Not quite. I've had it for some time, mostly as a curiosity. I picked it up in a shop that specializes in foreign objects. From the design, I'd guess it's Siamese. You're the only woman I've ever thought might be willing to carry it." He arched one eyebrow. "You *will* carry it instead of the pistol, won't you?"

"Yes, thank you." Pleased in spite of herself, she retracted the blade and folded up the fan. "It really is wonderful."

"Be sure to take it to Stokely's. And, speaking of the baron, considering his sudden interest in having you at the party, we should do our best to allay his suspicions about why I've chosen you as my partner." He held out his arm to her. "Come, my sweet, it's time to improve your skills at whist."

Chapter Twelve

◆◆◆

Showing indifference toward a man is the
surest way to attract him.
—Anonymous, *Memoirs of a Mistress*

Gavin couldn't decide which was worse—traveling to Stokely's Wiltshire estate in the rain or having Rosa join him and Christabel in the carriage. Christabel couldn't have come alone with him, of course; that would have ruined her forever in society. Bad enough that her reputation would be seriously tarnished by her association with him. She was only trying to preserve enough of what remained to have a decent future.

But it still chafed to be this close yet unable to touch her. He'd endured that for over a week now, and his control was stretched to the breaking point. Her and her maddening conditions—no caressing, no kissing, nothing that smacked of seduction if he was to continue preparing her for the party.

Insanity, all of it. He could tell from how she looked at him that she desired him. And God knew he desired her. He couldn't remember ever desiring a woman so much. Yet the bloody female persisted in holding him at arm's length.

At Stokely's, however, she'd have to let him touch her, if only to keep up appearances. And if Stokely behaved true to form, he would assign Gavin and Christabel to adjoining rooms, while Rosa would be sleeping in the servants' quarters with the other ladies' maids.

Gavin couldn't wait to see how Christabel reacted to having him just one connecting door away. After spending her days playing his mistress, she would be primed for spending her nights *being* his mistress. Christabel was too sensual— and too curious—a female to avoid his bed for long.

"What time is it?" Christabel asked, from across the carriage.

He drew out his watch. "Six. Damn this rain. I was hoping we'd arrive before dinner."

"When is dinner?" Rosa asked.

"Seven, usually."

"Will my lady have to dress for it?"

"Absolutely."

Rosa muttered a Spanish oath under her breath.

"My feelings exactly," Gavin replied. "If we miss it, it'll be catch-as-catch-can later. Stokely doesn't like the distraction of having a lot of servants hovering about to serve people at the card tables."

Christabel worried her lower lip. "Do you think I'm ready?"

He didn't have to ask what she meant. "Ready enough. You can hold your own with most of Stokely's set."

It was true. She'd come far after a week of unrelenting whist, played with two of his trusted servants who were excellent at the game. It hadn't taken her long to exceed their skill; she was a quick study.

A clever woman, oh, yes. And he found her cleverness intoxicating. Unlike his other mistresses, who'd used their cleverness in figuring out how to squeeze more gifts, more money, more everything from him, she'd used hers to improve her card-playing. He admired that. It was something *he* would do.

"How does this party work?" she asked. "We just play whist all the time?"

"We play every night until around three A.M., which is why we sleep until noon. After rising, we have a leisurely breakfast, then amuse ourselves with hunting, reading, whatever, until dinner at seven. Then the card-playing begins and continues until sometime after midnight, when we break for a late supper. Then it's back to the tables. That goes on for a few days. The eliminations don't start until halfway through the week."

"Eliminations?"

"In the first half of the week, the strong players prey on the weak, each individual team winning enough to keep going when others are pockets to let. Once the weak are thinned out, the games begin in earnest, a sort of tournament, if you will."

Her eyes had gone wide. Clearly, she hadn't realized this was the point to Stokely's little party.

"At that time," he went on, "there are usually around eight teams left. That's when the playing for money stops, although each player must pay into a pot for every hand they play. Once four teams reach a hundred points, the bottom teams are eliminated. Those four teams are paired off to play, and the two winning teams play for the pot. It usually numbers in the thousands of pounds by then."

She paled. "I hesitate to ask, but what amount do they pay into the pot?"

"The same as the stakes in the first part of the week— five pounds a game, twenty-five pounds a rubber."

Rosa gasped from beside her. "My lady, you cannot—"

"I'm covering your mistress's losses, Rosa."

"Perhaps I should bow out early," Christabel said, "so I don't cost you too much. I could claim to have reached my limit financially. Then I'd have time for . . . other things."

Like searching for those bloody letters. Her reluctance to speak of it in front of Rosa meant that even her maid didn't know about them. How interesting.

"If you bow out early," he retorted, "then as your part- ner I'll have to do the same, and that will rouse Stokely's suspicions. The winners split the pot, and for three years running, ever since he began this annual event, Stokely and I have been the ones to win it. Why do you think he keeps having it at his estate?"

"You mean, that ungodly amount of money is what Lady Jenner meant about your winning the pot?" she asked, a hint of panic in her voice. "Good Lord, what if I can't play well enough to get you that far? What if—"

"Don't worry—when I chose you as my partner, I knew I might lose the pot this year. But after the improve- ment in your playing the past few days, I'm not so sure." He grinned. "The two of us may even change the tradi- tion. If we do, you'll have more than enough to cover any of Haversham's lingering debts. Not to mention, repay me for my . . . efforts."

She relaxed against the squabs, with a small smile. "In that case, I suppose it will be all right. As long as I have time for my other activities."

"You'll have plenty of time." And so would he.

All he knew from his trip to Ilsley was that Christabel sought a pack of letters dated twenty-two years ago. Since then, he'd learned from other sources in London that on that date General Lyon had taken Christabel off to Gibraltar. They'd traveled with another officer posted to Gibraltar, the officer's wife and infant son, and a few servants.

The general, only a lieutenant at the time, had received his new posting rather suddenly. Probably that's what was in the letters—the reason for his posting.

It had to be related to some scandal Lyon and Prinny were involved in together, something Lyon had been escaping England to avoid. But what? If there'd been a scandal, not a breath of it had ever reached beyond the man's family circle.

And even though Gavin had tapped every source he knew, military and otherwise, no one had any inkling of a connection between Prinny and Roaring Randall Lyon. The man's rise to general *had* been rather quick, but Lyon had proved himself worthy of praise, so it was plausible that his own merits had fueled his promotions. He'd certainly acquitted himself well during the war, and was expected to return to England in a few months to a hero's welcome.

Yet he had a secret, one so explosive that his daughter would do almost anything to protect it. Gavin itched to know what it was.

Would Stokely tell him if he asked? Probably not. He'd refused payment from Prinny for the letters; he would undoubtedly refuse it from someone else. That meant Stokely intended to use them. But how? And why?

"Look, is that the place?" Rosa exclaimed, as the carriage turned off the main road and onto a gravel drive.

Gavin looked out, surprised to find that they'd made good time despite the rain. "Yes, that's it."

Christabel peered out the window. "Is it just the rain or is that building actually blue?"

"One of Stokely's idiot ancestors took a notion to cover the fine old stone in stucco, then paint it that awful color. Stokely wants to restore it, but the damned house is so big, it will cost him a fortune and take forever." He gave a half smile. "And he'd have to stay at home, instead of flitting from table to table in Bath and York and wherever else there's good gambling."

"Another respectable family ravaged by gambling," Christabel said woefully.

"Actually, although his illustrious ancestors probably turn over in their graves during his parties, Stokely has managed to increase his wealth through his gambling. That's why he can afford to hold this extravagant event for so many people."

"There will be a lot of guests?" Christabel asked.

"At least forty, if not more."

"And Lord Stokely has rooms for them all?" Rosa asked in astonishment.

Gavin bit back a smile. "Plenty of rooms, thank God. Otherwise, the wives would be forced to share their husbands' beds, and that would certainly put a damper on the fun."

"Byrne!" Christabel exclaimed, a fetching blush staining her cheeks.

"It's true. And just to prepare you, my sweet, I would advise you not to go looking for someone in their bedchamber unless you're expected. They're liable to be in another bedchamber entirely, with someone else residing in their own. You will merely embarrass yourself."

"Thank you for the advice," she said tartly. "I'll be careful not to take you by surprise."

"I didn't mean myself." He lowered his voice. "You're

welcome to enter *my* bedchamber unannounced at any time of the day or night."

"For pity's sake, Byrne," she murmured, jerking her head toward Rosa.

But Rosa was smirking, and her smirk only broadened when he added, "You're welcome to enter my *bed* unannounced, as well."

She lifted her eyes heavenward. "Any other lessons in immorality you wish to impart before we arrive?"

"Not at the moment." He swept his gaze down the beautiful day gown of sprigged muslin she'd chosen to wear, which the rain would render practically transparent. *If* Stokely's grooms didn't come running out with umbrellas. Which, unfortunately, they probably would. "But I'll be happy to impart some later in the evening."

When she scowled at him, he chuckled.

They drew up before the house, and grooms hurried to open the doors, regrettably bearing umbrellas. But luck was with Gavin, for the wind blew so hard that the rain was almost horizontal, and they got soaked anyway.

Dripping and sodden, they entered Stokely's imposing front hall to find the man himself waiting for them, cutting his usual dashing figure in a finely tailored evening dress of blue silk that made his prematurely white hair look almost blond in the candlelight.

"Byrne!" Stokely exclaimed as he came toward them, hand outstretched. "I was beginning to think you would miss dinner."

"So was I." Gavin shook his hand, then turned to Christabel, whose dampened gown clung to her lush form like a glove. Ignoring the sudden jump in his pulse, Gavin added, "Stokely, may I present—"

"Ah, but I've already met the lovely Lady Haversham."

Gavin's blood ran cold. Christabel had lied to him about that? Why?

But as Stokely took Christabel's hand, the confusion on her face made it clear that she was as surprised as Gavin. "I'm afraid I don't recall—" She broke off, her eyes going wide. "*You* were at Rosevine before Philip died. I remember it now. I only saw you that one time. I came into his study to ask him something, and he was with you." Her face clouded. "But he didn't introduce you. I assumed you were . . . that is—"

"You thought I was one of his creditors. It's perfectly understandable." Stokely's eyes narrowed. "But actually your husband and I were engaged in a . . . different sort of transaction."

Damn Stokely to hell. He was testing her to see what she knew. Gavin only prayed that she could brazen it out.

Apparently she could, for she flashed the man a game smile. "Oh, dear. Philip was asking to borrow money, wasn't he? I'm afraid every one of his friends had to endure that from him. I must apologize for my husband—"

"No need." Stokely slanted a glance at Gavin. "Besides, clearly I was not the only person from whom your husband borrowed money."

Gavin bristled at his implication. He'd been accused of many things, but never forcing a woman to his bed to repay her husband's debts.

Before he could level the man with an acid retort, however, Christabel slipped her hand in the crook of his elbow and cast Gavin what could only be called a fond smile. "Yes, thank heavens. Otherwise, I wouldn't have met Byrne. And he's been such a comfort to me."

"A comfort?" Stokely's expression grew calculating "That's a new way to put it, eh, Byrne?"

Gavin covered Christabel's hand with his. "It's growing late, Stokely. Perhaps you should have someone carry our bags to our rooms, so we'll have time to dress for dinner."

"Of course." Stokely waved a footman over. "Put Mr. Byrne's bags in his usual room. And put Lady Haversham's in the blue room."

Gavin scowled. "If I remember correctly, the blue room is in another wing from mine. In fact, it's right across the hall from the master bedchamber. Isn't that where you usually put *your* mistress?"

"We parted ways a few weeks ago. Since Lady Haversham was such a late addition to my party and I'd run out of rooms by then, I decided to put her there."

"You aren't trying to steal my partner, are you?" Gavin snapped.

"Of course not." Stokely's expression was impenetrable. "And about that, I've changed the rules for our games this week. I'm telling the others at dinner, but I suppose you can hear it now." He settled his black gaze on Christabel. "Whist partners for each rubber will be randomly selected. Until the eliminations begin, that is."

The blood pounded in Gavin's temples. "Why?"

Stokely shrugged. "As you know, that's how it's generally done in the clubs. It prevents cheating between partners who know each other well."

Ignoring Christabel's killer grip on his arm, Gavin said in a deliberately amused tone, "Are you expecting trouble with cheaters? It hasn't been a problem before."

"There's always a first time. Besides, that will give everyone a chance to observe their fellow players. Then, when it's time for the eliminations, they can choose their partners more . . . objectively before they start." He scanned Christabel's translucent gown with a decidedly lustful glance. "And it will lend more interest to the game."

"I thought the pot was what lent interest to the game," Gavin bit out. "Unless you've decided to change that, too?"

"No, but there is one other minor change that you will hear more about at dinner." He glanced at a nearby clock. "Which you will miss if you do not go to your rooms at once. Byrne, you can find your own way." With a smooth smile, he offered Christabel his arm. "I shall show Lady Haversham to her room myself."

As Christabel reluctantly took Stokely's arm, and they headed up the stairs with Rosa trailing behind, the most unsettling urge seized Gavin. He wanted to snatch Christabel free of the man, march her out to his carriage, and carry her back to London. He could scarcely keep from striding up the stairs after them.

What the hell had come over him? He'd known what to expect when they came here, and so had she. All right, so neither of them had guessed that Stokely had known her from before. Or might have invited her for that reason. Or that Gavin's half-jesting comment from a week ago, that Stokely might have taken a fancy to her, would prove to be true.

Damn the bastard. He didn't like how Stokely looked at her. He didn't like Stokely seeing her in that clinging gown, which showed her delectable shape. And he bloody well hated that she'd be sleeping a few yards away from the man.

Stokely could have any woman in the place . . . and often did. Most women found his combination of stark white hair and black eyes captivating.

In the past, Gavin hadn't cared if the baron shared an interlude with Gavin's companions, but it bothered him that Stokely might think Christabel equally accessible.

And why did it bother him? It must be because he hadn't yet bedded her himself. What other reason could there be?

There was only one solution—Gavin would have to bed her as soon as possible. He was *not* going to stand by and do nothing while Stokely played his nasty games with Christabel.

And once she was in Gavin's bed, he meant to keep her there for a very long time.

Chapter Thirteen

*Occasionally, one of my old lovers would
rise up to haunt me.*
—Anonymous, *Memoirs of a Mistress*

*C*hristabel could scarcely breathe as Lord Stokely led her up the stairs. She'd never dreamed that the white-haired man in Philip's study all those months ago had been Baron Stokely himself. She did remember overhearing Philip say, when she was outside the door, "She prefers Rosevine, and I prefer to have her here."

Lord Stokely had answered something she couldn't hear. But later when she'd asked Philip who he was, he'd told her the man was no one of importance. That's why she'd assumed Lord Stokely was a creditor.

Philip had probably sold the letters to him that very day, blast him.

"I hope you'll find your accommodations suitably comfortable, Lady Haversham," Lord Stokely remarked, as soon as they were out of Byrne's earshot. "You don't mind being on this end of the house, do you?"

"Wherever you put me is fine," she murmured, unsure what to answer.

"I was surprised to hear that you and Byrne are . . . friends. Your late husband said that you shot at the man."

She groaned. "Philip told you about that?"

"He mentioned it, yes. While he was explaining the reason for his dire financial situation."

"The reason for his dire financial situation was his gambling. And though I acted in a fit of temper when Byrne came to collect on my husband's debt, I did eventually realize that the person at fault was Philip, not Byrne."

Byrne was right about that at least. Her husband had brought his own ruin upon himself.

"Still, Haversham told me you disliked society, especially society of Byrne's sort."

She managed a laugh. "That's what he would have preferred, I'm sure."

"I did wonder if he merely wanted to keep you to himself." Laying his hand over hers, he stroked her fingers. "And now I understand why."

She had to choke down a sarcastic retort. Was every gambler in England a randy devil? And why did Byrne's flirtations heat her blood while Lord Stokely's just made her want to laugh?

Nonetheless, it wouldn't hurt to remain on the man's good side. "And now *I* understand why my husband didn't introduce *you*." She gave him a brazen smile. "No doubt he feared that your silver tongue would tempt me to . . . indiscretion."

He cast her a speculative glance. "Is that the only reason he didn't introduce us that day?"

Was he alluding to the letters? Did he really think she would admit to knowing that he had them?

With a look of wide-eyed innocence, she said, "I can think of no other reason, can you?"

He searched her face, then said, "Not at the moment." Then he halted before an open doorway leading into a spacious bedchamber. "Here we are, madam. I shall not keep you. Besides, we can talk more at dinner."

Blast. She was hoping to beg off so she could search his room while the others dined. But clearly he expected her there, and she dared not rouse his suspicions by disappointing him. "I'll see you then."

Only after he'd gone and she and Rosa were in the room with the heavy oak door firmly closed did she let out a breath. "Thank God that's over," she muttered. Then she caught Rosa eyeing her with disapproval. "What?"

"You were flirting with your host. What about Mr. Byrne?"

"I wasn't flirting. I was merely trying to be a congenial guest. And trust me, Byrne won't care anyway." It was true, but still a lowering thought.

Rosa snorted, but turned to hunt through the trunks that the footmen had carried up the stairs ahead of them. "Which gown will you wear tonight?"

"The rose one." Since she and Byrne had spent every moment of last week playing whist, her trip to the theater with him had never come to pass. So she still hadn't had the chance to wear it. "We'd better hurry, too." She glanced at the pretty Jasper clock beside her bed. "We've got only twenty-five minutes."

With a shriek, Rosa scurried to unpack the appropriate trunk. There was no time to ooh and ah over the rich azure damask draping the windows and French canopy bedstead, no time to admire the Persian rug spread before the massive marble fireplace. It took every minute of their allotted time to peel Christabel out of her sodden garments and dry her sufficiently to don a fresh chemise, corset, and evening gown. Rosa was nearly done cursing her way through repairing Christabel's sadly fallen coiffure when a knock came at the door.

"Come in!" Christabel called out.

Rosa finished just as Byrne entered. "Ready?" he asked.

Christabel rose, and he sucked in a breath, his gaze trailing slowly down the gown, then back up to fix on her décolletage. "Bloody hell. I should never have told Mrs. Watts to make you that gown."

Disappointed by his reaction, she thrust out her chin. "Whyever not?"

"Because you look too damned beautiful in it." He balled his hands into fists at his sides. "Stokely is going to salivate all over you."

She couldn't believe it—Byrne actually sounded jealous. A satisfied smile tugged at her lips. "Do you really think so?" she asked, surprised to hear a certain coyness in her voice.

He lifted his gaze to hers. "Let me put it this way—it's clear why the man assigned you the bedchamber across from his." He scanned the room with narrowed eyes. "He gave you the best room in the house. Do you realize that?"

"Did he?" She grabbed her fan and hurried to his side. "Let's go."

As they left the room, Byrne settled his hand in the small of her back with an oddly possessive gesture. "I tell you, the man is up to no good. He never puts a guest in the family wing, never."

"Perhaps it's just as he claimed—he ran out of rooms."

"In this mansion? Not bloody likely." Byrne slanted her a dark look. "Did he say anything to you?"

She related their conversation in full.

Byrne's lips tightened into a grim line. "Either he's playing games with us, or he's taken a fancy to you. Whichever it is, I don't like it. It'll make getting those letters all the more difficult."

Her heart sank. She should have known Byrne wouldn't be jealous; he was merely concerned about their purpose here.

Not that she wanted him to be jealous. She was already far too attracted to him as it was. If she thought for one minute that he might actually care for her . . .

That was dangerous thinking indeed.

They reached the bottom of the stairs where others waited to go in to dinner. Guests here and there hailed them, some of whom she recognized. The Talbots were there, along with Lady Jenner and a man who was probably her husband. Her lover, Lieutenant Markham, also stood close by, exchanging pleasantries with a raven-haired woman whom Christabel didn't recognize.

Laughing, the woman turned so that her profile was to them, and Byrne suddenly tensed. "Anna?" he said, his tone disbelieving.

The raven-haired beauty glanced over, then paled from the roots of her hair to the bodice of her fashionable emerald gown. She faced them slowly. "Gavin?"

She looked stricken. Byrne looked the same.

Christabel's heart sank. Was this another of Byrne's former mistresses? But no, she'd never heard him speak of any of them with that peculiar note of pain in his voice. And none of them called him Gavin. Or so he'd said.

"What are you doing here?" Byrne asked hoarsely, his fingers digging into Christabel's waist like iron talons.

"Lord Stokely invited me and Walter, of course." The

woman tugged on the arm of a man who stood near her. "Come, dear, I'd like you to meet someone."

Christabel found it hard to breathe past the tightness in her chest. Judging from Byrne's reaction, this was no mere mistress, whoever she was. But why could this "Anna" make him tense and angry when no other woman—including Christabel—touched his emotions?

The elderly man who turned around looked as if he'd rather be sleeping by a fire than waiting in a crowd to go in to dinner. "Eh? What is it?"

"Walter, may I present an old friend of . . . my family's, Mr. Gavin Byrne. Mr. Byrne, this is my husband, Lord Kingsley."

A muscle ticked in Byrne's jaw as he nodded at the gentleman. "Lord Kingsley. You're certainly a long way from home. Dublin, right?"

"Yes, Dublin." Lord Kingsley lifted his lorgnette to eye Byrne closely. "Have we met before?"

"No." Byrne shot Lady Kingsley a glance, then added in a voice thick with irony, "But I've heard of you."

Coloring, the woman said hastily, "Mr. Byrne owns a gentlemen's club in London, my dear. The Blue Swan. I'm sure he makes it his business to know everything about the most important men in England and Ireland."

"Quite." Lord Kingsley leveled a condescending gaze on Byrne. "Rather surprising that Stokely invited your sort, but I suppose that's to be expected. This being a gaming party and all."

"Yes." Byrne had apparently regained his composure. "Stokely likes to surprise people." He glanced beyond the Kingsleys. "And speak of the devil, here's our host now."

Lord Stokely approached, his face wreathed in smiles

as he slid between the couples. "Ah, Byrne, I see you've already met the Viscount Kingsley and his wife."

"Yes," Lady Kingsley said, casting Christabel a searching glance, "but we have not yet been introduced to Mr. Byrne's friend."

Lord Stokely performed the introductions as Christabel tried not to notice Byrne's stiff reactions. Or Lady Kingsley's stunning beauty. And elegant manners. And polished replies. The viscountess was everything that Christabel was not and could never be.

Indeed, it was all she could do not to laugh madly when Lord Kingsley turned into a fawning old fool the instant he heard Christabel was a marchioness. As he babbled his honor at meeting her and gushed compliments over her gown, Christabel fought to smile. His wife looked on with a pained expression, and Byrne stood there woodenly.

Their host seemed to find the whole thing vastly amusing. He clapped his hand on Lord Kingsley's shoulder. "Capital fellow, isn't he? We ran into each other last year at a card party in York. Lady Kingsley is an avid whist player, so I couldn't resist inviting her and Kingsley to my affair. We can use some new blood among our players, eh, Byrne?"

"That depends on how much of that new blood you're hoping to spill," Byrne quipped.

"Byrne, you wound me!" Lord Stokely exclaimed in mock reproach. "Lady Kingsley can hold her own at the tables, I assure you. And she'll prove a fine addition to our group." A calculating smile touched his lips. "She's full of fascinating tales about her coming out in London."

The sudden tension in Byrne was palpable. "Is she? Then she'll have to entertain us with them some night, won't she?"

"Indeed, she will," Lord Stokely said, with a smirk.

When Lady Kingsley looked ashen, Christabel wanted to scream. Who was she to Byrne, blast it?

Then Lord Stokely left the Kingsleys to offer Christabel his arm. "Shall we go in to dinner, Lady Haversham?"

She stiffened, but couldn't refuse. As Marchioness of Haversham she was the highest-ranking female currently present, so the host would naturally take her in to dinner.

Which meant Byrne would have to take in one of the lower-ranking guests—like Lady Kingsley, perhaps. Christabel couldn't prevent her surge of jealousy at even the possibility. She let Lord Stokely lead her off, feeling Lady Kingsley's eyes on her the whole way. It was slim comfort to know she wasn't the only one wondering about Byrne and his women.

Dinner was a lavish affair, which meant lots of French dishes, of course, so Christabel spent the early part trying to figure out what was what, without making a fool of herself. Even the lowly Talbots seemed at ease with the dizzying array of exotic dishes. Unsurprisingly, considering this company, it included not only oysters but pomegranates. And probably some Spanish fly—whatever that actually was—sprinkled among the dishes, too.

Thankfully, the woman to Lord Stokely's left kept him occupied, and although the man to Christabel's right should have been talking to her, he was too busy indulging in expensive delicacies to bother, so at least she didn't have to manage polite conversation.

Not that anyone else's conversation was terribly polite. Despite the presence of ladies, several rather bawdy jokes were told, only about half of which she understood. And no one protested them, not even Lord Kingsley, who looked the prudish sort. He was too engrossed in flattering Lady Jenner, who sat beside him.

Then there were some soldiers who actually took snuff at the table. She began to wonder why she'd worried about her manners; Lord Stokely's friends seemed rather ill behaved.

Except for Lady Kingsley, of course, who sat swanlike amidst the ducks, with back straight and lips pursed, taking tiny bites as she periodically cast longing glances down the table at Byrne.

Christabel wanted to slap her. Her only consolation was that Byrne didn't seem to notice Lady Kingsley's looks, or if he did, he hid it well. Indeed, he was one of the men telling the bawdy jokes.

Lord Stokely leaned over to Christabel just as the dessert was brought round. "They'd make an interesting couple, don't you think?"

She feigned ignorance. "Who?"

"Byrne and Lady Kingsley."

She stared him down. "Rather mismatched, I'd say."

"And what would you say if I told you Byrne once asked her to marry him?"

Struggling to hide her shock, she reminded herself that Lord Stokely was no more trustworthy than anyone else at this scandalous party. "I'd say you don't know Byrne very well."

"It surprised me, too, but I heard the story from Lady Kingsley herself. We had a . . . er . . . brief encounter in Dublin, and you know how women get when they're in the throes of such. Very confessional."

But that didn't mean the confessions were true. How could cynical, feckless Byrne have proposed marriage to anyone? If not for his intense reaction to Lady Kingsley, Christabel wouldn't believe a word.

Suddenly Lord Stokely glanced down the table, then

smiled. She followed his gaze to find Byrne staring at them with an odd fury in his face.

Had he guessed what Lord Stokely was saying? Or was something else making him regard their host with such venom?

"What happened between them?" she whispered, determined to find out what she could about Lord Stokely's claims. "I take it she refused him?"

"Of course she refused him." His eyes gleamed with delight at sharing a choice bit of gossip. "Lady Kingsley was a wealthy merchant's daughter. At the time of her come-out, Byrne had just opened his gentlemen's club. And though his contacts were solid enough to get him invited to the sorts of balls she attended, her family couldn't possibly countenance him as a son-in-law."

"How did Lady Kingsley herself feel about it?"

"If not for his situation, she might have accepted him, I suppose. Byrne can be charming when he wants. But he *is* a natural child, after all, with no relations that will admit to him. And her fortune was probably what attracted him, a fact that she and her family had to know."

Christabel couldn't see Byrne marrying to gain a fortune, for all his talk of having no soul. "Did she say that?"

"Not in so many words, but it's obvious. She was toying with a dangerous connection, so when Kingsley came along and took a fancy to her, her family aggressively pressed the match. In the end she did what any woman of sense would do—she married Kingsley."

Christabel repressed a snort. Woman of sense, indeed. Any woman of sense would have followed her heart. And clearly, the woman had once been in love with Byrne, perhaps still was. Was that why Lady Kingsley had allowed Lord Stokely to bed her? In personality he was something like Byrne, albeit a pale imitation.

Had he been in love with Lady Kingsley? Was he still?

As that question plagued her, she glanced over at Lord Stokely's gloating face, and another sickening realization struck her. "That's why you invited her, isn't it? To torment Byrne."

"I invited her for the same reason I invited *you*, my dear. Because you're both excellent whist players." A mocking smile touched his lips. "Or, in your case, I can only assume so from the fact that Byrne chose you as his partner."

If ever she'd needed a motivation for playing well, this was it. "You assumed correctly, sir. I mean to win the pot, if I can."

He leaned closer to press his mouth to her ear. "And if you don't, you can always try winning your host instead."

A chill swept down her spine, but before she could react to that disgusting statement, Byrne's voice boomed down the table. "What's all this about new rules for the games, Stokely? You've kept us in suspense long enough."

With a smile meant just for her, Lord Stokely rose and turned his attention to his guests. "Thank you, Byrne, for reminding me."

In a matter-of-fact tone, he explained that partners would be randomly chosen. The chorus of groans that followed did not deter him from moving on to the next change in the rules.

"Once we start the eliminations," he said, "the losers will be asked to leave the estate." His gaze settled briefly on Christabel. "At my discretion, of course."

Christabel fought to hide her panic. What if she hadn't found the letters by then? What if she didn't make it to the eliminations?

And what exactly did Lord Stokely mean by "at my discretion"?

Other people were furiously muttering complaints. Apparently, they'd all assumed they would be enjoying his hospitality to the end.

"Why the change?" Byrne's voice rose above the others' to pose the question no one else would ask.

Lord Stokely shrugged. "So that we don't have a lot of hangers-on milling about during the final games. There's too much potential for cheating."

Lady Jenner snorted. "Be honest, Lord Stokely. You're only doing this because Byrne changed partners. And the rest of us are being punished for his roving eye."

All eyes, roving and otherwise, turned to Christabel, who couldn't prevent a blush from rising in her cheeks.

Lord Stokely's demeanor changed suddenly, becoming icy cold. "I am doing this because last year there were complaints about Byrne and me always winning the pot. I will not have anyone accuse me or my friends of cheating. This merely makes everything more fair. And it is my house, after all. My house, my rules."

No one could argue with that, but it didn't stop people from grumbling as they rose and headed off to the evening's entertainment.

When they reached the ballroom, which had been turned into a massive card room for the week, Christabel was relieved to find herself partnered with Lady Hungate.

Lady Hungate didn't look quite so pleased. "I do hope you intend to show your true mettle *tonight*," the older woman remarked.

"I won't disappoint you," Christabel replied, remembering that afternoon at Lady Jenner's.

No, indeed. She wasn't about to risk being evicted

from the estate as one of the losers. Even if it meant flirting with Lord Stokely.

Damn Stokely and his manipulations. After five hours of
card play, Gavin still couldn't figure out what the man
was up to.

First, the changes in the rules, then his cursed interest
in Christabel. And the man had brought Anna here.
Anna, of all people. Gavin had hoped never to see her
again. That she was here now turned what was already
sure to be a difficult week into a potential nightmare.

Especially since Stokely clearly knew what she'd once
been to Gavin. Was that what he'd been whispering to
Christabel at dinner? The last thing Gavin needed was the
inquisitive little widow plaguing him with questions
about Anna. She already knew too many of his secrets for
his comfort.

Gathering up the trick he'd just won, he glanced over
to the next table, where Anna partnered Stokely against
Lady Jenner and Lady Hungate. What in God's name had
Stokely hoped to accomplish by inviting her? Did he hope
Anna would put Gavin off his game, now that Gavin had
chosen to partner someone else? If so, it wouldn't work.

Anna caught Gavin staring and shot him a brilliant
smile.

He tensed. Tearing his gaze from her, Gavin led a card.
In his youth, he would have fought a regiment of Cos-
sacks for one of those smiles from her, but she was thirteen years too late.

After his initial shock at seeing her, he'd realized that
she no longer had the power to move him. Or if she did,
she moved him to sadness. Because years of marriage to
the toad-eating Viscount Kingsley didn't sit well on her.

Yes, she was still beautiful, and yes, she still possessed a musical laugh that would melt most men's hearts. But it held a brittle edge now, as if tears always lay just beneath the surface.

She'd thrown him over for Kingsley, and look what it had brought her—a dull marriage to a pompous fellow whose only advantage lay in his title, since it had taken her own family's wealth to fill the man's coffers. So why couldn't he exult over her misery?

Because it seemed like such a waste of a fine woman. Suddenly he was tired of the waste, tired of watching women suffer from their husbands' neglect. He was tired of seeing once-hopeful young females turned into cold-hearted, dissipated bitches whose only choices were to pine away at home or live the same reckless lives as their husbands.

He was tired of watching good women forced to extreme behavior because of their gambling husbands' foolish actions. Women like Christabel.

As a magnet follows iron, his gaze swung to where she sat halfway across the spacious card room. Not once all night had he and Christabel been paired as partners, yet every moment he'd been aware of her. Where she sat. Whom she played. How often she laughed at a joke or responded to some idiot's flirtations.

He wondered how she fared. Was she winning? Losing? Panicking over losing?

That very real possibility squeezed his chest in a vise. He should never have brought her here. She didn't belong—seeing her with the others made that easily apparent. She could soak in a pool of debauchery for hours and still have none cling to her skin. And the truth was, he would hate to see her besmirched by it.

Why was that? Wouldn't it be easier to get what he wanted from her if she'd just slide down the slippery slope into sin?

Yes, but at what cost? Bloody hell, Christabel had said that very thing to him once—*but at what cost to his soul?* Now he was even starting to think like her. And that wouldn't do.

As if she felt his eyes on her, she met his gaze from across the room, and the vise around his chest tightened unbearably. Until she smiled, telling him that everything was all right.

"Byrne?" Talbot asked. "For God's sake, stop ogling your mistress and play your card. You'll have plenty of time for ogling later."

"If Stokely doesn't get to her first," said Talbot's present partner, Markham.

Biting back an oath, Gavin played his card. "You're assuming that Lady Haversham would choose Stokely over me. And that's not bloody likely."

Markham smirked at Gavin. "Unless she thinks it will help her gain the pot."

"Lady Haversham may not need Stokely for that," Talbot put in. "She and Lady Kingsley gave me and Lady Jenner a run for our money. We won, but only because we had better cards. And from what I hear, she and Hungate destroyed the two they played against."

Gavin couldn't squelch a burst of pride at Christabel's success. He'd known the woman could do it if she really put her mind to it.

"How did you meet Lady Haversham, anyway?" Colonel Bradley asked.

"I knew her husband," Gavin said evasively.

"That fool couldn't win at whist if his life depended upon it," Talbot said. "He should've made his wife partner him. Then he'd never have been in debt."

"Is that how the pretty widow landed in your bed?" Markham asked with a smirk. "Are you allowing her to pay off Haversham's debts with other services?"

Hearing that accusation for the second time tonight annoyed him. "Have you ever known me to need such tactics to get a woman into bed, Markham?"

"No, but you have to admit she's not your type." Markham glanced across the room. "Then again, a woman with diddies like that is any man's type."

An ungoverning anger seized Gavin at the idea of Markham even looking at Christabel's "diddies," and he could barely suppress a hot retort.

What the hell was wrong with him? He and Markham and Talbot had compared mistresses like this before— their "diddies," their mouths, their arses. But the idea of these idiots sullying Christabel with their coarse comments made him want to snarl at them to shut up.

It was merely pent-up lust—perfectly understandable. He should have bedded the woman the first chance he'd had. Letting her put him off was turning him into a blithering idiot.

"I'll tell you how he got her into his bed," Talbot put in. "He told her that he'd gain her a chance to win Stokely's pot. That would tempt any widow."

Bradley snorted. "If she fell for that, she's a fool. Any of us can tell her it isn't that easy to win Stokely's pot, even with Byrne for a partner."

"True," Talbot said, "but though she may not win the pot, I wager she'll be in the final four to play."

Stokely had been listening from the next table, and now he leaned over. "Is that a true wager you're offering, Talbot? Or are you spouting nonsense as usual?"

Talbot blinked, then dropped his gaze to his cards without answering.

"If he's not offering it, I am." Gavin flashed Stokely a taunting smile. "A thousand pounds says Lady Haversham will be in the final four."

The discussion had caught the attention of other players at the surrounding tables, and they stopped playing to see what Stokely would answer.

Stokely cast Gavin an assessing glance. Then he turned toward another part of the room, and called out, "Lady Haversham!"

She looked up, startled.

"Byrne here is wagering a thousand pounds that you'll be among the final four players. What do you think—should I take the wager?"

She recovered swiftly from her shock, pasting on an expression so unreadable it did him proud. "I can't tell you what to do, Lord Stokely," she called back. "Only you know if you can afford to lose a thousand pounds to Byrne."

That brought laughter from everyone, since Stokely could afford to lose several thousand pounds.

"So you think Byrne will win, do you?" Stokely asked.

Christabel's gaze locked with Gavin's across the room. "Byrne *always* wins."

Gavin's blood ran hot. He certainly meant to win this time. And not just the wager, either. "Well, Stokely? Will you take it or no?"

Stokely was quiet a moment, then said, "Why not? Contrary to what Lady Haversham thinks, you don't always win."

"True." Gavin tore his gaze from Christabel's to find Stokely regarding him with a speculative glance. "Only when it's important."

The gong suddenly sounded, jarring everyone, reminding them that this was their last game. Stokely always had a servant bang a gong at 3 A.M., after which no more new rubbers were to be started. It was the only way to ensure that everyone played roughly the same number each night; otherwise, some would play around the clock.

Gavin returned his attention to his cards. They were only halfway through this hand, and probably a game or two from completing the rubber. Bloody hell. Another hour before he could join Christabel in bed.

As he and Bradley won the hand, Gavin glanced up to see Christabel rise from her table. She was finished already?

She conversed a moment with her fellow players, then came to his table, where Talbot was shuffling the cards.

"How did you do, my sweet?" Gavin asked her.

She shrugged. "I won more than I lost."

"Good. That bodes well for my wager with Stokely."

She watched a moment, then said, "I'm all done in, so I think I'll retire."

"You could stay and give me luck," he teased.

She snorted. "As if you need luck. No, I believe I'll go on. But do stay as long as you must." She gave an exaggerated yawn and left.

Only then did it dawn on him why she'd been so eager to leave without him. She meant to snoop about Stokely's house alone while their host was occupied at the card tables.

Damn the woman. Didn't she have the sense she was born with? Searching the place while everyone was still

awake wasn't only foolish, but downright dangerous if
Stokely caught her.

He couldn't leave in the middle of a rubber without
rousing suspicions, but that didn't keep him from worrying. After Talbot dealt the cards, Gavin had to force himself to pay attention.

They were halfway through the hand when the table
next to them broke up. Stokely's table.

Gavin tamped down his concern. No reason to think
Stokely would deviate from his usual practice of staying
in the card room until the last guest had retired.

Two of the players at Stokely's table went off to bed
right away. Anna came to stand by Gavin. When he ignored her, she said good night and left. After Stokely
circled the room playing the attentive host, he returned to
Gavin's table and announced his own decision to retire
for the night.

"Perhaps I'll see if Lady Haversham wants some company," he said.

The other players tensed, recognizing the blatant challenge to Gavin. Gavin didn't care about Stokely's strut-
ting—he cared about Christabel not getting caught. "Go
ahead." Hiding his alarm, he played a card. "But I warn
you—once the chit is asleep, she sleeps like the dead. She
won't hear your knock."

"We'll see." Stokely saluted the others. "Good night,
gentlemen."

As he sauntered off, a surge of rage seized Gavin. While
he had to sit here and play the rubber out to avoid rousing suspicion, that arse meant to try seducing Christabel.

He scowled. That wasn't the point—it was the possibility that she could be caught that should concern him.
Because if she were, their attempts to regain her letters

would come to an abrupt end. Making sure *that* didn't happen had to be his first concern.

Not Stokely's interest in the woman. Not the fact that the handsome baron might try to put his hands—

Bloody hell, what was wrong with him? When had he begun putting a woman ahead of whatever scheme he was engaged in?

Well, no more. He would finish the rubber and win. Then he would find Christabel and explain in a calm, rational manner that she could not just go searching about the place willy-nilly.

And if Stokely should happen to get in the way of his fist in the process, so be it.

Chapter Fourteen

*There's nothing more satisfying than
having two men fight over you.*
—Anonymous, *Memoirs of a Mistress*

$\mathscr{C}$hristabel wished she could lock the door while she searched Lord Stokely's study, but that would rouse suspicion if he happened to come along.

She had to be careful, as careful as the baron himself had apparently been. Twenty minutes of searching had so far yielded her nothing. The man's desk drawers weren't even locked, which of course meant there'd been nothing of importance in them.

She turned to examining the few bookshelves, hoping one of them might conceal a secret safe. But even as she made her slow way along every shelf, despair gripped her. She hadn't realized how large his estate would be, how many places a man could hide something as small as a packet of letters. It could be anywhere. How on earth was she to find it in only a week?

Suddenly, she heard footsteps in the hall. She froze, then grabbed a book off the shelf and pretended to be reading it. Just in time, too, for the door opened, and a male voice said, "Ah, there you are. I thought you'd gone to bed. Then I saw the light from under the door and decided to check."

Lord Stokely. Heart thundering, she pasted a bored smile to her lips and faced him. "I hope you don't mind. I couldn't sleep, so I came looking for a book."

He stepped inside the room, and to her consternation, closed the door. "I'm glad you did. Now we have a chance to get to know each other better."

A chill ran down her spine. "Oh, I think I already know you very well, Lord Stokely," she said lightly. "You're the sort of man it's dangerous for a woman to be alone with." Tucking the book under her arm, she headed toward the door. "Now if you'll excuse me . . ."

With a toothy smile, he blocked her way. "Come now, my dear, no need to be coy. We both know why you're really here."

Fear churned in her belly. "Oh?"

Stepping nearer, he took the book from her and tossed it onto his desk. "You're looking for entertainment of a different kind. And since Byrne is too preoccupied with his cards to provide it . . ." He caressed her cheek with his forefinger in a move worthy of any fine seducer. "You came to find me. Poor Byrne should know that you're not the sort of woman to be kept waiting."

Her eyes narrowed. If Lord Stokely really was as attracted to her as he seemed, some mild flirting might gain her more information than hours of searching.

"Am I to judge from your silence that my assessment is correct?" Lord Stokely asked, eyes gleaming.

She forced a teasing smile to her lips. "I came here with Byrne. What makes you think I'd transfer my affections to you?"

"Perhaps because you like variety?" He bent his head to nibble her ear. Strangely, the motion left her cold. "Or perhaps because Lady Kingsley has arrived. She was still in the card room keeping Byrne company when I left."

Christabel fought to contain her jealousy. Even if the man spoke the truth, it didn't mean that Byrne was welcoming the woman's attentions. "As long as Byrne comes to *my* bed in the end, I don't care who keeps him company in the card room."

"Fortunately, *he* doesn't care who keeps *you* company in my study," Lord Stokely murmured in her ear. "Byrne and I have shared many a woman. He won't be bothered if you indulge yourself with me, I assure you."

He was probably right, blast him. But that didn't stop her from recoiling when the man slid his arm about her waist and pulled her into an embrace.

As he seized her mouth in a kiss, panic broke loose in her chest. It was one thing to flirt with the man to uncover his secrets, but quite another to let him seduce her. And would he even give her a choice? They were alone—if he wanted to, Lord Stokely could do as he pleased.

She tried to break the kiss, but he grabbed her chin to hold her still while he thrust his tongue against her closed lips. Just as she lifted her hands to shove against his chest, a knock came at the door.

"Christabel, are you in there?" Byrne called out.

Lord Stokely drew back with a curse. "I should have locked the damned door."

Relief swamping her, she called out, "Yes, Byrne, I'm here."

Byrne strode in, then halted, his eyes narrowing as he spotted her and Lord Stokely in an embrace.

Lord Stokely didn't even bother to release her. "As it turns out, Byrne, the widow wasn't sleeping after all."

"I see that," Byrne said tersely. "Ready to retire, my sweet?" He offered her his arm.

Only then did the baron release her. But as she hurried to Byrne's side, thanking God for her narrow escape, Lord Stokely said, "Care to amend your wager, Byrne?"

Byrne stared at the man with a steely gaze. "In what way?"

Christabel seized Byrne's arm as Lord Stokely ran his lustful gaze down her body. "If you win the wager, I'll pay you a thousand pounds. If *I* win, however, then Lady Haversham spends the last night in my bed."

"I can hardly amend the wager's terms in such a manner without the lady's consent," he said in a faintly bored tone.

"Lady Haversham?" Lord Stokely turned to Christabel. "Do you agree?"

Christabel was staring at Byrne in amazement. She meant so little to him that he would agree to her being offered as a prize?

Her temper flared. "I'll consider it," she said on impulse, though she didn't mean a word. Honestly, Byrne could be so unfeeling, it drove her mad.

"Give me your answer tomorrow then—" Lord Stokely began.

"No need," Byrne broke in. "I don't agree to the terms."

The murderous look in his eyes gave Christabel pause.

"But Lady Haversham said—"

"I don't care what she said. My wager is for a thousand pounds, nothing else."

Lord Stokely's eyes narrowed. "You'd rather pay a thousand pounds than share Lady Haversham?"

Byrne shrugged. "I can afford it."

He was back to sounding bored, but his hand now held hers in a killer grip, and he was clearly on the verge of strangling Lord Stokely.

A thrill shot through her. What had happened to Byrne's famous lack of jealousy?

"Well then," Lord Stokely said snidely, "I wish you joy of her. The bitch must have a gold-plated honeypot to have you wanting to keep her to yourself."

Byrne snapped, "You'll never get the chance to find out. I promise you that." And slipping his arm about her waist, he practically dragged her from the room.

As he hurried her away from the study, she marveled at the sudden fury that had seized him. If this wasn't jealousy, then she didn't know what it was.

"What the hell do you think you're doing, encouraging that arse?" he hissed at her, as they headed up the staircase. "Just because I wagered on you to end up in the final four doesn't mean you'll win, for God's sake. Do you *want* to share Stokely's bed?"

That was definitely jealousy in his voice. Her spirits lifting, she cast him an airy smile. "No, but if I happen not to make it to the eliminations, I'll have to leave the estate, and this way I could stay until the end no matter how badly I play."

He glared at her. "Stay. With him. As his bed partner."

"It would certainly help me in my efforts to find the letters," she said blithely. "I would have the run of the house."

With a curse, he dragged her into an alcove, where he pressed her against the wall. Bracketing her body between his arms, he growled, "You won't share my bed, but you'd share his? For the sake of those bloody letters?"

She met his gaze steadily. "Those 'bloody letters' are

gaining you a barony. Why do you care what methods I use as long as you get what you want?"

A muscle worked in his jaw. "There are better ways."

"Oh?" She pressed the issue, determined to make him admit his true feelings. "It would be simpler if I seduced Lord Stokely into—"

"No," he said flatly.

She bit back a smile. "I could just—"

"No." He leaned in close, eyes glittering. "I won't let you whore for the letters."

"Why not? You've always claimed you don't mind if your mistresses are unfaithful, and it's not as if you care for me. If I were to play up to Lord Stokely—"

"No," he said stubbornly. "No." He bent his head to hers. "Never."

Then his mouth was on hers, and he was kissing her possessively, as he'd never kissed her before. He'd never made her feel as if the world would end if he couldn't kiss her.

She threw her arms about his neck and gave herself up to it. It had been over a week since he'd kissed her, over a week since she'd promised herself not to let him do this to her.

How many times had she caught him looking at her with that barely banked fire in his eyes and felt her heart flip over in her chest? How many nights had she lain awake aching for just this taste of his mouth on hers?

"Christabel," he whispered against her lips, "God, woman, you're driving me mad."

At least it was mutual. He seized her mouth again, but this time his hands roamed up her ribs and down to her hips, stroking, seeking, caressing . . .

Someone passing by called out a coarse comment, and Byrne tore his lips from hers. "Come on," he growled, then tugged her down the hall.

She struggled to keep up with his furious strides. "Where are we going?"

"My room."

She dug in her heels. "Now see here, Byrne—"

"It's high time we discussed tactics for regaining your damned letters," he muttered. "And we can't do it in your room, with Stokely right across the hall."

"Oh." That made sense. Didn't it? Or was she merely so eager to plummet to her doom that she would do whatever he said?

She let him lead her down a series of halls until he ushered her into a lovely bedchamber where darkly burnished woods and antique brass created a decidedly masculine feel. Clearly he was a popular guest, for the servants had shown him the first attention. A fire blazed high in the hearth, a decanter of whiskey sat on a nearby writing table, and the vases overflowed with fresh flowers.

He seemed to notice none of it as he shut the door behind her, his expression grim. "I nearly lost ten years off my life when I saw you closeted in Stokely's study with him. I was certain he'd caught you going through his papers."

She sniffed. "I should hope I'm not so obvious as all that. I told him I was looking for a book, and he believed me."

"Did he?" Byrne edged nearer. "Then why was he so eager to change the wager? He's playing with you, Christabel—"

"If he is, I can handle him."

"You can always gut him with that blade I gave you, right?" he snapped, his voice heavy with sarcasm.

"If I have to."

He shoved his fingers through his hair. "You *don't* have to—that's the point. Just do your searching during safe hours."

"And when would those be?"

"After everyone's asleep, before the maids come round."

"From 4 to 5 A.M.? Don't be absurd. I'd never find them at that rate."

"Then at least make sure I'm with you when you go searching. We can always come up with some reason for being together in an odd part of the house."

Her eyes narrowed. "You sneaky devil, that's what this is about, isn't it? You're afraid I'll find the letters when you're not around. Then you won't get your chance at them. So you're trumping up this nonsense about the dangers—"

"I'm not trumping up anything!" He strode up to her, his eyes alight. "What did Stokely do while you were with him? Did he touch you, kiss you, caress you?"

"He kissed me, that's all."

His jaw grew taut. "Next time he finds you alone he'll expect more, especially now that you implied you might be willing."

He had a point. She thrust out her chin. "I'll just have to make sure he doesn't find me alone."

"When you're sleeping across the bloody hall from him?" he shouted. "He can creep into your room at any time of the day or night, for God's sake!"

"I'll lock the door."

"It's *his* bloody house. He has keys to all the rooms, remember?"

"Then I'll . . . I'll put a chair under the door or—"

"You'll sleep here, that's what you'll do," he ordered. "You'll sleep here with me, you'll go out on your little searching exhibitions with me, you'll—"

"For a man who doesn't care about the women he beds, you're beginning to sound very much like a jealous lover," she said quietly. "Do you hear yourself?"

That brought him up short. "Don't talk nonsense." He raked his fingers through his hair again in increased agitation. "I've never been jealous of a woman in my life."

"My mistake," she bit out. "And now that we've settled that, I'll return to my room."

She got as far as opening the door before he slammed it shut. "You're not going anywhere. You're staying here where I can keep an eye on you."

"Why?" she demanded. "Give me one good reason I should stay."

"Because I want you here."

"That isn't—"

He cut her off with a kiss, angling his body in close to trap hers against the door. But this time she didn't return it. This time she wanted more from him.

He was jealous and possessive of her, no matter what he'd claimed, and that meant he cared for her. But would he ever admit to feeling more for her than just desire?

It suddenly seemed very important to make him admit it. To find out if there really was a warm-blooded, feeling creature buried deep inside the cold and calculating debaucher. A man with a soul.

As if he sensed her withdrawal, he increased his erotic assault, letting his mouth drift down her jaw to her neck as his hands found the ties of her gown. "Stay with me tonight, my sweet." His tongue traced the curve of her ear, sending her pulse racing. "Share my bed. Enough of this foolish abstinence."

His hand slid inside her gown to thumb her nipple, and every muscle in her body came to life, wanting more. She choked down a sigh. "Admit that you were jealous when you saw me with Lord Stokely. Admit it, and I'll stay."

He paused in his caresses, then continued. "I won't admit something that's not true." He worked the ties free, and she felt her gown fall off her shoulders.

"Why not? You could lie, and I'd never know the difference. Go ahead, lie."

"I'm not going to bother lying about something as foolish as that," he bit out. But he wouldn't look at her as he shoved her chemise down far enough to bare her breast, then seized it in his mouth, sucking so greedily, it sparked her own greed. For him. In *her* bed.

"You won't . . . lie about it," she choked out, "because you know it . . . wouldn't be a lie."

"Think what you want." He swiftly turned her around so he could undo her laces, then strip off her corset. When she faced him once more, his eyes scoured her, hungry, needy . . . possessive.

"Admit it, Byrne," she prodded. "Admit that—"

He shut her up with a kiss, probably so he could remove her chemise and drawers without her protesting. Then he shamelessly fondled her breasts and her belly, sliding his clever, seeking hand between her legs . . .

Wrenching her mouth from his, she caught his hand to stay it. "Say the words. 'I was jealous.' Three words."

His eyes looked almost black in the dimly lit room. "I'll say it if you promise to spend your nights with me. To do your searching only with me."

"You know I won't promise that."

"Ah, but you will, my sweet," he rasped. "I'll make sure of it." Taking her by surprise, he caught her naked body up in his arms and carried her to the bed.

When he tossed her down atop the coverlet and tore off his coat, she considered whether to run, to escape him while she still could. But she wasn't ready to give up on him. Tonight she'd seen a glimmer of another Byrne, an uncontrolled one consumed by anger and jealousy.

And passion. He stripped quickly, raking her with a gaze so fierce and raw that it made her nipples ache. Yet she didn't fight the heated wine of desire flooding her senses. She lay there, relishing the sight of him baring his body in great strokes, like a painter working in a frenzy to reveal a corded thigh here, a bent elbow there.

For days, she'd worried that if they made love, he'd gain the power over her that he needed to discover—and exploit—her secrets. But might it not work both ways? If Byrne were capable of true caring, satisfying his desires might give her power as well. Power over him. The power to convince him that helping her was more noble than seeking to use her letters.

A power she might already have. "Admit that you were jealous," she pressed him. "Admit that you hated the sight of me with Lord Stokely."

"Promise me you'll never go off alone," he countered gruffly. Now naked, he joined her in the bed, lying on his side so he could caress her breast. "Promise me, lass."

"First admit you were jealous." Turning onto her side, she ran her hand down the line of hair on his belly until she reached the heavy length of him. As she clasped his magnificent erection, she whispered, "Admit it, Byrne."

Before she could even stroke him once, he caught her hand. "Oh, no, we're not playing *that* game again, you teasing wench."

Pressing her back, he used one of his hands to imprison both of hers above her head. Then he bent his mouth to her breasts and began to suck and tongue her nipples while his other hand found the yearning spot between her thighs and tormented it with silken touches and teasing caresses that were never enough to satisfy.

"Promise me," he tore his lips from her breast to growl. And all the while he roused her to a fever pitch of need, making her squirm and writhe and beg for more with thrusts of her hips against his too-gentle hand.

Yet still she managed to gasp, "Admit it . . . admit it and . . . I'll promise . . . whatever you wish."

"Damn you," he ground out as he hovered over her, inches from her mouth. "Damn you for being a stubborn minx."

She stretched up to kiss him, and he seized her mouth with a groan, slaking only some of her thirst with bold thrusts of his tongue. He insinuated one knee between her thighs, and she parted her legs to accommodate him.

Still kissing her, he braced himself above her so that his erection lay on her, warm, thick, promising release as he stroked it up and down against that tender little spot that throbbed and ached for him. "Promise me," he rasped against her mouth. "Promise me, lass."

She slid her freed hand down between them to grab his shaft, then gave it a long stroke she knew would drive him mad.

"Stop that," he hissed.

"Admit it." She matched his earlier, too-gentle strokes, caressing him as if he were as fragile as glass. "Admit you were jealous."

His gaze seared her even as he thrust against her hand. "No." He tried to pull her hand free, but she had a firm grip and wasn't letting go this time.

She rubbed her hard-tipped nipples against his chest, then arched up to his ear to whisper, "Admit it, Byrne."

Remembering what he'd done earlier, she laved his ear with her tongue. "Come on, admit it."

When she capped her sensuous assault with a torturously slow tug on his aroused flesh, he moaned, then said hoarsely, "All right, damn you, I admit it. Now let go."

She did, but though he probed between her legs with his shaft, she shifted her pelvis away, not quite satisfied with his answer. "Say the whole thing."

With jaw taut and eyes ablaze, he snapped, "Promise me you won't go anywhere here without me."

"I promise." She should at least give him that much.

Satisfaction filled his face. Reaching down, he found her entrance with his fingers, then drove his aroused flesh deep inside her. A groan of sheer pleasure erupted from his lips. "You're so tight and hot, my sweet. It feels so damned good to be inside you."

"Byrne," she begged, while she could still speak. "Say . . . the words . . ."

He withdrew, then thrust again, hard, furious. "I was jealous," he bit out. "I *am* jealous. Jealous of all those bloody idiots . . . in the card room. Who leer at you and . . . watch your arse while you walk—"

"Do they?" she whispered, surprised.

"And Stokely." His gaze bored into hers. "I hate the idea of Stokely touching you." He drove inside her again, so fiercely it made her gasp. "*I'm* the only one who should touch you. I'm the only one who should kiss you." His breath rasped against her ear. "*I'm* the only one who should . . . put himself inside you . . . like this—" He nipped her earlobe, then soothed the nip with heated swaths of his tongue. "If I believed . . . for one moment that you . . . would really countenance another man's—"

"No, never," she vowed against his cheek. "It's only you

I want." She wound her arms about his neck, arching up against him to find more of the glorious pleasure his delicious thrusts were rousing. "Only you."

"Christabel," he said hoarsely, then cast openmouthed kisses along her cheek, her jaw, her throat. "My God, Christabel . . ."

Byrne matched his kisses with wild, thundering thrusts, reaching down between them to rub her sensitive nub until she was falling, falling . . . falling into hell with the angel of darkness, the Prince of Sin himself. The man with no soul was plundering hers over and over, mercilessly, thoroughly, branding her with himself in every vein and muscle and limb, until she forgot where he ended and she began.

Now she was truly in trouble. She fancied she could feel the heat of hellfire on her face, smell the brimstone in the air, yet it was as sweet as fragrant roses to her. Lord help her, she didn't care where Byrne took her. Let hellfire consume her and the devil steal her soul. Because any hell with Byrne in it was better than a heaven without him.

"Damn you, lass," he whispered, his voice harsh and guttural. "Christabel . . . my sweet . . . my darling . . . mine . . . *mine* . . . *mine!*"

It was the exultant cry of the devil claiming her soul, yet all she could think as he spilled himself inside her and her body burst into flames was, *Mine, too, Byrne. You're mine, too.*

Chapter Fifteen

*I found it wise never to ask a lover about
his former mistresses, in case I did not like
his answers.*
—Anonymous, *Memoirs of a Mistress*

*G*avin lay sprawled on his back, staring at the canopy
above them as Christabel's sweet form curved against
him. He couldn't catch his breath, couldn't still the thundering of his heart. And it had nothing to do with his ex-
ertions of the past few minutes.

It was her and the things she'd forced him to admit.
Had that humiliating litany of jealousies really come out
of his mouth? And he hadn't even been lying to get her to
share his bed—he'd meant every word. Damn the chit.
Damn her!

Plenty of his mistresses had used lovemaking to coax
him into giving them jewels or gifts or excursions to exotic places. But none had ever used it to turn him confessional. Of course, none had ever made him want to
strangle a man just for looking at them with lust, either.

What the bloody hell had come over him? He might as
well slice open his chest and offer her his heart for the
plucking. *Here, my sweet, rip it out.* Colonel Christabel
wasn't satisfied with only his body, oh no. She wanted

everything. If he weren't careful, she'd turn him into a be-sotted fool.

He turned to stare at her, and his anger abruptly van-ished. She certainly didn't look like a wily temptress bent on his destruction. More like a purring kitten curled up against him, her face softly content, sleepily happy.

He was in trouble now. Because the truth was—he'd speak every humiliating word again just to see that look on her face. Imagine what it would be like to wake up to that look every morning. To have that smile shine for him every single day of his life.

His breath caught in his throat. Damn her for doing this to him! He mustn't let her guess what she'd done, or next thing he knew, he'd be married to her and sur-rounded with a passel of puling babes—

"Bloody hell!" He jerked up in bed. "I can't believe I forgot to use them!"

"Use what?" she asked, her contentment abruptly fading.

"Too late this time anyway." He settled back against the pillow, drawing her up to lean against his chest. "I forgot to use my French letters to prevent children, my sweet." Something else that had never happened with any other woman.

"Well," she said in a small voice, "it probably doesn't matter. I suspect I can't have children anyway."

A strange tightness seized his throat. "Why not?"

"I never conceived in all my years of marriage. So I'm probably barren."

"How do you know your husband wasn't the one at fault?"

"Men never are, or so the doctors told me."

He snorted. "What else would they say? If men could be at fault, women might start abandoning their husbands for not giving them children, and they couldn't have that. But if it takes two people to create a child, then it seems to me either person could be at fault for *not* creating one. That's merely logical."

"And you're nothing if not logical," she said dryly.

"Which is why we'll use my French letters from now on. And you'll use a sponge. I'm not taking any chances. I can't believe I took one this time." He stared down at her tumbled hair with an ironic smile. "That's what happens when a man goes days without a woman. He loses his capacity for logic."

She eyed him askance. "That would certainly explain why you never fail to be logical. I doubt you've ever gone more than one night without a woman."

For some reason, her assumption annoyed him. "I've gone weeks without a woman. I do have a life outside of the bedroom."

"I'd never know it, to look at Lord Stokely's guests. How many of your former mistresses are here? Two? Three? Ten?"

"Four," he grudgingly admitted.

She dropped her gaze from his, her hand tracing faint circles on his bare chest. "And . . . Lady Kingsley? How would you characterize 'Anna'?"

He stiffened. "What did Stokely tell you? I know he told you something."

"He said that you wanted to marry her, and she refused you." Her voice lowered. "He said you wanted her fortune."

"Damn the bloody arse. That's just like Stokely to speak half the truth. I didn't need her fortune, for God's sake."

"Perhaps he misunderstood her. He said he got the story from Lady Kingsley herself. Or perhaps that's how she looked at it. Especially since you'd just begun your club, and—"

"If she said I was after her fortune, she lied," Gavin ground out. "My club was already doing pretty well for the small concern it was, and she knew it. Nor did she refuse me, not at first. We were engaged. Secretly engaged. I'd already arranged for us to elope to Gretna Green, and she was ready and willing." He gritted his teeth, remembering. "Then the lofty Lord Kingsley came along, and her family pressured her into accepting his suit. And that was the end of our plans."

He hadn't realized how much bitterness was in his voice until she laid her hand soothingly on his shoulder. "You loved her, didn't you?"

Somehow he managed a shrug. "I was a young idiot. I suppose I fancied myself in love."

"And she loved you. She still does. I suspect she regrets letting her family convince her to choose Kingsley over you."

"Then she's a fool."

She stared up at him, wide-eyed. "Why?"

"The world is made for men. Women only succeed by marrying well, and I could never have given her the status she instantly achieved by marrying Kingsley. She would have been Mrs. Byrne, the Irish bastard's wife. Instead of Lady Kingsley, the Irish peer's wife."

"It wouldn't have mattered," she persisted. "You loved each other, and a woman should always choose love over other considerations."

"That didn't exactly work well for you, did it?" Her stricken expression made him curse his quick tongue. "I'm sorry, lass, I shouldn't have said that."

"Why not? It's true." She shifted out of his arms to lie with her back to him on the bed. "I loved Philip, and he trampled on my love. Perhaps you're right. Perhaps a woman should choose a man for more practical reasons, like money or status." Her voice lowered to a whisper. "Or how good a lover he is."

Yesterday, he would have exulted to hear those words. Now, all he could think was that he'd stolen something valuable from her—her wide-eyed belief in honor and beauty and . . . yes . . . love.

He bit back an oath. He hadn't stolen it—Haversham had. He was just furthering the education her husband had started.

That was a depressing thought.

"Byrne?" she asked.

He lay down beside her, tugging her body into the lee of his. "Yes, lass?"

"What happens now?"

"What do you mean?" he said, pretending not to know.

"With us."

Hardly realizing he did so, he tightened his grip on her. "We enjoy each other," he said fiercely. "We share a bed, we play whist, and we—"

"I mean later. After this is over."

"Nothing will change. You'll still be my mistress and share my bed."

She was silent a moment. "For how long?"

Damn her for asking that. Why did women always have to anticipate the end? "For however long we both want."

"But Byrne—"

"Enough," he broke in, covering her mouth with his hand. "Just let it be what it is for a while, all right? Can't you do that?"

She shifted to gaze up at him, her eyes glimmering with tears, but she nodded.

He let go of her mouth. "Good." He bent his head to kiss her, but she pressed him back.

"What time is it?" she asked.

"I don't know, four-thirty. Five. Why?"

"We should go look for the letters," she whispered.

For half a second, he thought she meant his French letters. Then it dawned on him what she was talking about, and a groan escaped his lips.

He really was far gone, to forget the very thing he'd come here to gain. That's what came of letting a woman get under one's skin.

He glanced at the clock. "It's nearly 5:00 A.M. The servants will be stirring."

"But we could wait until they've finished in the public rooms, then still have time to search the study or library while everyone is abed."

"I suppose," he said noncommittally. The truth was, he doubted they would ever find those letters by searching Stokely's huge mansion. They'd be better off trying to strike a deal with the arse. No, *he* would be better off striking a deal. He still meant to gain those letters for himself. It shouldn't matter to her in the long run—after he got what he wanted from Prinny, he would return them.

But he could only bargain with Stokely if he knew what was in them, knew their worth.

He pressed his lips to her forehead, then nuzzled her hair. "How many letters are there exactly?" He kissed a path to her ear, which he then caressed with the tip of his tongue until he felt her sigh beneath him. "How large a packet are we looking for?"

"I don't . . . know. Ten . . . twenty . . . not large."

Covering her lush breast with his hand, he kneaded the

nipple until it hardened to a fine point. "Is it bound with anything? Like string or ribbon?"

"A . . . a . . . yellow ribbon. I think."

He nibbled her ear. "I assume the letters are from your father to someone. A friend? The prince himself?"

Stiffening, she pushed him back. "You're trying to seduce me into telling you what's in them."

Damn her for being too clever—and wary—for him. "I'm trying to seduce you, yes. But I don't care what you tell me about the letters."

"Liar." She stared at him with an accusing gaze. "It doesn't matter anyway. Try all you wish—I'm not going to tell you."

Not now, anyway. He hovered over her, a faint smile touching his lips. "Does that mean you won't let me seduce you either?"

The sudden spark of heat in her was unmistakable. "We should sleep," she said, though her voice lacked conviction.

He bent his head to nuzzle her breast, then dragged his tongue over the nipple until she gasped. "We can sleep later," he said hoarsely. Then he added, "I'll be right back," and left the bed to find his French letters.

But by the time he returned to the bed, her eyes had drifted shut and her slow, even breathing signaled the end to tonight's lovemaking. He tossed the French letters on the bedside table with a rueful sigh. No matter; there was always morning. And tomorrow night. And the night after that.

For how long?

He shoved that question from his mind. But after he climbed into bed beside her, and was drifting off to sleep, it returned to haunt him. *For how long?*

Chapter Sixteen

❧❧

Do not trust anything your lover's former
mistress might tell you. Her motives for
what she says can never be pure.
—Anonymous, *Memoirs of a Mistress*

*O*n the third morning after Christabel had thrown caution to the winds and become Byrne's real mistress, she sat at the dressing table in her room, grimacing with every stroke of Rosa's brush. "Ouch!" she cried when Rosa pulled a bit too hard. "Are you trying to murder me?"

Rosa clucked her tongue. "These are the sacrifices you make for having a lusty lover." She cut her eyes slyly at Christabel in the mirror. "He makes love to you all night, no? That is why your hair is so tangled?"

"Not *all* night." But often enough to tangle her hair. And ensnare her heart.

A sigh broke from her. The trouble with Byrne was that whenever he made love to her, she could almost believe it meant something to him. He lingered over her for hours, bringing her to heights of pleasure beyond her most erotic dreams. After a while, she began to hope that he cared for her more than he let on.

But when they played whist with the others or when they searched Lord Stokely's mansion, he was that other

Byrne, the frighteningly efficient, calculating, ruthless gambler. And seeing that always plunged her into despair.

Wrapping a hank of Christabel's hair about her hand, Rosa briskly worked her brush through the snarled ends. "You are fortunate to be here with Mr. Byrne and not one of those other fools. He's good in the bedchamber *and* good at cards. Mr. Byrne will win you a fortune that you can well use."

"I don't know if I like gaining funds that way."

"By besting idiots like Lieutenant Markham? That man is an insult to the good name of soldiers everywhere, him and his phaeton and his airs. You should be pleased you and Mr. Byrne won his last pence. And his phaeton."

"I suppose." Last night had been one of the few times she and Byrne had been whist partners. The game had been a most potent illustration of Byrne's ruthlessness. "Byrne shouldn't have talked the man into staking his horses as well. That was unnecessary."

"Bah, Markham did not have to wager his horses. He did it because he thought he could win." Rosa smiled proudly. "He should have realized that you and Mr. Byrne are invincible."

Christabel snorted. "Hardly. Though I don't understand why Byrne was so determined to win his horses. Byrne told the man he 'liked the diddies on your nags.' Why would he say such a vulgar thing?"

Rosa shrugged. "It hardly matters why. The point is he won."

"But he should have at least allowed the man to keep his horses," she persisted. "Lord Stokely had already informed the lieutenant that he would have to leave, now that he'd lost all his funds. So the poor man has no means for returning to London. What will he do?"

"I heard he walked to Salisbury this morning and pawned his watch for a coach ticket."

"Oh no." But the lieutenant couldn't appeal to Lady Jenner for help, since her husband was present and unlikely to offer his carriage to his wife's lover. And no one else would wish to help him.

This was the sort of people she found herself among, with Byrne their Prince of Sin. Sometimes it disheartened her to think of how far she'd fallen. And for what? A few glorious nights in bed? A man who'd as much as told her he would never marry her and could almost certainly never love her?

Not that she wanted him to love her, oh no. She was taking no chances with a man who blatantly referred to himself as lacking a soul, a man who'd tried countless times to coax her into telling him what was in Papa's letters. She was proud she'd held firm, though she wondered if it even mattered anymore.

Because they couldn't find the blasted things. Byrne thought they were probably in a hidden safe, but they'd found no safe anywhere after going over every inch of Lord Stokely's library and study, as well as several other public rooms. Time grew short, and still nothing.

She hoped to change that today, however. "Are you done yet?" she asked Rosa impatiently.

"Almost. But what is your hurry? The men have gone out shooting, so it is not as if your Mr. Byrne can spend the day with you."

True, but he'd surprised her by suggesting that she use the time to search while Lord Stokely was occupied with the other men. Probably he thought she'd find nothing anyway. Or he was so sure of her that he believed she would tell him if she *did* find them.

Whatever the reason, she would take advantage of it and search Lord Stokely's bedchamber this morning—if the man kept a hidden safe, it might be there. And once she found it, she'd get Byrne to open it.

Rosa put the final pin in place, and Christabel leaped to her feet. "Thank you, Rosa," she called as she grabbed her silver fan and left the room. "I'll see you here again in the morning."

She'd been spending her wild nights with Byrne, then creeping back to her room before the other guests stirred. She wasn't sure why she bothered being discreet, however; no one else seemed to.

Out in the hall, she glanced both ways, then slid over to Lord Stokely's door. The downstairs servants would be occupied with serving the early risers breakfast, though it was past noon, and the upstairs maids would be helping those female guests who hadn't brought their own ladies' maids. Here in the family wing, the servants were done with the morning's work, so hopefully she wouldn't surprise anyone.

Still, as she reached for the door handle, she prepared a story for why she was walking into Lord Stokely's bedchamber unannounced.

The door was locked.

She couldn't believe it. She tried the door again, but it didn't budge.

Her eyes narrowed. Why would the man keep his door locked with only the two of them in the family wing? Unless he hadn't gone with the other men to shoot. Just to be sure, she knocked and called out, "Lord Stokely? Are you there?"

Rosa, curse her, stuck her head out Christabel's door and frowned. "I saw him leave with the shooting party this morning. And what would you be wanting with him anyway?"

Christabel glowered at her servant. "I need to ask him a question, not that it's any of *your* concern. And aren't you supposed to be seeing to the laundering of my drawers?"

Muttering to herself, Rosa closed the door, but Christabel knew the woman would now be listening for her to leave. Sometimes having a nosy servant was quite a nuisance. Tripping the blade on her little fan, she stuck it in the lock and poked around a bit, but her attempts brought her nothing.

She could think of no reason for Lord Stokely to keep his room locked, unless he was hiding something in his bedchamber. And what else could it be but her letters?

She would have to bring Byrne up here—if anyone knew how to pick a lock, it would be he. Somehow, they could work out a way to sneak into Lord Stokely's bedchamber when he wasn't there.

Still, in case she was wrong, she'd keep looking elsewhere. There was a private drawing room downstairs that hardly anyone used—it would be easy to search in there.

She hurried there, but when she walked in, she startled a group of women who were listening intently as Lady Jenner read to them from a slender book.

"Oh, Lady Haversham, you must join us!" cried Mrs. Talbot. "You will surely find Lady Jenner's new book as droll as we do."

She started to murmur some excuse, but Lady Jenner said, "You can add your store of information to ours."

"Information about what?"

"Lovers, of course," Lady Hungate put in. "We're comparing notes." She gestured to the volume in Lady Jenner's hand. "Some silly female has published a book of memoirs about her years as 'mistress to the loftiest of the *ton*,' and we're trying to guess who she might be."

Christabel was dying to hear more.

"You have to join us," Lady Jenner said. "Except for Lady Kingsley, the rest of us here have all been Byrne's mistresses at one time or another—we simply *have* to know if your experience of him is the same as ours."

Cursing herself for a fool, Christabel entered and closed the door. She'd been trying to convince herself that she meant more to Byrne than a mere mistress. Listening to his other mistresses would serve as a potent reminder that she was no different to him than the rest of his women. And she needed such a reminder just now.

"Oh, look and see if the author mentions Byrne!" Mrs. Talbot told Lady Jenner as Christabel took the remaining chair, near the door. "He might be in one of the later chapters."

"I doubt that," Lady Hungate said. "The writer is clearly a courtesan, and Byrne's mistresses are always married women."

"And the occasional widow," Lady Kingsley said archly.

Did she know that Christabel knew all about her and Byrne? Probably. Lord Stokely was too much of a gossip— and too intent on stirring trouble—not to have told her.

"I've read the whole of the memoirs," Lady Jenner said, "and there's no mention of Byrne."

"Perhaps he paid to be kept out of it," Mrs. Talbot said. "I heard that certain gentlemen received letters offering to keep them out if they paid a particular sum."

Lady Hungate laughed. "Byrne pay blackmail? He doesn't care who knows about his love affairs. Sometimes I think the man actually relishes the gossip about him."

"No doubt," Lady Jenner remarked. "He probably considers it a good thing to be known as the man with the warmest mouth and the coldest heart."

"He's not *that* bad," Lady Hungate chided. "And you have to admit that his prowess in bed makes up for any coolness of manner."

The women uttered a collective sigh.

Mrs. Talbot turned to Christabel. "Does he still do that thing with his finger where he—"

"Mrs. Talbot, really!" Lady Hungate protested. "I don't think we should discuss specifics."

"Why not?" the woman said stoutly. "Who else can we discuss such matters with? And you know very well you loved what he did with his fingers."

The fact that Christabel knew exactly what the woman was talking about chilled her. Because she loved it, too. Dear Lord, she really *was* just one of his harem, wasn't she?

"Byrne is wonderful, I'll grant you," another woman said, "but he's not the only man who knows what to do in the bedchamber. I once had this lover . . ."

The next hour was spent in the most embarrassing and enlightening discussion Christabel had ever heard. Some of the things they talked about, she hadn't even realized were possible. And some of them were quite intriguing.

She listened avidly, fascinated by the variety of ways a man could pleasure a woman. And vice versa. Perhaps if she could please Byrne in bed with some of these techniques, she might hold on to him after this was over.

She groaned. Hold on to him, indeed. Why did she never learn? And she ought to be ashamed of herself, thinking of an impossible future with Byrne when she should be worrying about Papa and *his* future.

"Getting back to Byrne," Lady Jenner said, "I'll tell you what I *don't* miss about the man—his insistence upon using French letters. I like the feel of a man's flesh inside me, and it's not as if I'm some whore teeming with disease. If it's siring children he wants to avoid, why not pull out at the end like the other men?"

Christabel hid her surprise. It never occurred to her that a man might do that.

"I like French letters myself," Mrs. Talbot retorted. "Less messy. Does he still insist upon it, Lady Haversham?"

Christabel's cheeks turned scarlet. "I . . . I . . . would rather not say."

"Look how you're blushing," Lady Jenner said snidely. "Do we offend you with our frank talk?"

"Not at all," she lied.

"But you haven't contributed much to the discussion. What does Byrne do that annoys *you*?"

She sought for something less . . . indelicate to share. "He steals the covers. I always have to steal them back in the middle of the night."

The other women exchanged perplexed glances. Lady Hungate leaned forward. "Are you saying that Byrne actually spends the night with you?"

"Yes, of course."

"There's no 'of course' about it," Mrs. Talbot put in. "Byrne never sleeps with anyone. He might doze, but never for more than an hour or two."

When the others nodded their agreement, Christabel's heart began to pound. "So Byrne has never spent a full night with any of you?"

"No, never," Lady Hungate said.

Lady Jenner gave a dismissive wave of her hand. "It's

only because she's a widow. He sleeps with her because she has no husband waiting for her."

"I don't think that's it," a young woman said. "My husband was always away, and my servants are discreet, but Byrne would never stay the night, even when I begged him."

Yet he stayed with Christabel every night, *all* night. Her blood thundered in her ears. Perhaps he *did* care, after all.

Then a lowering thought hit her: Byrne only stayed with her to keep her from being vulnerable to Lord Stokely.

"What always annoyed me about Byrne," Lady Hungate remarked, "was the way he insisted on calling me 'my sweet' or 'lass.'"

"It's the Irish in him," Mrs. Talbot said. "Irishmen are like that with the endearments."

"I don't mind his using an endearment; it's the ones he chooses. I'm a grown woman, for heaven's sake, not a 'lass.' And I'm certainly not 'sweet.'"

"I don't mind that so much," Christabel admitted. "And I rather enjoy it when he calls me 'darling.'"

Once again, there was that exchange of looks between the others. "He calls you 'darling'?" Mrs. Talbot said incredulously.

Finding all eyes trained on her, Christabel mumbled, "Sometimes, yes."

Lady Hungate sat back in her chair, eyes narrowing. "Well, well, isn't that interesting?"

"It means nothing," Lady Jenner snapped. "I'm sure he must have called me 'darling' a time or two. I just don't remember."

"I remember well enough," the young woman put in, a trace of envy in her voice. "He never called *me* that."

"Me either," Mrs. Talbot admitted.

"It seems Byrne has been showing Lady Haversham a different side than he showed the rest of us," Lady Hungate said.

"Nonsense," Lady Jenner snapped. "A leopard doesn't change his spots. If he behaves any differently with her, it's only because he wants something."

Christabel turned her fan over in her fingers. That was quite possibly true. Although she couldn't see how calling her "darling" helped him get anything.

"Nonetheless," Lady Hungate remarked, "Byrne is growing older. At some point a man does have to stop sowing wild oats and start sowing the more fruitful kind. Even his sort sometimes fall in love and marry."

"Byrne?" Lady Jenner said with pure contempt. "Interested in hearth and home? Don't be ridiculous. The man is incapable of love, much less marriage."

"That's not true," a quiet voice broke in. When everyone turned to Lady Kingsley in surprise, she colored but pressed on. "I once . . . er . . . knew a woman who said he claimed to love her, and even proposed marriage."

"The woman is either mad or a liar," Lady Jenner said stoutly. "Why, if you even so much as mention love to the man, that's the end of it. He might take you to bed one more time, but mention love, and you'll receive your congé the next day. It doesn't matter if you tell him you didn't mean it or were joking or—" She broke off, as if realizing how much she'd revealed. Then she thrust out her chin stubbornly. "If you want to end your association with him, all you need say is, 'I love you,' and he'll end it himself."

Christabel's throat grew raw at the very thought of Byrne cutting her off with such cursory disregard.

"It's true," Mrs. Talbot said woefully. "Never say those words to him if you want to remain his mistress."

Christabel's gaze shot to Lady Kingsley, who'd grown quite pale. Blast the woman. It was *her* fault that Byrne had become like this. How dared she trample on his heart for something as silly as status? She'd taught him not to care, not to let a woman close, not even to countenance talk of love and marriage.

Christabel sighed. That wasn't fair. She *had* hurt him, but other things had shaped Byrne, too: his hard childhood, the prince's betrayal of his mother—

"Do any of you know about the fire that killed Byrne's mother?" It suddenly occurred to her that these women might actually know. "How did it happen?"

"Some untended coal fire, I imagine," Mrs. Talbot said. "I'm friendly with the owner of the theater where Byrne's mother once worked, and he said it was one of those things—the lodging house was very mean, apparently, and fires like that happen often in the poorer part of town."

"But why wasn't Byrne in it, too?" she prodded.

"He was. It was late at night, and he was already asleep in the building when she returned from some jaunt to find it ablaze. She fought her way in and got him out, but her burns were too much for her, and she expired in hospital."

"You mean, Mrs. Byrne was burned?" Lady Jenner remarked with a cruel laugh. "That sounds like some child's ditty."

As Christabel's stomach began to roil, Lady Hungate said, "Eleanor, really! Have some respect for the dead."

"Don't be such a prig," Lady Jenner snapped. "You must admit it's an amusing coincidence. The Burning of Mrs. Byrne—why, it could easily be the title of some farce—"

"Excuse me," Christabel murmured as she jerked to her feet. She'd had enough of Lady Jenner's disgusting jokes and unfeeling manner. She had to escape the witch before she scratched her eyes out.

"Where are you going?" Lady Jenner demanded. "Planning to join the men at shooting? I understand you're quite the good shot. But then, shooting at people is easier than shooting at birds, isn't it? People provide bigger targets."

Christabel froze. So Lord Stokely had told everyone about that, had he? Beast. She faced Lady Jenner with a brittle smile. "Whenever you wish, Lady Jenner, I'll happily demonstrate my prowess with *both* sorts of target."

Mrs. Talbot tittered behind her hand, and Lady Hungate laughed outright.

But the countess's eyes narrowed as she rose. "Now is as good a time as any. Not for shooting at people, of course, but birds will do. And I've been known to fire a weapon a time or two myself. Why don't we all go?" She tossed down her book. "There's nothing very entertaining to do here, anyway."

"The men won't like it," Mrs. Talbot interjected.

"Nonsense," Lady Hungate said, with a surreptitious wink at Christabel. "Except for Lord Jenner, our fellows aren't the sporting sort. Mostly they wager on who will hit which partridge when, and how many bushes Mr. Talbot will fell with his flintlock. Might as well liven the afternoon for them, I say. Why not?"

Why not, indeed? Once the ladies were out there, the shooting party was sure to degenerate into another sort of outdoor entertainment, especially on this fine, dry autumn afternoon when an erotic interlude in a meadow would appeal to the decadent tastes of this crowd. Then she and Byrne could sneak off from the rest and come back to the house to search Lord Stokely's room.

"Just to make it interesting," Lady Jenner said, "I'll wager a hundred pounds against that silver fan Byrne gave you that you can't fell three birds before I do."

Christabel clutched her fan. "What makes you think Byrne gave this to me?"

"It's the sort of gift he gives—flashy and vulgar and entirely frivolous."

Little did the woman know. "If you find it so flashy and vulgar," Christabel countered, "why would you wish to gain it in a wager?"

"It obviously has some value, or you wouldn't carry it everywhere."

And Lady Jenner was exactly the sort to want to win a fan from a rival just for spite.

Did she really want to risk her only weapon in a silly wager?

Absolutely. It was high time the woman was taken down a peg. Besides, she could use the money—and it would make her feel less indebted to Byrne.

"Fine," Christabel retorted with a lift of her chin. "I accept your wager."

Chapter Seventeen

*It never hurts to shake up your lover with a
surprise appearance.*
—Anonymous, *Memoirs of a Mistress*

Out in Stokely's park, Gavin stood propped against a tree, vainly attempting to doze while his idiot companions placed bets on which partridge would alight first on an oak farther along the path. He was half-tempted to grab a rifle and scatter the whole damned flock just to end the silly wagering. What fueled this English obsession with frivolous bets? He preferred something more challenging for his wagers, like cards. Something that actually required forethought and skill.

He sighed. It used to amuse him that members of his club would wager on who would come in wearing a red waistcoat or which dog in a pack would be the first to piss on the nearest parked carriage. Lately, however, it had begun to irritate him. He'd spent years clawing his way up to where he was comfortable with this "esteemed" society, and for what? So he could stand around while they wagered on the flight habits of partridges? He'd rather be at his club settling accounts ... or at his estate talking to the steward about what winter crop to plant in the east fields.

And that scared him. Perhaps his half brothers were right—perhaps he *was* headed into his dotage. Why else had he begun to find Stokely's games so tiresome? Why else had he so viciously divested Markham of his rig last night, simply because the man had earlier referred to Christabel's diddies?

It wasn't old age setting in—it was *her*, his impudent new mistress. Clearly the woman addled his brain. He craved her constantly, thought of her even when she wasn't near. Having her in his bed should have sated his need or at least lowered it to normal levels. Instead it had honed it to a sharp, persistent ache. Damn the woman.

As if his thoughts had drawn her, he glanced over to see the women heading up the hill toward them with some mission in mind, Christabel at the fore. Look at her—the bloody chit stalked into battle like a Joan of Arc, only with lusher curves and prettier hair.

His blood quickened. He could easily get used to wrapping himself in that wealth of raven locks every night, to falling asleep with his hand on her hip, to waking with her snuggled close in his arms and making love to her while—

Damn, he'd grown aroused by the mere sight of her coming up a hill. What was next, maudlin spoutings of romantic verse and useless sentiment?

"Have a care, gentlemen," he said to his companions, who hadn't noticed what was going on behind them. "The hen brigade is approaching."

"What?" Stokely turned and spotted the women coming, then laughed. "Notice anything interesting about this particular group of women, Byrne?"

With a snort, Gavin pushed away from the tree. Stokely and his bloody sense of humor—one of these days, someone would pin his ears back for his idiocy. "You mean, other than the fact that they look rather determined? If I were you, Stokely, I'd be worried. Whenever women get together and start talking, it usually means trouble for the host."

"Ah, but that's *your* mistress heading up the pack," Stokely said dryly. "If anyone's in trouble, it's probably you."

Gavin scowled. Stokely might be right. It couldn't be good that every woman in the group had once been connected to him. "Good afternoon, ladies," he called down the hill. "Missed us, did you?"

Lady Hungate laughed. "Hardly, you rascal. We've come to join the shooting. Lady Jenner has challenged Lady Haversham to a match. They've even laid a wager on it."

The other men erupted into laughter, probably because they thought the woman was joking. Gavin knew better. Eleanor's husband might be a fool and entirely incapable of pleasing his wife in bed, but he was a true sportsman, and early in their marriage, he'd foolishly taught his wife how to shoot. Gavin knew for a fact that Eleanor had taken to it like a cat to cream. And Christabel—

"What are the terms of the wager?" Gavin asked, as the women reached the top of the hill and milled around Eleanor and Christabel.

Christabel met his gaze coolly. "A hundred pounds against my fan that she can fell three birds before I can."

That was all it took to have the other gentlemen placing their own side bets and the servants scrambling down the hill to fetch more rifles. Gavin shot Christabel a questioning glance, but nothing in her expression indicated the reason for this sudden wager. He'd thought she was searching the mansion all this time. Not that he'd expected her to find the letters, but he'd hoped that searching would keep her out of trouble while he went shooting with the gentlemen.

Yet here she was, surrounded by a bevy of his former mistresses, preparing for a shooting match. Even when Christabel tried to stay out of trouble, trouble found her.

"Byrne? Are you going to wager?" Stokely called out.

"Certainly. Put me down for twenty pounds on Lady Haversham to win."

Talbot duly noted that in the book he kept for these impulsive wagers.

"The same for me," Stokely said with a smirk. "I daresay any woman who can put a hole in a man's hat at fifty yards can shoot a partridge."

The men snickered.

"How do you know she was aiming for his hat?" Eleanor said with a sniff. "I'd have aimed lower."

"Could we not discuss the many areas of my person that women wish to shoot?" Gavin drawled. "It makes me nervous with so many loaded rifles lying about."

"If you weren't such a stickler for settling gambling debts at once," Talbot pointed out, "no one would ever want to shoot you."

Gavin knew the man was alluding to Markham, but he didn't care. "If I weren't such a stickler for settling gambling debts, I'd be poor. And the rest of you would have to go to White's and put up with bad food and even worse liquor."

Talbot chuckled. "True, true. But perhaps we should follow Lord Haversham's example and have our wives greet you with a flintlock when you come calling for your money."

"It was a repeater rifle," Christabel said grimly, "and my husband eventually paid his debt. As well he should have."

Gavin raised an eyebrow at her, but Lady Jenner snorted. "Perhaps if you had come to London with your husband from time to time, he wouldn't have been so free with his funds at the gaming tables in the first place."

As Christabel paled, Gavin prepared to retort, but Stokely beat him to it. "Haversham didn't want his wife in town. He told me that himself. He was a very jealous man—he feared she might fall under the influence of gentlemen like myself. And Byrne there."

"That's ridiculous," Christabel snapped. "He didn't want me in town because he didn't want me interfering with his visits to his mistress."

Stokely eyed her askance. "Mistress? He didn't have one. He certainly would have said something if he had. If anything, he was pathetically besotted with you. Couldn't stop boasting about his beautiful, clever wife whom none of us would ever get to meet because we weren't good enough for her."

Christabel looked thunderstruck. Gavin frowned. Damn it, what idiot had managed to convince her that Haversham possessed a mistress? And what purpose could it possibly have served, except to wound her feelings?

The servants had returned and were loading several rifles for each of the women. Christabel watched them silently, her face now impossible to read.

"Watch it, Byrne," Talbot said jovially, "Lady Haversham is eyeing those rifles awfully closely. Hope you didn't do anything last night to set her off, or she might take Lady Jenner's suggestion to heart and aim a bit lower." He punctuated his comment with a vulgar thrust of his hips.

Gavin glanced at Christabel, who merely rolled her eyes at Talbot. Hard to believe she was the same woman who'd been so shocked by the man in London. She'd adapted remarkably well, and he couldn't help admiring that.

He glanced over to find Anna watching him watch Christabel, and he gave the woman a cool nod. If Anna had been in Christabel's place, forced to masquerade for a cause . . .

He couldn't even imagine it. The woman hadn't had the spine to stand up to her own parents; she would hardly have the spine to embark on a scheme to save them from harm. Even now, she looked extremely uncomfortable with this adventure. But then she'd never been adventurous. Indeed, she'd been rather predictable, fond of gifts and outings and as frivolous as any other young woman at her come-out. Her father had spoiled her, and she was comfortable with that.

If they'd succeeded in marrying, she'd undoubtedly have been miserable within a month. Her father would have disowned her, so Gavin's early years as a gaming club owner would have been spent struggling to keep it afloat while his wife complained of his late hours and plagued him to spend money on lofty furnishings, a better house, and a barouche to impress her friends.

Perhaps Anna had unwittingly done him a favor. He would probably not be where he was now if he'd married her. And he couldn't have given her the title and status that she'd needed to be happy. Whereas Christabel . . .

He glanced over to where she was examining the rifles. What if he'd met Christabel all those years ago? What if he'd been the one to leap to her rescue in Gibraltar?

A nonsensical notion. He'd never leaped to anyone's rescue in his life. Still, if he'd met her at an assembly and courted her as he'd courted Anna, he suspected *she* would not have hesitated to hie off to Gretna Green with him, family approval or no. Christabel had an intoxicating tendency to throw herself heart and soul into everything she did. As a man who'd regulated all his actions for most of his life, he found that immensely refreshing, so refreshing that he could almost imagine—

An absurd idea. Christabel had told him she had no desire to subject herself to the rule of another man. He certainly had no desire to subject himself to the whims of a wife. Absolutely not.

His companions had now grouped themselves on either side of the ladies. Talbot offered to hand Eleanor her rifles, and Kingsley offered to hand Christabel hers.

Stokely dictated the rules. "The beaters will flush the partridges, and I will count down to the start. Talbot will keep track of the birds Lady Jenner fells, and Kingsley will keep track of Lady Haversham's. Once each has felled three, whoever fired last is the loser, and I shall determine who that is. All right?"

Everyone nodded their agreement. After asking the ladies if they were ready, Stokely ordered the beaters out to the fields. As the birds broke into flight, Stokely said, "On the count of three . . . One, two, three—"

The noise was deafening as each woman fired the one shot from her loaded rifle, tossed it aside, then grabbed another and so on until each had fired three times. Even before the smoke cleared, Gavin could tell that Eleanor had fired the last shot. So why was she beaming with triumph as she set down her rifle?

"Lady Haversham finished shooting first," Stokely declared. "Talbot and Kingsley, what is the count?"

"Lady Jenner took down three partridges," Talbot announced, gesturing to different points of the field.

Kingsley looked uneasy. "Lady Haversham shot down two partridges."

"And a blackbird," Christabel added. "That's three birds in all."

The dogs were indeed sniffing something in the grass where she pointed. Kingsley went to investigate, then announced cheerily, "It's a blackbird all right, neatly taken down with one shot."

Eleanor's expression turned thunderous. "Blackbirds don't count," she snapped. "Only partridges."

"I beg your pardon," Christabel retorted, "but the wager was for the first person to fell three birds."

"Three partridges," Eleanor countered.

"Sorry, Eleanor," Lady Hungate put in, "but you did say birds."

"The men are out here shooting partridges," Eleanor complained. "So I assumed that we meant partridges."

"If the point was to determine who was the better shot," Gavin said, "the point has been made, whether it's birds or partridges."

"But we all understood it to be partridges," Eleanor spat. "And she knows it." She stalked up to Christabel with her hand outstretched. "You know you lost, so give me that fan."

"I will not!" Christabel backed away from the woman. "And *you* owe me a hundred pounds."

Lady Jenner snatched one of the still-loaded rifles from a nearby servant and leveled it on Christabel. "Give me the fan, you little bitch."

Gavin's heart dropped into his belly. "It was just a bloody wager, Eleanor. If you want, we can do another trial and specify partridges—"

Stokely came up behind Eleanor and grabbed her gun, jerking the barrel up in the air. It went off, the ball hurtling up at the massive oak branch above them.

Seconds later, when Eleanor let out a bloodcurdling scream, Gavin realized that the ball had ricocheted off the branch to hit the trunk, then ricocheted back at Eleanor. The others turned just in time to see her lifting her skirts to reveal her left boot ripped open and blood gushing from her ankle.

Eleanor took one look at the blood and fainted. Chaos ensued—ladies rushed to her side or looked faint, while the gentlemen stamped about chastising Stokely for his precipitous action and belatedly ordering the footmen to empty the other loaded rifles.

"Stand aside!" Christabel ordered, striding over to where Lord Jenner sat in the grass, cradling Eleanor's head in his lap as the other ladies crowded round.

The ladies parted to let her approach. Eleanor was just coming to, but as she saw Christabel loom over her, she cried, "Keep the murderous woman away from me! She tried to kill me!"

"Don't be ridiculous," Christabel snapped as she knelt beside her. "You shot yourself. Now let me see that ankle."

Eleanor tugged her leg back from Christabel, then let out a yelp at the pain.

"Oh, for God's sake, let her look at it," Gavin seconded, coming up beside the women. "Lady Haversham spent years traveling with the army. I'm sure she's dressed a wound or two."

"Indeed I have," Christabel said. "Come now, it won't hurt to let me look."

Though Eleanor's expression was mutinous, she didn't resist as Christabel drew her leg out and examined it with surprising gentleness.

"It looks like just a flesh wound, but it will have to be cleaned before I can be sure that the ball didn't fracture a bone." Christabel lifted her gaze to Stokely. "You should call for a surgeon. This is beyond my limited skill."

"It shall be done at once," Stokely said, looking a bit green about the gills as he called a footman over and ordered him to Salisbury to fetch the surgeon.

"We need to get her inside," Christabel said, turning her gaze to Gavin.

Muttering a curse, he bent and picked Eleanor up, then carried her down the hill toward the house. He could have told one of the footmen to do it, but Eleanor was already accusing Christabel of shooting her—if anything happened to her between Christabel's brief treatment of her and the surgeon's arrival, she'd blame that on Christabel, too. He wasn't about to allow that.

Eleanor glared up at him. "Your new friend is a nuisance, Byrne. She doesn't belong here."

"No, she doesn't," he answered tersely. "She's too good for the likes of us. But she happens to be excellent at whist, and I happen to be fond of her, so I intend to keep her around. And that means I will be decidedly irritated if something were to happen to her." He cast her a cold glance. "Understood?"

Eleanor's face whitened before she glanced away. "Understood."

Thank God the bitch knew better than to cross him. Because right now, he could easily strangle her for threatening to shoot Christabel.

Once they got her inside, and the surgeon finally arrived, the man's examination revealed that the ball had only nicked the bone, but her flesh would require stitching. Although the surgeon advised her against participating in outdoor activities for a few weeks, he said that a night's rest would probably be all it took to get her up and around enough to play cards. He insisted that she not do any card-playing that night, a decree that sent Eleanor into wails of outrage, since the eliminations were to begin then.

Only after she'd elicited Stokely's promise to suspend the eliminations—and all whist games entirely—for one night did she agree to let the surgeon administer laudanum for the pain.

Then Gavin and Christabel followed Stokely, Talbot, and the surgeon out of Eleanor's bedchamber. As the other three men walked ahead of them down the stairs, in deep conversation with the surgeon, Gavin offered Christabel his arm.

"Congratulations," he quipped. "You managed to eviscerate Eleanor without turning a card."

She glared at him. "It isn't *my* fault that the woman shot herself. And you know perfectly well I won that match."

"I'm only teasing you, my sweet. Trust me, no one blames you. If anything, I blame myself. Eleanor isn't usually that foolish, but she was smarting over how I humiliated her lover. Since she chose to take it out on you, I concede that I probably shouldn't have pushed Markham so far last night."

"Or slept with every woman in creation," Christabel muttered.

"What?"

"Nothing. But now that we don't have to worry about cards tonight, I have the perfect way for us to spend the evening."

He took one look at the gleam in her eyes and groaned. "Please tell me that what you're thinking of involves bedsheets and a chilled bottle of good Madeira."

She eyed him askance. "I know where the letters are. They're somewhere in Lord Stokely's room. I went there to search earlier, but the door was locked. So all we have to do is pick the lock—"

"We? Do you have yet another skill I was unaware of?"

"Well, no, but surely you could—"

"I've had a relatively checkered past, I'll admit, but thievery wasn't part of it." That was perfectly true, but it didn't mean he couldn't pick a lock. Not that he wanted *her* to know that. He meant for her to be sound asleep when he searched Stokely's bedchamber. If Stokely was fool enough to keep the letters there.

"But you said you could get into any safe—" She broke off at the sight of a footman rushing up the stairs toward them.

He held out a sealed note. "An urgent message has come for you, sir."

His heart thundering in his chest, Gavin murmured a thank-you and took it. He read it quickly, then tucked it in his waistcoat pocket so she couldn't get a look at it. "I have to go to Bath."

"*Now?*" she asked. "But, Byrne, the eliminations—"

"They won't start until tomorrow. I can be there and back before then." He chucked her under the chin. "Don't worry, my sweet, I won't abandon you to the wolves at the card tables."

Her eyes narrowed. "And while you're gone, I can search Lord Stokely's room. I suppose I could try sneaking in while he's asleep—"

"Don't be ridiculous," he said, his heart skipping a beat at the very thought of her in Stokely's room in the dead of night. "And that won't be possible anyway. Because you're going to Bath with me."

Chapter Eighteen

I never allowed any man to insult me. Just because I was a mistress didn't mean I had to endure rudeness.
—Anonymous, *Memoirs of a Mistress*

Christabel could tell from Byrne's expression that he hadn't meant to say that. His dismay was almost comical. But then his eyes grew steely. "You're coming with me to Bath. Now."

She was tempted to refuse: At last she had a chance to search for the letters without him around. But getting into Lord Stokely's room could prove tricky, and if the baron had a safe there, she couldn't break into that. No matter what Byrne said, he probably knew exactly how to pick locks. So a trip to Bath would give her the chance to talk him into helping her do just that.

All right, so she was making excuses—the truth was, she wanted to go with him because she wanted to see his estate, wanted to get a glimpse of the real Byrne that no one else had.

"I'll have to take Rosa," she said.

"If you're worried about your reputation you'd be better off leaving her here, since we'll have to stay at my estate overnight. She can make the others think you never left. We'll only be gone one night, so you don't need a bag. If you meet me down the road, Rosa can tell anyone who asks that the incident with Lady Jenner left you feeling unwell. Then not even other servants will be able to enter your room to determine if you're there."

He had a point. And though she suspected that her reputation was already damaged beyond repair, it couldn't hurt to keep this trip a secret. "All right."

"I leave within the half hour. I'll meet you down by those hedges on the far lawn. They'll shield you from view of the house."

Then he was gone. She barely had time to stuff a few essentials into one of her old large reticules and instruct Rosa on what she should tell people, before it was time to meet Byrne.

Only after they were well away from Stokely's estate, did she relax. "Did you tell Lord Stokely you were leaving?"

Byrne nodded. "The bastard seemed inordinately pleased. He probably thinks he'll get the chance to seduce you, now that I'm gone."

"I don't understand his interest in me—though we might be able to use it."

A scowl knit his brow. "How so?"

"Well, you said you don't know how to pick locks." She smiled innocently. "If we can't figure out any other way to get into Lord Stokely's bedchamber, then I can always cozy up to him so that he brings me—"

"No," he said tersely. "You will not do any such thing."

"I'm not saying I would share his bed; just that I'd let him have a kiss and flirt a little until he invites me there."

Byrne's face was stormy. "Once there, you'd end up in his bed whether you wanted to be or not."

Christabel stiffened. "Don't you trust me not to allow a man to seduce me?"

"I'm not talking about seduction, lass. I'm talking about force. He'd call you a tease and do as he wished, feeling justified that any woman who came to his bedchamber meant to share his bed, no matter what she said. And no one would fault him for it, either."

"I can handle myself with him, and you can always stand outside and wait for me to call out if I'm in trouble—"

"No, it's too dangerous. I won't let you whore for those letters."

There was that word again. "Aren't I doing that already?" she asked quietly.

A deadly stillness came over him. "Are you saying you shared my bed only to gain my help?"

"Of course not. But the fact remains that thanks to this scheme, I began sharing your bed."

A curse erupted from him. "You are not a whore, Christabel."

"What am I then?"

"My mistress."

Like all the others. All the many others. Her throat grew painfully tight. "I see little difference between a whore and a mistress." Though the past two days with him had been mostly heaven, the reality of her position had plagued her conscience. "You're funding my part in these card games. You bought my gowns. Isn't a whore someone who exchanges her favors for financial gain?"

Anger tightened his features. "I'll grant you that a mistress does that, too. But there's a difference."

"Oh?" She trod dangerous ground—his mother had played that role for Prinny, after all. But she had to make him understand. "Aside from the fact that a whore has encounters with several customers and a mistress has several encounters with one, I'm not sure I see the difference."

The word "customer" made him flinch. "Then you haven't seen what I've seen, or you'd *know* the difference." He leaned forward. "I spent my entire boyhood around whores. You've never had a man beat you until you were blue. Or break your arm with impunity because he knew nothing would be done about it. You've never had to go out hunting for men just to gain the blunt to purchase a few hours sleep in a flea-ridden bed with three other women huddled together because there's no heat. You've never had to watch while a gin-soaked workman in the depths of despair slits his own throat, which, by the way, is the method of choice for killing oneself in Drury Lane—"

"Byrne, enough." Her heart ached at the thought that he'd seen such things probably before he was old enough even to understand them.

He breathed heavily, his eyes almost feral. Slowly, he calmed himself. After a few short breaths, he said, "The point is, you're not remotely a whore."

She hesitated. Should she continue to press him when he was so upset? She had to; he still didn't understand. "You seem to be saying that the difference between a whore and a mistress is one of station. Granted, the life of women in Drury Lane is pitiable, but that doesn't change the fact that both mistresses and whores take money in exchange for their favors."

A muscle worked in his jaw. "You're forgetting that one has a choice, and the other doesn't."

She thrust out her chin. "In what way does a mistress have a choice?"

"She can refuse to share her lover's bed, for one thing."

"She won't last long as a mistress if she does that often," Christabel said dryly. "And a whore can choose not to take a customer if she pleases."

"Damn it, you are not a whore!" he cried, clenching his fists in his lap. "Fine, you don't believe me? I'll show you the difference." Jerking down the window shades, he settled back against his seat, his eyes icily bleak. "Unbutton your gown."

She blinked at him. "What?"

"You're my whore, remember? I bought and paid for you. So unbutton your gown. Now!"

Her eyes narrowed, but her pride wouldn't let her back down and let him win the argument. "Fine." She did as he bade. "Anything else, sir?" she said, the words deliberately sarcastic.

His face was a rigid mask. "Show me your bubs."

Though the crude word brought her up short, it had another entirely unexpected effect. It aroused her. She couldn't imagine why, unless it was because it reminded her of stripping for him when they'd played Whist for the Wicked.

So although it took her some effort to get her gown and chemise unfastened and lowered to her short corset without any help from him, she managed it. And she gained a measure of satisfaction from his surprised look that said he really hadn't expected her to comply.

"Now touch yourself," he said hoarsely.

"I beg your pardon?"

The chill had left his eyes, replaced by a heat that sent the blood roaring through her veins. "Caress your breasts. Your nipples. So I can watch. That's what I like. To watch."

Fire leaped up through her, blooming into a blush in her cheeks. But she couldn't help noticing he hadn't called them "bubs" again. "All right," she said, her voice coming out sultry rather than merely compliant.

Gavin couldn't believe what he was seeing. Moment by moment he was losing control of the lesson he'd meant to teach her, but how could he have known the bloody wench would take to this so well?

Her eyes heavy-lidded, she rubbed first one breast, then the other, until the nipples tightened into tempting peaks. Until he had to forcibly suppress the urge to leap across the carriage and suck her lush breasts until she begged him for more.

He wouldn't do it, damn it! He wouldn't let her bloody stubbornness turn this into a seduction. He meant to prove to her once and for all that what they had wasn't the same as the sordid association between a whore and her customer.

Unfastening his trousers and drawers, he shoved them down just enough to free his rampant erection. "Now," he ground out, "suck my cock." Somehow he managed to add in a choked tone, "Whore."

That certainly had the desired effect. She blanched, her lower lip trembling. "I don't . . . understand."

"What's there to understand? You take my cock in your mouth, and you suck it until I find release. The same way I find release inside your . . . honeypot." He couldn't bring himself to use the crude word for that with her. He just couldn't. "Get down on your knees and suck my cock. That's one of the 'favors' I paid for, remember?"

For a moment, he was sure she'd balk. Even the most adventurous of his mistresses rarely performed that service for him, so he knew for damned sure Christabel would never do it.

Even after she fell to her knees on the floor between them, he thought a jolt of the carriage had thrown her there. But he should have known better—apparently Colonel Christabel would do almost anything to keep him from winning an argument.

He stared in unmitigated shock as she leaned forward and took the crown of his cock in her mouth. Bloody, bloody hell.

He caught her head in his hands, meaning to drag it away, but instinct made him urge it closer, until she'd enfolded most of him in her hot mouth. God, it felt so good. But when she began to suck, he knew he was in trouble, for it was all he could do not to explode right then and there inside her mouth.

"Enough," he growled, pulling her head back until his cock slipped free of her mouth. "You can't do this."

"Why not?" She gazed up at him with a mocking smile. Then abruptly it faded. "Oh, I'm doing it wrong."

Belatedly, he remembered what she'd said about her husband, about how she thought she hadn't pleased him in bed. "If you do it any more right, you'll pleasure me out of my mind, lass. That's not the point."

"Oh?" The mocking gleam had returned to her eyes. "Then what is the point? I'm only doing what you paid for me to—"

He hauled the determined wench up onto his lap. "You are *not* a whore." He seized her mouth to blot out the words she was sure to throw at him now that she thought she'd won this argument.

Not that she had. *Isn't a whore someone who exchanges her favors for financial gain?*

Damn her! He kissed her wildly, determined to erase from her mind the notion that she was his paid whore. She wasn't.

Then what am I?

He'd show her what she was. Even if he wasn't sure of it himself.

She tore her mouth from his. "Byrne—"

"Shh," he murmured, scattering kisses over her impossibly soft skin as he slipped his hand up under her skirts. "Let me make love to you, darling."

"No, it's my turn." Brushing his hands aside, she began to work loose his cravat. "I understand that a woman can make love to a man as easily as he can make love to her."

He drew back to stare at her in surprise. "And where did you hear that?"

"From your other mistresses." She removed his coat, then unbuttoned his waistcoat. "We had a very interesting conversation about how to please a man."

He groaned. "I'm not sure I like the sound of that."

Mischief filled her face. "Why not?" She took her time about undoing his shirt, which put him even more on his guard.

"Because given your military bent, you're likely to use such knowledge to bring me to my knees."

"You mean the way you brought me to my knees just now?" She tugged his shirt off over his head. Then she ran one finger down the center of his chest to his belly and lower.

But when she dragged her forefinger along the length of his cock only to tease the tip, he caught her hand, and growled, "Don't even think it, my sweet."

"What?" she said innocently.

"You are not going to pay me back for what I did earlier by tormenting me for hours with your devilish little hand. I want to be inside you. Now."

"Certainly, sir," she said, with that falsely compliant tone of before. "Anything to please the customer."

"Christabel—" he began in a warning tone.

"You didn't bring your French letters, did you?"

Damn. He hadn't. "Forget my French letters." He shifted her on his lap so he could divest her of her gown, then went to work on her corset laces.

"Ah, but do we dare?" she taunted him. "According to Lady Jenner, you never do without them, because you see your mistresses as 'whor—"

"To hell with Lady Jenner." He finished with her corset and practically ripped it off her. "And if you use the word *whore* in connection with yourself one more time, I swear I'll stop the carriage and make you walk to Bath."

She laughed. "No, you won't." She reached down to fondle his arousal. "Because then you couldn't satisfy *this*." When he merely glared at her, her smile faded. She kissed his mouth until some of the tension left him, then drew back, eyes solemn. "Why does it bother you so to think of me as a whore?"

"Because you're not one. And because I don't like your feeling that you are."

She stayed his hand as he reached to shove off her chemise. "You once told me you didn't care about the feelings of your mistresses."

"I don't," he said hoarsely. "But I damned well care about yours." God, she really was turning him into a blithering, besotted idiot. And at the moment, he didn't give a damn.

But she was staring at him with those solemn eyes again. "Why?"

Shrugging off her hold on his hand, he removed her chemise. "Why what?"

"Why do you care about my feelings, when you've never cared about the feelings of your other mistresses? How am I any different?"

Bloody hell. "I thought you were going to make love to me," he countered. He set her aside long enough to shove off his drawers and trousers in one quick motion, then pulled her back to straddle his lap. "So get to it, will you?"

The sudden gleam in her eyes should have warned him. But even after she'd lifted herself to come down on his cock, encasing him in her delicious heat, he didn't realize what she was up to. Until she stopped there, her gaze meeting his with mischievous intent.

"What makes me any different, Byrne?" she asked again. Slowly, she drew up on her knees, inch by inch making him groan.

"God preserve me from teasing wenches," he complained as he tried futilely to make her increase her motions.

Licking her finger, she rubbed it over her nipple. "You did say you like to watch. Or was that just a lie?"

His cock swelled to unimaginable hardness inside her. "Not a . . . lie . . ." With a low curse, he thrust his pelvis up at her. "Come on, Christabel—"

"How am I any different?" she asked again.

She was going to wring it out of him somehow, wasn't she? That's what he got for letting her anywhere near his former mistresses.

"You're honest and direct," he bit out. "You don't play games." He lifted one eyebrow. "Except in the bedchamber."

As a smile broke over her face, she began to move. It was slow, but steady, a torturous ecstasy that made him writhe beneath her. "What else?" she prodded.

He was nearly out of his mind already, and she'd barely started to make love to him. For a woman who'd only recently learned how to find her own pleasure, she certainly knew how to make a man work for his. But God, was it blissful work. "You . . . don't . . . treat me like . . . a never-ending . . . fountain of gifts."

She laughed. "Who does that?"

"Every mistress . . . I've ever had," he choked out. "Except you."

With a smile, she increased her motions until he thought he would die from the sheer joy of being inside her, hearing her laugh, seeing her face aglow and her eyes alight. For him. Because of him.

"A-Anything . . . else?" she managed as she rode him harder, her glorious hair a-tumble and her lush breasts bouncing so enticingly that he couldn't keep from grabbing one in his mouth and sucking it until she gasped. "Why, Byrne?" she whispered. "Why do you . . . care about . . . *my* feelings?"

He tore his mouth from her breast to rasp, "Because you . . . make me . . . want to be good. And no one . . . *no one* . . . has ever done that."

She clasped his head to her breast. "That's odd. You make *me* . . . want to be . . . bad."

He could feel his orgasm building, thundering toward the peak. Quickly, he reached down and fingered her between the legs until he felt her muscles tightening around his cock, milking it, urging him higher and higher.

"Then perhaps we . . . can meet . . . in the middle . . . my darling."

A cry erupted from her throat as she clutched him tightly to her breasts. He followed right after her, spilling himself inside her with a hoarse growl of satisfaction.

A long time later, after they'd finished and Christabel lay cradled in his lap, he realized he'd never felt such contentment in his life. The soothing rumble of the carriage wheels cocooned them in a private world he could stay in forever. In the past, being alone with a mistress after making love had made him restless.

With Christabel, it felt like heaven.

"Byrne?"

"Hmm?" he asked, stroking her arm.

"Was Lord Stokely right? Did Philip really not have a mistress?"

He sighed. That she could think of her husband right now somewhat dampened his enjoyment. "Does it matter?"

She lifted her gaze to his. "If he had a mistress, it means I wasn't enough to make him happy."

"No," he said fiercely, "it doesn't mean that in the least. It means he was too much an idiot to realize what a treasure he held in his hand."

She eyed him askance. "Is that why all your friends have lovers and mistresses? Because they're idiots?"

"Not *all* my friends are incapable of fidelity. Draker and Iversley are faithful to their wives, and their wives adore them."

"Yes," she said consideringly, "there is that."

There *was* that. If his brothers were any indication, fidelity was indeed possible in a marriage. But would it last? Could it?

"As for my other so-called friends," he said, "their marriages were built on practicality rather than affection. When people choose spouses for the financial and social assets they bring to the marriage, they may not always find ones whose company they actually enjoy."

Her voice turned bitter. "And sometimes, even when a marriage is built on mutual affection, one's spouse might come to dislike one's company enough to seek another's."

He held her closer, brushing his lips over her frowning brow. "Haversham clearly did like your company, from what he said to Stokely. If he had any mistress at all, it was gambling." He shook his head. "I've seen gambling turn father against son, mother against daughter, and husband against wife. It had nothing to do with you, my sweet. The obsession was probably there long before you came along. And once Haversham had the leisure to gamble whenever he pleased, there would have been no reasoning with him."

She curled against his shoulder. "So you don't think he had a mistress?"

"I never heard anything about him and other women. Apparently no one else did, either." When she merely digested that in silence, he added, "Who told you that he had a mistress?"

She reached for the carriage blanket lying folded on the seat across from them, then pulled it up to cover them both. "It doesn't matter. I probably jumped to conclusions—"

"Who, Christabel? Tell me."

She swallowed. "His Highness."

He stiffened. "Prinny? *He's* the arse who told you Haversham had a mistress?"

"It wasn't like that. I'm not sure he meant to imply—"

"Tell me exactly what he said." When she bristled at his commanding tone, he nuzzled her hair to soften her. "And how did you come to discuss such a thing with the prince, anyway?"

She sighed. "The first time I became aware of the missing letters was when I was called to London for a private audience. The prince claimed that my husband had apparently sold my father's letters. He was unsure how much I knew, but I admitted at once that I knew what letters he meant and what was in them. Then he said that Lord Stokely was threatening to publish them if His Highness did not . . . give him a certain boon."

"What sort of boon?" When she remained silent, Gavin took her by the chin and turned her face to his. "Come now, lass, surely it can't hurt for you to tell me what Stokely wants for them. I've already guessed that they concern Prinny as much as your father, so you won't be revealing that."

She stared at him a long moment before uttering a heartfelt sigh. "I suppose not." Her tone grew steely. "The impudent scoundrel wants His Highness to broker a marriage between him and Princess Charlotte, now that her engagement to the Prince of Orange has fallen through."

Gavin stared at her, stunned. "Is he insane?"

"Not entirely. She once carried on a clandestine correspondence with a handsome captain of the guards, so I suppose Lord Stokely figured that a baron would be an improvement over that."

"I seriously doubt that her father sees it that way. According to Draker, Prinny means for Charlotte to make a politically advantageous match."

Christabel nodded. "You can be sure that the prince has no desire to wed Princess Charlotte to Lord Stokely. But Lord Stokely seems determined to gain her as a wife."

"I suppose he's grown tired of being on the outside of society, even if he did put himself there with his scandalous house parties and wild living. Perhaps he thinks marrying a princess will erase his bad reputation."

"That makes sense. But it doesn't make his blackmail any less reprehensible."

"No," he agreed, though not wholeheartedly. After all, if he got his own hands on the letters, he meant to use them to gain something for himself, too. But at least he wasn't aiming to marry the princess and drag *her* into it. That made him less a villain than Stokely. Didn't it?

And why did it matter how much a villain he was, anyway? When it came to Prinny, any villainy against the man was justified. "Go on. Prinny told you about Stokely's threats, and . . ."

"I couldn't believe Philip betrayed my trust by selling my family's letters to Lord Stokely. So I told the prince that Lord Stokely had to be lying about having them. Even after the prince showed me the one letter Lord Stokely had sent as proof, I protested Philip's involvement. But he said it was either Philip or me or . . . or someone else close to him . . . like . . . like . . ."

Tears filled her eyes, making an unfamiliar knot form in Gavin's gut. "Like?" he prodded.

"Ph-Philip's mistress." She started to cry, and he wound his arms more tightly about her, cursing Prinny to hell. "I told him Philip didn't . . . ha-have a mistress . . . and he pointed out that I wouldn't know if he did . . . and the discussion ended there. I was too . . . shocked and numb . . . to ask who she was."

Brushing away her tears, she pulled herself together. After a moment, she continued in a muted tone. "I assumed that the prince knew for sure that Philip had one. But now that I look back, he was probably speculating. And after he raised the possibility, it made sense to me—Philip came to town so often, and he never wanted me to accompany him."

"Was it during that meeting that Prinny got you to agree to this scheme?"

She nodded.

"*Damn* him to hell. You were distraught, and he took advantage."

"You don't think he deliberately mentioned the mistress, do you?"

"I don't know. Possibly. But Prinny is so cynical about marriage and women that he could have merely assumed Haversham had one."

She stared up at his face. "You really dislike His Highness, don't you?"

"Hate and loathe would be more like it."

She caressed his cheek with her hand. "My father used to say that hatred only hurts the hater; it does nothing to affect the hated. Which makes it an impractical emotion."

It was the first time she'd mentioned her father in days, and her deeply affectionate tone gave him pause. "How badly would it hurt your father if these letters are published?"

She swallowed. "It depends on how the scandal plays out and which political party wins the ensuing fight. The best scenario is that he might lose his commission and be disgraced; the worst is that he'd be hanged for treason."

Bloody hell, what the devil was *in* these letters? And what would happen to *her* if Gavin got his hands on them?

Nothing would happen to her, he vowed as he tightened his arms about her. He wasn't going to publish the letters himself—just use them to make Prinny admit the truth about his mother to the world.

"Well, none of that will happen," he said firmly. "We'll make sure of that. *I'll* make sure of it."

As if that solved everything, she flashed him a tender smile, then rested her head against his chest.

But long after she'd fallen asleep, he continued to worry. What if he couldn't get the letters from Stokely—what would happen to her then? And was there anything he could do to stop it?

Chapter Nineteen

〜∞〜

Once in a great while, I would find a lover
with true hidden depths.
—Anonymous, *Memoirs of a Mistress*

Christabel was having the strangest dream. She was
floating up into the sky, carried aloft by some gentle
hand. Then it set her on a cloud, and her feet were released from their earthly bindings. A voice somewhere
above her said, "Let her sleep. She needs the rest. She can
stay in her gown a bit longer."

It was the sound of a door closing that awakened her.
Slowly, she opened her eyes to an unfamiliar room lit
only by a blazing fire in the hearth. It hadn't been a
dream. They must have arrived at Byrne's estate. He must
have carried her up the stairs and laid her in this bed with
its incredibly soft down mattress.

Sitting up, she winced as her corset pinched her breasts.
She vaguely remembered waking from her nap in Byrne's
arms to find they were nearing a town where he meant for
them to dine. Byrne had made love to her again, slow and
easy and wonderful. And after dinner, their long ride had
lulled her back to sleep.

She rubbed her eyes, then glanced around for a clock.

Midnight. They'd made good time. But where was Byrne? Did he mean not to share her bed while they were here? That didn't seem likely of her lusty lover.

She surveyed the room more closely. Come to think of it, this didn't *look* like a bedchamber prepared for the master's imminent arrival. Though the fire was starting to warm it, the air was still chilly, and bore the musty smell of a room long in disuse. Most of all, it was far too *pink* to be his, with lacy pink draperies, a pink canopy and coverlet on the delicate bed, and even a pink-and-cream rug. Not a Byrne room at all.

So where was he? Leaving the bed, she went to the door and opened it onto the main hall for the bedchambers. When she heard low voices from a few doors down, she went in stocking feet to explore.

As she drew nearer the last bedchamber, she could make out Byrne speaking to someone. "So the doctor has seen her again? He's sure she's improved?"

Her? Who might that be? Her heart sinking, Christabel edged nearer, careful to stay out of sight of the doorway.

"Yes, sir," said another voice. "I'm sorry that I sent for you."

"I *told* Ada not to," another voice complained, this one reedy and thin, though the tone somehow managed to be imperious. "It's nothing but a piddling cold."

"That's what you always say, even when you're coughing up blood," Byrne replied in the mildly indulgent tone of a man dealing with an invalid. "Fortunately, Ada has known you long enough to ignore you, Mother."

Christabel's heart began to hammer in her chest. Byrne's mother was alive? And living here on his estate? Dear Lord, she couldn't believe it!

What about the fire? Mrs. Byrne was supposed to be dead! Why did he continue to let the world think that she'd died? Though this did explain why he came to Bath whenever he was summoned.

"I'll be here until tomorrow, Ada," Byrne continued, "but I'll have to leave first thing in the morning. If you're sure she's all right."

"Dr. Mays says that she is, sir, but you did tell me—"

"Yes, and you were right to send for me. Thank you, Ada, you may go on to bed now. I need to speak privately to my mother."

"Very good, sir."

The woman's low murmur sent Christabel into a panic, but before she could even hide, the woman left the room and headed down the stairs away from where Christabel lurked in the shadows. She didn't even see her.

Uttering a silent sigh, Christabel edged back toward the door.

Byrne was speaking again. "I brought someone with me on this visit, someone I'd like you to meet."

"Another doctor? Please, Gavin, no more doctors. I'm doing better these days, no matter what Ada says, and Dr. Mays takes good care of me—"

"It's not a doctor," he broke in. "It's a friend. A woman."

"I see." A long silence ensued. "So you've told her about me then."

"Of course not. You vowed me to silence, and I've kept my vow until now." When his mother said nothing, Byrne went on in a tight voice, "I've always abided by your wish to live in the country when I could make you more comfortable in town, and I know how you feel about meeting new people. But I'm asking you to make an exception for her. Please."

A lump lodged in Christabel's throat. She'd never heard Byrne use the word *please* to anyone.

"All right," the woman rasped. "Before you leave in the morning, bring her to me, and I'll speak to her."

"I'll do that, thank you." His voice turned gruffer. "Now let's see about making you more comfortable. This room is too damned cold. And your water jug is half-empty, too. I'll call a servant to come fill it—"

That was all the warning Christabel had before Byrne came out the door and saw her. Caught in the act of being kind, he blinked at her like a fox startled by the hounds.

"Gavin?" his mother called out when he just stood there without summoning a servant. "What's wrong?"

He let out a breath. Then a slow smile curved up his lips. "It appears you'll be meeting my guest sooner rather than later, Mother."

"I-I'm sorry," Christabel stammered. "I didn't mean to pry . . . I woke up, and you weren't—"

"It's all right." He offered her his arm. "Come. Let me introduce you."

Painfully aware of her rumpled gown and her lack of shoes, she touched a hand to her fallen hair, and said, "Oh, Byrne, I don't know—"

"She won't care about that, I promise you," he said with a trace of irony. "Come on."

Taking his arm, Christabel let him lead her into the room. A massive half-tester bed presided over the darkest corner of what must have once been the master bed-chamber. Now it was a sickroom, the pungent odor of medicinal concoctions mingling with the sweet scent of freshly cut roses.

She couldn't see much in the dimly lit room, but the furnishings appeared feminine—delicate Windsor chairs, an elegant dressing table, and drapes in pretty prints that were probably cheery in the morning with the sun pouring in through the two massive windows. The bed itself wasn't cheery in the least, however, for its hangings draped its inhabitant in impenetrable shadows.

Byrne led her near it. "May I present my friend Christabel, the Marchioness of Haversham. Christabel, this is my mother, Sally Byrne."

"Good evening, my lady," his mother said in a taut whisper. "And where is your husband this fine night?"

"She's a widow," Byrne bit out.

Not sure what else to do, Christabel gave a little curtsy. "I'm very pleased to make your acquaintance, Mrs. Byrne."

Apparently that amused his mother, for a reedy laugh sounded from the depths of the bed. "Are you indeed? Never thought to have a marchioness in my bedchamber claiming the pleasure of my acquaintance." A gnarled hand emerged from the shadows, beckoning to her. "Come closer, dear. Let me look at you."

Swallowing, Christabel approached the bed. She could now make out a small form practically swallowed up by the night. But though the face was hidden, the eyes reflected the candlelight to play over her with an insulting scrutiny.

"She's a pretty one, I'll grant you that," Mrs. Byrne finally said. "But short."

"Mother," he warned, "be nice."

"It's all right," Christabel put in wryly, "there are plenty of times when I find shortness to be a defect myself."

The woman chuckled, then coughed. "I'm almost as short as you, so if it's a defect, it's one we share. Don't know how I managed to produce anything as tall as that rascal standing next to you."

Silence fell as they all thought the same thing: The prince was tall.

"Gavin," his mother added, "would you go fill that water jug for me while I chat with your friend?"

"Why?" he demanded. "So you can pummel her with questions about her character and her family?"

"Don't be impertinent, boy," the woman declared, though her affection came through in every syllable. "You're not too big that I can't still rap your knuckles."

That brought a reluctant smile to his lips. He turned to Christabel. "That was Mother's favorite punishment— knuckle-rapping. It's a miracle I can even hold a deck of cards."

"Indeed it is, since I had to rap them often enough, you rapscallion," his mother retorted. "Now go on, get that water." She coughed. "I'm growing more parched by the moment. And I could use some of that good brown bread I had at supper, too. Fetch it for me from the kitchen, will you?"

Byrne eyed her askance, but released Christabel's arm and headed for the door. Just as he reached it, however, his mother called out, "Don't you dare stand outside listening. I want a full jug of water and a nice slab of bread and butter. If you don't produce it in fifteen minutes, I'll know you've been eavesdropping."

Byrne cast Christabel a wry smile. "She knows me well."

As soon as he was gone, his mother said, "Sit down, Lady Haversham."

Her commanding tone with its faint hint of an Irish burr reminded Christabel so much of Byrne that she couldn't help smiling as she took a seat in the chair nearest the bed.

"Now tell me," Mrs. Byrne went on, "why is a woman of your station with my son?"

That wiped the smile off Christabel's face. What was she to say? How much would Byrne want her to say?

She went on the offensive. "Why shouldn't I be with him? He's a charming man and a hard worker—"

"Not something most marchionesses admire."

"I was a general's daughter long before I was a marchioness. So I *do* happen to admire a man willing to work hard."

Mrs. Byrne digested that a moment, coughing behind her hand. "But that doesn't explain why you're here with him when you could be moving in the highest levels of society."

Oh, if the woman only knew. Christabel tried for the most innocuous answer. "Your son has been helping me regain something my late husband . . . er . . . lost through gambling."

"So the marquess lost money at the Blue Swan, did he?"

"Yes, but that's not—"

"And you mean to pay off the debt by sharing my son's bed."

"No!" Christabel jumped to her feet. "I would *never* share a man's bed for money. And you insult your son by even implying that he would take advantage of a widow in such a scurrilous fashion."

"True." Those sharp eyes assessed her from the shadows. "So you aren't sharing his bed."

Christabel blushed, unsure how to tell a man's mother that she was his mistress. "I . . . well . . . it's just that . . ."

"You don't have to answer. I can guess that much." When Christabel groaned, she added in a dry rasp of a voice, "I'm not a fool, you know. I've heard about my son's mistresses.

Not from him, mind you—a man doesn't tell his mother such things, after all. But there's always the scandal rags, and Ada goes into Bath often to hear the gossip."

Mrs. Byrne paused to cough. "The thing is, Gavin has never brought one of his women to meet me, never even asked to introduce one to me. Never, do you hear?"

Christabel wanted badly to take heart at that, but she didn't dare. "I hate to disappoint you, but his bringing me here means nothing. He had no choice. He was forced into it."

Mrs. Byrne surprised her by laughing. "Forced? Gavin? Have you ever known my son to be forced into anything?"

That gave Christabel pause. "No."

"He brought you here because he wanted to, whether he admits it or not. So now I want to know why. What exactly do you mean to him?"

"I wish I knew," Christabel answered woefully. "But I really have no idea."

"Then tell me what *he* means to *you*."

That brought Christabel up short. What did Byrne mean to her? Merely a way of getting invited to Lord Stokely's party? Clearly not, since she'd started sharing his bed long after the invitation had arrived.

He was her lover, yes, but he meant more than that, more than she wanted. More than she feared he could ever reciprocate.

"I can't answer that . . . either." She couldn't keep her voice from cracking.

"Do you love him?" Mrs. Byrne asked, her raspy tone substantially softer than before.

Christabel's throat felt tight and raw. "If I do, I'm a fool. Because he will never love me back."

"Nonsense." She coughed a moment. "He fell in love with that idiot Anna, so how could he help falling in love with a sweet girl like you?"

She blinked. "But only a few minutes ago you implied—"

"I wanted to be sure of you, that's all. I trust Gavin not to choose a fool, but he is still a man and susceptible to pretty women."

"Not as susceptible as pretty women are to him," Christabel muttered.

His mother laughed. "True, true. The man has a way with women, I'll grant you. But none has ever touched his heart. If you mean to do it, then you should know some things about him." She gestured toward the fireplace. "There's a candle over there, dear. Light it and bring it here."

Sucking in a breath, Christabel did as Mrs. Byrne asked. As she approached the bed, the light from the candle fell full on the woman.

Though she'd half expected to find such a thing, Mrs. Byrne's face was so hideously disfigured that Christabel couldn't keep a gasp from escaping her lips, though she then tried to mask it with a cough.

"Stop that silly coughing, girl," the woman snapped. "I have a mirror—I know what I look like."

"I'm sorry—" Christabel began.

"Don't be. These burns are my badge of honor for saving my son. I wear them with pride." Her scarred lips twisted into a half smile. "Most of the time, anyway."

Now that she could see the woman better, Christabel was horrified at the pain Mrs. Byrne must have suffered to have such scars. Her ears were half-gone, and no hair grew on her scalp, which was simply a misshapen mass of healed flesh. "I heard that you were in a fire, but I cannot imagine how you managed to . . ."

"Live through it? That was hard, I'll grant you, but I was determined not to die. I couldn't leave Gavin with no one in the world."

"Then why did you let everyone believe you dead?"

"It's a long story." The woman beckoned her to sit on the bed. Taking the candle from her, Mrs. Byrne set it on the bedside table. "You see, right after the fire, there was a great deal of confusion. After I carried Gavin out, I collapsed. He didn't rouse for a few minutes, and by then I'd been taken off to St. Bartholomew's with others from the fire. They told him I was dead—most of those who survived the fire did die later, and we were unrecognizable when they carried us to the hospital. Indeed, it took weeks for me to recover enough to be able to speak my name and ask about him."

Mrs. Byrne took her hand, and now Christabel could see that it wasn't gnarled with age but twisted from the fire. "By the time I could find out about him," the woman continued, "he was living with a blackleg who'd taken him under his wing, and he was doing all right. I thought he'd be better off without a crippled and disfigured mother to support. So I ordered the people at the hospital not to say anything to him about me."

"Then how—"

She gave a rueful smile. "The boy is too clever for his own good, that's how. It was nearly a year before I could even leave St. Bartholomew's. Then a widowed nurse there offered me a place to stay in her cottage in the country. She had a chance at a lucrative position as nurse to a fine lady, but she couldn't bring her babe with her, so I agreed to be the child's nursemaid."

Her hand squeezed Christabel's painfully. "But I couldn't leave London without seeing my own dear boy. I didn't mean for him to see me, too, truly I didn't." She coughed a moment. "I went to the races in a hooded cloak, and I stayed well out of his way to watch him work, my fine strong lad, running an E-O table as if he'd been born to it, coaxing the country bumpkins into betting."

She shook her head. "Unfortunately, the races are a rough place for any woman, much less one like me, hobbling with a cane and dressed oddly. Some fool pulled down my hood to see what I looked like. You can imagine the reaction of those around me—a lot of silly screaming and such." Tears welled in her eyes. "But my boy . . . he just came up and pulled the hood back in place. 'There you go, miss,' he said. 'Don't you pay attention to that lot of fools.'"

Christabel was crying by then, too, the tears falling heedlessly down her cheeks.

"I only said 'Thank you, my boy.' But it was enough for him to realize who I was, to put everything together. You should have seen the two of us then, hugging and laughing and carrying on. People thought we were mad." She let go of Christabel's hand to wipe at her eyes with the sheet. "Look at me—it's been years, and it still turns me into a sniffling fool to remember it."

"That's all right," Christabel whispered. "Who wouldn't cry over a story like that?" Drawing out her handkerchief, she dabbed at her own tears, then handed the square of linen to Mrs. Byrne.

Mrs. Byrne blew her nose. "Gavin would laugh at us for crying, you know."

"Probably. Men don't understand." She waited until the woman had composed herself, then added, "So what happened then?"

"That's when I made him swear not to tell anyone I was alive. I told him I would disappear, and he'd see me no more if he didn't swear it. So he swore, the poor dear boy, and I went out to the country to live in Ada's cottage—she was the nurse, you see. And Gavin stayed in town."

"But why? You could have lived in town with him. You could have worn a wig and veil and gloves if people's reaction to your appearance bothered you."

She coughed into the handkerchief. "That's not why I wanted us to live apart. It was hard enough for Gavin before the fire, hearing people call me 'the Irish whore.' I told him it didn't matter as long as we both knew I wasn't one, but it mattered to him as soon as he was old enough to understand it. He got into fights over it, constantly in trouble for defending my honor to shopkeepers and idiots in taverns who bloodied his nose for his trouble."

Christabel gave the woman a half smile. "He is still rather . . . er . . . sensitive about the term."

"That doesn't surprise me. Only think how much worse it would have been if he'd had to hear people talk their nonsense about his mother being punished by fire for her sins. They said such things after they thought me dead, but once a person's gone, gossip fades." A cough wracked her. "If they'd known I was alive, he'd have had to hear it daily, to witness how people took my disfigurement, to endure the silly jokes about the 'burned Mrs. Byrne.'"

At Christabel's groan, she added, "You've heard it, too, haven't you? People are cruel sometimes. And I knew he'd need every ounce of his strength and will to survive in London. If he were a man alone, rootless, free, he might do it, but if he had me to take care of—"

"But he was only a boy," Christabel protested. "Twelve is so very young."

"Not for Gavin. He'd already spent months taking care of himself, already found a way to support himself. I couldn't help him in London—I could only be a burden to him. As it was, I was lucky I could care for myself at Ada's cottage."

"You could have taken him with you to the country."

"To do what? Labor in the fields? Serve as apprentice to a blacksmith? He was too clever for that, too ambitious. And while Ada could earn enough as a nurse for me and her babe, she couldn't support him, too."

Her lips tightened into a grim line. "Do you think I liked being apart from my son? Living from monthly visit to monthly visit? Not knowing whether he was hungry or hurt or—" She broke off with a raspy cough. "But look at him now. Would he have come so far if I hadn't left? I don't think so."

Christabel wasn't so sure, but she'd never been in a situation where she had to make such a hard choice. What would she have done?

Mrs. Byrne's voice filled with pride. "He grew up to be a fine, strapping man, a true son of a prince." She patted Christabel's hand. "You know about his father, don't you?"

"Yes. Byrne, however, doesn't seem so pleased by the connection."

She sighed. "I know. He blames Prinny for everything."

"He has good reason."

"Perhaps. But he doesn't see that his suffering and mine made him what he is—strong, fierce. Who would he have been if Prinny *had* kept up the annuity? An actress's bastard son, that's all, living off the fruits of his birth. But now he owns his own club, and he's done so well that he bought this place so I could—"

"—banish yourself to the outskirts of Bath," Byrne said from the doorway. Entering with the jug of water and a plate, he glanced from the candle fully illuminating his mother's face to Christabel's damp cheeks, then added gruffly, "Have you been telling her the whole sad tale, Mother?"

"She had to," Christabel retorted. "*You* never would."

"I couldn't." He strode over to the bed. "I made a vow."

"You see?" Mrs. Byrne remarked. "Isn't he a good son?"

"A very good son," Christabel answered, her heart full as she watched him set the plate on the bedside table, then fill the cup with water.

He sat down in the chair Christabel had left and flashed both a rakish smile. "Keep that under your hat, or you'll destroy my reputation for ruthlessness. Then I'll have gentlemen refusing to pay their debts right and left." He winked at Christabel. "Or sending their wives out to shoot me."

"Byrne," Christabel warned him, "don't you dare—"

"That's how we met," he said, pure mischief shining in his eyes. "Lady Haversham shot at me when I came to collect on her late husband's debt."

"Did she really?" Mrs. Byrne chuckled. "That explains why you went after her. Your philosophy has always been if you can't beat them, bed them."

Byrne groaned. "For God's sake, Mother—"

"I wasn't born yesterday. I know what you do with your women." She coughed. "Same thing I did with your father, though I can't regret it, since it gave me you."

"And a life of pain and misery," he said in a hollow voice.

"Pish, everyone's life has a measure of pain and misery. If I've had a greater share of it from time to time, I've also had a greater share of joy." She patted Christabel's hand. "Especially tonight."

When she followed the comment with a fit of coughing, Byrne rose. "We'll let you sleep now." He bent to kiss her cheek, then turned to offer Christabel his arm.

As she rose and took it, his mother said, with an edge to her voice, "Which room did you put Lady Haversham in?"

"The pretty pink one."

His mother smiled her approval. "At least you have *some* sense of decorum."

Christabel choked back a laugh. For a woman who knew so much about her son's mistresses, Mrs. Byrne was surprisingly concerned about appearances.

Then again, here at his estate Byrne might be an entirely different person—the lord of the manor, a respectable gentleman. Christabel could hardly imagine it.

"Good night, Mother," Byrne said.

They started to leave, then on impulse Christabel broke from him and ran back to the bed to place a kiss on Mrs. Byrne's scarred cheek. "Thank you for telling me about him," she whispered.

Tears filled his mother's eyes. "Thank you for trying to understand him."

When Christabel returned to Byrne's side, he was watching her with thinly veiled curiosity. As soon as they left the room, however, he said, "I take it you and my mother had a very emotional chat. I suppose she bombarded you with questions about your association with me?"

"What we discussed is private."

"And I hope it will stay private outside of this house as well," he said tersely, as they strolled together down the hall.

"I would never betray your confidence, or hers. Surely you know that."

He shot her a shuttered glance. "I wouldn't have brought you if I'd thought otherwise. Though I do wish she'd allow me to tell people about her. I'd like to have her in London, where she could be better cared for."

"What does she suffer from?"

"Weak lungs. The doctors say it's unrelated to the fire, but I have my doubts. In recent years, she's been plagued by agues and pleurisy during the autumn and winter. They've brought her near to death a few times, so I often have to make emergency trips to Bath."

He brought her to a halt outside her bedchamber door, and his manner changed. "I . . . er . . . that is . . . tonight you'll—"

"Be sleeping alone." She gazed up at him, eyes twinkling. "I gathered as much."

"I suppose you find this very amusing," he grumbled.

"That the wicked Mr. Byrne would put his mistress in a separate bedchamber out of respect for his mother?" she teased. "No, indeed. Why should I find that amusing?"

With a dangerous glint in his eyes, he pressed her against the door. "Perhaps I should remind you how I got my reputation for wickedness in the first place—"

He kissed her, so deeply and soulfully it roused a painful ache in her chest that had nothing to do with desire. When he drew back long moments later, she could see in his eyes that he felt something else, too.

But all he said was, "Thank you."

"For what?"

"Treating my mother like a person."

She stared at him. "She *is* a person."

"I know. But people confronted by a monstrous face tend to treat the person beneath it as a monster, too. Thank you for being better than that."

"You're welcome," she said softly, a lump in her throat. When he bent to kiss her again, she stopped him. "But if you keep kissing me, I may be tempted to make your sacrifice to propriety all for naught."

He laughed. "Then I'd better say good night, darling."

"Good night . . . Gavin."

He started to walk away, then stopped as it registered that she'd called him by his Christian name. He glanced back at her, one eyebrow raised.

She shrugged. "So you have *two* women calling you that—why not?"

"Why not indeed?" he answered. But his eyes burned into hers a long moment before he walked down the hall and entered his own room.

"Sleep well, my sweet prince," she whispered after his door was closed.

Her dear, sweet Prince of Sin. Christabel entered her own room, feeling bereft not to have him there with her. He was rapidly proving to be not so sinful after all. He was proving to be a man she might be able to trust, to care for . . . to love.

Never say those words to him if you want to remain his mistress.

Blinking back tears, she unfastened her gown, then stripped off her stockings and sat down on the bed. What was she going to do about Gavin? About *loving* Gavin? Because she did love him. She saw that now. And she began to believe that in time he might actually be capable of loving her, too.

But they didn't have time. The letters lay between them like the proverbial elephant in the room. Now that she knew the full extent of why he hated the prince, she knew he would never give up until he learned what was in them, even if he had to deal with Lord Stokely privately to do so.

She groaned. Gavin and Lord Stokely could make plans together, and she would never know. She couldn't be with Gavin every minute of every day, and as time grew short, she wasn't the only one who'd grow more desperate.

Well, she could fret over how he'd act if he got to them on his own and realized their massive significance. Or she could trust him with the truth. She could take a chance that if she told him everything and impressed upon him the seriousness of what would happen if he tried to use the letters, he might let his conscience be his guide.

A week ago, she wouldn't have attempted it. But that was before she'd seen the side of Gavin that understood how important it was to save one's family. If she made him understand that she must protect her father as he'd protected his mother, she might get through to him.

Or she might not. Did she dare risk it, with Papa's life hanging in the balance?

Did she dare not? She needed him to get the letters— that grew more painfully clear with each passing day. And the barony wasn't enough to motivate him to remain on *her* side—having a title wouldn't take away his mother's pain, a pain that so clearly ate at him. Gavin wouldn't stop until he'd avenged her.

Unless Christabel could show him that vengeance brought only more pain.

You make me want to be good.

Oh, Lord, she prayed he'd been telling the truth. Because now was his chance. And if he decided to use the knowledge for vengeance instead . . .

He *had* to do the right thing. He *had* to. This wasn't a gamble she could afford to lose.

Chapter Twenty

*The man is always the last to know when
Cupid has struck him.*
—Anonymous, *Memoirs of a Mistress*

*G*avin wasn't sure how to read Christabel's mood. Ever since they'd left Bath this morning, she'd been staring out that bloody window as if the answer to her troubles lay in the softly carpeted hills and autumn-hued trees they hurtled past.

Perhaps he shouldn't have brought her to meet his mother. But now that it was done, he couldn't regret it. Unless it was Mother's tale that haunted her. How much *had* his mother told her about those dark, early years?

"What's wrong, lass? Why so quiet?"

"I'm thinking about what will happen when we return to Lord Stokely's."

He relaxed. Now, *that* he understood. "You're worried about the eliminations, I suppose."

Her gaze shot to him. "I wasn't. Should I be?"

"It depends on who's left to play."

"You and I will be partners from now on, won't we?"

He cast her an indulgent smile. "Of course, my sweet. Tonight Stokely will gather everyone who has the money to stay in the game. When he asks us to choose our partners, we'll choose each other, simple as that. From then on, it will be the two of us, for better or worse."

"Until death do us part," Christabel said dryly. Before he could react to that astonishing comment, she asked, "Is that why you never partnered with any of your mistresses? Because even that bespoke a more permanent connection than you wished to have?"

"I never partnered with any of my mistresses, darling, because Stokely's a better player than any of them."

"Including me," she said with a frown.

"*Until* you," he corrected her.

She snorted. "If I didn't have to play to stay—and if you hadn't made that wager with Lord Stokely—I would quit right now. Because I know I can't play well enough to beat everybody who's left."

"Nonsense. When you put your mind to it, you're as good as any of them. The only one who might pose a problem is Eleanor, because she tends to rouse your temper. But perhaps fortune will be with us and her injury will take her out of the game entirely.

"As for the others, Lady Hungate plays better than you, but she lacks your aggression. And when you play Lady Kingsley, remember that she tends to save her trumps. That should help you best her. *If* you pay attention. Which I begin to think might be a problem."

"It won't. By tonight, I'll be ready to focus on the game." She dragged in a heavy breath. "But first, there's something important I must discuss with you."

"Oh?" He eyed her warily. After last night, he had no idea what to expect. Especially after her comment about "until death do us part." Was that what she wanted from him? Marriage? Did he *want* her to want it?

That was the crux of it, wasn't it? He began to think he wanted far more from her than a short affair. Or even a long affair. She made him yearn, and that scared the hell out of him. He'd taught himself long ago not to yearn for anything he wasn't absolutely sure he could have.

"Let's put our cards on the table, Gavin," she said. "So to speak."

His pulse began to race. "Why not?"

"If you could gain the letters right now, what would you do with them?"

He blinked. The letters. She was talking about the bloody letters. "What do you mean?"

"We both know you want them for yourself. If you had them—if I could give them to you—what would you do with them?"

"It would depend on what's in them."

"Suppose I said it was something that could damage His Highness."

"Create a scandal, you mean?" When she didn't answer, he debated whether to tell her the truth. But after last night, surely she'd understand and sympathize with his aims. "I'd use them as leverage to force him to make a public apology to my mother, among other things. To declare that she wasn't the liar and the whore he painted her, but the true mother of one of his by-blows."

"You know it's highly unlikely that he would ever agree to that," she pointed out. "His reputation is soiled enough right now; it would damage him too much before the people to be painted as a liar and a cheat."

"Which he is."

"Yes," she admitted with a sigh. "What you want isn't unreasonable. And perhaps he might grant it if you can obtain the letters." She stared at him. "I've decided to tell you what's in them."

That he had not expected. He gazed at her with suspicion. "Why now?"

"Because I'm hoping that once you understand their importance, you'll treat them with the proper care. Perhaps you'll even show some mercy toward your father, despite his many sins."

He wasn't about to tell her that she was wasting her breath, not when he was this close to hearing the truth.

She swallowed. "I'm praying that any man who cares as much for his mother as you obviously do could never harm another mother who sacrificed for the good of her child."

His eyes narrowed. "What other mother?"

She squared her shoulders, clearly gathering her strength. "Maria Fitzherbert. Whom some still consider to be Prinny's lawful wife."

"Mrs. Fitzherbert has no—" He broke off, his blood thundering in his veins. "She has a child?"

"A son. In Gibraltar. Where my father took him twenty-odd years ago, along with a soldier and his wife who took him in. The letters are from Mrs. Fitzherbert to my father, discussing their plans for . . . er . . . removing the child from England and having him become known as the soldier's son."

The ramifications of her words shook him with the force of a tempestuous sea. "Bloody, bloody hell. Prinny has a *son* by Mrs. Fitzherbert. You know what that means."

"Of course. Why do you think they had him whisked out of the country and hidden all these years?"

"If the child is really his by Mrs. Fitzherbert, the succession would be in danger." He leaned forward, hardly able to contain his excitement. "This is no by-blow of a mistress. The Catholic Church *still* considers their marriage valid, which means plenty of people would consider the boy a legitimate heir to the throne. And neither George III nor Parliament would let the crown pass to Prinny when Prinny's own heir is in question."

She nodded. "Exactly. That's why His Highness is so desperate to regain the letters. Because if they're published now, it would put an end to any hope that he'd ever be king."

"My God," he crowed, "I'd hoped for leverage to force him to admit the truth, but this is far better! A way to rid the country of the bastard once and for all!"

She'd gone white as ash. "Gavin, listen to me. I don't blame you for hating him, but surely even you can see why these letters must *never* be published. You have to think of more than yourself in this."

"Why?" he snapped. "That arse has never thought of anyone but *himself*. The country would be better off without him: He's a bloated, self-serving cancer eating away at the good name and reputation of England. Plenty of people would thank me for making it impossible for him to succeed to the throne."

"But others, like the Tories, would champion him. It would embroil England in chaos for years, Gavin. *Years*. The dispute over Charles II's succession went on for over fifty years and caused the Glorious Revolution, not to mention the Jacobite rebellion a mere sixty years ago. Why do you think Mrs. Fitzherbert agreed to send her son away? Because she didn't want him at the center of such a storm. Because she loved him too much to put that burden upon him."

"No, she did it because Prinny forced her to. Because she let that arse pull the wool over her eyes." He'd be damned if he'd accept her comparing Maria Fitzherbert's sacrifice to his mother's. "And once again, Prinny gets what he wants. But don't you understand? This is the chance to rid England of him. To make him suffer—"

"For what he did to you and your mother." Her eyes filled with tears. "Gavin, all you want is vengeance. But wreaking your vengeance would split the country apart."

"You're wrong. They'd simply put Prinny's brother Frederick on the throne, and that would be that."

"Even if you're right, and I'm certainly not willing to take that chance, have you even stopped to think what it would do to *you* if you take on the Prince of Wales? You'll be denounced as the man who brought scandal upon the crown for his own purposes—"

"What do I care about that? Nothing they say could be any worse than what's been said of me before."

"Yes, but you have a measure of success and respectability now. Will your mother, who takes such pride in how far you've come, enjoy watching you be vilified in the press?"

That gave him pause. "She'll understand," he said through gritted teeth. "She'll cheer me."

"Will she? All the nasty things they said about her will be amplified tenfold. The press will surely find her, too."

"At least she'd finally get justice."

A look of sheer desperation swept over her face. "And what about me? And my father?"

"What do you mean?" he said hoarsely.

"I told you before—if the letters are published, Papa could lose his commission. And if he's arrested for treason—"

"He wouldn't be arrested, damn it. Even the Whigs who despise Prinny wouldn't attack a war hero for loyalty to the crown."

"Interfering with the line of succession is a treasonous offense, punishable by hanging." She swallowed. "You don't think Prinny would pursue that? And succeed? He might lose his chance to be king, but he'd still be a prince with influence. Papa had been instructed to burn the letters, but he didn't. So His Highness would have him punished one way or another." Her voice dropped to a whisper. "And me, for telling Philip about them in the first place."

Gavin ruthlessly ignored the instant punch to his gut that her words delivered. "He couldn't touch *you,* my darling. I wouldn't let him." He leaned forward to seize her hands. They were so cold they were like icy fingers of fear squeezing his heart. "As for your father, I wouldn't let anything happen to him, I swear it. I'm not without influence myself. Between me and my brothers—"

"Brothers?"

Damn. He hadn't meant to reveal that.

"I know about Lord Draker but—" She broke off, awareness dawning in her face. "Lord Iversley is one of the prince's by-blows, too, isn't he? I did wonder at the closeness between the three of you."

"Yes, and Iversley is an earl, which counts for something. Between the three of us, we can protect your father, and I know I can protect you. I have plenty enough wealth to take care of you *and* your father. I can't believe the general would lose his commission, after all his service to his country, but if he did, he could live on my estate. As could you."

She dropped her gaze from his. "I'm sure Papa would be delighted to live with his daughter and her lover."

"And if I were your husband? What then?"

He hadn't meant to say the words, but now that he had, he let them stand. Christabel as his wife. The possibility that he'd sneered at only a couple of weeks ago, had come to seem like a dream. If they married, none of this could touch them—they'd have each other. And then who cared what anyone said?

Her face was shadowed with disappointment, and her hands trembled in his. "You are so desperate for those letters that you would make this patently spurious offer?"

"No!" He refused to release her hands when she tried to draw them from his. "It's not a spurious offer, and it's certainly not intended to get me the letters. Why not marry me? We could make a good marriage, you and I."

She lifted a haunted gaze to him. "You and I and your current mistress."

"No." He dragged in a weighted breath, hardly able to believe what he was about to say. "I'd be faithful to you." When she looked skeptical, he added fiercely, "I'd be faithful, I swear it."

"And to gain this position as your wife, I need only stand by and watch as you betray my country, sentence my father to a life of condemnation—"

"It has nothing to do with us!" he cried.

"It has *everything* to do with us," she hissed. "If you steal those letters to publish them, then you are not a man I can marry."

His eyes narrowed. "You would take the side of that selfish arse—"

"It's not for him, blast it!" Frustration wracked her face. "Forget, for a moment, what this would mean for His Highness and the country. Forget what it would mean for me and Papa. Consider what it would mean for Cameron."

He jerked his hands free of hers. "Who the bloody hell is Cameron?"

"Mrs. Fitzherbert's son. The one those letters concern. He's spent years believing that an army captain and his wife are his parents. They've treated him kindly, given him a loving home. And now you wish to destroy that—"

"Correct me if I'm wrong, but this 'boy' is about twenty-two now, is he not?"

"Yes. What of it?"

"I was twelve when I lost my pathetic excuse for a home, and when, for all practical purposes, I lost my mother. Don't ask me to feel sympathy for some lad who's had a loving family and comfortable home until now. Because of Prinny's favor, he probably has fine prospects. Do you know what prospects *I* had at twelve?"

"Gavin—"

"Do you know that days after the fire, the blackleg who'd taken me in actually made several appeals to my dear 'father'? That he told His Bloody Highness I was alone in the world and could use some assistance? And that Prinny ignored every appeal?" Gavin snorted. "Prinny no doubt feared that if he gave me any money, it would be a tacit admission of our connection."

Gavin's anger burned in his gut like a hot brand. "And the prince wasn't about to admit that he'd been, as you put it, a liar and a cheat, that he'd grievously wronged my mother. No, it was much better to ignore the plight of a boy who he *knew* was his child, to let his mistress's name continue to be so vilified that she felt she could only help her son by abandoning him."

Christabel's face now filled with such pity that he had to look away. "You saw her, lass. Surely you realize how much she suffered from his neglect." His voice grew hoarse. "Do you know how she got so badly burned?"

"I know she saved you," she whispered.

"Yes. Late at night, she returned from some piddling job she'd managed to find. When she heard I was still inside, she wrapped herself in a wet rug and came in after me. She found me asleep and couldn't wake me. Since she couldn't carry me out while keeping us both wrapped in the rug, she chose to wrap *me* in the rug and face the flames herself." The old pain rose to choke him, acrid as the smoke that had clung to his clothes for weeks afterward. "And for her sacrifice, she suffered months of pain, still suffers even today."

Violently he fought the tears stinging his eyes. He had never let them fall before and wasn't about to do so now. He could at least be as strong as his mother had been that cruel night.

His hands balled into fists as he swung his gaze back to Christabel. "If not for His Bloody Highness, she would have been living in some comfortable brick house in a decent part of town where fires didn't happen with appalling regularity. I wouldn't have been left alone at night while she slaved at some menial job. She deserves justice for what he did to her, and I mean to get it for her."

"But she doesn't want justice," Christabel protested. "Whatever hatred she felt for him is long gone. You've got to put that part of your life behind you, and getting vengeance won't do that."

"It might. How can I *not* avenge her, when every time I look at her face—"

"She's happy, Gavin. Can't you see that? If you do this, do you really think it would improve your life? And what about your brothers? I take it they don't share the same difficult relationship with the prince as you do—will they be pleased to watch you destroy His Highness's chance at being king?"

"If they aren't, they ought to be," he growled.

"And me?" she whispered. "You know how *I* feel about it. I can't just stand by and watch while you destroy everything I've worked for, no matter how much I love you."

Love. The word dangled between them, a glittering promise. With other women, he'd only seen it as a signal that a pleasant affair was about to turn into a prison. But with her, it was an invitation to a life he'd never expected to want. A life he began to think he might want after all.

And that terrified him. Because it meant he would have to be a different man. Marrying her was one thing—it was practical, even sensible. But *loving* her? Bloody hell.

"Don't say that," he rasped.

She paled. "What? That I love you? I can't help it. It's true."

Panic swelling in him, he tore his gaze from her. "It's not. What you think you love is an illusion. Meeting my mother put some notion in your head that I'm noble and unselfish and all those damned things you admire. But I'm not. I only survived those years of poverty by beating my conscience into silence and trampling my heart."

"But you don't have to do that anymore. You have a successful business and friends and family—"

"The point is, it's done. I can't regain what I lost, Christabel. This is all that's left, this . . . this creature of will with no heart, no conscience. If you can accept that, then we can probably have a decent marriage. But if you want more, then I can't be what you want. I'm the man with no soul, remember?"

"I don't believe that." She caught his chin, forcing him to look at her. "I've seen you be kind to your servants and generous to card cheats and fierce in the defense of those you love. If that's not a man with a soul, I don't know what is."

The love shining in her eyes was so bright, it hung before him like a palpable temptation. But to live up to her belief in him, he'd have to give up his chance to make Prinny pay. And he couldn't. He simply couldn't.

"See what you want to see, but that makes it no less an illusion." Tearing his gaze from hers, he said in a hollow voice, "I've never before let talk of love override my reason. I'm not about to do so now."

The low moan she gave, like that of a wounded beast, cut him so to the heart that he nearly wished the words back. But if they were to have any sort of future, she would have to realize what he was.

"You mean to publish the letters, if you find them," she whispered.

"I mean to use them however I can to strike at Prinny."

"I can't allow that," she said in a small voice. "So I'm afraid that from now on, we must part ways."

His heart thundering, he shifted to stare at her. "What do you mean?"

"I'll look for the letters alone. And I can no longer . . . share your bed."

An unreasoning rage seized him. "My other mistresses have tried to manipulate me by withholding their favors, my sweet. It has never worked before, and it won't work now."

The hurt in her face made a hard knot fist in his gut. "I'm not trying to manipulate you. I'm simply telling you that I can't bear to stand by and watch while you bring the world down about your ears. And that means I can't bear to share your bed. It would be too painful."

"Fine," he snapped, his rage so murderous that he feared what he'd do if he stayed there a moment longer. He knocked on the ceiling. "Driver! Stop the coach."

"What on earth are you doing?" she said, her face showing alarm.

As the coach shuddered to a halt, he reached for the door. "Since you can't bear my presence," he said snidely, "I'll ride the rest of the way up top."

He leaped out, then paused to glare at her, his hand still on the handle. "But good luck finding those letters without me. Or should I say, finding them *before* I do. Because I mean to get my hands on them one way or the other."

Chapter Twenty-One

Some lovers never give up.
—Anonymous, *Memoirs of a Mistress*

One way or the other.

For the hundredth time in two days, Christabel wondered what Gavin had meant. Did he plan to bargain with Lord Stokely for the letters? The two men were at cross-purposes, so she doubted that would work. Lord Stokely didn't really want to publish them—he wanted to marry the princess. Whereas Gavin definitely wanted to publish them to prevent His Highness from gaining the throne.

A lump settled in her throat. He would never understand, never be able to see past his vengeance. She'd gambled and lost.

Yet she didn't regret telling him everything. At least now, if he found them before she did, he might think before he acted. He might remember what she'd said, let it break through his wall of anger.

"Cut the cards, Lady Haversham," said a taut voice across from her.

She looked up to find Gavin and the other players watching her. Forcing her attention to the game, she cut the cards and pushed them back at Gavin, who began to deal.

Despite everything, he'd chosen her as his partner. He'd given her no chance to protest or choose someone else—after their return from Bath, he'd simply announced before the assembly that he and she would be partners.

Though she'd realized he probably just wanted to keep her in his sight at all times, she hadn't protested. It was crucial that she stay at Lord Stokely's as long as possible, and she always played her best with Gavin. They seemed to understand each other on a level deeper than most players. And she learned so much just from watching him.

Playing with him these past two days had taught her something else, too: how difficult it must have been for him to turn himself into the man with no soul. Because at the card tables, she'd had to turn herself into the woman with no soul. It was the only way to stay in the game—by thinking of him merely as her card partner, blotting out the emotions that swelled in her whenever she looked up to find him hard and cold and remote.

Like now, when he arranged his cards with methodical precision, like a mechanical toy in circumscribed motion.

Hard to believe that the same man had actually offered her marriage. If he'd even meant it. Even if he had, by now he'd certainly rethought the words he'd spoken in a vain attempt to bring her over to his side.

A sigh escaped her lips.

"Bad cards, Lady Haversham?" Colonel Bradley asked.

She blinked at the man. "If it were, I'm not fool enough to admit it."

"Well, if you mean to signal Byrne with your sighs," the colonel retorted, "I'll make sure Stokely hears of it."

Gavin's eyes narrowed. "Are you implying that Lady Haversham and I cheat?" he asked in that velvet-over-steel voice that never failed to make her shiver.

Colonel Bradley blanched. Men fought duels over such accusations. "Just making idle conversation, old chap."

"The colonel is merely annoyed that we're winning," Christabel put in. Gavin's temper had been dangerously close to explosive lately, and anything might set him off.

Besides, she and Gavin *were* winning. They'd made it into the top eight teams, and the competition had been fierce. Fortunately, Lady Jenner had indeed been forced out of the game because her injury kept her abed. But that had left several others of equal competence. So although she and Gavin were closing in on a hundred points, they had to reach it soon. Two teams had already made it—Lady Hungate and her lover, and Lord Stokely and Lady Kingsley.

That last pairing had surprised some of the other players, but not her. Clearly, Lord Stokely hoped to unnerve Gavin, his main rival, by having Anna as his partner. And since the woman's idiotic, unsuspecting husband regarded Lord Stokely's choice as a compliment to his wife's superior playing, he hadn't blinked an eye as he'd toddled off to the nearby inn where the other banished guests were staying.

Christabel meant to avoid ending up there herself. Gritting her teeth, she walled off her emotions, and turned herself into a card-playing machine like her partner. How Gavin had done it for years, she would never understand. But it did explain how he'd become the man of sheer, unadulterated will who sat across from her.

No one spoke as they played. There was none of the earlier banter and jokes, none of the possibilities for distraction. Everyone was too busy fighting for a chance at the pot, which, last she'd heard, was up to forty thousand pounds.

They won the game just as the gong sounded. When Christabel breathlessly asked to see the tally, Gavin said with a satisfied smile, "We've reached a hundred, my sweet. We've made it to the final four teams."

Tallies around the room revealed that the team below them still lacked nearly thirty points to reach a hundred, so they'd have a few hours' reprieve from play tomorrow when the others sat down.

That meant some solid time for searching and another chance to thwart Lord Stokely. But time grew short; at most, they had another two nights and one full day.

Colonel Bradley and his partner wandered off in search of entertainment, leaving her and Gavin alone at the table. She rose, eager to escape him before she was tempted to round the table and kiss the grim line from his lips.

But as she turned away, he asked in a low voice, "Have you found them?"

She glanced about the room, but the only people left in the room were Lord Stokely and a few others in conversation several yards away. "I wouldn't still be here if I had. Have you?"

"No."

The clipped word frustrated her. It told her so little. She eyed him speculatively. Perhaps if she told him what she knew, he'd unbend enough to tell her the same. "I searched the drawing room and some of the guest rooms. I still haven't been able to get into Lord Stokely's room, however. He keeps it locked."

"They aren't there. I searched it while he was drinking with the others after last night's games."

She lowered her voice to a whisper. "You picked the lock?"

He nodded. "And yours, too," he said dryly. "Then I tried your door, but it wouldn't open."

"I've been wedging a chair under the handle because of Lord Stokely."

"So you gave up on flirting with him to gain access to his room?" he asked in a tight voice.

"Yes."

He let out a breath. "Thank God for that." Turning the deck of cards around in his hand, he stared at her. "It's rapidly becoming apparent that we aren't going to find them this way. We'd be better off striking a deal with Stokely."

"He won't give them up," she murmured, with a glance in the baron's direction. "And offering a bargain would only put him on his guard."

"I know. That's why I haven't done it yet. But if the choice is leaving here without the letters or striking a bargain—"

"I have nothing with which to bargain—nothing he'd want badly enough to give them up. You, on the other hand, have money and connections—you might have something he'd want. And it's not as if I can stop you from . . . dealing with him."

Throat tight, she turned to leave, but he spoke again, his voice softer, almost tormented. "Please, lass, I need to know . . . Are you all right?"

"As well as can be expected." For a woman whose heart was breaking.

"You look tired."

Under the circumstances, his concern angered her. "I find it hard to sleep when the possibility of disaster looms over me and my family."

"And I find it hard to sleep without *you*."

Her gaze shot to his, and the yearning she glimpsed in his eyes banished her anger, rousing a bone-deep longing for him in her chest. It had been three full nights since they'd shared a bed, three nights of restless tossing, anxious dreams, and fiery, unfulfilled needs that drove her to drown her woes in tears.

It would be so easy to give in, to tell him she didn't care what happened as long as she had him, didn't care if her father lost his commission, his reputation . . . his life.

Ruthlessly, she pushed the temptation away. "Try laudanum. I understand it works wonders for the sleepless."

"Christabel, please—" he choked out.

"Lady Haversham!" a voice called out, dragging her attention from Gavin.

She stifled a groan as Lord Stokely approached, especially when a quick glance around revealed that everyone else had left.

The baron flashed them both a patently false smile. "I understand that the two of you will be playing in the next round."

"We'll be winning the next round," Gavin said.

"We'll see." Lord Stokely settled his gaze on her, and it grew decidedly lewd. "I hope your partner told you that in the final stages, we meet right after breakfast to play. So the others will be starting at one o'clock."

"I told her," Gavin interjected.

Lord Stokely ignored him. "I'll send a servant for you once the next round begins. Of course, we may start later than one o'clock if I have another more entertaining prospect tonight that keeps me up until the morn." He offered her his arm. "Would you join me for a glass of wine in my study, Lady Haversham?"

She actually considered it. Perhaps if she got Lord Stokely drunk—

No, she couldn't do it, not with Gavin sitting there watching, assuming the worst. Besides, the more she saw of Lord Stokely, the more convinced she was that Gavin was right about him. He *was* playing with them. He would never tell her anything, but he might very well be capable of rape. It was too dangerous to risk.

"Thank you," she said, ignoring his proffered arm, "but I'm tired after the long day. I believe I'll go on to bed now."

She started to walk past, but he caught her arm. "Come now, don't be so—"

"Let go of her," Gavin said, each word clipped like pistol fire as he rose to his feet behind them.

Lord Stokely's grip on her arm only tightened. "Don't be an ass, Byrne. I know you kicked her out of your bed, so now that you're done with her—"

"First of all, what happens in our bed is none of your concern." There was no velvet with the steel in his voice this time. "Second, I am far from done with her, and even if I were, you would have no right to manhandle her."

"I'm not manhandling her."

Gavin's eyes narrowed to slits. "If you don't remove your hand from her arm this minute, I will break it finger by finger until you do."

Lord Stokely released her with amazing speed. "Christ, you're mad." His resentful gaze shot to Christabel. "We'll talk again when you don't have an angry ex-lover hovering about."

As the baron stalked from the room, she heard Gavin mutter, "The hell you will, you slimy bastard."

They were entirely alone in the cavernous card room. Wary of his mood, Christabel started to leave, but he added in a low voice, "Don't go."

She faced him wearily. "Gavin, there's no point to this."

"No point?" He strode up to her, then caught her head in his hands and kissed her, slowly, achingly. But when she only stood there woodenly, fighting the surge of feelings that his mouth sent coursing through her, he drew back with a curse. "The point is that we belong together. I miss you. And I can see from your eyes that you miss me, too. Why must you be so stubborn?"

"Why must *you*? I'm trying to protect everything I hold dear—"

"I've already said I'll not let any harm come to you or your father. But my mother deserves justice."

"Don't lie to yourself that you're doing it for her."

"You think I'm doing it for me?" He released her abruptly. "I'm giving up the barony my bloody sire offered. And as you pointed out before, I could lose what little position I have in society. So what advantage will I gain from it?"

"An end to your guilt."

He looked stricken. "What do you mean?"

"I've thought about it constantly ever since Bath. You blame yourself for your mother's disfigurement, don't you?"

A muscle worked in his jaw, but he didn't answer.

"You blame yourself for not rousing—"

"I shouldn't have slept through a fire, damn it! I shouldn't have left her to carry me alone."

"You weren't asleep, Gavin," she said gently. "You were overcome with smoke, which is common in a fire. Don't blame yourself for making it necessary for her to wrap you in the rug. That was the fire's fault, not yours, no matter what you've told yourself through the years. She had a hard choice to make, and she did what any mother would do—sacrificed for her son. But that doesn't mean you should feel honor-bound to make it right."

"How can I not?" he said hoarsely. "It's more than just the fire. I wasn't by Mother's side in those difficult months in the hospital when I should have been. They told me she was dead, and like a fool I believed them."

"You were twelve! You might have been running an E-O table by then, but you were still a child, and you thought like a child. The people in authority told you she was dead—why shouldn't you believe them? No doubt you saw enough bodies come out of the building that night."

She laid a hand on his rigid arm. "You have every right to be angry and hurt and bitter, my love. But wreaking havoc on His Highness won't fix that. It certainly won't help your mother."

His body tensed, and he refused to look at her. "She'd have been better off if I'd never been born."

Dear Lord, he truly believed that, didn't he? "Oh, my love, don't even think it. You're the center of her life. I know she doesn't regret one minute of having you. She would certainly not want you to do this and ruin your chances at a decent future. All she wants is for you to have a happy life." She lowered her voice to a whisper. "That's what I want, too."

His gaze swung to hers, fiery, furious. "You have an odd way of showing it. You refuse to share my bed, you refuse my offer of marriage—"

She snorted. "As if you really meant it."

"Of course I meant it," he protested. "I still do."

She dropped her gaze from his. "I thought you might change your mind when you'd had a chance to reconsider."

"Well, I didn't." He slid his arm about her waist and pulled her close, then added in a husky rasp, "You're the only one keeping us from having a respectable connection, the only one putting conditions on our marriage. I want to marry you no matter what happens."

She gazed up at him, torn between love and fear. "Then you must think beyond your vengeance to your future. How can we have a happy life with this cloud hanging over our heads?"

"All that matters is us. If we don't care about public opinion—"

"What about our children? What about *their* future? Do you really want them to grow up hearing slurs against their father, the man who caused the greatest scandal in royal history? And their grandfather, the disgraced general? You, of all people, should know how sensitive children are to criticism of their families."

Judging from his stunned look, he hadn't thought about children at all.

"N-Not that I'm even sure I can have children," she stammered, disconcerted by his expression, "but I would like to try. I-I would hope that if we married . . ." When he continued to stare at her without speaking, her heart sank. "You probably don't even want chi—"

The door swung open behind them to admit Mr. Talbot and Colonel Bradley, clearly in an already inebriated state. "Byrne!" the colonel cried. "You should try some of Stokely's— Oh, Lady Haversham. Didn't mean to interrupt. We thought we'd see if Byrne would join us in a drink."

"It's all right," she murmured, grateful for the reprieve. At least she wouldn't have to hear Gavin admit that he never wanted children, an admission that would shatter her in her already fragile state. "I was just heading off to bed."

Before they could say anything else, she fled.

Gavin watched her leave, too stunned to do more than stare after her. Children. With Christabel. He couldn't believe he hadn't thought of it beyond his efforts to prevent it by using French letters.

"Come on, Byrne," Talbot said, weaving on his feet. "The lady is gone, so come have some brandy with us. Stokely's broken out the best stuff."

Gavin whirled on them, his frustration with Christabel twisting into fury at them. "Of course he has. He's hoping that if you drink enough tonight, you'll be too bloody cropsick tomorrow to play decently, and then his team will win the pot. He does it every year, and you fools fall for it every time. Why do you think he and I always win?"

He surveyed them with a sudden surge of disgust. "I don't know why I even bother with the lot of you. You're idiots, every last one. You deserve to have Stokely fleece you. Good night, gentlemen. Enjoy your drink while you can. Because after tomorrow, you won't be able to afford brandy for some time."

"Now see here, no need to be an ass—" Talbot began, but Gavin was already out the door and in the corridor, looking to see if he could catch Christabel.

But no, she'd disappeared. He would think that she was searching, except that she preferred to sleep a few hours first and do her work after there was little chance of running into Stokely. Unlike Gavin, she wasn't used to late nights. Which meant she was presently in her room, where between Rosa and the chair she kept propped against the handle, she might as well be behind a castle moat. So there was no chance of trying to change her mind by kissing her and making love to her and talking of marriage and the future.

And children.

A groan escaped him as he stared up the staircase that led to the family wing. *He* could have a family wing—the house at Bath was large enough for it. And if he had his barony, he could pass the title on to his son—

Damn it, he wasn't going to get the barony, not if he followed his plan for vengeance.

Gritting his teeth, he strode off toward the other part of the house, trying to blot Christabel's words from his head. *What about our children?*

He'd never wanted children before. Why should he want them now?

An image rose unbidden, of her nursing a babe at her breast, of a little lass with red curls perched on his knee or a dark-haired boy calling him Papa—

Damn her! Christabel was driving him insane with her talk of their future.

Raucous laughter assaulted his ears, and he gave a wide berth to the drawing room from whence it came. Stokely was in there filling the men's bellies with drink. Then he would send them to bed stinking drunk, where they'd get into rows with their wives or mistresses. And no one would awaken in any condition to focus on a card game. Except Stokely, of course.

For the first time, he felt sickened by the scheming and manipulation and outright chicanery involved in the man's little games. And his disgust stretched beyond the baron to the women who'd been making advances to Gavin ever since they'd heard that Christabel wasn't sharing his bed. To the supposed "gentlemen" of his club, who scoffed at him behind his back for being in "trade" even while they drank his liquor and ate his food and took advantage of all the amenities of his club as if it were their due.

Damn them all. Once he had his barony, he'd tell them to go to hell.

No, he reminded himself again, he wasn't going to have a barony. Instead, he was going to heap calumny on his own head by unseating Prinny from the throne. And for what?

Don't lie to yourself that you're doing it for her.

Of course he was doing it for her.

All right, so his mother had never asked for vengeance, had never prodded him to seek it. Although she'd cursed the prince in her early days, she'd changed after the fire. She'd said that having her life spared had made her realize that life was too precious to spend it hating.

And why should she? He'd done all the hating for her—hating those who'd unjustly called her a whore, hating Prinny . . . hating himself.

He walked up the stairs to his room in a daze. Yes, hating himself. For sleeping through the fire, for not being able to protect his mother, for being born. Christabel wasn't far wrong—part of the reason he wanted this so badly was to quell the guilt he'd felt ever since he'd been old enough to know he was a bastard, to know that his very existence had altered his mother's future.

Yet she was right about something else, too. His mother *did* want him to have a happy life. Otherwise, she wouldn't have made such sacrifices for him.

Now he meant to reward her sacrifice by destroying any possibility of a happy life for himself. Because if he couldn't have Christabel, he couldn't be happy.

He stopped outside his bedchamber as a hollow pain settled in his gut. He couldn't take this anymore—being without Christabel, going off to his empty bed alone every night, not having her to tease and provoke and hold. Only two women had ever looked at him with true love in their eyes. Only two women had ever looked beneath his defenses to see a man of worth, a man capable of more than he'd shown the world heretofore.

And he would disappoint them both, destroy his future and theirs—and the future of his children—just for the chance to thumb his nose at a man who didn't deserve to breathe the same air as they. He must be insane.

Abruptly, he turned on his heel and headed back down the stairs. No more—it was time to put an end to the nonsense. He'd find those letters if he had to spend all night searching. And if that didn't work, he'd bargain with Stokely.

No matter what he had to do, he would get the letters back for Christabel. And only for Christabel.

Chapter Twenty-Two

*If you find a lover who can be faithful to
you, hold on to him with all your might.*
—Anonymous, *Memoirs of a Mistress*

The next day, Christabel slipped into the main drawing room as the clock struck one. Except for the two
teams who'd won early and were probably still abed, the
other players would be at the tables. Lord Stokely would
be overseeing his guests, even though he was done with
this round. And she'd seen Gavin dozing in the music
room.

But she couldn't think about him right now. Or the
fact that she'd passed Lady Kingsley heading for the
music room. An assignation? With the only woman he'd
ever loved?

She couldn't bear to think it. But she had to face the
prospect of a future without Gavin, of hearing about him
with some new mistress, while she and Papa weathered
whatever awful prospect lay before them.

Shaking off the icy fear stealing down her spine, she set
her fan on a console table near the door. She'd been using
the fan as her excuse for being in any room. If a servant
came in or one of the guests, she said, "I was looking for

my fan—have you seen it?" Then she'd pretend to find it and leave the room.

After so much time searching, she'd developed a routine. Begin at the door and work steadily around the room twice. In the first time around, she examined the furniture, though she doubted she'd find the letters just sitting in some drawer. The second round was for the walls. She searched every panel and molding within reach, looking for anomalies in paint and trim and design, anything that might hide a safe. Of course, once she found one, she'd have to deal with Gavin, because he could open it, and she couldn't. But she'd cross that bridge when she came to it.

She'd just opened a drawer when she heard the door open behind her and a voice say, "You won't find them in there, Lady Haversham. What kind of an idiot do you take me for?"

Whirling to face Lord Stokely, she felt her blood freeze as he reached behind him with a cold smile to turn the key in the drawing room door, then drop it into a coat pocket.

"I don't know what you're talking about." She fought not to show fear as she edged toward where her fan lay on the console table. "I was looking for my fan."

His hand came down on hers just as she reached for it. He pocketed her fan, too, and her heart sank.

A chilling laugh escaped him. "We both know you weren't looking for any fan, my dear. You and Byrne must take me for a complete idiot. I know what you want—and you can be sure that you will *never* find those letters just lying around in some drawing room. I have them in a very safe place, I assure you."

Oh, Lord, he knows everything.

He shocked her by lifting her bare hand to his lips and kissing it. "Of course, you might persuade me to share the fruits of my labors if you make the effort. You might as well receive something from this scheme, too. The letters did belong to your family, after all."

When he closed his mouth around her forefinger and sucked, it was all she could do not to punch a hole in his palate. But she wasn't ready to draw the battle lines—she'd find out what she could while they were still on good terms.

So she swallowed her disgust, and asked coyly, "What do you mean, you could help me get something, too?"

He lifted his head, but didn't release her hand. "I knew you would see reason. Especially after Byrne kicked you out of his bed." His eyes gleamed. "Your dear Philip didn't leave you with much, did he? And the prince is no doubt breathing down your neck for the letters."

She schooled herself to show no response. "What is your offer, sir?"

His eyebrows shot up. "Greedy little spitfire, aren't you? I think you'll like what I propose. If you'll tell Prinny that you'll authenticate the letters if I'm forced to publish them, then I will make you rich beyond your wildest dreams."

"Byrne offered me riches, too," she lied. "Why should I take *your* offer?"

"He doesn't have the letters. And I do. When Prinny marries me off to Princess Charlotte—"

"He'll never do it," she broke in. "His Highness has loftier husbands in mind for her."

The baron snorted. "Given the choice between marrying his daughter to me or losing his chance to be king, the prince will never choose Charlotte, I assure you. And if he *is* fool enough to do so, then I can sell those letters to a publisher for a hefty sum." He entwined his fingers with hers and drew her close. "Especially if you agree to tell your side of the story. They'll be fighting over who gets to publish the book. You were what age when you and your father sailed off to Gibraltar with a prince's son? Six? Seven?"

"Eight," she said tightly.

"Perfect. A child's perspective."

She fought down the roiling of her stomach. "You forget that my father is still alive. And he could be hanged for treason if they're published."

Lord Stokely shrugged. "Your father's a general—he could flee to America or any number of places from France, and no one would ever find him." He bent his head to her ear. "*You* are the one you should be thinking of, my dear, not your father."

When he placed a wet kiss to her ear, she eased her head away from him with a shiver. "And I suppose a friendship with you would be part of this bargain."

"Of course." His eyes bored into hers, lust shining in their depths. "I will be a most generous lover, my dear. I know you have nowhere to go, but I would set you up in any house in London that you choose, a slew of houses if you want. Princess Charlotte comes with a substantial dowry, so I could afford to shower you with jewels and gowns and—"

"There's only one problem with that," she said, extricating her hand from his. "I don't particularly care for jewels and gowns and houses in town. And I have no desire to be your mistress."

"Holding out for marriage, are you? Not sensible, you know. A penniless marchioness is of little more use to a man than a penniless milliner." He ran his slimy gaze down her. "Some fellow might marry you for your obvious charms, but beyond that, you're little good to a man."

"Then why would you want me for a mistress?" she snapped.

"Because I happen to like obvious charms." He slid his hand about her waist. "And you've shown that you prefer men of my sort."

"Not really." Time to get out of his. She wrenched free of his hold and backed toward the door. "I'm afraid I'll have to refuse your generous offer, Lord Stokely. Being one man's mistress is more than enough for me." She searched for something that might make him open the door. "In fact, Byrne and I had planned to meet here to search for the letters. He's probably on the way even as we speak, and since he's adept at picking locks—"

"Good try, Lady Haversham, but it won't wash. I saw him heading out into the gardens with Lady Kingsley right before I came in here. Why do you think I chose that moment to speak to you?" As he stalked her, his smile sent a shiver down her spine. "Ever heard the phrase, *divide and conquer*? Lady Kingsley is interested in renewing her acquaintance with your good friend Byrne."

He lunged forward and caught her around the waist again. "And I'm interested in beginning one with you."

She shoved against his chest, not only to force him away but in hopes of finding where he'd stuck her fan. "But I'm not interested in beginning one with you."

"You will be. As soon as I show you I can be an even better lover than Byrne."

He lowered his mouth to hers. Blast, he gave her no choice.

She reached down and grabbed his ballocks, squeezing them more tightly than she'd squeezed Gavin's that first time. No one could say she didn't learn from her mistakes.

It must have been the right amount of pressure, for he jerked back, his eyes popping wide. "What the devil—"

"Let go of me, sir," she commanded.

"You little bitch—"

She squeezed until his curse turned to a squeak, and he released her waist. Then she backed toward the door, dragging him by the ballocks the whole way. "You just couldn't listen, could you?" she snapped. "When a lady says no, she means no. Perhaps next time you'll remember that."

The veins stood out on his face, and his jaw was taut enough to bounce a penny off of. "Y-Yes," he choked out. "Just . . . let go."

When she reached the door, she felt inside his coat with her free hand until she'd retrieved her fan and the key. Then she unlocked the door and opened it. "Thank you for the enlightening discussion, Lord Stokely." Then she gave an extra squeeze and released him, leaving him doubled over and groaning while she rushed out the door and locked him inside.

Pocketing the key and her fan, she hurried out of the house with her heart racing. That had been much too near for comfort. She had to get as far away from the scoundrel as possible, before he came after her.

At least it would take a few minutes for him to make himself heard—once he recovered—and another few minutes for the servants to find the key and let him out.

She headed to the gardens. She had to find Gavin. There was no point to their searching anymore—Lord Stokely had made that painfully clear. So they had to strike some bargain with him. But only Gavin had the wherewithal to deal with the man. Somehow she must convince him to give up his plans for vengeance and help her. She simply must make him listen!

Voices came from the gazebo in the far corner, so she headed there. But as she approached near enough to recognize the voices, she hesitated. Lord Stokely hadn't lied— Gavin *was* with Lady Kingsley.

Something kept her from bursting right in on them. Heart pounding, she edged around the gazebo until she found one of the fanciful shuttered windows, still closed from the night before. She eased the shutter open enough to look inside, though she felt like a fool for eavesdropping. But how could she not? Lady Kingsley had been the love of his life.

"Enough, Anna," Gavin was saying. "You've babbled on now for ten minutes about why you listened to your parents years ago. I keep telling you, it doesn't matter to me anymore. I've forgotten it—you should, too. And if you dragged me out here just to beg my forgiveness or some such nonsense—"

"Forgiveness! No, it's not forgiveness I want from you."

Christabel peered around the edge until she could see them both in profile. Once again, she was struck by how hauntingly beautiful Lady Kingsley was. A lump settled in her throat. No wonder Gavin had loved her.

"Then what?" he snapped. "I have to return to the house."

"For what?" Lady Kingsley countered. "That hoyden you call a mistress? I hear she's not even sharing your bed these days."

He stiffened. "Who told you that?"

"Lord Stokely, of course. He heard it from his servants."

"Ah." He arched one eyebrow. "You and Stokely seem rather . . . cozy now that your husband is in town."

"Are you jealous?" she said hopefully.

"Afraid not, my sweet. Those days are long past."

At his words, the tightness around Christabel's heart eased some.

But they brought a frown to Lady Kingsley's delicate brow. "You needn't worry about me and Lord Stokely. He's not my sort. And she's not yours. Surely you see that. You need a woman with finesse, sophistication, a woman like—"

"You?" he said dryly. "Thank you, but I've had my fill of women like that."

"Oh, Gavin." Her aching whisper set Christabel's teeth on edge. "I don't blame you for hating me. I should never have listened to my family."

"But you did, Anna," he said, his voice decidedly more gentle. "And you were right to do so. A marriage between us would never have worked. You would have fretted over my constant absences and the enormous amount of time I spent at the club in the early years. You would have chafed at the lack of money—"

"I'm not so shallow as all that," Lady Kingsley said petulantly. "I would have understood about your financial situation."

"Perhaps," he said, though he sounded merely placating. "But I couldn't have succeeded while worrying every moment about you. We were too young, and I couldn't give you the things you wanted. There's a very good reason men wait until they're older and established to marry. Because then they have the time and money they need to devote to a wife and family."

"Or a mistress?" She lowered her lashes provocatively as she sidled up to him. "It would take very little for me to convince Walter to buy a house in town. Then you and I could meet whenever we pleased." She reached up to unknot his cravat. "You loved me once—"

"That was long ago," he said firmly, removing her hand from his cravat. "And I don't want a mistress. I want a wife."

Her gaze flew to his. "You mean to marry Lady Haversham?"

"If she'll have me," he said in a hoarse whisper.

Christabel couldn't breathe. He'd meant it? He really did mean to marry her?

That didn't seem to alter Lady Kingsley's purpose. "There's nothing to say you can't have a wife *and* a mistress. Most men do. Marry the chit if you crave respectability, but you could still—"

"No, I only want her. You're right—she's not my sort, thank God. She's kind and generous and honest, far too good for the likes of me. But that's not going to stop me from marrying her, no matter what it takes."

Christabel's blood thundered in her ears so loudly, she was sure they would hear it.

Lady Kingsley looked decidedly ill. "If it's a wife you want, I could . . . try to convince Kingsley—"

"To divorce you?" Gavin gave a harsh laugh. "Don't be absurd. Even if he would, you'd be a fool to risk it. I wager you don't like scandal any more now than you did then." He softened his tone. "And I hate to tell you this, Anna, but if you showed up on my doorstep tomorrow free as a bird, I wouldn't marry you. Our time has passed, my sweet. Lady Haversham is the woman I want, the woman I *need*. And nothing you say or do will change that."

"I don't believe it." Lady Kingsley threw her arms about his neck. "You still love me—I know that you do. And I can prove it, too."

As she pressed her lips to Gavin's, a searing rage roared through Christabel. She rounded the gazebo, threw the door open, and hissed, "Take your hands off my fiancé this minute, you scheming witch."

Gavin was already setting the woman away from him, but as Lady Kingsley whirled to face her, Christabel jerked out her fan. "You had your chance with him, and you lost him. You don't get another." Flipping the catch to release the knife, she brandished the blade. "And if you don't leave him alone from now on, I swear I'll gut you like a fish the next time I see you."

Lady Kingsley let out a squeak.

"Better take her words to heart, Anna," Gavin said dryly. "She's liable to do exactly what she says."

"Oh, yes," Christabel said in her fiercest voice. "You see, women who lack 'finesse' happen to possess boldness in spades. We don't sneak behind our rivals' backs to steal their lovers. We have the courage to *fight* for the men we love, a character trait that sophisticated women like you have apparently failed to acquire."

Gavin looked as if he were struggling not to laugh. "You'd better go, Anna. Lady Haversham and I have some matters to discuss in private."

Lady Kingsley gave a tight nod, then edged warily around Christabel before darting out the door.

As soon as she was gone, Gavin dropped his gaze to Christabel's blade. "You can put it away now, lass. Unless you're planning to go on a rampage and threaten my former mistresses, too."

She retracted the blade. "I'm sorely tempted."

He stepped closer. "You do know, darling, that I wasn't trying—"

"Yes, I realize that. I heard the pertinent parts." When

he reached for her, she brushed his hands aside. "But I didn't mean to . . . I didn't come here for that. I came to tell you what I found out about the letters."

His smile faded. "Right now, I don't give a bloody damn about those bloody letters. Christabel, I—"

"Lord Stokely knows that we've been looking for them."

That brought him up short. "I'm not surprised. But how can you be sure?"

Swiftly, she related the encounter she'd just had with the baron, leaving out the parts that might send Gavin into a rage.

It sent him into a rage anyway. "He wanted to make you his mistress?" He headed for the door. "It's time I set that bloody arse straight once and for all."

"Forget Lord Stokely's flirtations for a moment," she said, grabbing him by the arm to stay him. "I came to tell you that he seems to think having me on his side would help him. He mentioned that I could authenticate the letters."

That gave Gavin pause. "Did he?" He turned toward her, eyes narrowing. "That means he's beginning to doubt whether he could convince a publisher to print them without other proof." He grabbed her by the shoulders. "Do you know what this means?"

She eyed him warily. "N-Not really."

A slow smile lit his face. "It means we have something to bargain with."

"I don't follow—"

"Don't worry," he said, "leave it to me. If we can't go to the letters, perhaps we can make the letters come to us."

"You have a plan!"

"I have a plan." He removed her fan from her fingers

and tossed it aside, then slid his arms about her waist to draw her near.

She strained back from him. "What is it?"

"I'm not telling you."

Her heart sank. "Because you mean to get them for yourself."

"Have a little faith in me, darling," he said softly. "Have a little faith in yourself. Did you think I could remain immune to your heartfelt pleas forever?"

"Actually, I did," she said, with a lift of her chin.

"Then you don't realize the effect you have on me. What you said last night made sense. I *was* doing it for myself, when all I ever wanted was justice for my mother. But if using the letters would hurt her more—would hurt *you* more—how can I do it?"

A cautious hope sprouted in her chest. "So you're going to help me get them back? And let me return them to the prince?"

At the mention of His Highness, his face grew pained. "I'll do whatever you want, darling. Just don't expect me to enjoy it."

Hope sprang to full flower. "Oh, Gavin!" she cried, throwing her arms about his neck and showering his face with kisses. "Thank you, my love, thank you!"

After a moment, he drew back, a suspicious gleam in his eyes. "I'm not done, lass. I do expect you to meet one condition before I'll help you."

She eyed him warily. "Oh?"

"You have to agree to marry me."

Marry him. The word *yes* was on the tip of her tongue before she caught herself. She'd leaped into marriage without a thought once before—she was not going to do so again without settling a few things first.

Nor did it bode well for their future that he would use the letters to try forcing her into marriage. "Let me see if I understand you—you will only help me regain the letters and return them to their rightful place if I agree to marry you."

"Exactly."

"That's blackmail, you know."

"Of course," he said without an ounce of remorse in his face. "By now, you should know I'm capable of worse."

"So if I refuse to marry you? Would you then go off to get the letters on your own and ruin my family?"

"Absolutely."

She frowned. "You wouldn't help me out of the goodness of your heart?"

"Let me tell you a secret, lass." He bent close to her ear and added in a whisper, "I don't have any goodness in my heart."

When he then proceeded to kiss a path along her jaw, she said, "Then why should I marry you?"

"Because you want to."

"I'm not sure that I do," she said, peeved that he could be so certain of her. He reached for the buttons at the back of her day gown, and she added, "Stop that! We don't have time for—"

"We have plenty of time," he assured her. "The next round of games won't begin for another hour or two, and we need only a few moments with Stokely. So we have all the time we need to . . . work out the terms of our agreement."

He slid her gown off her shoulder and pressed an openmouthed kiss to the flesh he'd bared. "Besides, I'm not leaving here until you agree to marry me."

As his hand slid inside her gown to cup her breast through the chemise, she sighed. It had been too long since he'd touched her, too long since he'd caressed her. "But what if . . . your plan doesn't work, and you can't retrieve them?"

"Then we renegotiate." He dragged her gown off. "But don't worry, I'll get them back somehow. As long as you agree to my terms."

When he circled around behind her to unlace her corset, she became aware of her surroundings. "Gavin, if someone sees us—"

"Don't worry, they're playing cards." But after dropping her corset beside her, he strode over to close the gazebo door. "So? Will you marry me?"

"I don't know why I should," she grumbled. "It will quite ruin me in society to be married to a scoundrel like you."

He laughed. "As if you care about society."

She thrust out her chin. "And I have some terms of my own."

He arched one eyebrow as he came toward her, shedding his clothes piece by piece. "I hope you're not going to ask me to close my club."

"Why would I do that?"

"Because of Haversham and his penchant for gambling," he said tightly.

She snorted. "*You* would never lose a fortune at the tables. No, I'm not worried about you on that score." When relief showed in his face, she couldn't resist saying, "But if that were one of my conditions, would you do it?"

He approached her, eyes narrowing. "You're going to be a stubborn minx and make me beg, aren't you?"

"After all you've put me through?" she said lightly. "Absolutely."

She backed away from him, only to come up squarely against the pillar that held up the gazebo. Wearing nothing but his drawers, he reached out and flicked her chemise off her shoulders. As it slid down her body, he dropped to his knees, and said earnestly, "I'll do anything it takes to have you in my life."

"Anything?"

"Anything." He slid her own drawers down, then leaned close to press a kiss to the curls that already grew damp. "I want to make you mine."

His mouth closed hotly over her, sucking, caressing. "I want to take care of you, have you take care of me," he murmured against her. "Have children with you."

Her blood raced as she clutched his head. "Oh, Gavin, what if I can't?"

"It doesn't matter. It's you I want."

"*Only* me?" she whispered. "You have to admit you're used to having a rather . . . wide variety of women at your disposal."

He sat back on his heels and stared up at her, eyes solemn. "Sometimes a man must sample a variety of women to learn what he really wants. And I want you. Just you. From now on, until death do us part."

She swallowed, still hesitant. "No mistresses, no ladies of the evening—"

"I don't need them anymore, my darling. They were all practice for you." Then he covered her with his mouth, and began to show her exactly how much he'd learned from his "practice."

"Ohhh, Gavin . . ." she murmured, as the ache built in her, the ache that only he could soothe, that only he roused. "Please . . . please—"

"Marry me." He brought her just to the edge, then kept her there hanging, yearning . . ."Marry me, Christabel."

There was one thing he hadn't said, but she was afraid to ask for it. Because if Gavin couldn't love her—

"Marry me, darling." He tugged her down, laying her out on the cushions scattered about the gazebo floor. After shoving off his drawers, he knelt between her legs and entered her with one fierce thrust. "I can't promise I'll make you happy, but I sure as hell will try."

"What if I need something more to make me happy?" she asked hesitantly.

"Something more?" His eyes searched hers. "Ah yes, something more." He drove into her deeply, then said in a husky rasp, "I love you, Christabel. More than I ever imagined possible, I love you."

Her joy exploded, making her arch up into him in an urgent need to be closer to him, to have him filling her so completely that they could never be torn apart. "Oh, Gavin, I love you, too."

His gaze grew fierce, hungry, the gaze of a man who knew what he wanted and would move heaven and earth to get it. "Then marry me, my love." His voice was an aching whisper as he thundered into her. "Marry me . . . marry me . . ."

And as the need soared in her, finding an answer in his wild and passionate thrusts, she cried, "Yes . . . yes . . . oh yes, Gavin, yes!"

Then they were reaching release together, the flood of pleasure swamping her, washing away any doubts and uncertainties until the only thing remaining was the bedrock of the love she felt for her dear, strong Gavin.

The aftermath was sweet indeed. Gavin dragged her into his embrace, where they lay, hearts pounding, until their blood began to cool and their passion to ebb.

Still hardly daring to believe the joy that stole through her, she whispered, "Did you mean it?"

He tipped her chin up to him, and the warmth in his eyes made it clear that he knew exactly what she was asking. "I love you. I love how you throw yourself into any endeavor with the strength and enthusiasm of an army marching to war. I love that you try to be honest in everything, that you hire damaged soldiers as servants, that you're loyal to your family. I adore the fact that you went after Anna with a knife." His amusement faded to earnestness. "I love that you look at me and don't see a bastard or a coldhearted gambler or a licentious fool. You see a man worth saving. I love that most of all."

Her throat grew tight as she stroked his cheek. "Tell the truth, my love. If I'd refused to marry you, would you still have agreed to help me get the letters back to Papa?"

He flashed her a rueful smile. "Yes." When she began to smile, he added gruffly, "But only in hopes that I could convince you later to marry me."

"Nonsense," she teased. "You do have a conscience, for all your protests otherwise. *And* a soul."

"If you say so," he muttered. "But if you think that means I'm going to start forgiving people's debts and doing fool things like going to church and—"

Her kiss cut him off. When it rapidly flared into something hot and raw and he slid his hand down to fondle her breast, she broke free to whisper, "Enough of that for now. We'll have plenty of time for it later." Sitting up, she found her chemise and drew it on. "Now tell me how we're going to get Papa's letters back."

With a sigh, he propped his head up on one hand. "All right, darling. My plan isn't foolproof by any means, but here's what I was thinking . . ."

Chapter Twenty-Three

*If your lover is a gambler, you must be
prepared for anything.*
—Anonymous, *Memoirs of a Mistress*

As Gavin ushered Christabel into Stokely's study right behind the baron, he tamped down his unease. He must sound convincing to a man who knew him far too well. If this didn't work—

It had to. He gazed down at Christabel, at her luminous eyes and fear-tightened mouth, and felt a punch in the gut at the thought of failing her.

She cast him a sudden glance, a hesitant smile, and his heart constricted. He had to convince Stokely one way or the other. He refused to disappoint her as Haversham had.

"So what's this about, Byrne?" Stokely asked as he took a seat behind his desk. "You mentioned a proposition?"

"I want to buy Lady Haversham's letters from you."

Stokely didn't even bother to pretend he didn't know what Gavin meant. "Why would I sell them to you when I wouldn't take Prinny's money for them?"

"Because if you don't," Gavin retorted, "I'll make them useless to you."

The baron's eyes narrowed. "What do you mean?"

"Christabel and I will tell the press about some forged letters making the rounds that insinuate that Prinny had a child by Mrs. Fitzherbert. We'll claim that Christabel's husband had them forged so he could sell them to pay off a gaming debt. And that will leave you with nothing to blackmail Prinny with."

Stokely shot up from his chair, his face a cold, hard mask. "You wouldn't dare. The minute you raise the possibility of there being such a child, the press will descend in a swarm to examine every aspect of General Lyon's past and Lady Haversham's marriage. They'll unearth the truth, and the prince would never allow that."

Gavin stared at him coldly. "I don't care what Prinny would allow—I'd just as soon see him destroyed. Why do you think I want the letters for myself? So I can ruin his chance of being king."

Stokely, of all people, knew how much Gavin loathed the prince. But that didn't mean he'd fall for this. "I seriously doubt Lady Haversham would conspire with you in any effort that would destroy her father, too."

"As you said earlier," she retorted, "my father can flee anywhere he pleases."

"If you truly didn't care what happened to your father," Stokely snapped, "you would have taken me up on *my* offer."

Gavin could cheerfully kill the man for that offer. Especially since he sensed she was hiding the worst of what had happened.

No matter. Once they had the letters, Gavin would take great pleasure in making sure Stokely paid for his actions.

Stokely was eyeing her now with suspicion. "You'd never let Byrne raise the subject of Prinny's child in the papers, not when it might destroy your family." The baron rounded the desk to stare Gavin down. "And while you may not care about Prinny, you care about *her*. I'm not a fool. This is a bluff, and a feeble one at that."

He started toward the door. "The letters are not for sale, not now, not ever."

Time for drastic measures. "Then I'm afraid I shall have to call you out, sir, to defend Lady Haversham's honor after the insult you gave to her earlier today."

"No, Gavin!" she cried. He hadn't told her of his measure of last resort, because he knew she would protest. But Stokely couldn't use the letters if he were dead, after all.

Unfortunately, Stokely merely laughed at the suggestion. "Duel over the honor of a whore? Don't be absurd."

As rage exploded in Gavin, Christabel grabbed his arm. "Perhaps another sort of duel would appeal to you more, Lord Stokely," she said quickly. "A duel more suitable to your talents. And ours."

Gavin stared at her. What was she up to?

At least her words had kept Stokely from leaving. He eyed her with the faintest hint of interest in his face. "Go on."

"Why not add the letters to the final prize of the games? We'll forgo the pot—you and Lady Kingsley can keep it for yourselves even if you lose—but if we win, we get the letters. And if *you* win, you keep everything."

Gavin suppressed a smile. Leave it to Colonel Christabel to come up with a strategy that might actually entice Stokely.

"You're not even sure you'll make it to the final round," the baron pointed out.

He was actually considering the offer. Good. "You're not even sure *you* will," Gavin countered.

Stokely snorted. "Lady Kingsley and I have been ahead of you the whole way."

"Exactly," Gavin said. "So why not agree? You're far more likely to win than we are. Of course, if *you* don't make it into the final round, we would still expect the letters to be part of the prize. And if *we* make it, I'll forgo my thousand-pound wager with you, too. Think of it—no matter whether we win against you or lose, you get to keep the thousand pounds and the pot. That's a rather hefty consolation prize."

Stokely frowned. "How is this any different than if you pay me for the letters?" His lascivious gaze settled on Christabel. "Of course, if Lady Haversham's . . . affections were thrown into the bargain, I might consider—"

"Absolutely not," Gavin bit out. "She isn't part of the bargain." And by God, when this was over, he'd tear the man's lungs out for even thinking of it.

"However," Christabel put in, "I *will* offer one additional inducement. If we lose, then I'll attest to the authenticity of the letters. That's what you wanted from me anyway, isn't it?"

"Not entirely," Stokely said.

"It's all you'll get," Gavin snapped. When Stokely bristled, he forced a modicum of civility into his tone. "This way you'll gain nearly everything you wanted."

"*If* I win. And if I can trust the two of you to hold to your part of the bargain."

"Have I ever cheated on a bet before?" Gavin snapped.

"There's always a first time."

"If you want, we'll sign something saying that the letters are authentic. If you win, we'll hand that over. If *we* win, you give us the letters."

Gavin could see the conflict in Stokely's face. He wasn't quite as sure of his position as he'd led them to believe. He couldn't entirely assume that Christabel would keep Gavin from prematurely revealing to the press what was in the letters. After all, Gavin had never shown such loyalty to a mistress before. Why would he start now?

Besides, Stokely wanted the letters free of any encumbrances. And Christabel's offer made that possible.

"Come now, Stokely," Gavin said, "it's a fair proposal, and you know it." His tone grew condescending. "And you *are* a gambling man, aren't you? You have a choice: Gamble on the final game or gamble that we don't go back to London and spread tales about the letters that would make them useless to you. Which will it be?"

Stokely glanced from Gavin to Christabel, then back. "All right," he said at last. "We'll play for the letters."

Ruthlessly Gavin resisted the impulse to crow.

Now all they had to do was win at cards.

Christabel couldn't believe it. Heart pounding, she stared down at the trick they'd won, the trick that had just catapulted them into the final round past Lady Hungate and her partner. Perhaps the good fortune that had always evaded Philip had amassed itself to rain down on her and Gavin in their hour of need.

With a groan, Lady Hungate lifted her gaze to Gavin. "I swear, Byrne, you have the damnedest luck."

"True, but in this case it wasn't luck, Lady Hungate." His eyes met Christabel's. "It was skill."

Lady Hungate cast Christabel a grudging smile. "You may be right, sir. You may just be right." She turned to her partner. "Come, my dear, let's go drown ourselves in Stokely's brandy. No point to abstaining from it now that we've lost any chance at the pot. Again."

When she and her partner rose, Lord Stokely looked over from where he was standing with the team they'd just beaten, waiting for the outcome. "Do we have a winner then?"

"Of course," Gavin said, eyes glittering. "It's just the four of us from here on out, Stokely."

Lord Stokely came over with Lady Kingsley. "Shall we go on to the final rubbers now? Or do you wish a brief period of respite?"

"I don't need any respite," Gavin said. "What about you, darling?"

"I'm ready now," Christabel answered. Or as ready as she could ever be for a game where so much was at stake.

"But before we begin," Gavin told Lord Stokely. "I want to see the prize."

"I thought you might." Reaching inside his pocket, Lord Stokely drew out a packet and threw it on the table in front of him.

Her blood began to thunder in her ears. So close and yet still miles away.

Gavin strode up to the table and reached for them, but Lord Stokely stayed his hand. "*If* you win, and not before."

"How do we know they're the right ones?"

Lord Stokely glanced beyond him to Christabel, one eyebrow raised in question.

"It's them," she confirmed, her throat dry. She would recognize that faded yellow ribbon and the crumbling paper anywhere.

"What's this about?" Lady Kingsley asked.

"Nothing you should worry your pretty head over," Lord Stokely told her. "Just play to win, my dear. Play to win."

"I always do," she retorted.

"Shall we begin?" Gavin asked.

"In a moment," Lord Stokely answered. "But first . . ." He waved over two footmen who'd been standing at the ready inside the door. "Mr. Byrne keeps a knife inside his boot. Make sure you relieve him of it. And search the chit, too—she's been known to carry a pistol from time to time."

Gavin's lips twisted in a smile. "Don't you trust us, Stokely?" he said, as the footmen searched him, removing his knife.

"Not for one minute."

A maid was called in to search Christabel, discovering her fan in her apron pocket.

"You can keep that, I suppose." Lord Stokely gave a cruel laugh. "You might need it when the game grows heated."

Lady Kingsley looked as if she might say something about the fan, but Christabel shot her a threatening glance that the woman thankfully took to heart.

"Now it's my turn to search *you*, Stokely," Gavin said.

Lord Stokely looked offended. "I'm a gentleman. I don't carry knives hidden in my boot."

"All the same, I'm sure you won't mind if I look for myself."

Lord Stokely hesitated, then gave in with a nod.

When Gavin had satisfied himself that Lord Stokely indeed was weaponless, he added, "Same terms for the game as always? We play the best two rubbers out of three?"

"Of course." Lord Stokely waved toward the chairs. "Ladies."

As Christabel found her seat, her pulse began to race. So much was at stake—the letters, her father's honor, even her future with Gavin. If Lord Stokely won and kept the letters, there was no telling how or upon whom His Highness would wreak his fury. He might not stop with her and Papa. By agreeing to marry Gavin no matter what, she'd put him firmly in *her* camp, and the prince had already done so much to hurt him that she couldn't bear to see him do more.

They had to win. It was as simple as that.

Her hands shook as she pulled out the chair. Then suddenly Gavin's hand was covering hers, helping her with the chair. And in the process, giving her a brief caress. As she sat down, she gazed up at him.

His mouth crooked up in a smile. "Good luck, my love," he murmured. Then he left her to take his own seat.

It was enough to steady her hands and her nerve.

She forced herself to concentrate, to remember every card played. Earlier in the week, she'd partnered Lady Kingsley a few times and even Lord Stokely once. She dredged up every memory of how they'd played, every strategy they'd exhibited. And she put it to good use.

They lost the first rubber. But Lord Stokely and Lady Kingsley lost the second. It was down to one.

They were in the final game, nearly even in points, when Lord Stokely said, "I suppose you told Byrne about our encounter this morning, Lady Haversham."

"Of course." If he was trying to rattle her, she wouldn't let him.

"And the caresses we shared. Did you tell him of that?"

Now he was trying to rattle Gavin. "*Shared* implies that both of us participated, Lord Stokely. But as I recall the only caress I gave you was of the painful variety."

Gavin laughed. "Grabbed you by the ballocks, did she? You'd better be wary of Christabel, Stokely. She can bring a man to his knees, and not in a good way."

In the end, the only person rattled by the interchange was Lord Stokely, which gave her immense satisfaction. After that, he kept his opinions to himself. Which was a good thing, because the cards took all her concentration.

Still, they kept fairly well apace with Lord Stokely and Lady Kingsley, although the couple had the lead.

Then disaster struck. She stared at the abysmal hand she'd been dealt, praying that Gavin had a better one.

She glanced over the table at him, but his face showed nothing as he examined his own cards. Just once, she wished he would break his stoic manner and give her some sign of how good his cards were. But if he did, there was always the chance that the other side could see, too, and that would be dangerous.

They were four points behind Lord Stokely and Lady Kingsley, four tiny points. Yet it might as well be a hundred with a hand like this. She could feel the panic rise in her throat, feel the terror building.

Then Gavin's voice came to her from that long-ago night when he'd first started teaching her to play. *Whether ten pounds or ten thousand ride on your hand, you must leave emotion out of it. Play to the cards you have. Always.*

So she did. She forced herself to block out her fear and concentrate on the cards.

Lady Kingsley was saving her diamonds, no doubt, since diamonds were trump, so Christabel must save bigger ones. She let a jack of clubs pass that she could have

taken with a two of diamonds, barely suppressing a sigh
of relief as Gavin took it with the king of clubs.

And that's how it went, each of them playing to the
other's strengths like an old married couple. They won
that trick and the next, until with a final flourish, Lady
Kingsley brandished the queen of diamonds.

And Christabel topped it with her only good card—
the one she'd saved so carefully—the king of diamonds.

Gavin smiled widely. "We won, my love. We won."

"It can't be," Lady Kingsley whispered, her gaze fixed
on the king of diamonds. "I was sure Lord Stokely had it.
From the way you were playing, I didn't believe . . . I
couldn't imagine—"

"It's all right, my dear," Lord Stokely said, seeming
oddly unperturbed. "We changed the terms of the game,
so you and I still get to keep the pot. They merely get to
have these."

When he tossed them across the table at Christabel
with nonchalant unconcern, she grew suspicious. She
picked them up and thumbed through them, her delight
turning rapidly into fury.

"What is it?" Gavin asked.

"Three are missing." She shot Lord Stokely an accusing
glance. "And knowing you, they're probably three of the
most damaging."

The baron shrugged. "Your husband must have kept
them out for that reason. These are the only ones *I* have."

"You blasted cheater," she hissed. "You'd better produce
those other three letters, or I swear I'll—"

"What? Tell all of London about them and risk your father's neck? Not likely, my dear." His eyes gleamed at her.
"But thank you for the pot, both of you. I can always use the
funds when I go to court my . . . ah . . . future royal wife."

"I don't understand," Lady Kingsley put in. "What on earth is this about? What are those?"

"Nothing you need worry about," Lord Stokely reassured her.

Out of the corner of her eye, Christabel saw Gavin reach for the knife in his boot, then realize it wasn't there. When his gaze met hers, she understood, and instantly slid her fan across the table.

Gavin caught it, and seconds later was on his feet behind Lord Stokely, jerking the man's head back by the hair so his other hand could press the blade to the man's neck. "The missing letters, if you please," he growled.

Lord Stokely's surprise rapidly twisted into fear. "I don't have them."

Gavin stared down at his old "friend." He didn't believe for a minute that Stokely didn't have the other letters. Especially since Christabel's expression showed that she didn't believe it either. "Then what happened to them?"

"I . . . I don't know."

"A pity." Gavin pressed the blade closer. "Now I'll have to kill you so you can't use them."

"You wouldn't dare," Stokely whispered, though his hands were shaking, and sweat had broken out on his brow. "For God's sake, Byrne, I'm a lord of the realm. Kill me, and you'll end up on the gibbet."

"Not when Prinny hears of it. He wouldn't hesitate to free the man who acted to save his throne." He lowered a blade a bit. "But you do have a point—if I kill you, I won't get the other letters, and someone else might stumble upon them who could use them."

"Yes," Stokely said, breathing a little easier.

"So I'll just have to remove pieces of you until you recover your memory." Gavin slid the knife around until it lay directly beneath Stokely's left ear. "Shall I start with this?"

"You wouldn't—"

"You forget where I was raised." Gavin could feel both ladies watching him in horror, but he dared not respond to that. Stokely had to believe he would do it. "I learned all sorts of things living in Drury Lane. Did you know that a man can survive very well without his ear? And if you're worried it might make your head look uneven, I could always remove the other—"

"Enough," the man said hoarsely. "The other letters are in the safe. Behind you. In the mantelpiece."

"Where exactly?" Gavin demanded. With his free hand, he grabbed Stokely's ear and dragged him up out of the chair by it. "Show me." Gavin drew back the blade just enough to allow Stokely to edge toward the mantel.

The baron pressed something, and a piece of the marble swung open to reveal a safe.

"Right here in the card room," Christabel said in disgust. "How you must have enjoyed knowing that we were looking everywhere but here, that we were playing cards a few inches from your safe."

Stokely's shrug ended when Gavin pressed the knife against his neck once again. "Open it."

"I thought you knew how to open a safe," Christabel said.

"This is how." Gavin shot her a faint smile. "You can get any man to open a safe if his only other choice is losing his life." He shifted the knife to beneath Stokely's ear. "Or parts of his anatomy."

Stokely stiffened but complied.

The safe swung open to reveal not only the pile of pound notes that constituted the pot, but the missing letters. "I always like a man who pays his debts," Gavin growled. Reaching inside, he ignored the money and took the letters. Then he retracted the blade, pocketed the fan, and thrust Stokely aside. "It's been a pleasure, Stokely, but we must be on our way."

Gavin scooped up the other packet of letters where Christabel had left them.

"What will you do with them?" Stokely asked, his voice less shaky now that he no longer had a blade at his throat.

But Gavin didn't hear him. It had finally dawned on him what he held in his hand. Power. The power to hurt Prinny. The power to avenge his mother. If he had them published—

"Give the letters to me, Gavin," Christabel whispered.

Her voice penetrated his consciousness, drawing his attention. He looked over to find the blood draining from her face.

She stretched her hand out to him. "Gavin, please, think what you're doing."

"Yes, think," Stokely prodded with a malevolent smile. "You could ruin His Highness forever."

"He could ruin *himself*," she said hoarsely. "Be quiet, blast you."

Himself. She was worried about him being ruined. Not her father or even her, but *him*. Had any woman, other than his mother, ever considered him and his needs first? Or put his welfare and future ahead of her own?

The weight of that love rained down on his long-dried-up soul, renewing and restoring it, until he realized he had no choice but to honor it.

He stepped over to the fireplace, then looked at her again. "Yes?"

As always, she understood without his having to explain. She nodded.

He tossed the letters into the fire, feeling peace steal over him as they burst into flame. One fire had begun his torment; it was only fitting that another should end it.

Stokely shot up from his chair. "You're insane! Do you know what those are *worth*?"

"Yes. That's why I burned them. As long as they're intact, someone can and will use them." Gavin flashed Christabel a rueful smile. "I can't take the chance it might be me."

Her heart shone in her answering smile, as wide and giving as any man could wish for in a sweetheart, a lover . . . a wife. Coming to his side, she stretched up to press a kiss to his mouth, then took his hand. "Come, my love, I think it's high time we go home."

Home. He didn't bother to ask if she meant his town house or hers, or even the estate at Bath. Because it didn't matter. From now on, home was wherever *she* was.

Chapter Twenty-Four

*Occasionally, a man will actually marry
his mistress, but that is rare enough as to
be remarkable.*
—Anonymous, *Memoirs of a Mistress*

So much had happened that Christabel could scarcely believe it had been two weeks since Lord Stokely's house party. First there'd been the quiet wedding at Gavin's house in Bath, with his mother meeting his half brothers and their wives for the first time.

Then she'd reported to His Highness about the outcome of the mission, though he didn't yet know that the letters had gone up in smoke. She was waiting to reveal *that* until Gavin received his part of the bargain. She didn't trust the prince any more than he did.

All week she'd been busy settling her household matters so she could move out of the Haversham town house and into her new husband's. Not to mention planning for today's ceremony.

She glanced over at Gavin, who stared pensively out the window of the waiting room at Westminster Palace. Her heart swelled with love. What a dear he was. Marriage suited him.

"Clearly His Highness isn't going to meet with me privately as he promised." Gavin turned from the window to face her. "I knew he'd renege on that term of our agreement."

She didn't blame him for his skepticism. The ceremony to bestow his barony on him began in only thirty minutes. His half brothers were already inside, taking their seats with the rest of the lords.

"He'll come." Going to his side, she tapped his arm with her fan. "If he doesn't, he'll force me to use this."

A faint smile touched his lips, the first in the past hour. "Assaulting a prince is a treasonous offense. You'd hang, my sweet."

"Nonsense," she teased. "How could he possibly hang the wife of his son?"

Gavin's smile faded. "His son, whom he has yet to acknowledge and never will." He took her hand in his. "At least he's giving me the barony. That's something, I suppose."

But then the door opened, and His Highness entered. He'd kept his promise after all.

Christabel dropped into a deep curtsy, but Gavin, for better or worse, just stood there and stared. He'd never met his father, had he? The very thought of not knowing one's own father made her heart ache for him.

Especially when the prince said in a remotely formal voice, "Good afternoon, Mr. Byrne, Lady Haversham."

"Mrs. Byrne," she corrected him fiercely. "I've taken my new husband's name."

"Ah, yes, I'd heard that the two of you were married. But I rather thought you'd prefer to continue going by Lady Haversham."

Widows of high rank had a choice when they married a man of lower rank, and plenty of them chose to retain their loftier appellation. Christabel had been thrilled to rid herself of the title of marchioness.

"Of course," His Highness went on, "you will shortly be able to don a new title—Lady Byrne." The prince turned to Gavin. "You still wish to have Byrne as the name of the barony?"

Gavin nodded. "It's the least I can do to honor my mother."

At the mention of Sally Byrne, His Highness stiffened. "I suppose that's why you wanted the private meeting with me. So you could blackmail me with the letters into admitting—"

"The letters are gone," Gavin snapped. "I burned them."

His Highness gaped at Gavin.

"That *was* what you wanted, wasn't it, Your Highness?" Christabel said hastily. "For them to disappear?"

"Of course, but—" The prince eyed Christabel skeptically. "You *saw* him burn them?"

"Yes. So did Lord Stokely and Lady Kingsley, if you need witnesses."

His Highness's expression shifted to one of incredulity. "Did Mr. Byrne know what was in them when he burned them?"

"He did, Your Highness. Yet he burned them right there before Lord Stokely's very eyes."

The prince released a long, heavy breath. "That would explain why Stokely fled the country."

"Did he?" Gavin asked.

"Went to Paris. He wasn't waiting to see what measures I'd take to ruin him." His Highness gave Gavin a cold smile. "But he'll find out eventually." He paused to assess Gavin. "When you first agreed to this scheme, Mr. Byrne, you said you wanted to meet with me privately. Why?"

"Why do you think? Because I wanted—still want—something from you."

"Oh?" the prince said stiffly. "The barony is not enough?"

"To repay him for how you treated his mother?" Christabel put in. "How you left him friendless to—"

"Hush, my love, it's all right." Gavin took her hand, rubbing his finger along her wedding ring, which matched his own. He turned to the prince. "You owe my mother an apology for many things, but especially for how you called her a whore to any who would listen. My mother didn't deserve that. You and I both know she wasn't one." When the prince said nothing, he went on, "I don't expect you to make a public declaration—I know that it wouldn't be politically prudent. But among your friends—the ones who matter, the ones who gossip—I want you to set the matter straight."

The prince inclined his head. "I suppose I could do that."

"Secondly," Gavin went on, "I expect you to fulfill your promise to pay her an annuity. I want you to pay it in full, going back to when you first stopped it, and continuing it until her death."

Christabel blinked. She hadn't heard about this.

The prince's eyes narrowed. "Yes, Draker told me about your mother's surviving the fire. He says you keep her comfortable at your estate at Bath, so I don't see why she needs an annuity."

"That isn't the point," Gavin ground out. "It's the principle of the thing. So I want you to establish a charitable annuity in her name, to be paid to St. Bartholomew's Hospital for indigent women. St. Bartholomew's took care of her after the fire. And your establishing the annuity will show to the world that she wasn't the sort of woman you made her out to be."

"All right," His Highness said, his expression showing that this new demand had caught him by surprise. "Anything else?"

"No," Gavin said tightly.

"One more thing, Your Highness," Christabel put in. Her proud husband wouldn't ask for himself, so she would ask *for* him. "After all that Gavin has been through, the least you can do is privately acknowledge him as your son."

"It doesn't matter," Gavin told her. "I did what I did for you, not for him."

"I know, darling. And I also know it *does* matter to you, in your heart." She turned back to the prince, who was watching them with interest. "Please, Your Highness, just this once admit who he is."

The prince let out a heavy sigh. "Of course you're mine, Gavin. No one with eyes could ever doubt it." Then he stiffened. "And we will never speak of it again."

"Of course not . . . *Father*," Gavin retorted, clearly unable to pass up his one chance to annoy his sire. "Don't worry, I've lived this long without a father—I certainly don't need one now."

But his hand gripped hers, and his voice shook. He might not need a father—but he needed to know he had one.

"Speaking of fathers, I almost forgot," the prince said, turning toward a nearby door that led to an adjoining room. "Come in, General. You were right—there was no treachery involved after all."

"Treachery? What do you m—" Christabel broke off as a man stepped into the room. "Papa!" she cried, and ran to his side. "Papa, you're here! You're back!"

"Yes, dearling, I'm back." As he enveloped her in his embrace, all the changes and difficulties of the past two months swamped her until she couldn't restrain her tears. Her father gripped her tightly and said in a voice gruff with emotion, "There, there now, Bel-bel, since when does my brave little soldier cry?"

"You must forgive my wife," Gavin said tersely. "She's been worried sick about you."

"Oh, Papa," she choked out, "I am so sorry . . . for everything. For showing Philip the letters . . . for betraying your trust—"

"Nonsense," he whispered, "do not blame yourself. Your fool of a father should never have kept those letters in the first place." He lifted his head from hers. "A point that His Highness has made abundantly clear."

She turned a wary gaze to the prince. "You don't mean to punish him, do you?"

"For serving England?" the prince said dryly. "Routing Napoleon? Protecting his regent? The country would probably take up arms against me if I did, especially since all is now well."

"Then why did you mention treachery?" Gavin snapped.

Her father was the one to answer Gavin. "When His Highness heard that you were married, he assumed you had somehow coerced my daughter into sharing the content of the letters with you. And that the two of you meant to tender your own demands in exchange for them. As soon as I landed at Dover two days ago, he had men waiting to bring me to London to witness this meeting, so that if anything went wrong, I could coerce her into doing the right thing."

"I take it His Highness doesn't know my wife very

well," Gavin said. "I haven't met a man or woman alive who could 'coerce' Christabel into anything."

Her father eyed Gavin consideringly. "Still, she does have a kind heart, and it sometimes leads her to trust the wrong sort of man."

As Gavin bristled, she left her father's side to go to his. "Not this time, Papa." She slipped her hand in Gavin's. "I know that you have good reason for your concern, and until you know him better, you won't believe me. But Gavin is the finest man I've ever known."

Gavin squeezed her hand. "I swear I would never let harm come to your daughter, sir," he said in the most solemn tone she'd ever heard out of him, except for perhaps when he'd spoken his wedding vows. "And if you give me the chance, I'll prove I can be a good husband to her."

Papa looked at them together, his face wary but resigned. "We'll see, Mr. Byrne. We'll see."

"The ceremony will begin in ten minutes," the prince said. "Ladies are not allowed in the gallery, so you will have to wait here, Mrs. Byrne."

"I'll keep her company," Papa said. "We have much to tell each other."

"Yes," she told her father, "but if you could give me a moment alone with my husband first before he goes in—"

"Of course."

After he and the prince left, she turned toward Gavin, her heart swelling with pride. "So my wicked Prince of Sin is to be a baron, is he?" she whispered as she straightened his cravat and brushed a speck of lint off his fine black coat. "Your mother will be so happy."

He gazed down at her tenderly. "As a wise woman once told me, my mother will be happy if I am happy."

"And are you happy?" she whispered.

"I was. Until you told your father that I'm the finest man you ever knew. Are you certain I can live up to that, darling?"

"I'll make sure that you do," she said lightly.

"And how do you mean to do that? By shooting at me?" Though his dry tone held a hint of the old Byrne, the bitter cynicism was gone.

"By loving you."

His eyes darkened, and he kissed her, long and slow and tender. "Now that, my sweet, is a prospect worth re-forming for."

Epilogue

London
July 19, 1821

❦

Marriage changes a man, and not always for the worse.
—Anonymous, *Memoirs of a Mistress*

The cannons and gunfire and other celebratory explosions had gone on all afternoon, which was why Gavin didn't hear his butler's approach until the man spoke.

"The first of the guests has arrived, my lord."

Gavin had been a baron for five years and still couldn't get used to being called "my lord." "Thank you." He closed the account book for the Blue Swan and laid it aside on the desk in his study.

Gone were the days when he spent hours at the club poring over the books. It was just as easy to do it at home, especially now that he'd hired a manager. Just as easy . . . and far more pleasant.

His butler still stood nearby.

"Is there something else?" Gavin asked.

"Shall I inform her ladyship of the guests' arrival?" the butler asked. "Or would you prefer to do it yourself?"

"She's not down there already?"

"No, my lord. She was called to the nursery. Something about another Tweedledee emergency, I believe." His butler was trying hard not to smile and failing miserably.

"I'll fetch her," Gavin said, chuckling. "You go explain to the guests about Tweedledee emergencies. If you can."

The butler headed off downstairs, while Gavin went in the opposite direction. As he approached the nursery, he heard Christabel speaking in even tones. "I told you, your papa is too busy right now to decide who will be Tweedledum. He'll do it later. And if you don't behave, I'll make you both Tweedledee."

"Papa has to do it, or it doesn't count," answered a child's voice.

Smothering a laugh, he paused in the doorway to watch. As always, at the center of the family contretemps was his black-haired, four-year-old daughter, Sarah, who'd inherited her father's deviousness and her mother's temper. Toddling after her was his two-year-old son, John, whose hair already held a hint of red and whose stubborn insistence upon doing whatever his sister dictated had landed him in trouble more than once.

Trying futilely to reason with them was his wife. His beautiful, adorable wife, whom he loved more every day. And to think he'd almost thrown her away for some vengeance that would have brought him naught but grief.

"If you won't let me do it," she said, "then you'll have to be patient and mind Nurse until after dinner—"

"It's all right," Gavin said as he entered the room. "I'm here."

"Papa!" his children cried as they raced over to throw their arms about each of his legs.

He swallowed the lump that stuck in his throat every time he looked down to see those faces light up with joy.

"Make *me* Tweedledum, Papa," Sarah cried.

"No, *me*, Papa," John said.

He ruffled their hair. "If I make you both Tweedledum, will you stop plaguing your mother?"

He must have been mad when he'd first read them the nursery rhyme and encouraged them to play the parts. But who would have thought they'd turn it into the competition of the century?

"We can't both be Tweedledum," Sarah complained. "John has to be Tweedledee. He was Tweedledum last time."

His son's lower lip began to tremble. "John Tweedledum. Not Sarah. John."

"That's not fair!" Sarah protested.

Gavin hid a smile. "I tell you what—you can be Tweedledum for the first hour, and John can be Tweedledum for the second. All right?"

Sarah nodded solemnly, which meant that John instantly followed suit.

"Jane?" he said.

Their nurse came forward, her face filled with exasperation. "I'm sorry the children disturbed you and my lady, but Miss Sarah ran downstairs to fetch her mother when my back was turned—"

"It's all right. I know what a slyboots my daughter can be sometimes."

"I wonder where she got *that* from," Christabel muttered.

"Watch it, wife," he teased, "or I'll make *you* Tweedledee."

"Mama can't be Tweedledee," Sarah said loftily. "She's just Mama."

When Christabel rolled her eyes, he stifled a chuckle. "Jane," he said, "I hereby endow you with the authority to designate Tweedledums and Tweedledees. If either John or Sarah misbehaves while their mother and I are dining with our guests, you have my permission to turn them both into Tweedledees until they agree to behave themselves."

"Very good, sir," Jane retorted.

He cast his children a stern look. Or attempted to, anyway. "And if I hear one word about your giving Nurse any trouble, I'll tell Grandmama Byrne and Grandpapa Lyon. They'll be very disappointed to hear how their grandchildren are behaving." He turned to offer Christabel his arm. "Shall we, my love?"

She took it, but as soon as they'd left the room, she said in a low voice, "Tell Grandmama Byrne and Grandpapa Lyon, indeed. As if that would do anything—they spoil the children almost as much as you do."

"Every child deserves some spoiling," he said.

She glanced up at him with a soft smile as they headed down the stairs. "Yes, I suppose they do."

"But I wish I knew why they consider Tweedledee to be 'bad' and Tweedledum 'good.' In the bloody nursery rhyme, the two are interchangeable."

Christabel chuckled. "Ah, but they're children, Gavin. Logic doesn't enter into it. Sarah decided that Tweedledum sounds like drums, so she associates it with Grandpapa's tales of battle. Whereas, according to her, Tweedledee is the sound a bird makes, and that's just 'silly.'"

"And if Sarah says it, John follows right behind."

"That won't last once he's old enough to assert himself, I suspect."

He laughed. "True, true." They'd reached the next floor and were heading for the staircase that led down to the drawing room when he suddenly pulled her into an alcove and kissed her hard.

As he drew back, she was staring at him, bemused. "What was *that* for?"

"For marrying me. For giving me two beautiful children." He settled his hands on her waist. "For believing in me when no one else in their right mind would have."

It was her turn to kiss *him*, her mouth so warm and sweet that their kiss soon erupted into something hotter. This time when he drew back, her face was flushed, and her breath came in little staccato gasps that only enflamed him further.

"We don't have to go downstairs right away," he murmured. "We could keep them waiting a few minutes more."

"Don't tempt me," she warned, pushing him out into the hall and tugging him toward the stairs. "You know what happened the last time we kept your brothers waiting. We never heard the end of their teasing. 'So, Byrne, did you and Christabel get lost on the way down? Perhaps we should send you a floor plan for next time. The drawing room is the one that *doesn't* have a bed.'"

He laughed at her fairly accurate imitation of Iversley. "Point taken. My brothers are idiots."

She snorted. "You're as bad as they are with your swaggering answers."

"You do know we only say such things to make our wives blush."

"Yes, I know very well the whole lot of you are wicked scoundrels."

Yet despite her grumbling, she'd never wavered in her faith in his character. She'd never been the clinging, distrustful woman she'd threatened to be as his mistress. And oddly enough, her trust in him made him even more determined not to disappoint her.

He bent to press a kiss to her ear. "That's why you never find us boring."

She gazed up at him with an earnest expression. "Do you ever miss your old life, Gavin?"

"You mean my whining mistresses, long, lonely nights at the club with drunken cardplayers, parties at Stokely's where I had to be on my guard against treachery every waking hour—"

"That's a no, I take it," she said with a small smile.

"A definite no."

They'd reached the drawing room now, but he paused outside the doors to take her hands in his. "Never doubt for one minute that I love my life, I love my children, and I love you."

"I don't doubt it," she replied, her own love shining in her eyes. "But we'd better go in. I am *not* going to be fodder for their teasing again."

"I'm not sure you can ever entirely avoid that. You're married to *me*, after all, and it will be some years before my brothers stop making me eat crow for the many times I swore never to marry."

How true it was. The minute they walked in, Draker hailed them with a smug smile. "You know, Byrne, once you marry, your appetite is supposed to decrease, not increase."

"And how's that working for you?" Gavin shot back, as one of his footmen offered him a glass of wine.

"Here we go again," Christabel murmured under her breath.

But then a cannon shot from outside the window made them start.

"They've been at it all day," Iversley said, gesturing to the window with his own glass of wine. "Prinny has been ruling for years already, yet you'd never know it to hear them."

"Did you attend the coronation?" Gavin asked Draker.

"I did. The Queen turned it into a damned fiasco."

"One thing you can say for Prinny." Gavin remarked, "He's never boring."

"Rather like his sons," Christabel said from beside him.

Gavin smiled. "Yes. Exactly." He took a glass of wine from the footman and handed it to her, then lifted his own. "On this day, of all days, we need a toast, don't you think, gentlemen?"

"Absolutely." Iversley lifted his glass, and said, "To the Royal Brotherhood of By-blows."

They echoed the toast as one, even the ladies.

As they drank, Gavin looked round at the men who'd truly become his brothers and at their wives, who would walk through fire for one of their own. Just like his mother.

Just like his own wife. He stared down at Christabel, who was beaming at him, her face brimming with love. He raised his glass again. "And to our royal sire. Long live the king."

Author's Note

 umor has it that George IV and Maria Fitzherbert did indeed have a son, James Ord, who was given to a ship's captain and his family to raise, first in Spain, where the captain was given a job as a dockyard inspector by George's brother, then in America. Supposedly James Ord wrote Mrs. Fitzherbert once to ask if she was his mother. She never replied. And with good reason—since her "marriage" to the prince had always been disputed, if she'd admitted to having a child by him, it would have seriously damaged the prince's chance to be king. England could not afford any more disputes over successions.

At the time of my story, Princess Charlotte had indeed broken her engagement with the Prince of Orange, but at this point was already considering Prince Leopold of Saxe-Coburg, whom she married in 1816. So she definitely wouldn't have liked being forced to marry Lord Stokely!

$\mathscr{L}$ady Amelia Plume spotted a gentleman pushing his way throught the crowded ballroom toward her. "Oh no. *He's* here."

Her plan to elicit information from Major Lucas Winter vanished in the wake of her sheer need for self-preservation. "Excuse me," she said and released the major's arm, "I have to go."

He hurried after her as she swept toward the nearest glass door that led out onto the gallery. "Go where?"

"Away from Lord Greedy—I mean, Greeley. And please don't follow me outside. You're hard to miss, Major Winter. You'll lead him right to me."

Thankfully, he heeded her request. As soon as she'd reached the gallery, she turned and peered back through the door. Major Winter had vanished but the Marquess of Greeley had halted to scan the area. When his eyes fixed on the glass doors, she jumped back.

Glancing about her, she spotted a pillar and slid around to the other side of it. She kept her gaze fixed on the crack between the pillar and the wall, through which she could just see the glass doors.

"Did I miss anything?" came a voice at her elbow.

She nearly jumped two feet. Whirling to find the major grinning at her, she cried, "You beast! You gave me the most horrid fright! And what are you doing here?"

He shrugged. "I came through another door." His eyes gleamed at her. "Too bad you couldn't find a pillar to hide behind upstairs when I found you, or you could have avoided—"

"Shhh," she hissed.

And just in time, too, for they could both hear the glass door opening just beyond the pillar.

She shrank back from the crack as a voice called out, "Lady Amelia?"

Her gaze shot to Major Winter. As if to protect her, he edged closer. A smile touched her lips despite the scare he'd given her moments ago. It really was rather exciting, hiding out here behind the pillar with the major.

A long silence ensued, during which she envisioned Lord Greeley surveying the area around the gallery with his perpetual sneer. When she heard the click of his heels on the stone coming closer, she flattened herself against the cold marble, struggling to keep her breathing quiet.

That was no small feat with the major standing mere inches away. Somehow his hand had found her waist, and he stroked it absently, silkily. She swallowed hard.

The major's gaze fixed on her throat, and again there was that delicious flicker in his eyes. But the moment was broken by Lord Greedy's muttered curse. As Amelia held her breath, the footsteps receded and the door closed.

The moon illuminated the major's lips as they quirked

up in a wry smile. "Do you mind telling me what that was all about?"

"I can't stand Lord Greeley," she breathed, still worried he might come bounding out and find them there.

"I guessed that much. The question is why? He seemed all right to me." Major Winter added acidly, "For an Englishman."

"That's because he's not after *your* fortune."

"That's why you're not married yet? You don't want to marry a fortune hunter?"

His hand still rested on her waist. She knew she should move away, but she couldn't bring herself to do so. "Who does?"

He leaned his forearm against the pillar beside her, his expression turning calculating as he stared down at her. "Then I guess that means *I* don't have a chance."

Reminding herself that she was supposed to be playing the flibbertigibbet, she flashed him a silly smile. "Don't you have money?" she asked, holding her breath for his answer.

"I did once." His voice turned hard and cold. "But it all vanished a few years ago."

"You should have been more careful," she said lightly, though her blood pounded in her ears. Had his money "vanished" because of her stepmother, Dolly? Amelia had to know more. And that meant not driving him off by implying he had no chance with her. "Of course, you have other compensations that make up for your lack of fortune."

"Do I?"

She slanted a gaze up at him. "What woman could resist a big, strong marine like you, who's had such exciting adventures? Hearing your tales would keep a woman entertained when many other, duller husbands would not."

"And you would marry a man just because he'd had adventures?" he said skeptically.

"Certainly! It would be great fun." Sliding away from him, she strode down the gallery. It was easier to play the flibbertigibbet when he wasn't so close. "Especially if my husband took me on some adventures, too."

She could feel his gaze on her, probing her. "Then I'm surprised you never married one of the English officers."

"Most of them are only interested in my fortune, and the few adventurous officers either don't want wives or are already married." She gave a dramatic pout. "Even the married ones expect their wives to stay at home like good little girls and never see the world while they go sailing to the West Indies and beyond."

"Trust me, Lady Amelia," he said coldly, "you wouldn't enjoy seeing the world if it meant spending your days in a cramped ship's cabin or long hours on a camel's back or—"

"You've ridden a camel? What's it like? Can they run like horses or is it more like a trot? Do they really go for hours?"

He stared at her. "Camels are smelly and dirty and cantankerous. You wouldn't like riding one."

Oh dear, she was giving herself away again. An interest in camels was decidedly not a flibbertigibbet attribute. "You're probably right," she said. "Smelly things make me ill."

"I suppose you got this interest in adventure from your stepmother," he said coolly.

She caught her breath. He kept turning the conversation back to Dolly. He *must* suspect her of something.

"My stepmother?" Walking over to the gallery rail, she gazed down into the garden to hide her agitation.

He came up to lean against the rail beside her. "I'm sure she told you all about her own travels to France and Canada—"

"I said nothing about France and Canada, Major Winter," she retorted, her blood pounding in her ears. "It was Spain, remember?"

"Right, during the war. I forgot." He searched her face. "You must be very close to your stepmother if you adopted her philosophy."

"I can't imagine what you mean," she hedged. It became clearer by the moment that he really was after Dolly. But until she knew why, she didn't know how to answer his questions safely. She had to get him off the subject.

"I know your stepmother couldn't have been married to your father for more than two or three years, but—"

"Major Winter," she broke in, turning toward him. "Are you going to just stand there babbling about my relations? Or are you going to kiss me?"

He blinked. "I beg your pardon?"

Turn his head, she reminded herself. *Away from Dolly.* Her heart thundering wildly, she walked her fingers up his coat lapel. "Generally, when a man follows a young lady onto a gallery, he has something other than conversation in mind. We're alone, and the moon is high. You couldn't ask for a better opportunity." With her other hand, she grabbed his and placed it on her waist.

Though he didn't remove his hand when she released it, he dragged in a sharp breath. "How old are you?"

"Twenty-two."

"Too young for me," he said hoarsely.

"Nonsense. Lord Greeley is nearly forty and it didn't stop *him* from pursuing me." She lowered her eyelashes in what she hoped was a provocative manner. "Of course, if you find me unattractive—"

"No man in his right mind would find you unattractive, Lady Amelia," he ground out. "But that doesn't mean I'm fool enough to kiss you."

Her gaze shot to his, and some insane instinct possessed her. "Then you leave me no choice, sir. If you won't kiss me, I shall have to kiss *you*."

Every muscle in Lucas's body went taut as a full sail. God have mercy. The little flirt actually rose up on tiptoe to press her lips to his. Damnation, she was young enough to be . . . well, at least a younger sister.

But she didn't kiss like a sister, that was for damned sure. She had the softest, sweetest lips he'd ever tasted, and that was saying something. Bad enough that he'd spent the whole waltz they'd just shared reminding himself she was only part of his investigation and *not* a fine-looking young woman with sparkling eyes and a pretty little treat of a body that made him want to run his hands over more than just her slim waist. Now this.

For half a second he considered thrusting her away and lecturing her about offering men things she wasn't willing to give. Then he caught a whiff of her honeysuckle perfume, and his control snapped. To hell with it. If the lady wanted kissing—

Slipping his arm about her waist, he moved his mouth on hers, testing, tasting, enjoying. But before he could even get going, she drew back, a blush touching her cheeks.

It figured—females like her were always teases, especially where unsuitable fellows like him were concerned. They liked to try things out . . . things they never meant to act on.

Not this time.

He trapped her against the rail. "If that's your idea of a kiss, Lady Amelia, it's no wonder you crave adventure." As the scent of her perfume engulfed his senses once more, he seized her chin, then growled, "*This*, sweetheart, is a kiss." Then he brought his lips down on hers again.

She had one hell of a mouth—as tender and sweet as a Virginia peach. And she didn't deny it to him, which was a shock in itself. In his experience, highfalutin females like her didn't kiss so openly or melt so swiftly in a man's arms. So the way she was kissing had him wanting things—

Damnation, it had been way too long since he'd held a woman. She was an English lady, for God's sake, and a flighty one at that. Not the kind of woman who generally attracted him.

So why couldn't he stop kissing her? Splaying his fingers over her back, he thrust his tongue between her parted lips—

She jerked back, surprised, but didn't pull out of his embrace, just stared up at him with those luminous eyes that reminded him of liquid chocolate. "What are you doing?"

For a flirt, she sure seemed innocent. "I guess no one's ever kissed you like that." He ran his thumb along her lower lip. "With their whole mouth."

"No," she breathed.

"Then maybe it's time somebody should."

He kissed her again, and this time when he probed between her lips, she let him in. As he repeated the motion, driving his tongue deeply inside her luscious mouth, she melted in his arms like freshly churned butter.

Kissing her was like sinking into warm molasses. He forgot she was English, forgot whose stepdaughter she was. He didn't care if he burned for it later, he had to sate himself on her mouth.

When she lifted her arms to encircle his neck, crushing her soft breasts against his chest, he dragged her hard against him and let his hands roam up her back, then down to her shapely hips, then up again until his thumbs brushed the undersides of her breasts—

"We must stop this," she drew back to murmur, her face flushing and her breath coming quickly. "Someone will soon notice that we're both gone from the ballroom, and if anyone catches us here together, I'll be called 'fast' or worse."

"That's the price you pay for adventure, darlin'."

"Then it's too high. You get to leave whenever your work in England is done, Major, but I still have to live here. Being ruined in society isn't an adventure if that's all you have. It's just foolish."

For a flighty girl, she sure found some sense when it came to her reputation. When she tried to pull from his arms, he refused to release her. Somehow he had to either keep her here or figure out a way to see her again, so he could ask about her stepmother. "Dance the rest of the dances with me."

"I can't."

"Why not?"

"It's considered improper unless a couple is courting."

When she gazed at him steadily, he tensed. "I'm not in the market for a wife, Lady Amelia."

A faint smile touched her lips. "I rather thought not. So if you'd be good enough to release me——"

She pressed her hands against his chest, and he reluctantly let go, but not before she felt the shape of the dagger in his coat pocket.

Eyes narrowing, she ran her hand over the bulge. "What's this?" Without waiting for him to answer, she opened his coat and peered inside. She lifted her gaze to his with a smile. "Do you always carry a dagger to a dance?"

"Do you always check a man's coat for weapons?" he countered.

Just when he was beginning to think her not so flighty after all, she cast him one of her vacant smiles. "Of course not, you silly man." She wagged her finger at him. "Though you really shouldn't carry it, you know. Arming oneself for a ball is considered terribly gauche, Major."

"Lucas," he said tightly, inexplicably annoyed by her sudden formality after the kisses they'd just shared. "Call me Lucas. It's my Christian name."

She lowered her lashes demurely. "That isn't proper either, sir."

That's when it hit him—the perfect excuse for continuing his association with her until he could get his questions answered. "You English have an awful lot of rules. I'm more at home with pistols than promenades, but maybe you can help me with that. You seem to know a thing or two about society."

Her gaze shot to his, suddenly wary. "What do you mean?"

"I'll be in town for a while consulting with the authorities about the Algerians." It was the bargain he'd made with his superiors. He would discuss the Algerian issue with the French and the British if he was also allowed to pursue his investigation.

He went on. "I've been invited to all kinds of social events, but as you figured out, I'm not exactly an expert on English society. Maybe you could tell me what's acceptable. Teach me how not to insult every officer I meet." He flashed her a smile. "Admit it, Lady Amelia, I badly need lessons."

A surprisingly calculating gleam appeared in her eyes. "Yes, you do."

"And who can teach me better than you?" The one woman who could lead him to Dorothy Bates. And from there, with any luck, to Theodore Bates.

"Who indeed?" She fluttered her lashes at him. "But what have *I* to gain from these lessons if you're not interested in marriage?"

He thought quickly. "Tales of adventure, of course. You did say you found them amusing."

Apparently he'd struck gold, for her face lit up. "You'd tell me about the Barbary pirates? And your adventures as a marine?"

She was a strange one, wasn't she? One minute she acted like a silly female, and the next she showed surprising depths. He couldn't figure her out.

But at least now he knew how to turn her chatty. "I'll do you one better. I'll give you some adventures of your own. How about that?"

Her smile faded. "By adventures, you don't mean what we just . . . "

When she trailed off with a blush, his blood turned to fire. "Only if that's what you want, darlin'," he drawled.

She blinked, then her expression turned coy. "What I

want doesn't matter. Ladies must consider their reputations."

Too bad. He already itched to taste her again.

If women were wines, Lady Amelia would be champagne, the kind of bubbly froth that went right to a man's head. Besides, uncorking the virgin vintage wasn't exactly an entertainment he approved of. "All right. I'll see what else I can drum up."

How much adventure could a lady like her actually crave, anyhow?

She broke into one of her captivating smiles. "Why don't you call on me tomorrow at Papa's town house, so we can start your society lessons and my adventures. I'm sure your cousin can give you the direction." She glanced back toward the glass doors. "Now I'd best go in, before someone comes looking for me."

When she walked off, he started to follow and she stopped short. "We can't go in together or people will assume—"

"That we were out here doing something we shouldn't?"

"Exactly." She gazed at him from beneath seductively lowered lashes. "And let this be your first lesson in English society—nobody ever lets on to other people that they've been doing something they shouldn't."

"In that case—" He brushed his hand down the back of her dress, over her nicely rounded—

She leaped away with a blush. "What are you doing?"

"There's dirt from the railing on your gown. So if you don't want anybody knowing what we were doing . . ."

"Oh." She backed away, dusting off her gown. "In future, you really should *tell* me what to do, not take it upon yourself."

"All right. Next time I'll let you brush off your own bottom." Her shapely, fits-perfectly-in-a-man's-hands bottom.

A laugh bubbled out of her. "And you certainly shouldn't say the word 'bottom' in society."

"You'd rather I said 'ass'?"

She cast him a reproachful glance. "You're not supposed to refer to any part of a person's body at all."

"So I can't offer to give you a hand? Or take your arm? Or lend you an ear?"

"You know very well what I mean."

"According to your countrymen, I don't know a damned thing about civilized behavior. I'm practically a savage."

"Even savages can learn to behave." She gave him a flirty little wave. "I'll see you tomorrow . . . Lucas. And don't forget—you owe me an adventure."

He stared after her as she darted from the gallery. Oh, he'd give the little flirt an adventure, all right. And somewhere between feeding her tall tales, quenching her thirst for excitement, and letting her play at taming the American savage, he'd be sure to get the information and answers he wanted from her.

Love
historical romance?
So do we...

No Longer a Stranger
Joan Johnston
Can a heart as wild as the West
be tamed?

Highlander in Disguise
Julia London
Naked desire can never
be disguised...

A Woman of Virtue
Liz Carlyle
Handsome Lord Delacourt is
vain, vindictive, and merciless.
But he always honors his bets—
and follows his heart.

To Pleasure a Prince
Sabrina Jeffries
Passion is this prince's only
pleasure.

The Wedding Raffle
Geralyn Dawson
He who holds the winning ticket
wins the prize—but loses his heart.

Secondhand Bride
Linda Lael Miller
To win his father's ranch, a
hard-living cowboy settles
down and takes a wife—
another man's wife!

A Loving Scoundrel
Johanna Lindsey
This Malory rogue has finally
met his match.

My Surrender
Connie Brockway
Scandal. Deception. Passion.
Sometimes it's best just to
surrender...

If You Dare
Kresley Cole
He's looking for revenge.
She's looking for passion.
Do they dare love each other?

Available wherever books are sold.

11901